CALIGO

Elanor Miller

Also by Elanor Miller

TENEBRIUM

For everyone who gave TENEBRIUM a chance

FLAPPERS AND FALSE GODS
BOOK TWO

In Caligo City, mere men can be gods...

This edition was first published in 2024

Independently Published

Caligo is the second novel from Scottish writer Elanor Miller
@elanormiller

ISBN: 9798871594438

Cover Design by Celin Chen - www.celingraphics.com
Edited by Belle Manuel
Copy Editing by RJ Ruth
Formatting and design by Damian Jackson
Developmental Editing by Lauren Duddridge

GLOSSARY OF TERMS

ARC: *The Augmentation Regulation Committee*

Aegis: *A device that creates a shield of energy, protecting the wearer.*

Aug: *A person with an augmentation or augmentations.*

Augmentation: *Cybernetic and/or Biomechanical devices that blend human bodies with robotic technology.*

Cicada: *Cochlear Implanted Communication and Data Appliance. A device implanted into the ear that functions like a smartphone.*

Console: *Similar to a computer. A terminal that allows access to the datastream.*

CPD: *Caligo Police Department*

Datastream: *The evolution of the internet.*

Ghoul: *A person who has used Styxx or Quietus and succumbed to its effects; a person in a rabid state of addiction.*

Gold Legion: *A cult of the rich that tried to eradicate the poor and take over Tenebrium City by force. The legendary predecessors of the Onyx Legion.*

Grim Sweeper: *A person who cleans crime scenes and transports bodies to morgues or for disposal.*

Index: *A device implanted into the wrist, that allows users to interact with technology around them, answer calls, search the datastream – much like a smartphone.*

Inmutationphobia: *The dislike and/or strong prejudice against people with augmentations.*

Jonk: *Short for Jonckheere Transporter, a Jonk is the evolution of the car. A transporter that can fly.*

Onyx Legion: *A privatised military force under the control of the Mayor and the District Attorney in Tenebrium City.*

Neo-Prohibition: *The reincarnation of Prohibition from the 1920s and 30s. The act of outlawing something, in this case drugs and alcohol*

Quietus: *A variant of Styxx that turns users into ghouls if they stop taking it.*

See®: *Surgical Eyesight Enhancement – Pronounced 'Seer'.*

SSA: *Supervisory Special Agent*

Styxx: *A highly addictive drug which has been found to turn users into rabid, zombie-like creatures.*

TPD: *Tenebrium Police Department*

Una Anima: *The Church of the Single Soul*

Zealotism/Zealotry: *Extreme, excessive and/or fanatical devotion to a person, cause, or belief, that usually results in the refusal to tolerate other perspectives.*

PROLOGUE

An excerpt from *'The Beautiful and the Damned: A Chronicle from Caligo'*

— A Historical Journal by Anthony Oubier

In the winter of 2189, fire rained from the sky. Historians would call this catastrophic event, and the culmination of Climate Change, 'The Scorching'. When the ash had cleared and those who survived took stock of what was left, it became clear that the human race could no longer live on the surface of the earth. What were they to do? Search for another planet? Drill into the earth's core? Build bases on the moon? These options were no doubt pondered by the boldest and brightest of the time, but what transpired was the colonisation of the oceans.

Huge conical structures dubbed 'Stygian Colonies', made from gleaming silver metal, were built into the ocean floors, like lances thrown from the sky. Three at first, housing only the wealthiest of survivors; there are thousands now at time of writing. Each colony has hundreds of floors, each home to a city, both above and below sea level, and while history has undoubtedly played out in each and every one, only two have carved their legacies in the blood of their citizens.

This Chronicle from Caligo must start in Tenebrium City, for as all roads lead to Rome, what transpired in Caligo in the late 2420s could not have happened without the fall of Tenebrium in 2425.

The first city to be completed after The Scorching, Tenebrium was the jewel of Colony Six. The city was intended to be a haven for the rich only, but refugees from the earth's surface flocked to the new city chasing the promise of prosperity. Tenebrium might have opened its doors to the common folk, but most who went there found themselves forced into low-paying jobs or consumed by the insatiable and unforgiving culture of excess. Poverty was as prevalent as opulent plenty, and those in power did all they could to keep it that way. The rich got richer at the expense of the poor.

This money-before-all-else ethos came to a head in 2425 when the Gold Legion, a cabal of the elite helmed by Medicorum Medical Services CEO Chester Maxwell, tried to supplant the government and take the city by force. Their campaign was long and cost many lives, particularly those who lived in the city's Poor Quarter, for the Gold Legion's true aim was to eradicate the impoverished and restore Tenebrium to what they saw as its former glory.

In the years leading up to the coup, Tenebrium's citizens were subject to Neo-Prohibition and harsh capital punishment laws among other measures designed to target the most marginalised and vulnerable. The effects of these measures were not only felt by the poor, however. By October 2425, anyone who wasn't part of the elite felt the brutal impact of these policies. The culmination of which was a bloody city-wide battle between Legion sympathisers and a small number of law enforcement who remained loyal to the metropolis.

The worst thing the Gold Legion did, however, was not its open assault on Tenebrium, nor was it how the sect's members bought, killed, and threatened their way into positions of power. It was the drug known as Styxx.

Distributed in secret through the city's shady underbelly, the drug wrought horrific changes in those who took it. Causing a dream-like state of bliss at first, users would quickly become mindless monsters, overcome by a rabid hunger for human flesh. The authorities dubbed these addicts 'Ghouls' and, after declaring an epidemic, proceeded to quarantine all those affected in the SubLevel—a system of maintenance tunnels that ran under the city.

Even after the coup was thwarted and the city was handed back to its citizens, the so-called ghouls remained quarantined, with no cure in sight. And they remain there to this day.

Now that you understand Tenebrium's secret shame, for what I have detailed above is far from public knowledge, we can delve into the harm Tenebrium's legacy inflicted on Caligo.

The late 2420s saw the sale and implantation of augmentations rise exponentially. A once luxury item available only to the extremely wealthy, augmentations became accessible to the general populace on several of the ocean colonies for the first time in 2426.

After the dismantling of Medicorum Medical Services in Tenebrium City, the patents for human upgrades, which had previously been jealously guarded by the pharmaceutical giant and, more importantly, the cultists that owned it, were sold as part of the reparations owed to the denizens of the once besieged city.

The majority were purchased at auction by one Travis Mercer, a philosophy professor turned philanthropist. Championing equality and the benefits these augmentations could bring to those suffering from physical ailments, Mercer published the blueprints for the technology held within these patents, ensuring that augmentations were now able to be mass-produced, lowering the prices considerably.

For the first time in the history of the colonies, anyone who wanted to be upgraded had the choice to do so. This was a massive boon to those suffering from a range of illnesses, to those with limb differences, and a definitive stride forward in the realms of medical equality. Progress, however, is always met with opposition, and there were many who thought that the potential dangers of having augmented humans outweighed the medical benefits.

The first place to offer these new affordable upgrades was the city of Caligo.

Caligo, founded in 2409, was still in its infancy in the late 2420s. Built to ease over-crowding in its sister city, Tenebrium, Caligo was not subject to any of the problems that plagued Tenebrium or laws like Neo-Prohibition, yet strangely, it still adopted Tenebrium's love of jazz, short hair, and shorter skirts. Historians posit that this 'Jazz Age' aesthetic was pushed by those in power as it made adopting and enforcing stricter laws and policies more palatable.

Tenebrium's problems were sweeping and widespread. Corruption ran rampant with a very heavy and obvious human cost. Caligo's troubles, on inception, were far more subtle in their malevolence. It wouldn't be until early 2429 that they would be laid bare, and the true effects would be seen by all.

The city's legend would be forever tarnished when religious zealotism clashed with the fight for body autonomy. The rise in augmentations was initially met with curiosity, which, for some, quickly turned to fear and outrage. The more advanced augmentations became, the more the most radical among the religious factions claimed they were 'affronts to God'. Those prone to zealotry thought that the right to choose was superseded by the will of God and expressed these views vocally.

Initially, there was concern among the public when it was announced that the augmentations would be rolled out to tactical divisions of law enforcement, but it was not until they were visible among the general population that violence became part of the debate.

Una Anima, the Church of the Single Soul, had been particularly vocal in their opposition to augmentations from their introduction. While the church purported to have been victim to a smear campaign headed by the augmented minority, many claimed that it was Una Anima who entreated violence against the augmented population, not the other way around, and by mid-2429, the church and its founder were implicated in several grisly murders, as well as bribery and blackmail on a colony-wide scale.

When removed from the events of that time, it is easy to see the link between the church's preaching and the anti-aug violence that swept Caligo City in early 2429. From their fear-mongering by spreading misinformation to their thinly veiled calls to action, the part that Una Anima played in the anti-aug movement cannot be understated.

The church's beliefs can be split into two major ideals. The first of which is that a person only has one soul and that replacing any part of the body with an augmentation damages that soul, and therefore makes the augmented person less human. The second is that augmentations unfavourably change what it means to be human—in their minds, a human should be flesh and bone only—and that this change was the first step to the extinction of the human race. With those two concepts in mind, the picture of the tensions at the time becomes troublingly clear. Una Anima even clashed with other religious denominations within the city, who stood in solidarity with the augmented and took umbrage with Una Anima's damaging rhetoric and Plutus-like penchant for hoarding wealth. Never before, and likely never again, will there be such a polarising and divisive faction as the Church of the Single Soul. They were the flashpoint that ignited the city of Caligo.

The official record states that a single perpetrator was responsible for not only the murders but the anti-aug sentiment that led to still more violence. This, in my mind at least, strains credulity. However, a source closer to the ground agreed to tell me what they call the 'real story', and it is that story which I present to you here.

Once again, I ask you to delve with me into the realms of hearsay. I cannot confirm that the tale you are about to hear is true, though I believe it to be so. What I can do is ask you to take a moment to consider the possibility that it is.

THE PAST

Seventeen years ago...

Cynthia Wayland had never been in a casino before, let alone one run by the mob. Clutching her pearl necklace with one hand and her small handbag in the other, she made her way between the Blackjack and Roulette tables, careful not to make eye contact with anyone she passed.

Bourbon Street Casino and Bar was the haunt favoured by gangsters, and the rich when boredom pushed them to walk on the wild side. Located in Tenebrium's Pleasure Quarter, it had a reputation for all the wrong reasons. Violence, extortion, and illegal liquor were always on the menu. If you couldn't pay what you owned, you didn't leave unless it was in a body bag.

Cynthia could feel many sets of eyes following her as she made her way across the smoky gaming floor to the poker section in the back.

Three round tables engulfed in a smog of cigar smoke sat in semi-darkness next to the rear exit. Only one of the red, felt-covered tables had a game tonight, however. Luckily, it was the game she was looking for.

Omaha was high stakes poker. Even the richest of Tenebrium weren't foolish enough to join this game. It was only for those who counted themselves as part of the Russo family, or those with a death wish.

The head of the Russo family and the man Cynthia had come to see, was sitting with his back to her, facing the exit.

"Excuse me, Mr Russo," she said quietly. He didn't respond. "Mr Russo—"

He raised a massive hand commanding silence. "Wait," he said in a snarl as silky as it was fierce. Cynthia did as she was told; it didn't occur to her to disobey. Nervous sweat was forming around her hairline; she dabbed it away gently with a silk handkerchief, hoping no one would notice.

She was made to stand like that for the best part of an hour, but she did so without complaint. Finally, when the losers had paid their dues and the pot had been split amongst the winners, Vincent Russo turned to face her.

He was a hulking presence standing well over six feet tall. He was White with dark hair that was going prematurely grey at the temples. One of his eyes was a brown so dark it was almost black, and the other was milky white. A thin and twisted scar bisected his eyebrow, telling gruesome tales of how he had been blinded.

"Follow me, please," he said as if he were a gentleman. "We can talk privately in my office." He walked between the tables at a comfortable pace, with Cynthia trotting behind. Two men materialised as if from thin air and followed at her back.

Vinny's office was actually a storage space. The ruddy, bare brick walls were covered by metal shelving holding bottles of every kind of bootlegged booze imaginable, and the light overhead was a single yellow-ish bulb that hung low in the centre of the room. The desk in the storeroom-come-office was large and expensive, rather at odds with the rest of the décor. The accompanying armchair, which could have comfortably sat three, was even more so.

"Get the lady a chair," Vinny said to one of the men who had tread on their heels, as if he had been rude to a treasured guest.

When a chair was finally produced, Cynthia sat down, so nervous now she was shaking. The two men posted themselves at either side of the door and Vinny settled himself behind his desk, every bit the king of the castle.

"You have me at a disadvantage, ma'am. You know who I am, but I don't know you." Vinny looked Cynthia up and down, a carnal glint in his eye.

"Cynthia Wayland," she said, boldly extending a hand. Vinny smiled and clasped it. His hands were large, rough, and very warm, though not sweaty.

"Well, Cynthia, what brings a beautiful lady in pearls to the Pleasure Quarter?"

"I need your help, sir." She was scared, but her resolution held her voice steady.

"'Sir'?" He chuckled and licked his lips. "What do you need help with?"

"My son was in an accident. He was badly hurt...his injuries are...terrible. He needs more medical attention than we can afford."

"Is that how you lost your arm? The same accident?" Vinny asked with what seemed like genuine curiosity as he eyed her prosthetic.

"Yes. It was a transporter crash. The banks don't care, and I'd heard—"

"What have you heard?"

"That the Russos will give loans to those the banks turn away." Her voice faltered a little.

"You heard right. How much d'you need?"

"Two hundred and fifty thousand—"

"Two hundred and fifty large," he let out an unkind laugh. "Bad accident."

Cynthia hung her head and stared at her fingers twisting in her lap. This had been a mistake, and she knew it. Fear was bringing tears to her eyes, but she didn't want the mobster to see.

"There, there," he said, startling her as he stood up and came around his desk to sit on the edge in front of her. "I'm sorry. I'm an awful, rude man. I didn't mean to scare you. I'm sure we can come to an arrangement." He put his hand on her knee and rubbed it gently with his thumb. "Of course I can front you the credits for your poor son."

This change in attitude was jarring and did nothing to calm her heart as it pounded against her ribs. "Th-thank you," Cynthia stammered, with a weak smile. "We can pay 200 credits a week and we'll pay you more whenever we have it. My husband has a good job and I work part time—"

"Forget about the money. Keep it." His hand shifted a fraction higher on her leg.

"How will I repay—?"

"Come to my home for dinner every Thursday night until I say otherwise. I'd like to get to know you. You have a way about you." He didn't have to leer, or wink, or put any crass inflections on his words; Cynthia knew exactly what deal he was proposing.

"That sounds lovely," she said, wiping her eyes with a tissue from her purse as her skin crawled at the thought of the man before her. "Thank you."

No one, even her husband, would have been able to tell that the smile she affixed to her face was fake.

THE CHURCH OF THE SINGLE SOUL

Snow blanketed the steps of the Una Anima Church as fresh white flakes continued to fall. The crowds gathered out front seemed immune to the cold as they waited with bated breath for Levi Seward to give his sermon.

Press and devout followers alike craned their necks and stood on the tips of their toes to get just a glimpse of the preacher where he stood silently behind a golden lectern framed by the church's impressive wooden doors.

Levi was White and in his early fifties. His dark hair was slicked back, and his jaw clean-shaven. He wore a black shirt complete with a priest's collar, matching dark slacks, and silver-tipped cowboy boots. He said nothing as he basked in the waves of anticipation that rolled off the mass of bodies before him.

To his right, positioned strategically among his entourage, was Agent Thea Williams. Shivering with her hands stuffed in her pockets in a small attempt to ward off the chill, she scanned the sea of bodies, looking for any potential threats. In her opinion, the man whom she was tasked with protecting was far more of a threat than anyone who might be armed and possessed of malintent within the crowd.

He was the worst kind of zealot—the kind with money. He used obfuscation and double-speak to preach hate and intolerance, all the while projecting an air of benevolence and charitableness. In reality, credits were the only thing he truly believed in, and his followers seemed to worship him more than they did any deity. When Thea had left Tenebrium City three years ago, she had thought she was leaving that sort of cultish and greedy villainy behind, but as it turned out, corruption was everywhere, and Caligo was in no way immune. Wealth, it seemed, would always be that which was most coveted.

For the size of the crowd, Thea thought the security detail was uncomfortably light. One ARC agent—her—, two police officers and three 'personal guards', whatever that meant. It didn't bode well should something untoward happen, and it gave Thea an uneasy feeling in her stomach.

The painfully acute sound of microphone feedback pierced the eerie silence, drawing Thea out of her dark musings. Levi Seward was ready to be heard.

"Caligites," he boomed, his drawl thick like cold honey. "We are a city under siege. We are bedevilled by the plague that is augmentations. Technology has not only invaded our cities and homes, but our bodies. Everyone from our law enforcement to our doctors is tainted by technological advancements that have no place in any kingdom under God." The crowd made impassioned and indiscriminate noises of agreement. "The body is meant for the Lord alone; it says so plainly in the bible. Our bodies are his temple, temples for the holy spirit, not man-made creations. If God had wanted us to have these powers, he would have given them to us."

"That's right!"

"Amen!"

"But this," Levi continued, gesticulating wildly, "is about so much more than our bodies. It's about our children, our safety, and our souls. These augmentations are not only affronts to God, but they are weapons more powerful than any gun, and they are in the hands of predators and criminals. Don't be fooled by those who say they are a medical breakthrough. The augmented population is not made up of the sick—it is made up of the blasphemous, of the evil. The soulless! For augmentations taint the immortal soul. Our city, and so many others like it, has given superpowers to dangerous criminals. These devices will be used to kill, hurt and steal—and no conventional weapon will protect you. I'm afraid. I live in fear of what these 'augs' are capable of. We should all be afraid..."

"I can't believe we're protecting this prick," Alex Wyndham said from behind Thea, as if they had read her thoughts. "God didn't invent pacemakers, but here we are." Alex was impossibly tall and Black. Their tightly coiled hair was cropped close to their scalp, and large golden hoops hung from their ears. They were a detective with the Caligo Police Department and the first friend Thea had made in the city.

"Careful," Thea muttered out of the corner of her mouth, nodding to the assembled press as the flashes of a hundred cameras caused her to squint. "You're being watched. You do not want to be a target for these people."

"I urge you," Seward said loudly, drowning out any reply from Alex. "To shun augmentations and the augmented predators who stalk our streets. We must take back our bodies—"

BANG

A shot rang out, the sound reverberating all around.

Chaos erupted on all sides. The crowd screamed and scattered, searching for cover. People pushed and shoved, slipping in the snow as they ran in all directions, trying desperately to get out of the line of fire.

Another shot rang out, then another.

Thea raked the scene with her eyes, but she couldn't find the culprit in the maelstrom of bodies and continued snowfall.

"I'm on Seward," Thea said, touching a hand to her ear to activate her Cicada implant. She would be damned if she let a man like Seward be martyred.

Thea pushed her way through the throng of people, including Alex, who had encircled Seward like a human shield.

"Come with me," Thea commanded, taking the preacher by the elbow. He didn't protest as she led him over to the church's large front doors. A shot splintered the wood just above Thea's head as another embedded itself in the lectern behind her.

"Keep low," she said, pushing Seward, who had been frantically looking around, down into a crouch.

She pulled on the handle, but the heavy doors remained shut fast. Thea examined the lock; something corrosive had twisted and warped the metal. Whoever wanted to kill Seward had made sure he couldn't retreat into the safety of his church.

Cursing, Thea reached for the preacher, who was cowering, huddled against her legs. "Get under there." She all but dragged him to the lectern and forced him underneath.

More shots rang out, and Levi pulled Thea down so he could hide behind her.

"Where are you going?" He shrieked, grabbing onto Thea as she tried to stand.

"Get off me, you idiot," Thea spat, wrenching herself free of his grip.

Thea had barely righted herself when she heard yet another shot. This time, it hit a human target. Her.

She felt a sharp, burning pain as the bullet grazed her cheek, quickly followed by the warm, wet flow of blood as it streaked down her face and onto her neck.

She saw him then, the shooter, standing at the edge of the steps. He had sneaked up the side in all the chaos. He was young, or at least he looked it. He was White with sandy hair that was tousled and slightly damp. There was a smattering of patchy stubble on his jaw, which only added to the picture of youthfulness. His eyes, however, were black. Entirely black. Even as he stood some fifty feet away, Thea could see that there were no whites or coloured irises. It was as though his pupils had enveloped the entire eye.

The pair of them stood there for a moment, stock still, watching one another as bodies moved frantically around them. Then, as one, they dashed forwards, pushing their way through the crowd towards each other. The shooter seemed to sense that to get to Levi, he would have to go through her.

Thea slammed her hand onto the centre of her chest, depressing the button hidden under her shirt as she ran. A pale glimmering light erupted from the spot and took shape in front of her, forming an aegis of gold. Thea began counting backwards from ten, knowing that the shield couldn't be sustained for long. Ten. Moving with her, the shield of aurulent light deflected every shot the black-eyed man fired at her.

Nine. Eight. Seven. Six. Five. They were only twenty feet apart now. Four. He continued to fire. Three. Rage contorted his boyish features as the bullets continued to bounce off the ethereal barrier. Two. Thea was in close. She saw her opening. One. As soon as the shield dropped, Thea brought up her own gun and fired a single shot. The stun round hit the black-eyed man squarely in the chest and he dropped to the ground, unconscious.

No one noticed the danger had passed at first as the crowd continued to panic, but as Thea kneeled down to handcuff the black-eyed man, Levi's booming voice cracked the air, bringing a fresh wave of screams and shouts with it.

"We are saved!" he cried. "You are safe, my friends. Be still. We have been saved. This is God's will. Those of us with untainted souls are his chosen!"

The fearful exclamations were quickly replaced by the clicks of cameras as Thea was blinded anew by the dazzling flashes. Seward came forward and grabbed her hand with both of his. "I don't know how to thank you," he said, not looking at her, but out into the press gallery that had hastily reassembled itself. "You were an agent of the Lord this day." Thea tried to pull her hand away, but Seward redoubled his grip. "Smile," he muttered through clenched teeth.

THE AUGMENTATION REGULATION COMMITTEE

The city of Caligo was a spectacle of gothic Art Deco. Stained glass windows, pointed arches, and flying buttresses abounded underneath a blanket of smoke and steam. Gargoyles loomed from every rooftop watching over the denizens, like stone demons perpetually ready to strike. Trams travelled across long wires high in the sky and glimmering brass cogs and gears allowed entire buildings to move around the city at will.

Thea tore her eyes away from the beautifully intricate metropolis to look at the black-eyed man. They were sitting opposite each other inside a transporter headed for The Orchard. Now that they were in close proximity, Thea had decided that the black-eyed man was a little older than he first appeared, not eighteen or nineteen, but maybe in his early to mid-twenties; though this too was a guess. He hadn't said a word since he had been arrested and refused to give any form of identification. He just stared unblinkingly at Thea, reflecting her own face back at her from the depths of the inky pools.

The Orchard was the headquarters for the Augmentation Regulation Committee, so named because the building had been built into the roots of a colossal cherry blossom tree. Hundreds of metres in the sky, the pale pink flowers were perpetually in bloom, petals trickling down to the ground like snowflakes. The building itself was teal glass framed by white brick and silver metal, with the shimmering branches weaving across its face.

As the transporter landed, the black-eyed man stood with the air of being walked to the gallows. He didn't struggle or say a word as Thea marched him through the sea of fallen petals. He just stared unblinkingly as he was led through the entrance and into the booking centre. It was unnerving. He seemed coiled, like he was ready to strike—but he made no sudden violent movements and did nothing other than what he was bid.

The Booking Centre comprised several small rooms that led to the containment facility in the underground levels. Each room represented a stage of the process. First, the suspect would be searched for any dangerous weapons. Then, they would be identified via fingerprinting or retinal scanning. After that, they would be checked over by a member of the medical team before they were given a change of clothes and sent down to the holding cells to await interview or transport. It was a long process that would incur much paperwork.

"I'll take him from here. You should get that seen to," Emmanuel Jones said, pointing to the cut on Thea's cheek that still oozed lethargically when she spoke. He was Thea's favourite of the Booking Agents, or Tour Guides, as they were called within the department. He was short and Black, with thick twist braids and lime green fingernails. Emmanuel ran a tight ship, preferring to book suspects himself, which made Thea's job a hundred times easier; but more than this, he was kind and could be trusted not to be more hands on than necessary. Thea hadn't approved of manhandling suspects when she was a detective, and she still didn't now that she was an agent; the law be damned.

Thanking Emmanuel again and bidding him farewell, Thea made her way from the Booking Centre to the lifts. The view on the way to her office was spectacular. The interior of the elevator shaft was overgrown with twisting roots; they tangled themselves around the many crystal-shaped lights. The car itself was glass, giving anyone inside a glimpse of this amazing mix of man-made and natural. It was like stepping into another world for a few seconds a day.

Reality dawned as it always did, however, when the doors opened onto the Investigation Wing. Thea's office, like that of the other Supervisory Special Agents, was in the centre of the seventy-seventh floor. Twelve identical glass-walled rooms, arranged like a clock face, opened out into a common area filled with screens, information terminals, meeting areas and coffee machines. The idea was to give investigators a place they could work in peace that was never too far away from somewhere they could collaborate with their teams.

Thea's office took the 9 o'clock position. Like all the others, the walls were made of lightly tinted glass. A metal bookcase that contained every procedure manual imaginable sat against the back wall, and a black desk complete with matching armchair took pride of place in the centre. There was a single pot plant in the corner and no personal effects. The carpet was a dark grey-blue, like the brick walls of the wing.

When Thea arrived, Alex was already waiting inside. They were perched on the edge of her desk holding a MedKit and looking concerned.

"Our fearless hero returns," they said dryly, waving the kit. "You're all over the news. The anti-aug crowd are big fans."

"Don't remind me," Thea groaned, taking up the seat behind her desk. "What are you doing here? I thought you'd be at your precinct."

"I wanted to make sure you were okay, and I knew you wouldn't have bothered going for medical attention."

"You spoil me," Thea said, pulling back her hair and leaning forward to allow Alex to clean the graze left by the black-eyed man's bullet.

"This is shallow, but I'd get Medicus to look at it. Wouldn't want to scar that pretty face," Alex said as they applied butterfly stitches.

"Thanks." Thea touched her cheek gingerly. It was tender, but it would be fine in a few days.

Alex set the Medicus Kit down. "I don't like this. Any of this," they said, moving their hands in circles. "We're supposed to be out there helping people. Solving crimes. Since when do we protect nutjobs? He preaches hate and violence and doesn't even pretend to hide it. 'We must take back our city'—like that wasn't a call to action."

"Seward must be paying people off. It always comes down to money," Thea said with a sigh.

"If our agencies don't start curbing this bullshit, people will die. It's only a matter of time before one of Seward's flock brings his message to fruition."

"I know, but I don't know what to do about it. I can't find any dirt on him and, believe me, I've tried. He walks the line very carefully. Says just enough to get his message across but not quite enough that we could arrest him."

They both fell silent for a moment, contemplating the rock and the hard place they were between.

"Think he pays his taxes?"

Thea snorted. "You should get someone on that."

"Who's that?" Alex said.

Thea followed Alex's gaze. Through the glass she saw a handsome man with tanned skin the colour of Sahara sand. His pointed jaw and slicked-back hair were unmistakable as he crossed the common area with a wide smile on his face.

"Drew," Thea said, opening the door to hug Andrew Torrez. "When did you get back?"

"Just now," he said, taking a step back to look at her. "What happened to your face, Querida?"

"Guess you haven't seen the news," Alex said with a smirk. "Alex, by the way." They gave Torrez a mock salute.

"Andrew," Torrez said with a nod before turning back to Thea. "Have you been getting into trouble again?"

"I'll explain later. It's good to see you. But you didn't come all the way here just to see me, right?" Thea said, narrowing her eyes in suspicion.

"Of course I came all this way just to see you," Torrez said, feigning outrage. "Because I need a favour."

"Whaddaya need?"

"I have a meeting with a client. It's supposed to be a straightforward adultery case, but something isn't sitting right with me. I think there's more to it." Torrez scratched his chin thoughtfully. "I was hoping you'd let me use your fancy agent access to do some digging."

"Sure. But try to be discrete. I have to go brief AD Castillo."

Alex followed her out of the office as Torrez set to work at Thea's desk.

"You didn't tell me you were seeing someone," Alex said, their tone probing.

"I'm not." Thea kept up a brisk pace as she made her way through the winding corridors to the Assistant Director's office.

"So, you and Andrew is just a casual arrangement?"

"It's not like that," Thea laughed. "He's my best friend. That's Torrez," Thea added when Alex raised their eyebrows.

"That's Torrez?" They repeated.

"Yes, that is Torrez."

"You never mentioned he was handsome."

Thea shrugged.

"He calls you 'Querida'. Isn't that Spanish for 'beloved'?" It was clear that Alex wasn't convinced.

"It started out as a joke, and it just stuck. He called me it when I was a rookie cop."

"He's a detective?" they said, with an intensity that surprised Thea.

"He was. He's a private investigator now. Long story."

"More things you can't talk about? You make being your friend really hard sometimes."

They had reached the door to the Assistant Director's office.

"Sorry, but duty calls," Thea said, nodding towards the door. "I'll give you all the dirty details later."

"There's dirty details? To be continued, then." And with a wink, Alex turned and began to walk back towards Thea's office. Shaking her head, Thea knocked once on the plain wooden door, then entered.

Assistant Director Mateo Castillo was sitting behind his desk waiting for Thea. He was a few years north of fifty and wearing very well. He had tanned skin and his once dark hair was now salt and pepper. Castillo had a charming way about him that tended to mean he got what he wanted. Not with Thea, however; she was immune to his silver tongue. It was because of this that she was surprised when she had been promoted to SSA and given a team of her own. AD Castillo, it turned out, seemed to like to be challenged and forced to think of different ways to do things and for that, he had Thea's tentative approval.

"Agent Williams, thank you for coming. Are you all right? Have you been to the MedBay?"

"I'm fine, thank you, Sir."

"I'm glad to hear it. Well done today, Williams. You did the department proud." He lent back in his chair in a self-satisfied sort of way.

"I'm ready to give you my report."

"It can wait. I have something else I need you to do first."

"Sir?"

"Levi Seward is holding a press conference in front of the building. He wants to thank us—well you—for saving his life. I think it would be excellent PR for the department. We are so rarely touted as heroes."

"With respect, I wholeheartedly disagree. I think aligning ARC with someone like Seward sends entirely the wrong message. He preaches hate, and we're supposed to stand for tolerance and unity."

"Your views are noted, but I insist. This will be good for us."

"I'm not a show dog. I won't be paraded publicly."

"As much as I enjoy your lack of deference, SSA Williams, you will, in fact, do exactly as I have asked because it is your job."

"Press conferences—"

"Finish that sentence at your own peril," Castillo said, his composure perfectly intact. "This isn't up for discussion."

Ten minutes later, Thea was back in her office watching Torrez work at the console on her desk.

"What's wrong?" Torrez asked shrewdly as Thea paced the room. "What happened?"

"I think I'm about to do something very stupid." Thea stopped her back and forth and perched on the edge of the desk.

Torrez drew his eyes away from the holographic screen to survey Thea. "Do you want talked out of it, or into it?"

"Neither. I've already decided. What my boss wants me to do doesn't feel right."

"Okay," Torrez said, getting up from behind the desk. He moved to stand in front of Thea and took both of her hands in his. "I am a leading authority on stupid decisions. Me, I think with my heart—"

"Heart?"

Torrez chuckled but continued without comment. "You think with your head and your instincts. If something feels wrong to you, trust your gut. It probably is."

"Come with me."

"Where are we going?"

Thea left the office, Torrez hot on her heels. Together they made their way quickly to the lobby and out onto the front steps of The Orchard. Just like at Una Anima, Levi Seward stood behind a gold podium before a mass of journalists. This time, however, the anticipation was more of a low hum. Thea could feel the excitement from the newshounds. It was like they knew something was about to happen that would keep them in articles for a month.

"You sure about this? Last chance to be a good little agent," Torrez asked with no real conviction.

"Stand off to the side," Thea said, stepping into what felt like the line of fire.

As soon as the preacher spotted her, a wide grin spread across his face. He clapped, and the assembled crowd followed suit. "There she is," he called over the din. "The woman of the hour." The clicks of a hundred cameras filled the air, like the chirps of crickets on a warm summer's eve.

Thea walked quickly to stand beside him as the hubbub died down.

"Agent Williams, everyone. I am alive today because of her. I can't thank you or your organisation enough for what you did. Putting your life on the line to save mine. It's God's work you do, and it was his will that we meet. I think he knew I would need protection from those who seek to silence his word. I have said all along that those with augmentations are dangerous, soulless, and today proved that—"

Thea stepped in front of Seward taking hold of the microphone and nudging him out of the way. He laughed as if this delighted him and the press laughed with him, but Thea could sense his anger. The preacher didn't like to share the spotlight.

"I would like to thank the preacher for his kind words. I was just doing my job. It's no more or less than anyone else in my situation would have done—"

"Don't sell yourself short," Seward said, trying to regain control of the microphone. "Your bravery cannot be overstated—"

"I would also like to thank the preacher," Thea cut across him. "For trying to use me as a bullet shield. For trying to hide behind me while he bravely cowered away from the danger his violent rhetoric creates and for trying to force me into a photo op, while I tried to detain the shooter. These are, without a doubt, the actions of a selfless man who cares about the lives of others."

There was a moment of silence as her words sank in before an eruption of sound. Voices called her name over and over, begging her to comment further, screaming questions and demanding quotes. "The department has no further statement on the incident and I will not be taking any questions at this time. Thank you."

Thea made a beeline for Torrez, ignoring any further attempts to elicit a comment.

"You are my hero," he said with a huge grin on his face, taking her by the arm and leading her away as if he was her personal security.

CALIGO IN CRISIS

This message is brought to you by The Church of the Single Soul

'Levi Seward is our link to God' – The first tenet of Una Anima.

Augmentations Are The First Step To Extinction

We only have one body and one soul. The more technology we add, the more our souls are damaged and the less human we become.

What is it to be human without a soul?

We were made in God's image. Pure and untainted. When metal replaces what God granted us, we take the first steps towards the extinction of the human race as we know it. Evolution, for evolution's sake, is not a stride forward, but a stride away from the path of God.

Those who have tainted their bodies with augmentations have sacrificed part of their immortal soul in exchange for power. Neither Heaven nor Hell will accept them, and neither should we. They are no longer fit to call themselves human. They should not be allowed the same rights and protections as the rest of us. They are a danger to righteous folk. Less than human, they are more susceptible to the Devil and will use their ungodly powers to enact his will on earth.

If they are to endure, they should be kept separate, away from the good God-fearing people that they currently terrorise. We cannot allow any 'person' with augmentations into our hospitals and schools to mix with our children and the vulnerable lest they taint them with their lies. Any parent who furnishes their child with augmentations should face the full might of the justice system for their abuses. We must take back our city and take back what it means to be human.

The message will not spread itself. Stand with us against the destruction of what it means to be human.

Donate to The Church of the Single Soul today and show that you still love God as he loves you. The greater the donation, the greater the blessing.

Join us at midday, every day, at Una Anima or via stream, for a sermon with Levi Seward.

One Body
One Soul

THE NIGHTJAR

The Nightjar was a beautiful bar in Caligo Heights. Near enough to the Entertainment District and several shuttle ports, it was frequented by travellers and Caligites alike. It was the place to be for drinks and dancing, having perfected the delicate balance between bar and nightclub.

Caligo, unlike Tenebrium, had never been subjected to Neo-Prohibition and, as a result, had a much more relaxed drinking culture and a much more enjoyable nightlife.

The inside of The Nightjar was glimmering dark antique bronze, with red upholstered booths and moody lighting. The bar itself was made of old barrels and the partition between the tables and the dance floor was made up entirely of empty whiskey bottles.

Cleo sat at their usual table, waiting. Slim, Black and beautiful, she had dyed her short hair a warm honey-blonde since Thea had seen her last. She smiled and waved Thea over as she entered. Cleo had been a medical researcher for Medicorum Medical Services before getting cold feet when she realised what they planned to do with the drugs they were creating. She had been punished grievously for this and suffered a great ordeal in the SubLevel of Tenebrium because of it. Against the odds, the friendship between the two women had blossomed to the point where Thea counted Cleo as part of her inner circle.

"Hi!" Cleo stood to give Thea a warm hug.

"Sorry, I'm late. It's been a day." Thea said, returning the hug.

"No shit. Look at your face!" Cleo gently touched Thea's cheek, concern drawing her eyebrows down.

"It's nothing," Thea said with a reassuring smile. "Really."

Looking dissatisfied, Cleo sat back down. "Did I see Andrew?"

Thea took her jacket off and followed suit. "He's meeting a client nearby. So, how long are you in town for?"

"Couple of days this time. I'm presenting my findings to the medical association and begging them to give me more funding. It's all very dull. I...saw you on the news."

"Which time?" Thea said, taking a large gulp from the glass Cleo pushed towards her. She wasn't sure what the cocktail was, but the red liquid tasted like fiery cinnamon—it was divine.

"Both. You just can't help yourself, can you?"

"I'll worry about it tomorrow. Tell me how you've been. What's new?" Thea said, waving the subject away.

They spent the next couple of hours catching up, laughing and dancing, but it wasn't until they were several cocktails in, that Cleo, her face flushed from the heat and the alcohol, finally said, "I do have some news, actually," with a small nervous smile.

"Yeah?" Thea asked encouragingly.

"I'm seeing someone." Cleo blushed; it wasn't like her.

"That's great," Thea said, taking a swig of her latest cocktail.

"It's very new, and it's complicated, and you are the only person I've told." Cleo babbled.

"Complicated how?"

Cleo shook her head. "It's Marielena," she blurted.

"Torrez's wife Marielena?"

"You think it's too messy?"

"No such thing, if you're happy."

"I'm worried it won't work."

"They're separated and look at us. Our friendship shouldn't work—I had an affair with your husband..."

"And now you're one of my closest friends."

"Exactly. It only has to be as complicated as you make it."

"I just...it's going so well. Neither of us planned it, but I'm happy. *We* are happy."

"That's all that matters. Congratulations to you both."

They clinked the rims of their glasses together.

"Please don't tell Andrew," Cleo said, suddenly anxious.

"Of course not. It's none of his business."

Thea watched as Cleo fiddled with the straw in her drink.

"What's wrong?"

"Andrew. He's going to be hurt, isn't he?" Cleo said at last.

"Maybe, but they haven't been together for over three years. I love Drew, but this has nothing to do with him. She left him and he would tell you himself she was right to. He loved her, but he didn't treat her like he should have. Maybe he'll be upset—I don't know, he's seeing someone now—but mostly, I think he'll just want her to be happy."

"Thank you," Cleo said, reaching across the small round table to give Thea's hand a squeeze. "I've shared. It's your turn. What happened today?"

"Nothing that hasn't happened before." Thea drained what was left in her glass.

"What d'you mean?"

Thea sighed. "I left Tenebrium because I thought it would be better, or at least different in another city. But it's not. Caligo is the same. Beautiful on the outside but rotten to the core."

"I'm sorry, but Thea, you must know that's naïve. Corruption is everywhere. The people in power will always do bad things to keep it because the system is broken. And unless there is a cult calling the shots—Caligo *is* better."

"Ever heard of The Church of the Single Soul?"

"Unfortunately, I have." Cleo leaned in conspiratorially. "Is it really that bad?"

"No. And, yes. I don't think they're plotting to take over the government, but I think that they have some vested interest in anti-aug tensions. I don't know what their angle is yet, but their leader—Levi Seward—he wasn't even on the map two years ago. No record. No affiliations to any church I could find and then suddenly he's anti-aug Jesus. Something else is going on here, but I can't quite put my finger on it, and even ARC is afraid to get involved. I don't get it. The city is a powder keg about to explode. It's gonna be bad when it does."

"Whenever there's trouble, wherever there's a battle to be fought, there you are. Right in the thick of it."

"What if I don't wanna fight anymore?"

"I don't think you have a choice. It's who you are. I don't think you're capable of walking away."

"But I wish I was. Life would be so much easier."

"You care—I hope you never lose that."

The rest of the night passed in a whirl of dancing and laughter as both women let go of their worries, for a little while, at least.

ARSONIST'S LULLABY

Night had only just fallen when Mr Denver stepped out into the street. The air was cold and crisp, the remnants of the morning's snowfall still lay on the cobblestones. He spent a happy moment watching his breath coil in front of him, before turning his collar up and pulling the thick black mask over his face.

It was uncomfortable and took only moments for his breath to dampen the fabric. He could smell the tobacco on his breath more strongly as the soggy fabric tickled his nose. His wife was right, he should quit the foul things. Lamenting his last cigarette, he set off on his way.

He mingled with the crowd, careful to be forgettable, keeping his pace neither fast nor slow and his head down.

The Kelpie Clinic was on the outer edge of the Downtown area of Caligo. The building itself had once been a library but had since been converted into a free medical centre. It was kept open by donations and provided augmentations and aftercare to those in need.

Mr Denver hated the place. It disgusted him. It frightened him. He couldn't fathom why anyone would want to have metal grafted to their body. Why they would want to replace the parts nature had given them with cold man-made devices, like they were Frankenstein's monster. He imagined touching his wife's cheek with cold steel fingers. The thought enraged him.

He had spent the last week surveying the building and memorising the layout. Making sure that he knew exactly where the exits were and how to block them.

Moving resolutely to the clinic's entrance, he pulled a crowbar from the inside pocket of his jacket, glanced over his shoulder to make sure there was no one around, then used it to jam the front door shut.

Quickly, he made his way down the alley off to the side. Even though he had seen it many times now, the mural painted on the side of the building still made his lip curl in anger. It showed the story of a young boy losing his legs. The boy had dreamed of running marathons and he cried because he thought that dream was over, but then he was given new augmented legs. He was learning to walk again, learning to run. The last image in the flowing story showed the boy raising his arms in triumph as he crossed the finish line of a race with a crowd of thousands cheering him on.

Cheater, Mr Denver thought, tearing his eyes bitterly away from the mural.

Emerging from the alleyway onto the small patch of grassy land behind the clinic, Mr Denver headed straight for the heavy metal dumpster that was pushed off to one side. Over the last three days, he had been sneaking bottles of diethyl ether and hiding them inside.

He pulled one of the bottles out and splashed its contents on the back door before pushing the heavy dumpster up against it. Pulling matches from his pocket, he struck the whole book and threw it into the dumpster. It caught fire immediately with a roar of heat. It took only seconds for the flames to spread to the door and start licking at the walls.

Heady triumph washed over him as he watched the flames grow, the heat caressing his body.

The final part of his plan was the Cicada Jammer hidden in the depths of his dark overcoat. With the push of a button, Mr Denver could block any and all communication signals from Cochlear Implanted Communication and Data appliances. No one inside would be able to call for help.

Mr Denver stepped back to admire his handiwork. It surprised him that it took several minutes for anyone inside the cursed place to notice anything was wrong. Then, the hammering started on the doors and windows, but it wasn't until those inside realised they were trapped that they began to scream.

Mr Denver whistled happily as he walked home, a smile on his face and a spring in his step.

JOURNALIST LOST

Mrs Idina Baker-Singh lived at 223 Stein Street in Uptown. It was a nice, though slightly cramped, area. Homes were generally small and expensive, as the location was very desirable to those seeking status.

The Baker-Singh household, however, was on the outskirts of the area where the houses, while still modest, were far more affordable. This displeased many of the snobs in central Uptown, so much so that they would try to claim that Stein Street, and its neighbours, weren't really part of Uptown at all, but rather an extension of Caligo's Pleasure District.

Whether this bothered Mrs Baker-Singh, Torrez never found out, and it was the farthest thing from his mind as he knocked on her door.

Idina, as it turned out, was a White woman in her early sixties. She was tall and slender, her short grey hair styled in intricate finger waves. Torrez got the impression she took great pride in her appearance and had possibly worked in the fashion industry. There was something about her long-sleeved, high-neck, floor-length black dress and pearl earrings that gave Torrez the impression of an artist. As if to compound this image, the house was immaculate inside. Every wall was adorned with beautiful paintings, and every surface had the styled look that could only be gained with the help of an interior designer.

Idina led Torrez through her beautiful home to a small room that looked out over the garden. It was nothing like the rest of the house. Messy, with newspaper clippings covering the walls, it was clearly a home office for someone who worked in the news cycle.

"If you are any kind of PI, I assume you have realised that I wasn't entirely honest with you when we spoke yesterday," she said, gesturing around the room. "My husband did not run off with a woman from work."

"But he is missing. I always do my homework," Torrez added when Idina looked surprised. "Why haven't you taken this to the police? They don't have any records of a report."

"I did. They say that there is no evidence of foul play. My husband is younger than me...people make assumptions." Torrez could tell that the admission hurt her pride and could imagine that she and her husband had been forced to defend their relationship often.

"But if you were younger, and he was older, they wouldn't say a word. People are judgemental when they have no right to be."

Idina smiled at that. "Yes, they are."

Sensing that he had gone some small way to gain her trust, Torrez said, "What do you think happened to him?"

"When paying for your services, can it also be assumed that I am paying for your silence?"

"Of course."

"Ranveer is an Art Journalist. That's how we met," she said with a small smile. "He's well respected and as such he has been getting invited to Demytrus for years—it's a very exclusive underground art show, where the artists are anonymous—this year he discovered a sculptor going by the name of Chiparus. He was captivated and fascinated by their sculptures. He wanted to meet Chiparus, but, well, that's not how Demytrus works. He's been obsessed with discovering Chiparus' identity for months."

"What's so special about these sculptures?"

"They are bio-mechanical depictions of the human form."

"Augmentations?"

"Exactly. The sculptures are made using discarded augmentations."

"How does an underground art show lead to him going missing?"

"Augmentations. He became as obsessed with them as he was with the art. The deeper he delved, the more involved he became with the augmented community and the discrimination they face. His angle is appearances. How augmentations should be worn with pride, how they shouldn't have to look God-given to be acceptable."

"He's Lalique. The pro-aug activist."

"How did you know?" Idina said in surprise.

"Educated guess. I bet Lalique—Ranveer—isn't very popular with the anti-aug movement."

"No, he isn't."

"Especially after the cyber theft he committed."

"He used those funds to help an aug shelter," she said, firing up at once. "So many have been pushed out of their homes and jobs because they have augmentations. People don't understand that, in most cases these aren't electives. The rich can afford super strength, but most everybody else just wants a better quality of life." Her passion impressed Torrez.

"I'm not judging you. I agree with you."

She paused to regain her composure. "He's been getting threats on his blog—but to report them he would have had to come forward and—"

"Police reports are public record, not to mention that would mean outing himself as Lalique."

"Yes."

"When did you last see or hear from him?" Torrez asked, peering into one of the many boxes piled up on the desk.

"It's been two days. He was supposed to have a meeting with his editor at midday, but he never arrived. No one has seen him since."

"And what were the threats?"

"Things like 'You will devour your sins, lest they devour you.' And 'a gilded tongue speaks no lies'. The last one was 'You shall be fixed to the cross'."

"Do you mind if I use his console? I want to see if I can get a beat on whomever was posting the threatening messages."

"Anything you need. Please, just find him."

LEGACY

Thea stood under the blistering water, hoping that it would wash away the fog in her mind caused by the several cocktails too many that she and Cleo had enjoyed the night before. It wasn't like either of them to drink to excess, but it was all right to let go and have fun once in a while. And it had been fun. Cleo was a dear friend and a welcome escape to life in Caligo. Thea refused to grudge or feel guilty about a very rare hangover.

Thud. Thud. Thud.

"Can you get that?" Thea called from the shower as the insistent knocking continued. "Cora, are you here?"

Thea waited, but she received no response. Apparently, her twin sister had left their shared apartment before Thea had gotten up for work. The knocking turned to hammering. Cursing, she threw a towel around herself and made her way to the front door, leaving watery footprints on the wooden floorboards.

"What?" Thea said, wrenching the door open. Then, "Mom?"

Athena Williams stood at the threshold, dressed all in powder blue. She looked very much like her twin daughters. She was White, with the same dark brown hair, high cheekbones and full lips that both Thea and Cora had inherited. Where she differed from her children was the eyes. Athena's eyes were a deep and startling green. Thea and her sister had gotten their golden-brown eyes from their father.

"Is Cora here?" Athena said, not looking at Thea.

"No."

"I see." Athena turned on her heel and walked back towards the lifts.

"Mom!" Thea called, still dripping as she stepped out into the hall.

"I have nothing to say to you."

"I got shot yesterday. How about, 'are you okay?'"

"You seem fine," Athena was careful to keep her voice low.

Thea let out a derisive laugh. Her mother was not a woman who liked to make a scene. She would have died of embarrassment to have one of Thea's neighbours come upon them arguing in the hall. It made Thea want to shout louder, just to spite her. She suppressed the childish urge.

"So what? You're just going to avoid me for the rest of our lives?"

"Keep your voice down," her mother hissed predictably as she closed the gap between them. "You're naked. Get back inside."

Thea allowed Athena to herd her back into the apartment. She didn't speak again until she had slammed the door.

"You betrayed—"

"Don't start with that again."

"—your father. You betrayed him when you told that court all those horrible things."

"True things, Mom."

"That's not the point!" Athena was yelling now. "You owed him loyalty—"

"That is the point! Dad was a villain. He was one of the bad guys. People tell their kids horror stories about men like him. Thousands of people died because of him—some of them he killed himself. He gave Cora away as a bargaining chip to a cult! He was willing to let me die if it meant keeping power and he cheated on you every chance he got. I get it, you married the devil, and you don't know how to deal with that, but he's dead, Mom. You don't have to keep making excuses for him."

"Don't you dare. Our marriage is none of your business, so you can scratch that off your list of reasons to hate him. He wasn't perfect, but he was my husband, and he was your father. How could you do it? How could you stand there in front of that court—those strangers—and rubbish his legacy?"

"His legacy? He was willing to kill off half the city if it meant he could have more money and more power. He helped turn people into monsters, people who will never get back to their families. I was doing my job. And it's not like it even makes a difference. The court documents are sealed. I was served a gag order. No one wants to talk about how they let a cult take over the city—so his secrets are safe."

"You stood up and defended...that man. The man who killed your father. Where was your compassion for the man who raised you?"

"Maxwell killed dad, and I *did* take the stand against him."

"You are more loyal to Tenebrium than you are to your family."

"And you are more loyal to a dead cultist, a man who is responsible for the deaths of thousands of people, than you are to your own daughter. You don't even know what family is."

"Thea..."

"I'll tell Cora you stopped by."

"Thea," Athena said again. This time, the plea in her voice was unmistakable.

"Goodbye, Mom."

Thea turned her back on her mother and returned to the bathroom to finish her shower, but it was several minutes before she heard the front door close.

Thea was late.

As she tapped her foot on the tram's grubby metal floor, she more than ever missed Jonks. Caligo did have Jonckheere transporters, but in an effort to curb traffic, workers were encouraged to commute using public transport. What would usually have been a peaceful journey, where Thea could enjoy stunning views of the city, was now an irritation. Why did they move so slowly? The fact that both methods of transport were equally eco-friendly made being pushed to use the slower alternative even more irksome.

When the tram finally landed, Thea had to sprint through The Orchard's atrium and down into the booking centre.

"You here for the black-eyed man?" Emmanuel said from behind his desk. Today his nails were pink, but otherwise he looked as he always did.

"Yeah," she said, still panting slightly. "I'm here to conduct a suspect interview."

"You just missed him."

"Sorry?"

"He was bailed out."

"His bail was set at fifteen million credits. Who bailed him out?"

"Levi Seward. Hey, don't start with me," Emmanuel added as Thea opened her mouth to argue. "Take it up with Castillo."

Assistant Director Castillo was a night owl. He tended to work late, rarely leaving the office before midnight, which meant he wasn't often seen in The Orchard before midday. It was only half-past eleven, but Thea chanced her luck regardless.

As it turned out, the assistant director had not come in early. He had left his office door open, however, as was his custom. AD Castillo liked to style himself as the only trustworthy suit. He was careful to project the air of having nothing to hide. The office was large, not ridiculously so, but still larger than those of Thea and the other SSAs. The walls were the same dark blackish-blue as the rest of the wing and the floor was concrete, with a thick rug covering the centre of the room. There was a brown leather wing-back chair sitting behind the large mahogany desk and a pot plant in the corner.

Thea hovered at the doorway, waiting. It wasn't long before AD Castillo appeared, dusting petals from the brim of his hat.

"Close the door," Castillo said, as if he had been expecting to see Thea.

Thea did as she was bid, while the assistant director took off his coat and hung it over the rack nearby.

"Seward bailed out the shooter."

"I know," Castillo said with a sigh as he slumped into his armchair. "Everything about that incident stinks. Why would the supposed victim of an attempted murder drop fifteen million credits to bail out the person who tried to kill them?"

"I was hoping you would know."

"I'm a lot of things, Thea, but I'm not dirty and I'm certainly not on Seward's payroll."

"I never accused you of being dirty, sir." The conversation had taken a turn Thea hadn't anticipated or intended.

"You never say it outright...you just sort of imply it from time to time."

"I'm sorry if I've given you the impression that I don't trust you."

"So, it's just authority you have a problem with? Not me personally. You are a natural born leader, I get it." Thea didn't know what to say. Before she could think of something, Castillo went on. "You were right. Yesterday. Not about how you handled the situation—we'll talk about that later, but you were right about Seward. This unit should not be associated with a man like him and I'm sorry I pushed you to do that press conference."

"I don't understand."

"I want us to be one the good guys, but this job doesn't always make that easy. We all answer to someone—myself included. I've decided to take a leaf out of your book and push back. It might not always seem like it, but you can count on me to be in your corner."

"Is something happening?"

"No, I just like to know who my allies are and I like to take responsibility for my mistakes."

"Sir—"

"So," he cut across her. His entire demeanour changed from tired and worried to his usual business-like and upbeat. It was jarring. "What is your plan for the shooter, Joel Curtis?"

"I still need to interview him."

"That won't be easy. His release form put his address the same as Seward's and the preacher doesn't want to press charges."

"This was nearly another mass shooting—that's not up to him. And even if he could have the attempted murder charges dropped, the kid shot me."

"Seward may refuse to testify."

"We don't need him. There were over a hundred witnesses, including Detective Wyndham."

"And if he pays off those witnesses and commands his followers not to cooperate?"

"You know something, but you aren't supposed to say."

"I just want to know what you'll do if this case proves more difficult than we first imagined."

"Whatever it takes."

"Good. Keep me posted."

Castillo placed his hand on his desktop, summoning the datastream, then began annotating a report. Feeling like their conversation had given her whiplash, Thea left the office more confused than when she had entered.

CELEBRATING TWO YEARS OF THE PRO-AUG BLOG

(And 1 million subscribers!)

For those of you who don't know—my name is Marielena, I'm thirty-nine, and a brain infection called Encephalitis left me with one of the worst cases of Chronic Fatigue Syndrome that the doctors in my hometown of Tenebrium had ever seen. I was housebound, barely able to get out of bed most days. I got breathless walking to the bathroom; I could barely find the energy to walk down the stairs. Sex with my then-husband was a rare event, and when we did manage to be intimate, I was never able to give my all. The disease isn't why we parted ways, but that's a story for another time and another blog. I lived like that for nearly six years, if you could call it truly living.

Just when I had resigned myself to a life filled with headaches and joint pain, dizzy spells and constant tiredness, the patents for human augmentations ended up in the public domain. I thought nothing of it at first. How could augmentations help me? I wasn't missing a limb; I wasn't blind or deaf. I was just indefinably broken, or 'out of order' as I used to joke.

It was six months later before I gave augmentations another thought. I was having dinner with a dear friend at my home, when I got so tired she had to carry me to bed. That was when she asked if I had explored augmentations. I explained that I wasn't a suitable candidate, and her reply changed my life.

'Are you sure?'

I told her I was, and she let the subject drop, but over the next few days, I couldn't get her question out of my mind. Augmentations were my every thought, like an itch in my brain I couldn't scratch. The truth was, I wasn't sure. When I finally gave into curiosity, I found I had never been more wrong. Augmentations could do so much more than I had ever imagined.

Most augmentations are powered by the body they are in, using the same energy that would have moved an organic body part. This is the most common way to power an augmentation—but it isn't the only way. My body lacked energy, though my limbs still worked. I spent weeks researching if there was some variation that could help fix my tired body. Finally, when I was ready to give up on cruel hope, I came across M-Pulse.

M-Pulse is a device that artificially simulates electronic impulses throughout the body, brain and nervous system. It allows people like myself to run off a bank of artificial energy, which dramatically decreases the effects of conditions like CFS. M-Pulse devices, however, are not easy to come by.

From discovering M-Pulse, to researching whether it was right for me, finding a supplier and a doctor who could fit the device, to actually having the procedure done took a little over nine months. It was during this time that I had my first taste of the anti-aug movement.

The anti-aug movement is complicated and multi-layered. Though an extreme minority, there are some in the movement with reasonable concerns, but most are scared and ill-informed. Should people be allowed to have eye lasers and machine guns for hands? Probably not. But should the fact that that's now theoretically possible impact whether a child can walk again? No. And that's the crux of the problem. The anti-aug movement likes to focus on possible worst-case scenarios, instead of reality. And it is expressed in ways that vary from rude comments on blogs like this one, to all-out hate speech. More than this, there has been a worrying trend of violence not only against the augmented community, but those who openly show support for it.

It was because of this foray into the dark world of the anti-aug movement that even after I found a doctor who could perform M-Pulse procedures it was yet another month before I talked myself into setting a date. I urge anyone considering augmentation to seek out the pro-aug community—hate isn't the only thing out there; I promise. I urge any of the anti-aug movement to respectfully seek out stories like mine. You may find that once you see that your fear is misplaced and that augmentations don't make a person less human, that your hate drifts away with your misconceptions.

Having weighed up all the options and wading my way through both the pro and anti-aug camps, I was finally ready to have the life changing M-Pulse augmentation fitted and on March 28th, 2427, that's exactly what I did.

I won't go through the procedure here as I have detailed it in several other posts on this blog, but it was intense, and the learning curve was steep. Two years on, however, it is the single best decision I ever made. I am happier and healthier. I have the freedom to pursue my dream and goals. I don't need to be accompanied when I go out. I feel like I've been reborn as the person I was supposed to be. My only regret is that I let fear stop me from doing it sooner.

It's hard to believe how far I've come in the last two years, and I'd like to thank each and every one of you who has come on this journey with me. The support and friendship I have found within the pro-aug community has been irreplaceable. Here's to many more years together.

THE ZEALOT

Torrez stood at the door of his bedroom watching his partner sleep. The soft, rhythmic sound of Joseph's breathing was hypnotic. It filled Torrez with a sense of peace and comfort.

When Torrez had decided to become a Private Detective, he should have known that Tenebrium was not the place to do it. Too many people remembered him as a dirty cop. Clients had been easy to come by; information had been near impossible. Everyone whom he thought he could count as an ally shut him out, and the only cases he had the clout to complete were those that involved photographing cheating spouses. It had seemed natural after that to follow Thea to Caligo City on Colony Eleven. After his wife had left him, she was the only person in the world who still cared about him.

Not long after he arrived, he had met Joseph. Beautiful Joseph. Joseph was muscular and Black. He had flawless full lips, and the kind of smile that could give a person palpitations. He was smart, kind, and the sex was amazing, but hard as he tried, Torrez didn't love him. He wanted to, but he just didn't. He cared for him greatly; he wanted him sexually, and they had lived together happily for nearly two years, but in his heart of hearts, Torrez knew something was missing. Or rather, someone else was taking up the space that should have been reserved for Joseph.

Sighing, Torrez turned away from the world's most perfect man, and made his way into the living room. Their apartment wasn't as big as the one he had shared with Marielena, but it wasn't small either. The walls of the den were bare brick, with dark wood furniture and black leather couches. There was a small gold bar against one wall, filled with bottles of booze—it still felt strange to Torrez that he could display it openly—and a gramophone in the corner.

Torrez dropped restlessly onto the couch nearest the bar. He pulled a cigarillo from the case in his pocket and lit it. He took a few draws, blowing the smoke out slowly before he pushed up his shirt sleeve to reveal the small metal implant on his wrist. It looked like two triangles inside a circle and was his connection to everything on the datastream. He tapped his Index and the datastream sprang to life in the air in front of him, composed of a rainbow of light. He tapped his Index again and the notes he had made using Thea's console appeared beside it. He had used her resources to find who had threatened Ranveer and discovered a recurring visitor to the journalist's website who called themselves 'The Zealot'.

Painstakingly, Torrez followed the trail from The Zealot's threats on Lalique's blog to their origin—an address in the Church Ward. Caligo had so many people from so many different backgrounds, with so many different religious beliefs, that there was a whole section of the city devoted entirely to faith and worship. These different creeds lived together side by side, enjoying a previously unheard-of harmony. As well as places of worship, there were charity buildings and in one such abandoned building, the person or persons who had styled themselves 'The Zealot' had set up shop.

Finishing his cigarillo, Torrez adjusted his suspenders, grabbed his overcoat and hat and made his way out into the night.

BURNED

It had taken the firefighters nearly twenty-four hours to get control of the blaze, and when they finally doused the ravenous flames, The Kelpie Clinic was barely more than a charred husk.

As Alex walked through the water-sodden and fire-blackened rooms of the clinic, they could barely hold back tears. The devastation of reckless hate was evident everywhere they stepped. They had been tasked with search and rescue, but as soon as Alex had seen the building, they had known that no one could have survived the inferno.

"Sick bastard barred the exits," Detective Erin Fry said from behind her oxygen mask. "Have you found anyone yet?"

Alex shook their head, and the detective headed to the next room over. Alex followed the hall they were in to the end.

They let out a strangled cry, muffled by their fire mask, as the smell of rancid and overcooked meat hit them from the doorway. Alex was afraid to step into the room from which the odour originated, but they knew they must.

They closed their eyes and let the smell wash over them as they stepped inside. Counting themselves down from five, Alex finally opened their eyes.

It was worse than they had expected. Huddled against the back door was a charred mass of bodies, both adults and children, all burned beyond recognition, with wide mouths forever screaming. Alex had seen their fair share of horrors in their time, but this would haunt them forever.

Unable to stand it any longer, Alex all but ran out of the building. When they reached the relative fresh air of the street outside, they wrenched the mask from their face and vomited on the concrete. The sickeningly wet splashes hitting the ground, mixed with the images of the victims inside the clinic, had Alex throwing up all over again. When they could vomit no more, Alex straightened.

Taking deep, shaky breaths, they touched their tragus implant and waited for a response.

"Agent Williams, here."

"Thea...I..."

"Alex? Are you okay?"

"No."

"Where are you?"

"You better get down here."

"What's happening, Alex? Where are you?"

"It's a crime scene."

"What?"

"We need ARC. Someone burned The Kelpie Clinic. They're all dead."

"I'm on my way."

THE CELIA SHORT CONFERENCE CENTRE

The conference centre was cold. Cleo stood shivering on the stage in front of the small but captive audience. They stared at her with stereotypically bland corporate expressions.

"So, in summary, you have only succeeded in curing yourself and the four other patients who were affected by the Styxx variant Quietus. You have made absolutely no progress with the ghouls who are still contained in the SubLevel. Is that correct?" asked the chair of the medical research committee, Everard Hyde. He was a tall and slender White man in his late fifties, with, in Cleo's experience, a permanently grim disposition.

"Yes, and—"

"And now," he cut forcefully across her. "You wish to abandon your penitent studies to move into the contentious field of augmentation?"

"I haven't given up on the ghouls."

"I should hope not, considering they are of your creation."

"But," Cleo said loudly, making it clear she would not be interrupted again. "Science needs to advance in order to let me do that. My team is the boldest and the brightest, chosen by yourselves, and we haven't made a single stride forward when it comes to the ghouls. Augmentations are a new and expanding field, capable of so much more than we ever imagined. I think it would be valuable to shift the focus of the research conducted by my team and I to include augmentations. We've tried everything else. An implant or device may be the cure needed for those still affected by Styxx."

"And this has nothing to do with 'The Augmented Journey Blog'?" Everard asked with a sneer.

"My personal relationships are not the Committee's business and have no bearing on my research."

"Indeed. I was unaware you were romantically involved. I merely meant that you are a cited source on that blog and several others. It appears you have already shifted your focus."

"My focus has always been and will always be the ghouls," Cleo said, pushing her embarrassment aside. "We have hit wall after wall with every avenue we've tried. Wasn't it you who said, 'leave no stone unturned' when you hired me?"

A slightly bitter smile twisted Everard's lips. No one liked being asked for more money, and no one liked being out manoeuvred. "As you wish," he said after a pregnant pause. "I will extend your funding for another six months, subject to monthly reviews, and make available to you and your lab what you will need to broaden the scope of your research to include augmentations."

"Thank you, Mr Hyde."

"Don't thank me yet. Should you make no positive and quantifiable progress within the next six months, I will terminate your funding and your position. Good day, Ms James."

Everard and his silent companions rose from their seats in eerie unison and filed from the room without a backwards glance. Cleo stood where they had left her feeling suddenly like she was being edged closer and closer to the precipice of a steep cliff.

MOLTEN METAL

The Church Ward at night was a beautiful and sombre place. Quiet at this late hour, and dark in contrast to the rest of the neon city, most of the buildings had turned off any lights that would denote welcome. Tall streetlamps brought only dull illumination through the mist of the cold winter's eve.

Torrez made his way along the deserted thoroughfare and into a narrow snicket between a blue-domed mosque and a red brick synagogue. The closeness of the buildings in the Church Ward blocked out much of the lamplight from the Main Street and it made the chill in the air seem more oppressive.

Following the map his oculus implant showed at the corner of his field of vision, Torrez pressed on along the tight alleyway until it finally opened out into a small square. There were no streetlamps here, and Torrez had to squint to read the signs on the buildings, but it didn't take him long to spot the warehouse he was looking for.

The abandoned Una Anima building was the biggest and flashiest, even in its current state of disrepair. Torrez would have expected no less. A large, tarnished bronze sun hung over the doorway and Torrez could see, even from a distance, that the padlock on the front door had been cut. For an organisation that was extremely wealthy, it appeared to skimp on security.

He wasn't sure what he was going to find inside, so it was with more caution than usual that Torrez made his way into the building. He waited until he had crossed the threshold to pull his gun, on the off-chance that someone else might be prowling the abandoned streets.

The warehouse was pitch dark, like Torrez had stepped into the void. He blindly tapped his Index and then blinked. When he opened his eyes, everything was hues of black and green.

The warehouse was filled with what could only be described as copious amounts of junk. There were boxes and boxes of out-of-date flyers. Bunting and other decorations that were commonplace at church fairs lay unused and unopened on row after row of sturdy but basic metal shelves. There was no order to the warehouse, which struck Torrez as odd. He wondered if the tall shelves had always been placed in such a pell-mell way, or if they had been moved to create a sort of maze.

There were mannequins that bore a disturbing and clearly deliberate resemblance to Levi Seward, next to many unmarked packing crates. As Torrez wended his way through the chaotic shelves, he heard nothing but his own footsteps. The place appeared abandoned, but something, perhaps the instincts he had honed as a detective, told him that there was something amiss.

The first hint that his gut had been right came in the form of a strange metallic scent coupled with an odd odour that reminded him of roast beef. Following his nose, Torrez made his way through the ever-tightening labyrinth of shelves, his gun held tightly at his side.

When Torrez finally made it to the centre, he recoiled in horror. Even dulled by the night vision provided by his Seer, it was a sight that would haunt his dreams for years to come.

A cross, made of many different lengths of mismatched wood, has been erected against one of the metal shelves. Crucified upon it was the body of a man. He was Indian and in his mid-forties, and though Torrez could tell none of this due to the horrendous disfigurement he had suffered, he was sure he had just found Ranveer Baker-Singh.

Crude metal stakes pinned his hands and feet to the cross, and a mesh of barbed wire held his head in an upright position, staring at the ceiling. All of this was abhorrent, but nowhere near as chilling as what had clearly killed him. Molten metal had been poured down his throat, spilling onto his face and chest. It had blistered the skin and burned away his lips, revealing his teeth and jawbone.

Whether post or antemortem, Torrez couldn't tell, but the letters crudely carved into Ranveer's chest were a clear message.

'Those who speak false will choke on their lies.'

SUNKEN

Thea wasted no time with the trams now, but she still tapped her foot impatiently in the back of the Jonk as it zoomed towards The Kelpie Clinic. The name 'AD Castillo' flashed blue in front of her eyes a fraction of a second before her Cicada buzzed in her ear.

"I'm already on my way to the clinic," Thea said, without preamble.

"I've sent Rosenberg to the clinic. You're needed elsewhere."

Billy Rosenberg was Thea's second in command. He was good at his job and had long since gained Thea's trust, but she still would have liked to check on Alex herself. Despite her personal wishes, Thea said, "What's happened?"

"A murder, and a grisly one at that."

When Thea arrived at her diverted location, Tenney Stevens Elementary School, there was already a full police cordon in place. She knew by looking at the bleak expressions on the faces of the beat cops manning the perimeter that whatever she was going to see inside would be unpleasant.

Caligo, unlike Tenebrium, did not use the old-fashioned yellow crime scene tape. Instead, they used connected beacons that, when activated, created an impenetrable barrier of translucent red light.

Thea stepped up to the edge of the cordon. An officer she didn't recognise asked for her badge. She showed it to them, then followed them into the school. They were quiet as they led Thea through the locker-lined halls and only nodded towards the door marked 'Swimming Pool', before returning to their post without a word.

Tenney Stevens must have been a very expensive private school; Thea had never known an elementary school to have a pool. Her suspicions were confirmed when she stepped through the double doors.

The pool looked like she imagined a Roman bathhouse would. The walls were a sandy stone and the floor, like the pool, was a beautiful blue and green mosaic. Statues of ancient gods and goddesses stood watch over the waters.

The room was alive with activity. Tables and evidence stations had been set up in all four corners and there was a buzz of chatter as officers conferred with CSIs. A large white sheet hung from tall metal frames, blocking the shallow end of the pool from view. There were floodlights hovering high in the air, silhouetting the movement behind the screen.

Thea walked steadily, careful not to slip on the slick tiles, over to the officer holding the logbook and signed in.

"Agent Thea Williams. ARC."

"Badge number?" The officer asked pleasantly. The tag pinned to her chest told Thea her name was Rachel Martin.

"T-W-zero-one-four-nine."

"The lead detective is Andrea Shill. She knows you're coming."

Thanking Officer Martin, Thea made her way over to the water's edge, where a dark-haired woman, wearing a forest green suit, knelt at the poolside.

"Agent Williams?" the detective asked with a tight-lipped smile. She was tall, with a long straight nose and copper skin.

"Thea, please," Thea said, holding out a hand, which the detective shook firmly.

"This is one you'll probably need to see for yourself. You okay with getting wet?"

"The body is still in the pool?"

"More or less."

Thea took off her jacket, shoes, socks and holster and laid them on a nearby table before following Detective Shill behind the cordon.

A White man in his fifties was nailed to a make-shift cross, made from what looked like children's desks. Bunches of pencils nailed his hands and feet to the wood. He was already very bloated, and his skin, which was purpling, had started to blister. The corpse was half submerged in the shallow end, having clearly been dredged from the depths of the pool. Going against the sick feeling in her stomach, Thea jumped into the water. She waded towards the CSIs and when she was near enough to see his face properly she let out a curse.

"Nothing prepares you for something like this," Shill said, walking beside Thea. "I don't care how long you've served for."

The skin on the man's face was peeling and parts of it appeared to have been burned away. His tongue was lolling out of a hole in his cheek.

"He was down there for a couple of days, right?" Thea asked the nearest Crime Scene Investigator. "Judging by the bloating."

"Yes, Ma'am. Two at least before we found him, and the Grim Sweepers had real trouble getting to him."

"Any idea what killed him? Did he drown?"

"No. It looks like molten metal was poured down his throat before he was thrown into the pool."

"Jesus," Thea said. The depravity of humankind was shocking.

"There is something carved on his chest, but it's hard to make out."

"Show me."

The CSI pulled back the sopping fabric of the victim's shirt. Thea immediately saw why it had been hard to read. The bloating had stretched and deformed the crude letters.

"Those...who speak...false...will choke...on their lies," Thea said as she squinted at the letters.

"We think that's what it says, but we won't know until we get him back to the morgue."

"Thank you," she said to the CSI. "Shall we discuss this dry?" she asked Shill.

Five minutes later, Thea was wrapped in a warm towel sitting in the teacher's lounge at a table opposite the detective.

"I've seen a lot of things in my time..." Shill let the sentence hang.

"Do we know who he is?"

"Travis Mercer. That's where you come in," Shill said as comprehension dawned on Thea.

"Why here? Why leave him at a school? Why not leave him outside the Mayor's office, if whoever is doing this is trying to make a statement?"

"His daughter is a student here."

They sat in silence for a moment.

"The Kelpie Clinic was burned down today." Thea said as she towelled her hair.

"You think it's connected?"

"Connected? Definitely. But whether it's the same person or not, I don't know. Anti-aug sentiment is growing and it's being stoked by people like Levi Seward. We need to catch whoever did this, and quickly. If we're seen to be languishing, it's only going to bolster the anti-aug factions and make the augmented minority think we don't care about them."

"I don't think there's anything more we can do here. I'll call you when we have some leads."

THE PAST

Four years ago...

The afterglow was fading. Even though their bodies were still joined, Bastion could feel the ugliness of their circumstances forcing its way between them. Like dark smoke, it seemed to slither around them, its tendrils strangling the brief happiness he had felt until it was snuffed out entirely.

"We can't do this again," Bastion said, easing himself from Cora and rolling onto his back. "It's not right."

"You are as much a prisoner as I am," she said.

"No, I'm not. I chose this."

"You didn't know what you were choosing, and now you're trapped. Just like me." She reached for him, but he pulled away. They had discussed the ethics of their arrangement more times than Bastion could count. He knew he should say no, but he never did. Every time he took what was offered and every time it made him feel monstrous. Like the worst kind of predator.

He looked at Cora, drinking her in. The light from the single lamp they had made love by cast a warm glow over her pale skin. She was beautiful. "I knew," he said, tearing his eyes away from her lest he let himself be pulled back into the bliss of her embrace.

He stood to avoid the hand that again tried to pull him back to her and made his way to the en suite bathroom.

Like the bedroom, it was decorated in emerald green with gold and white accents. He crossed to the hugely deep free-standing tub and started the tap running. He sat on the edge as he tested the temperature of the water.

"You are not like them," Cora said fiercely from where she stood in the doorway. Her dark hair fell in soft waves on her shoulders. Her eyes were bright golden brown and filled with fire. She was ready for a fight.

"Don't be naïve. I am exactly like them," he said, not looking at her. "I knew they planned to kill people. I knew they would do anything to gain power, and I didn't care because we wanted the same things. I still don't care. My cold feet have nothing to do with an attack of conscience. My heart doesn't bleed for the people of Tenebrium. Maxwell is threatening to hurt Walt, and if I intervene, he hurts you. I only care when it affects me and the people I love. Think about that the next time you invite me inside of you. I'm holding you prisoner, Cora. This whole situation is fucked up."

"Maxwell is holding me prisoner. My father is holding me prisoner. You don't hold me here, you don't lock the doors or tie me up, but we both know that if I left, there would be a price to pay. I don't run because I love you. You aren't my jailer. You're my cellmate."

"You don't know what you're saying," he said, shaking his head sadly.

"Don't be a cad," she said sulkily. "I'm not the one who isn't thinking clearly here. I know what I want, and I'm not ashamed to admit it."

"I am ashamed. Damn well ashamed. It's not right for me to want you. You say it's what you want, but how can I ever really know if that's the truth?"

"The same way everyone else does it. You have to trust me." She moved into the room and slid onto his lap before he could stop her.

He wrapped his arms around her in spite of himself. "You're going to wake up one day and realise that this is wrong. I'm far worse than a cad for letting this continue."

The conversation was circular, and it always ended the same way. Cora would swear that her feelings for him were real, and that they were not born out of fear, stress or desperation, but a genuine connection they had both been surprised to find. Bastion for his part, even though she never truly managed to convince him, would let himself be talked around because Cora was one of only two people in the world whom he loved, and the thought of being without her was just as crushing as the thought that what they shared was something dark and insidious.

"Can I join you?" she asked, wiggling slightly in his lap in an attempt to distract him.

"The bath was for you," he said, gently pushing her to her feet and standing himself. "I'll take a shower later." He kissed the top of her head and left, feeling like he would need far more than a shower if he ever wanted to be clean.

THERAPY

"I think about him all the time," Cora said, not looking at Dr Fraser.

"What do you think about him?" the doctor asked.

She was sitting in the doctor's spacious office. The room was decorated in calming greys and greens and filled with plants. Cora sat on a chaise longue facing the stocky White doctor who sat in a comfortable recliner next to the window. They had dark hair with a long beard to match and wore dazzling gold eyeshadow.

"I think about how we never got to say goodbye," Cora continued. "I think I loved him. I really loved him. I know how we met was troubled, but it's been three years. I feel more together, more myself than I ever did, and I still miss him. My sister would say that it wasn't real. That I loved him as a way of coping, but I think I just loved him. He was good to me. He protected me, listened to me. Confined to that house, I was more at peace than I ever had been out in the world."

"You seem to worry a lot about what your sister thinks," Fraser observed.

"She's the best person I know. She saved me and she saved Tenebrium. There are thousands of people out there in the world who owe her their lives and most don't even know it. She never lets injustice stand. She never turns her back on a fight. She always does the hard thing, the right thing. She's always in my corner. She's the one person I can always count on."

"She sounds like an amazing person."

"She is."

"I believe it. But she isn't you and she doesn't get to tell you how you feel."

"Sometimes I wish I was her. She's so together."

"She hasn't been through what you've been through."

"She's been through worse."

"But she isn't you," the doctor said firmly. "You gain nothing from comparing traumas. We all deal with things differently."

"I suppose."

"Last session, I asked you to take up things you loved before. Things that you feel make you—you. Have you?"

"I've been singing again. Just to myself. It feels private. Before, I loved to be on the stage, but now, it feels like it's just mine and I like that."

"Is it helping?"

"I've been sleeping better."

"Good. Any more episodes?"

"No. None since the last one."

"Great. Same time next week?"

"Same time next week."

INITIATION

It had been a very long night. After the elementary school, Thea had made her way to the remains of The Kelpie Clinic to check on a very shaken Alex, only to be called away to the Church Ward where she had been surprised to find Torrez and another modern-day crucifixion. The arson and the two murders were so clearly linked to the anti-aug movement that the cases had been automatically claimed by ARC. AD Castillo had predictably assigned them to Thea and ordered that she investigate at once. The attack on Levi Seward would have to wait.

By the time she had gotten back to her apartment, it was well into the next morning.

"You look awful," Cora said when she caught sight of Thea. "Are you okay?"

"I'm fine. Three crime scenes in one night, one of which was a swimming pool," Thea said, throwing herself gracelessly onto the couch beside her twin sister.

"That explains your hair," Cora said with an exaggerated grimace.

Thea laughed. "Shut up."

Cora was Thea's identical twin sister, and while when they were younger it had been nearly impossible to tell them apart, the different paths their lives had taken showed on each face. Like Thea, Cora was White, with golden brown eyes and full lips. She had dyed her dark hair blonde of late and it suited her, as well as further distinguishing her from her sister. There was a battle-born hardness to Thea that Cora lacked. She was softer, less cynical, and more hopeful. She had been through a terrible ordeal in Tenebrium that had left an indelible mark on her, but it hadn't managed to kill the dreamer in her. Thea couldn't say the same.

"Are you taking a shower or heading straight to bed?"

"Shower then bed...or maybe I'll sleep right here." Now that she had sat down, the effort of moving seemed herculean.

"Go to bed."

"I will."

"Thea?" Someone was shaking her gently by the shoulder. "Thea."

Thea opened her eyes with a groan. Her neck hurt and she had pins and needles in one of her arms. It took her a moment to reorient herself. It was dark, so it must have been some time in the evening, as the winter days in Caligo were short. As her eyes adjusted, she realised she was still on the couch in the living room.

"I thought you were kidding about sleeping out here," Cora said as she turned on one of the frosted bulb lamps that sat in the corner of the room.

"I was. How long was I out?" Thea sat up and rubbed her eyes.

"I've been to work and back...so...nine hours. You must have really needed the rest."

A year or so after they had moved to Caligo together, Cora had begun to feel restless. She had made impressive strides in both her physical and mental recovery, but she still felt like something was missing. She couldn't go back to her old life as a sex-worker. It was tied too closely to her trauma, and while she didn't regret her time in Tenebrium's Pleasure Quarter, she needed something different. That was when Thea had offered to get her a job at ARC, not an agent like Thea, but in the data division. Cora had loved the idea, as it meant Thea was close, but not so close that Cora couldn't stretch her wings. Two years later, Cora was flourishing in her role as an intelligence expert.

"I'd better shower. I don't want to be late again."

"You need to eat and get some proper sleep. In a bed."

"I know, but it will have to wait until tonight. I'll pick up breakfast—I guess it's dinner now—on the way."

As Thea dragged herself gracelessly to her feet, a thought occurred. "Hey, Cora?"

"Yeah?"

"Have you heard anything at work?"

"Like what?" Cora muted the television she had just turned on.

"About AD Castillo or Una Anima?"

"No. You think something is going on?"

"I'm not sure yet. If you hear anything, will you let me know?"

"Of course. I told you about Roshni and Callisto and they made me pinky swear."

Thea laughed, then headed to her en-suite bathroom to shower and get ready for yet another shift at the Augmentation Regulation Committee.

Not for the first time as she stepped out into the Investigation Wing, Thea thought that The Hive would have been a far more accurate name for ARC HQ than The Orchard. The entire building was buzzing with activity. The cacophony of voices all around and the droning hum as bodies moved at top speed to achieve their various tasks gave the place an almost anthill-like quality. Usually, the hustle and bustle was soothing to Thea—it felt like justice at work, but now it felt like a front for something more insidious. She couldn't quite put her finger on it, but something wasn't right and now that the seed had been planted in her mind, she couldn't get rid of it.

As Thea crossed the common area to her office, AD Castillo fell in step with her. He looked flushed, as if he had run to catch up.

"Morning, Sir. Everything all right?"

"Deputy Director Vargas is waiting for you in your office."

"Should I be worried?"

Castillo tugged gently on Thea's arm pulling her to a stop. He leaned in close as he said, "I think I gave you the wrong impression the other day. I was dealing with some personal issues, and I let my flair for melodrama get the better of me."

"Okay," Thea said after a pregnant pause because it was clear the assistant director was waiting for a response.

"Everything's fine."

"Okay," Thea said again, careful to sound sincere.

AD Castillo nodded, surveyed Thea through narrowed eyes for a moment, then turned on his heel and walked briskly in the direction of his office.

Deputy Director Vargas was a formidable woman. She was of Puerto Rican descent and in her early sixties, with long chestnut hair and purple eyes. Her violet irises were a recent addition. She had been diagnosed with retinitis pigmentosa and decided that rather than wait for her eyes to degrade over many years, she would have them removed and replaced with fully functioning augmentations. The effect was both eerie and quite beautiful.

"Apologies for ambushing you like this," she said from her perch on the edge of Thea's desk. "But I have a matter that needs immediate attention. It's delicate. I'd like you to go alone, as a large ARC presence may make matters worse. With your... history, I think you're the best choice for this mission."

"Mission?"

"Strictly reconnaissance. We've had some reports of...odd initiation practices at Una Anima. With how prevalent the Church of the Single Soul is in the media at the moment, I'd like you to take a subtle investigative approach. If we barge in there guns blazing and the reports are false..."

"It would look bad for ARC," Thea said indifferently.

"Exactly." Vargas gave Thea a bland smile.

"What sort of initiations?"

"The reports are muddled and quite frankly—ludicrous. Augmentation conversion therapy. Unlicensed medical procedures...it's hazy, but if even ten percent is true, we should be worried."

"When is the next...event?"

"Tonight, and remember, don't engage, observe and report back. That's all."

"Yes, Ma'am."

The Church of the Single Soul was the biggest and grandest building in the Church Ward. It was made from glimmering golden-brown stone with green and purple stained-glass windows. A colossal bronze sun hung above the tall carved wooden double doors. It would have been impossible to enter covertly through the large doors, and upon reflection, Thea thought perhaps that was the point.

Instead, she headed around the side where she found a far less grand service entrance. She was surprised and grateful to find it unlocked. Thea carefully slipped inside, closing the door behind her.

This new area definitely felt like being 'behind the scenes'. There was none of the usual grandeur or portraits of Levi Seward. Just grey walls and beige crates. It was a storage area, much like a small warehouse in appearance. Two members of the church were taking stock of a recent delivery, but they took no notice as Thea walked past them and deeper into the church.

The stockroom led into a bright corridor. The walls were a yellowish-white and the floors were covered by an inoffensive buff coloured carpet. Thea could hear voices echoing nearby and knew she was on the right track. She followed the sounds until it led her to an ornate door marked 'Chancel'.

Thea pressed her ear to the door. Though it was hard to tell, she was almost positive that the voice she could hear pontificating wasn't Levi Seward himself, but one of his underlings. 'Cast off your old life. Remove sin from your body and restore your immortal soul,' it was saying.

Gently, Thea opened the door and found herself behind the altar. There was a large glass cross, flanked by portraits of Levi Seward.

The pale pews had been pushed to the side and a ring of around forty Una Anima members wearing white hooded robes stood in a circle around five others. Four people, three men and a woman, all with augmented limbs, knelt in their underwear in front of the fifth, a White man of around thirty with curly red hair and rather sharp features.

"Are you ready to prove your loyalty to Una Anima, to the Lord, and to Levi Seward?" He demanded as he stood over them.

"Levi Seward is our link to God," the initiates said together.

The red-headed man smiled and turned to take the case that was offered to him by one of the robed figures. He laid it at his feet in front of the initiates, then knelt to open it. Inside were four long stainless steel surgical blades.

"Rid yourselves of your sins."

The first initiate to pick up a blade was a Black man, with greying locs and an augmented arm. The other three followed quickly after.

"Rid yourselves of your sins," the red-head man repeated.

The man with grey locs took several deep breaths that were almost shouts, then plunged the blade into his shoulder where the metal met his flesh. He screamed as blood pulsed from the wound, but he didn't stop his attempts to carve out his augmentation.

Thea jumped out from her hiding spot behind the altar, holding her badge in one hand and her gun in the other. "Everybody, stop what you are doing right now. Put the blades on the ground and put your hands in the air."

The three initiates who hadn't started to mutilate themselves looked nervously at each other but didn't drop the blades. They didn't start to cut either. The man with locs continued his assault on his shoulder, his pained grunts and shrieks echoing in the large chamber.

"This is a private religious ceremony. I don't care what agency you represent; you have no right to be here. Please leave."

"This is illegal. Encouraging and facilitating self-harm is a crime. Requiring mutilation as an initiation is a crime. Stop this now. Sir." Thea turned her attention to the man with locs, who had succeeded in cutting down to the metal where it fused to his bone. "Put down the knife before you bleed to death."

"I can do what I want to my body and I want to be pure. I am a private citizen." His voice was breathy and threaded with pain. It was clear he was having trouble cutting through the bone, though whether due to blood loss, a poor tool, or the awkward angle it was hard to tell. Either way, he was likely to pass out before he succeeded.

"You'll be privately dead if you keep that up. This is insane."

"You have no right to comment on our religious practises," the red-headed man said, his voice dripping with superiority.

"If this was a religion, I'd agree, but this is a cult. Screw it." Abandoning caution, Thea holstered her badge and gun and marched forward. She pushed the white-robed onlookers out of her way as she made her way into the centre of the circle. In his weakened state, it was easy for her to wrestle the blade away from the man. Thea threw the bloodied knife to one side and forced the man onto his back as she pulled off her jacket. She crumpled it up and used it to apply pressure to the wound. Up close, the man with locs was pale and his skin slick. If she had waited any longer, he probably wouldn't have survived.

"Call Medicus," Thea shot at one of the robed figures nearby. "Now!" She bellowed when they hesitated. As they did what she ordered, Thea used her shoulder to activate her Cicada. "This is Agent Williams. I'm declaring a major incident at The Church of the Single Soul. There is one casualty with life-threatening injuries. We'll need teams on the ground and press liaisons."

SCARS

Someone was kissing their way up Walt's back. He opened his eyes, but didn't move, enjoying the sensation as he lay on his stomach in bed.

"What are you doing?" he asked softly.

"Counting your scars."

"You'll be there a while."

Walt rolled over to look at Fen. She was gorgeous. Her glossy black hair was tousled and strands fell from the bun she always slept in, framing her face. She was Chinese and in her late thirties, a reporter and a surprise. He hadn't been looking for a relationship with anyone, but she had been persistent, and he was grateful. It was still very new. They had only been seeing each other for a few months, but Walt was happier than he could remember being in a long time.

"Morning," she said, giving him a quick kiss on the lips.

"Morning," he said with a smile.

At her gentle nudging, he allowed himself to be pushed back onto his stomach.

"What are all these little ones?" He shivered enjoyably as her fingers traced the small scars across his shoulder blades.

"I was thrown through a window."

"What about this one?"

He tensed slightly as she touched the long thin scar in the small of his back, behind which the metal cage that held his spine together resided. "Broken back."

He rolled over to face her again.

"And this?" She placed a gentle kiss on the circular mark on his stomach.

"Gun shot."

"Are you lying to me?"

"Nope." He shook his head. "Being a cop in this town is tough."

He sat up and captured her lips. She put her hands on his chest and pushed him back into the pillows, then slung a leg over his hips so she was straddling him.

"I'm going out of town for a few days," she said, breaking the kiss. "For a story."

"What story?" Walt asked, kissing her neck.

Fen sat up and tapped her nose, then lent back down to take his earlobe between her teeth.

"You're gonna keep me in the dark? But when *you* want information, you're very demanding," he said breathlessly, watching enraptured as she licked, sucked and kissed her way down his chest.

"What if it's not information I want?" She slipped her hand between them just as his Cicada buzzed in his ear.

"Hold that thought," he said with a groan.

"Just the thought?"

"James, here." He said, his eyes never leaving Fen's. They were alight with desire.

"Sir, we need you at a crime scene. It's bad."

"I'm on my way," he said with a sigh as he ended the call. "Rain check?" he asked Fen with obvious regret.

"I'll see you when I get back." She gave him a final deep kiss, then got out of bed to get dressed. He followed suit, knowing that his day could only get worse from here.

MUTINY

Mateo Castillo was not a brave man, at least not anymore, but he was a good one—somewhere deep down. He had diligently worked his way up to assistant director by not making waves. He did enough to be thought of as competent, made enough of an impression to be considered well liked, but never truly stuck his neck out or took a stand. It had served him well. Now, however, it was becoming harder and harder to sit on the sidelines, especially when he knew his own position was at risk.

He had always had a good relationship with upper management; it was one of the perks of being charming, yet inoffensive, but now he could sense something was troubling the waters. It made him uneasy. It made him uneasier still when he had been urgently called to the Deputy Director's office.

It was with sweaty palms that he knocked on Natalia Vargas's door. While some found her new irises pleasant, they unnerved Mateo. He had much preferred the deep, rich brown they had been in the past.

"Mateo," she said warmly as she opened the door. "Thank you for coming in at such short notice."

"Not a problem. What can I help you with?"

"I need you to take control of Agent Williams' team for the day and prep them for a mission."

"Why?" Mateo said bluntly, too surprised to employ his usual tact.

"I sent her on another mission. It was supposed to be simple, but things rarely go as planned. Oh, she's fine," Vargas added, correctly reading his facial expression. "She's just busy. This one is a bit much for the other SSAs. If I can't have Thea, I need someone else who I have complete faith in."

"We used to be friends, didn't we?" They had been more than friends a long time ago, but it hadn't worked out and both had gone on to get married. Vargas still was.

"I don't know what you mean. We are friends, aren't we?" Vargas made a valiant attempt at shock, but it didn't quite ring true.

"Then as a friend—why are you blowing smoke up my ass?"

"I had forgotten what you were like before you settled behind a desk. I like the old you."

"Something is going on. I can tell. I know you, remember."

"You're being paranoid. That's a trait of the new you."

Mateo was sure she was lying, but he also knew when not to push. "What mission does the team need prepped for?"

Vargas smiled like she knew the conversation wasn't over but pressed on regardless. "I—well, you are sending them to The Tiernan Shelter on Kip Street."

"Tiernan is a shelter for vulnerable augs."

"We have had reports of weapons within the complex."

"Reports from who?"

"It was anonymous."

"Then how do you know if it's credible or not? This isn't the kind of thing we want to go in blind on. We could cause real harm here."

"The tip is anonymous on the record..."

"But you know who it is."

"I do and I trust him—it. Friends we may be, but this is an order. I've already briefed the team. I just need you to make sure they do as I instructed. You don't have a choice here, AD Castillo."

And there it was. She'd won, like she always did, because just as when they had dated, the power was always hers.

Mateo liked Thea, maybe slightly more than was professionally acceptable, but more than this, he respected the hell out of her. She fought for what she believed in and never backed down from a fight. Her personnel file read like fiction, but when he had finally met her, he had realised she was every bit as impressive as her history made her sound. He admired her courage, but he didn't have it. This would undoubtedly be bad for her, but he needed his job. He had his daughter to think about.

The Mission Hub was where tactical teams, like the one Thea headed, went to prepare for missions. It was all metal, with lockers for guns and armour.

When Mateo arrived, he was surprised to see the eight agents whom Thea was in charge of already geared up for the mission. All eight were wearing black tactical gear that reminded Mateo of Tenebrium's Onyx Legion.

"You are the leader of this team when Williams is absent, Correct?" Mateo shot at Rosenburg. He was White with auburn hair and medium in all senses of the word- medium height, medium build. Even his hair was the happy medium between red and brown.

"Yes, sir," he said, standing to attention like the soldier he'd been.

"I'm halting this mission until further notice."

"But sir, the order came from Deputy Director Vargas..." Rosenburg let the sentence trail off but both men knew what he was implying.

"This mission has been eighty-sixed. Am I making myself clear?"

Looking extremely uncomfortable, Rosenburg leaned in so that only Mateo could hear him. "With all due respect, we are far more afraid of Vargas than we are of you."

"You walk out that door—you're all suspended."

"She'll do worse. I'm sorry, sir, but I'm willing to risk it."

Mateo watched on helplessly as the team filed out of the locker room towards the transporter bay.

Thinking quickly, Mateo brought his hand to his Cicada. "Thea," he said as soon as she answered. "We have a problem."

SPIN

Levi Seward stared at his reflection in the mirror, pleased. He looked good, better than good. Handsome and refined, but not so much as to seem flashy. He had cultivated the perfect image that appealed to all facets of his audience because he knew what they wanted. He knew how to prey on their fears and speak to their values. He knew how to twist them around his little finger.

"Two minutes, Mr Seward," the PA said, peeking their head into the lavish dressing room.

Levi nodded and waved the assistant away. He gave himself a final once over and, unable to find any flaws in his perfectly polished façade, made his way into the studio proper.

The set of Caligite Socialite was brightly lit by many studio lights and filled with camera equipment and crew. Though there was seating for a live audience of around three hundred, the rows and rows of chairs sat empty; today would be a far more intimate affair. The usual long discussion table had been replaced by two velvet armchairs that framed a holographic fireplace.

Caligite Socialite's host was a self-professed 'Southern Belle' by the name of Sadie Moore. Sadie was White and in her early sixties. She was everything a flapper wasn't; all big hair and cleavage wrapped in a cloak of demureness and hospitality. She was already waiting for Levi when he sauntered onto the sound stage.

"Levi!" Sadie exclaimed, running to meet him. When they came face to face, she hugged him tightly, pressing her breasts into his chest, air-kissed each of his cheeks and straightened his lapels. Had he been attracted to women, he imagined it would be quite an effective display, and while he wasn't moved, he respected a fellow hustler.

"Sadie, darling," he said, returning her enthusiasm with interest.

"You ready, Cher?" Sadie said, in a far more business-like tone.

"Always." Levi winked.

"Well, all right then. Bobby over there will tell you when."

"All right everyone, this is your ten second warning," the aforementioned Bobby called from the gloom behind the spotlights.

Sadie sat down in the leftmost armchair, facing out into the empty audience. Three cameras and an abundance of dazzling lights beat down upon her.

"We are live in five, four, three, two..." As Bobby mouthed 'one' the red 'ON-AIR' light flashed.

"Good evening, Socialites," Sadie beamed. "As you all know, I'm Caligo's own Southern Belle, Sadie Moore and, boy, do I have a show for you tonight. Instead of my usual panel, I have just one guest for y'all, but I promise you will not be disappointed you tuned in. Unless you've been living under a rock, you have heard him speak, you have seen him on the news, you know his face and you've probably been wooed by his charms—please join me in welcoming the leader of The Church of the Single Soul, Una Anima, and Caligo's very own Levi Seward."

At Bobby's signal, Levi walked into shot and joined Sadie in front of the virtual fire. They performed the same greeting as they had seconds before, then Levi took up his armchair, crossing his legs and leaning back as if it were a throne.

"Thank you for joining me."

"Thank you for having me."

"Before we get into it—how are you? You've been through quite the ordeal." Sadie patted his knee in a supportive, if slightly suggestive, way.

"I'm all right. I was lucky. Thank you."

"How did it feel? What's it like to be shot at?"

"It's frightening, and it's frightening to think that that level of violence is what anyone with dissenting opinions needs to be prepared for, but they can shoot at me all they like. I will not stray from the path."

"Speaking of the path," Sadie said, steering the conversation like a master host. "You are the leader of Una Anima. Can you explain what you and your church stand for? What is the single soul?"

"What we believe is simple," Levi said, touching the tips of his fingers together in a way reminiscent of prayer. It was a practised move, and it worked. "God designed us in his image and altering that image is against his will. To replace what the Lord gave you with metal—or biomech or whatever folks want to call it—damages that person's soul, and we only get one. The more bits of their body they replace, the more they damage their soul, and a soul is what makes us human. To be augmented is to be less human, and if we keep accepting these things, because we are too afraid to hurt feelings, the human race as we know it will cease to exist. It will be replaced with a race of soulless augs, more machine than man, and for me that's not only sacrilege, it's the stuff of hellish nightmares."

"Is it fair to say you hate the augmented? That's certainly what's reported."

"No. no, it's not fair to say that at all. I don't hate these people. In fact, I love them and that's why I'm trying to save them. Without a full soul, they cannot enter the kingdom of Heaven. Their spirits will wander in purgatory eternal, and I wouldn't wish that on anyone. 'Save our souls' has never had more significance than right here and right now."

"Do you have a message for the augmented community?"

"It's not too late. Remove the impurities from your body, live as you are, and repent. God will forgive you, and so will I."

Sadie nodded and raised a hand as if she was testifying.

"I'll say it again. God is forgiving," Levi went on. "That is why I went to meet the man who tried to kill me."

"You did not!" Levi couldn't say whether Sadie's shock was real or yet another thing that carefully curated for the cameras, but he appreciated the prompt nonetheless.

"I did, and I forgave him. I refused to press charges. I even paid his bail. He has strayed from the path, but he's just a little lost."

"Do you think it's in your power to save a man like that?"

"Well, he agreed to meet with me again, and we've had some great chats. He's even interested in joining the church. That's the power of Una Anima. Of God. You are only damned if you choose to stay lost. I will welcome with open arms anyone who wants to rejoin the path. There is no sin that cannot be cleansed by repenting."

"Stay tuned for the preacher's full account of the near fatal attack on his life and an in-depth discussion about the dangers of augmentations after these messages."

GHOSTS

In the three years after what historians would call 'The Battle of Medicorum', the building itself had lain abandoned and untouched. There had been no one to reclaim anything left behind and no one willing to rebuild. Consequently, the white marble monolith loomed over the Eltham District like the ghost of the Gold Legion. Passersby avoided looking at the husk, and squatters who had taken up residence in most abandoned buildings nearby gave the place a wide berth.

As Walt stepped through the front doors, his heart skipped a beat. It was like stepping into purgatory. Nothing had changed. Rubble and broken glass covered the once gleaming floors, and the walls were cracked and pock-marked by bullets and pulse rounds. He tried not to think about the things that happened there as he walked through the atrium of the medical wing.

The room was haunting. The columns that punctuated the vast space were crumbling. The glass lift that led to the mezzanine was hanging precariously by a single wire. Shards littered the floor below it, coated in dried blood. Walt couldn't help but see Bastion lying there, broken; his words still echoed in Walt's ears. "It's easy, isn't it? Loving her."

Now, there was a large fissure in the floor near the stairs, easily wide enough to climb down. It was surrounded by TPD personnel.

"It doesn't feel right being back here, does it?" Detective Orion Martin said, breaking away from his colleagues to greet Walt. Orion was bald, Black, and long-serving. He could have retired five years previously, but police work, it seemed, was in his blood.

"We should've had this building demolished," Walt said, nodding. "What have we got?"

"You haven't seen anything like this before, I guarantee it," Orion said, taking Walt over to the aperture.

Orion was right, Walt had never seen anything like it. Hanging from the exposed rebars was a woman. She had a metal rod passed through her shoulders, crucifying her over the crevasse. Her chest was bare, and the words carved there read: "Liar".

"I know her," Walt said, squinting at the decaying face. "That's Helena Cutter."

"The actress?"

"She's an activist now. It can't be a coincidence she was posed here. Was she killed here?"

"Yes. There's a secondary crime scene in one of the procedure rooms down the hall."

Rubbing his eyes, Walt stepped away from Orion and touched his hand to his Cicada, then tapped his Index. A small square of light appeared at face height.

"Walter?"

The square of light flickered slightly, then an image of Torrez, looking tired and dishevelled, filled the space. Clearly, was in bed; an arm was draped loosely over his waist.

"It's early."

"I found your missing woman."

"Helena Cutter?"

"Yeah. You filed the missing person's report and, if I remember correctly, she has no family, except an estranged husband. I need you to ID the body."

"Damn." The image blurred slightly as Torrez extricated himself from his partner and moved into what Walt could only assume was his bathroom. "Was she crucified?" His voice echoed softly off the tile.

"How did you know?"

"There are two more victims in Caligo. Both vocally pro-aug."

Walt walked back over to Orion and leant over the crater so Torrez could see the body.

"Yeah. That's her," he said regretfully.

"All right, thanks for doing this. I'll contact local PD in Caligo and see if we can liaise. Three makes a serial killer." He sighed.

"Actually, this is aug related. Crossing city lines makes it an ARC case."

"Shockingly, I don't trust big flashy organisations."

"Thea is an agent with them now. I assume you still trust her."

Walt and Torrez had come to something of an understanding in recent years, to the point where Walt might even call him a friend. One of the many things that made that possible was the fact they never talked about Thea.

"It's been years."

"Fine," Torrez said, all but rolling his eyes. "I'll make the call."

"No. I'll see to it."

HOMECOMING

Marielena picked the two glasses she had just filled with wine up from the sideboard and carried them over to where she had left Cleo on the loveseat.

"Thank you," Cleo said, accepting the offered glass.

They were sitting in Marielena's plant room, surrounded by green fronds, delicate leaves, and terracotta pots.

"So, what happened?" Marielena said, pulling Cleo's feet into her lap so she could massage them.

"It was awful. We aren't making any progress with the ghouls and the board just loved pointing out how I have achieved next to nothing in the last three years. I had to beg them to fund more research. If we don't make some headway this time, they'll cut my funding, which is the same as firing me."

"I'm sorry, Mi Amor. I wish I could help."

"Honestly," Cleo said, a lump in her throat. "I'm just not sure it can be done. What I helped create with Styxx...people have died because of me. People are as good as dead because of me. Hundreds of thousands of people and their families and I can't do a goddamned thing about it. I am good at my job, and my team is amazing, but I don't think it can be done. And if it can't be done, I'm a murderer. The people they were are gone and all that's left is a monster that I made."

Tears streamed down Cleo's face, and Marielena slid along the sofa so she could cradle her.

"It's going to be okay," she said, brushing a tear from Cleo's cheek.

"I have no right to be upset. This didn't happen to me—I did this."

Marielena knew there was nothing she could say. No words could fix this. Instead, she brushed her lips against Cleo's cheek, slowly making her way to her mouth. She had meant to soothe only, but as her tongue found Cleo's, Marielena felt a shift between them. Their relationship was new. It was a bad idea to have sex like this, with Cleo so emotional, but the pull Marielena felt towards the woman was hard to deny.

They had no time to act upon the desire that had bubbled up in Marielena's stomach. There was a thunderous crash and the tinkling sound of shattered glass hitting a hard wooden floor.

"What the hell was that?" Cleo said, getting to her feet, tears forgotten.

They made their way into the living room. A brick lay cracked on the dark floor. It was clear it had been launched through the small window from a Jonk.

Marielena stopped to pick it up. Rusted metal nails had been hammered into the ruddy clay, and there was a note haphazardly attached with elastic bands.

"Take down the blog or else," Cleo read over her shoulder.

"It's to the point, I suppose. What a mess," she added, looking at the broken window.

"They're just trying to scare you," Cleo said, placing a chaste kiss on the side of her neck.

"It isn't working."

"Be careful."

"I won't censor myself for the benefit of thugs and bigots."

"I didn't say censor yourself; I'm saying take care of yourself. You should report this."

"I'll call Walt."

Cleo nodded and gave a strained smile, and Marielena knew exactly why. She and Walt had ended their marriage on surprisingly good terms. In fact, both she and Marielena would describe Walt as a friend, but neither of them particularly wanted her ex-husband involved in their relationship in any capacity, even a professional one.

THE RAID

The silence in the back of the tactical transporter was tense. Rosenburg could feel the tension that had taken hold of his fellow agents. It didn't sit well with them going against Thea. It didn't sit well with him, either. Nor did their mission. To have ignored a direct order from AD Castillo didn't feel nearly as daunting as betraying Thea.

ARC was a complicated agency. In general, it tended to be on what Rosenburg called 'the right side of things', but it still needed money to function, and as with all institutions that relied on donations to top up government funding, sometimes it had to bend the rules and cross lines. This was one of those times. But ignoring the odd misdemeanour was not the same as victimising already marginalised and vulnerable people.

Thea wouldn't do this.

Thea wouldn't do this.

Thea wouldn't do this.

He couldn't get the thought out of his head.

As the transporter landed beside the Tiernan Shelter, Rosenburg's team got to their feet as one. All was quiet on the street outside. He directed his comrades to their agreed entry points with a nod of his head. No one spoke; they didn't need to.

Rosenburg would be taking point. As his subordinates scattered, he stayed where he was, looking at his watch.

Twenty seconds passed as he stood there in front of the main entrance.

Three. Two. One, he counted to himself.

When the time came, he raised his leg and slammed the sole of his boot into the door. With the recent augmentation he'd had fitted to correct an old knee injury, the power he generated was immense. The door was blasted off its hinges. It hadn't even hit the ground when Rosenburg stepped inside.

"Augmentation Regulation Committee! Nobody Move!"

Similar cries and shouts echoed from the other points of entry as windows were breached and doors broken down.

"Down on the ground!"

"Hands behind your head!"

"Eyes on the floor."

The room Rosenburg had entered appeared to be a refectory of sorts, but there was also bedding on the floor and makeshift partitions made from tattered sheets. The obvious poverty here made Rosenburg's heart ache. *We should not be here*, he thought.

There were sixty or so people dotted around the bare room. Most were sitting at long tables that would not have looked out of place in a school canteen, eating some kind of stew. Some had very obvious augmentations, metal limbs or chrome plates affixed to their skulls, while others were subtler, perhaps a silver eye or thin gleaming strands of light passing under the skin. They all looked scared. Those at the tables sat with their hands behind their heads, those who had been lying on the rough-and-ready pallets, knelt with their hands raised.

We should not be here.

"My name is Billy Rosenburg. I'm with the Augmentation Regulation Committee. We have had reports of illegal weapons being held at this facility. We aren't here to hurt anyone. We ask that you remain where you are while we conduct our search. If you co-operate, we will be out of your hair as soon as we can."

"If we're so safe, why did you bust in here with assault rifles? There are children sleeping in the other room." The man who had spoken was very tall, well-muscled, and Black. He had long, dark locs pulled back into a ponytail that fell to the middle of his back.

"What's your name?"

"None of your business. We haven't done anything wrong. There are no weapons here."

"Just let us do our jobs and we'll leave."

"What about our doors and windows? It's winter."

"I'll see what I can do."

"Sure you will."

"Leave it alone, Bast," a small blonde woman with dwarfism to his left said, tugging on his elbow. She was White with a buzz-cut and an entirely silver arm.

"No, ma'am. He's right. We've come into your home and I'm sorry but—"

Commotion in another room made Rosenburg stop short.

"I said don't move! Don't move! I'll shoot," they heard a muffled voice yell.

"No!" Rosenburg roared, tearing from the room. The man and his companion following suit. "Stand down!"

A burst of gunfire rent the air and Rosenburg saw a teenage boy sprinting down the corridor, Agent Yull, the newest member of the team, close behind him. "Get back here," he yelled.

"Stop!" the blonde woman yelled. "He doesn't understand! He's just scared!"

"Stand down!" Rosenburg bellowed.

He was bowled out of the way by the tall man with locs. His huge strides allowed him to catch up to Yull faster than Rosenburg ever could. As soon as he was close enough, he tackled the man, and they both tumbled out of the broken back door into the street.

Recovering quickly, Rosenburg tore after them.

When he stepped outside the teenage boy was cowering next to a dumpster, Yull was on his feet, with a bloody nose, pointing his rifle at the unknown 'Bast', and there was a ring of Caligo Police officers fencing them in, press dotted amongst them.

"Fuck," he muttered, pulling off his helmet and roughly tousling his sweat-damp hair.

Stepping away from their fellow officers, a detective moved to stand in front of Yull.

"Stand down," they said. "I'm Detective Alex Wyndham with the CPD. We have had credible reports that a false tip was given to ARC in the hope of stoking anti-aug sentiment."

This had Thea written all over it, and had he not been sure that he was in very big trouble, he would have been impressed.

The blonde woman went to comfort the teenage boy, and the man with locs got to his feet. He radiated a power that made Rosenburg sure he could have flattened Yull if he had wanted to, augmentations or no.

"All right everyone," Rosenburg said, resigned to the shit-storm that was brewing. "Let's move out. We're sorry for the trouble," he added to the Tiernan residents, who were now standing in the doorway watching on.

Hanging his head, Rosenburg did the walk of shame through the shelter and out the front door he had kicked in. He had expected what faced him—this was Caligo City, but it was still overwhelming. He was met with a tide of journalists.

"What do you have to say about the incident?"

"Was this an accident or is ARC finally showing its true intentions to the augmented community?"

"Who gave you the tip?"

"False tip, that seems convenient. Do you have anything to say?"

"Who's your commanding officer? You aren't allowed to not answer that one. It's the law."

"Supervisory Special Agent Thea Williams."

THE PAST

Seventeen years ago...

"Please don't go," Derrick Wayland begged his wife.

"I have to," Cynthia said, placing her hand on his cheek.

She had known this was coming. He had watched her get dressed and apply her make-up with the air of someone attending a funeral.

"I don't want you to sleep with him," he whispered, his lip quivering.

"I don't want to, but I have to." She wouldn't cry; she refused to do her make-up for that monstrous man a second time. Resigned to what she had to do, Cynthia pulled her most expensive coat from the cupboard and slipped it over her red silk dress.

"No, you don't. Stay. Our son's operation is tomorrow. He needs his mother."

"If I stay, how will we pay for the surgery?"

"We'll find a way." Derrick reached out and took her prosthetic hand, holding it tightly so she couldn't make any further moves to leave.

"And when the repo-men come and rip it from him, what will we do then?"

She knew she'd won when his hand fell away from hers.

"I love you," she said, unable to look him in the eye.

"Come back to me," he muttered, turning away, seemingly unable to watch her leave.

The Jonk ride to the home of Vinny Russo was the shortest of Cynthia's life. The tighter the knots in her stomach became, the faster the transporter seemed to travel. All too quickly she was landing in front of a fortress-like mansion.

High brick walls surrounded a large garden of perfectly manicured grass and flowers. A long, white cobbled path led to the biggest house Cynthia had ever seen. It was wide and stunningly white, with a mix of round and rectangular windows across its several floors. The entrance was bowed and framed by pillars with carved floral reliefs surrounding the gleaming glass door.

A rat-faced White man was waiting to greet Cynthia as she stepped out of the Jonk.

"Right this way, Ma'am," he said, extending a hand which she accepted out of fear.

The man led her gently up the front steps, through the door and into the foyer. It was a vast space with rounded archways leading off into other parts of the expansive complex. A huge spiral staircase coiled high above.

Cynthia was led under one of the archways and through a set of gleaming black double doors into the sort of dining room she would have expected to find in a palace. It was all black. The floors, the panelled walls, the velvet curtains, even the long table was black and glossy. Only the chairs provided contrast. All twenty-four of them were a deep purplish-red.

"He'll be with you shortly," the man said as he exited, closing the door behind him.

Now that she was alone, the magnitude of the situation hit her. Cynthia clasped a hand over her mouth to stifle the sob she let out. She took deep, ragged breaths as she tried to calm herself. She was sure her fear, however justified, would be seen as an insult or rejection, and she didn't want to offend the mobster lest he renege on their deal or worse.

There was a single candle placed at the far end of the table and two places set for dinner. Cynthia moved over to the setting that was clearly meant for her and sat down.

It felt like an eternity as she waited for the vile brute to show himself. She couldn't help but let her mind wander to the things she was going to have to do with him. The thought of his lips on hers, his caress, their bodies joined, made her shiver in disgust.

"Are you cold?" Cynthia let out a squeak of fright. "I'll add another log to the fire."

Vincent Russo looked just as he had the first time she'd seen him, hulking and scarred. She watched apprehensively as he moved slowly around the table to the fireplace. She was surprised by how quiet his entrance had been and even more surprised by the grace he walked with; she hadn't noticed it before. He picked up two dry logs and tossed them into the flames before turning back to look at her properly.

"You look lovely," he said softly. He sounded nervous, but that couldn't possibly be right. "I'm sorry I'm late. I had...things to attend to."

"I'm sure you did," Cynthia said. She was so afraid it was making her bold, but Vinny let out a low chuckle.

"Are you hungry? I didn't know what you liked, and I didn't want to presume, so I had the chef from Deco come here for the night. He'll make whatever you want. My cousin Dill raves about the place." Cynthia didn't say anything. She didn't understand. "Why are you looking at me like I have two heads?"

"You...you want to eat. Before..." she couldn't finish the sentence.

"Before what?"

"Before we have...sex."

"When I said dinner, I meant it," Vinny said, taking up the seat opposite. "Just dinner. I know my reputation and most of it is true. I'm not a good man. I've done nasty twisted things and I'll tell you about them if you want, but I just want to get to know you. If you want to have sex, we will. The thought of it makes me...but not unless that's what you want. I'm not asking you for anything other than your company."

"You're rich, powerful...dangerous, you can have anyone. Why me?"

"That's the thing. I can't have anyone. My lifestyle is one I chose, but it's a lonely thing."

"I'm married."

"Lucky guy."

"At the casino...you made it seem..."

"A man in my position has to keep up appearances. I know what they call me. Beast. Cyclops. Frankenstein. Is it how I'd like to be perceived? No. But it's effective. In my line of work, image is everything. Nobody is brave enough to cross an honest to God monster."

"Why were you late?" she asked, meeting his eyes for the first time. Both the milky white one and the rich brown one seemed to radiate sincerity.

"The truth?"

Cynthia nodded, certain she didn't really want to know.

"I was punishing a thief. He stole a lot of liquor from one of my casinos, not to mention a wad of cash."

"What did you do to him?" It was barely more than a whisper.

"I took a pair of clippers to his fingers, then I used a rusty saw to take his hand at the wrist. I wanted to send a message."

Cynthia's heart was beating as fast as a hummingbird's. The way he held her gaze told her every word was true. She knew she ought to look away, but something held her steady.

"I'd like a steak—if that's all right," she said finally.

"How do you like it?"

"Rare."

VULTURES

Caligo City was run by the press. There were government officials, Civil Servants and Law Enforcement all dedicated to shaping the way information was given, but public attitudes changed at the whim of the media. Gossip columns, glamour rags, and news outlets controlled perceptions and everyone in the city was desperate to be in the know.

To Thea, it felt like every person in Caligo was a journalist. Wherever she went, she was bombarded by the press. Since her name had been broadcast as the leadership behind the raid on Tiernan less than 24 hours ago, she could go nowhere without being followed by press-men and newshounds. She was embroiled in a whirlwind of sensationalism and tabloid gossip. With all outlets ignoring the crux of the problem–Caligo was not safe for those with augmentations. Instead, even though there was irrefutable evidence to the contrary, the press discussed at length whether Tiernan really had been hiding deadly weapons and if Thea was old enough to hold the position of SSA.

"No comment," she said for the hundredth time, pushing a reporter roughly aside as they tried to stop her getting inside The Orchard.

It was another cold Caligo morning, but the frosty air and the damp from the previous night's rain did nothing to deter the now ever-present crowd outside ARC headquarters.

"Vultures," Thea muttered to herself as she finally made it inside the atrium. Ignoring any greetings, she all but ran to the lift and stepped inside, pummelling the button for the Investigation Wing. Thea's respite was barely more than a second, however. Just before the doors closed, a beautiful Chinese woman slipped between them, trapping herself and Thea alone in the lift.

Thea knew immediately that she was a journalist.

"Agent Williams," she said, shoving a recorder in Thea's face. "I'm Fen Yeoh with the Tenebrium Times. I'd love to hear your account of what happened at Tiernan."

"I wasn't there, and you shouldn't be here. Go back downstairs to the press office," Thea said through gritted teeth, barely able to contain her temper.

Fen hit the emergency stop and the elevator shuddered to a halt.

"Seriously?"

"The raid is just another in a long line of worrying anti-aug trends. Do you have any words of reassurance for the augmented community? Can ARC really keep them safe when it's just adding to the persecution they face on a daily basis?"

"No comment." Thea pummelled the keypad again, restarting the lift.

"Just days ago, you saved the life of prominent anti-aug figure Levi Seward only to publicly condemn him, then yesterday your team took part in an illegal raid. Where do *you* stand? Where does ARC stand? How can the augmented community trust an organisation that seems to have a foot in both camps?"

"I didn't order the raid. Deputy Director Natalia Vargas did, based on a tip she knew was false. Levi Seward is a scumbag, and I am firmly in support of the aug community," Thea said. The lift doors opened, and she gratefully stepped out.

"That's on the record," Fen said, surprised, holding up the recorder.

"No, it isn't. You can't record inside this building." Thea folded her arms over her chest and smirked slightly.

"You're going to deny you said that, aren't you?" Fen said shrewdly.

"Sure am. But that doesn't mean it's a lie. Now go back to the press pit. You have news to report."

To ensure that Ms Yeoh actually went where she was supposed to, Thea accompanied her to the press pit before making her way back to the Investigation Wing.

She wasn't sure why she had told the journalist what she had. Maybe it was that Ms Yeoh seemed more concerned about the welfare of those with augmentations than her colleagues. Maybe it was just that, after Tenebrium, Thea'd had enough of conspiracies and subterfuge, of obfuscation and the company line. Either way, she had done yet another thing that would probably get her fired. She was erring on the side of recklessness, and she knew it.

As the elevator doors opened, she found herself face to face with Natalia Vargas. It was rather like being confronted unexpectedly by a fire-breathing dragon.

"May I have a word?" Her tone was so light it was dangerous.

Thea was sure Vargas knew she had been the one to call in CPD and put an end to the raid, but she wasn't sure what Vargas could do about it.

"Of course, Deputy Director."

"You aren't going to like what I am about to say, but please believe I'm doing what I think is best."

"Ma'am?" Thea felt wrong-footed.

"I think it's best that CPD handles the initiation mutilations that you witnessed at Una Anima. I want you to take point on the crucifixions instead. Two prominent pro-aug figures have been brutally murdered and I think we can both agree that it's an important case."

"Why can't another ARC agent take on the mutilations?"

"In light of the fallout from Tiernan, I think it's best that we keep a safe distance from the augmented community until we can regain some of their trust. The false and malicious tip will be investigated and whomever made it will see justice in line with the city's hate crime laws." Vargas stared Thea down as if daring her to ask the question they both knew was on the tip of her tongue.

Thea refused to balk. "Will you yourself be subject to a review for your part in the order?"

"Yes. I am voluntarily submitting to an ethics review and I'm confident that they will see I had no idea that the tip was malicious."

Thea nodded, not trusting herself to say any more.

"Well," Vargas said brightly. "You have your new case. Please keep me abreast of any progress."

"Yes, Ma'am."

Thea had taken barely a few steps away from Vargas when her Cicada buzzed. "UNKNOWN" flashed at the corner of her eye.

"SSA Williams, here."

"Hi, this is Dr Montgomery from the TPD. We have a body that I believe is linked to one of your open cases. Would it be possible to meet?"

THE PAST

Six years ago...

"Not here," Thea said, smiling as she pushed Walt away from where he had cornered her in the TPD breakroom.

"Are you sure?" he asked with a grin, kissing his way along her jawline. They were alone, for now, but the TPD was not a place known for privacy. Any one of their colleagues could come in and find them in a compromising position.

"I'm sure," Thea said, giving him another half-hearted shove.

"C'mon, isn't the danger part of the fun?"

"Not for me it isn't," she said, stepping away from him finally. "And if that's all you're here for, I'm not interested."

"It's not," he said, closing the gap again. "It was a bad joke. You know it's more than that."

He pressed his lips softly against hers in apology.

A throat was cleared behind them and they jumped apart so fiercely that Walt hit one of the many tables, knocking a cup to the hard tile floor. It shattered like the moment they had shared.

Thea's face felt hot, and she was sure it was bright red as she turned to face the inopportune interrupter. She relaxed slightly when she saw Bill Fenske with his large moustache and penchant for tact. He would disapprove but he could be trusted to keep secrets; Bill wasn't in the market for office gossip.

"Flynn's finished with your mass shooting. I loaded the autopsy reports onto your console," he said, as if he hadn't noticed the intimate moment or the spilled coffee.

"Thanks," Thea muttered as she left the room, unable to look at either man.

Walt caught up with her moments later in the corridor that led to the detective's bullpen.

"Thea—"

"I don't want to talk to you," she said, brushing him off.

"I can't leave it like this. It's a thing now—I can tell by the way you're not looking at me."

"If it had been anyone but Bill," Thea said, struggling to keep her voice low. "That could have been the moment that cost us both our jobs. What the hell are we doing, Walt? You're married. You're my superior."

"We can't have this conversation here. Please come over tonight. Cleo's out of town. We can talk then." There was the merest hint of a plea in his voice, but it was enough.

It had taken Thea several hours to go through the medical examiner's reports fully, and by the time she found herself on Walt's doorstep, it was nearly ten o'clock. She knocked gently once and opened the door.

Walt was sitting at his dining table surrounded by reports, with a half-drunk glass of whiskey beside him. He was taking notes in the air. Every time he moved his hand words appeared on the virtual whiteboard beside him. He dismissed his work, and all the reports and notes disappeared with a wave of his hand.

"I was starting to think you weren't gonna show," he said, draining the last of his drink and getting to his feet.

"Sorry, I was held up at the station." Thea closed the door and moved deeper into the room.

"So," he said with a knowing smile.

"We got here sooner than I thought we would." Thea moved further into the room so that the only thing between them in the open living space was the couch.

"And where are we?" Walt said, crossing his arms over his chest.

"The end," Thea said simply.

"It's not about the danger. For me. It's not about the danger or the sneaking around."

"I know that," Thea said, holding his gaze to make sure he believed her. "We were stupid. We never should have started something that neither of us had any intention of seeing through."

Walt's face was unreadable, as always. He said nothing. He just stood there with his arms folded.

"Say something," Thea said as the silence stretched on.

"I can't." Walt gave a wry smile. "If I say what I want to, what I've been trying desperately not to, it really is over."

"It's over anyway. Don't say it."

"I have to," he said in a resigned sort of way. "At least once."

"Please don't." She could see the cliff edge upon which their relationship was so precariously balanced, and she wasn't ready to watch it fall. "It'll make this so much harder."

"I love you," he said clearly.

"Damnit, Walt," Thea groaned.

"I don't want to. I try not to, but I do."

"Why did you have to say it?"

"Because it's true," he said, smiling slightly at her apparent annoyance. "I have no illusions about what we're doing here. It was never supposed to get this far, but it has."

"You're married," Thea said. It was the simple truth that should have put a stop to their relationship in the beginning. "I'm gonna leave and I'm not coming back. I'll ask for a new partner tomorrow."

Thea felt numb as she turned away from him and made her way to the door.

"I know it shouldn't make a difference," Walt said quietly. "But do you..." he let the sentence trail off.

"Love you?" She stopped.

She saw him nod out of the corner of her eye.

She should have left. She should have kept walking, but instead, she turned to him and said, "Yes. I love you," in a voice so low it was barely audible.

He closed the distance between them in long strides. His hands found her face and pulled her lips to his as he used his body to press her into the door frame. She could feel his excitement.

"Say yes," he breathed. It was a clear plea.

"Yes," Thea said against his lips.

His passion for her mirrored Thea's for him, and she reciprocated in kind. Her hands found his waistband and roughly freed his shirt. He moaned as she ran her hands up his back, only to drag her nails down his spine.

"Take your clothes off," she commanded breathily.

He obliged at once making quick work of his waistcoat, tie and shirt. When his torso was bare, Thea dropped to her knees in front of him. His eyes lit up, but she only undid his belt before standing again.

"Ladies first," she teased.

"Yes, ma'am," he said with a familiar fire in his eyes.

When he finally buried himself inside her with a groan of pleasure, they both knew there was no going back. They were long past the point of no return. Separation was unimaginable.

THE RETURN

Tenebrium hadn't changed. It was like a time capsule, trapped in a by-gone age. The streets and buildings looked the same. The neon signs flashed as they always had and music still filled the air. So many different tunes from so many different places that it was indistinguishable from white noise. Thea had hoped never to go back there, and yet it felt like she had never left.

Tenebrium had taken so much from her. Her father, her sister for a time, her home, the man she had loved and now, because of what had happened there, it seemed her relationship with her mother was irreparable. In another time, in another place, maybe all of those stories could have ended differently.

She was glad of Torrez by her side as she walked through the achingly familiar streets. He put an arm around her shoulders as if he could sense her discomfort.

She had watched the city besieged, all but burned to the ground, but looking at it now, there was no trace of the destruction wrought by the Gold Legion. It was disquieting.

Torrez came to a stop, pulling Thea to a halt with him.

"What?"

"Are you really not gonna see him while you're here?"

"Who?"

"Don't even try that with me, Querida. Walt."

"No. Why would I? I'm here to speak to the ME."

Torrez shook his head in obvious disapproval but didn't comment further.

Before they knew it and far before she was ready, they were standing outside the Tenebrium Police Department.

"It's like going back to high school after you've graduated, no?" Torrez said, looking up at the building that was so familiar to them both.

Thea nodded; it was oddly like taking a step backwards in time.

The atrium of the TPD was a huge high-ceilinged room made from glimmering white agate. Benches were bolted to the polished floors, several of which had ne'er-do-wells handcuffed to them, waiting to be booked. Instinctively, Thea headed straight for the elevators, but she and Torrez were stopped moments later by a receptionist she didn't recognise.

"Excuse me! Visitors are required to sign in."

"Visitors," Torrez repeated with a grim glee.

"Right. Of course, sorry. I'm Det—Agent Thea Williams and this is—"

"Thea? Walt's Thea?" the receptionist said, looking at her more closely. "His old partner? I've heard some amount of stories about you."

"I'll bet," Thea said stiffly. "This is Andrew Torrez."

"Another TPD survivor," Torrez added.

Once they had been given their visitor passes, they headed back to the lift, this time unimpeded.

"'Walt's Thea'?" Thea repeated, nettled. "I've been back in this city for ten minutes."

Torrez drew his fingers across his lips as if zipping them shut.

Thea's heart gave an uncomfortable flutter when they arrived on the detective's floor.

"Why are we stopping here?" Thea asked.

"Nostalgia."

The bullpen was exactly as it had been when she had left three years previously. Dark panelled walls, hanging screens showing the innumerable news networks, posters of pin-ups intermingled with evidence photos, wanted posters and the odd family picture. Her desk was as it had always been, still slightly scuffed from the numerous times boots had rested on top of it. Then again, it wasn't her desk anymore.

"Thea," a warm voice called. "You are a sight for sore eyes."

"Orion? You still haven't retired."

"I'm a die with your boots on kinda guy," Orion said, getting up from his desk to shake Thea's hand. "Here's more home than home is." Being a detective was a tough and time-consuming job. It was hard on marriages and Orion's had fallen victim to the strain.

"I remember that feeling all too well."

"You work for the Augmentation Regulation Committee now, right? Good for you. Want me to tell the captain you're here?"

"No, that's okay. I'm just headed to the morgue."

"I won't keep you then, but it's great to see you. Torrez," Orion added stiffly; the two men had never gotten on. Orion was as strait-laced as they come and hadn't liked the way Torrez conducted himself as a detective long before he had been outed as dirty.

"You, too." Thea smiled. "Can we go now?"

Thea was keen not to linger in the bullpen. The journey to the morgue was a short one, but when the doors opened, it was into unfamiliar surroundings. What had once been a long white corridor with only a few doors was now a small antechamber with a metal gate manned by two guards. Through the gate, Thea could see the morgue doors she recognised, but there was no getting there without surpassing the guards.

"Excuse me—" she began.

"I'm sorry, sir, ma'am, but you can't be here," the rounder of the two guards said, stepping forward to meet them as they disembarked from the lift.

"I'm Agent Williams—"

"That's nice, but you can't be here."

Torrez let out a stifled laugh that he quickly turned into a cough.

"I was called by your ME and asked to meet with her."

"Do you have an appointment card?"

"No, but I have a pass."

"That might get you to the canteen, but it's not getting you into the morgue."

"Okay, how about you stow the attitude and check with Dr Montgomery. She'll be able to clear this up."

"We have no visitors scheduled for today," he said with a smirk, making it clear he had no intention of checking.

"You know that off the top of your head?"

"Look, I've had just about enough of you journalists trying to sneak in here."

Thea pulled her ARC badge from her waist and thrust it forward. "As I said, I'm Agent Williams. I work for the Augmentation Regulation Committee—"

"We got a problem here, Bart?" The voice caused the hairs on the back of Thea's neck to stand on end.

"Just another journo trying their luck, Captain."

Thea turned to see Walt standing in the lift, arms crossed over his chest. Of all the things in Tenebrium that hadn't changed in the last three years, Walt was not one of them. He looked good, better than good. Handsome. Happier. Healthier; much more like the man she had known when she first became a detective. The self-loathing alcoholic with a death wish he had become latterly seemed to have vanished. It was unnerving. His hair was well kept and his blue eyes bright. He had adopted a short stubble beard instead of the clean shave Thea was used to; it suited him.

"Maybe we should discuss the case in my office before you meet with the doc," Walt said.

REUNION

Walt had known she was coming, heard her voice already, but nothing compared to seeing her in the flesh. She was as beautiful as he remembered. Her dark hair was slightly longer now, and she had a thin graze on her cheek, but she was still Thea.

"Shall we?" Walt said, gesturing towards the lift. "Torrez." He added with a nod that was returned without enthusiasm.

Torrez stepped into the elevator looking half amused, half uncomfortable. Thea followed him inside without a word, refusing to look Walt in the eye. It was maddening.

Images of the past flashed through his mind. Their first kiss. Their affair. Getting caught by his wife and all that followed. Their relationship falling apart. Him falling apart. His descent into alcoholism. Thea sponging her father's blood from his face after Walt had been forced to murder him.

He had done so many awful things. The last time he had seen her, he'd told her he loved her, and she, not without reason, had rejected him. "We ruined each other, you and I," she'd said. And it was true, they had. Thea had left Tenebrium not long after that, without saying goodbye. He hadn't taken it well. It had taken everything he had to maintain his fledgling sobriety at the time. Somewhere along the way, however, as he dealt with the aftermath of everything that had happened and everything he had done, being sober stopped being about Thea and started being about him. Over three years later, his sobriety, a battle he would never be done fighting, was holding firm. It shook ever so slightly as he looked at the woman who, at one time, had been as vital to him as air.

"You were really gonna come back here and not see me?" Walt couldn't help himself. "After everything." Even he was surprised to find how angry he was in that moment.

Thea shrugged. She still wasn't looking at him.

"You thought you could just come into my house without me knowing? Work cases with my people, but avoid me?"

"You know," Torrez said, discomfited. "This isn't how I imagined this would go."

"This is exactly how I thought it would go," Thea muttered.

When the elevator doors opened, Walt stormed out, leading the way to his office. The air felt charged as Thea and Torrez followed in his wake, like they were exuding tension. He opened the door and held it for them. Thea's eyes lingered on the nameplate that read, "Captain Walter James", for a moment, but she didn't comment.

"How did you even know I was here?"

"Torrez gave me the heads up when you arrived."

"Thank you for that," Torrez said with an expression that reminded Walt of a deer caught in headlights.

"I'll bet he did. It doesn't matter. We're here now. Let's just focus on the case."

"I think we have a few things to talk about first."

"I'm going to wait outside," Torrez said, sweeping out of the room before anyone could stop him.

They stood in silence, the slam of the door seeming to echo in the space between them. Thea's eyes never left the carpet.

"For fuck's sake, would you look at me?"

"What?" Thea said aggressively. It was more like a taunt than a question, but when those golden-brown eyes finally settled on his, the electricity was palpable.

"What do you mean 'what'? You just up and disappeared. You left without a word. I had no idea what'd happened to you. And then, you swan back into my town, my precinct after three years and you can't even do me the courtesy of a 'hello'?"

"Don't be so dramatic. Betty and Torrez knew where I was going. I doubt you were organising search parties. And Tenebrium is 'your town' now?"

"I thought we were good. After everything we put each other through. I thought we forgave each other."

"We did."

"You owed me a goodbye."

"I owed you. I owed you?"

Their voices had gotten steadily louder with every rejoinder so that they were both nearly shouting.

"Look," Walt let out a long sigh. "I'm sorry. I didn't realise I was still pissed until I saw you. I thought it was all in the past, and it is. It really is," he lied.

"When I left, it wasn't about you. It wasn't...entirely about you."

Walt laughed softly. "I know."

"I didn't know how to say goodbye. I don't think there are enough words to encompass everything that happened. You would have tried to stop me leaving and we both know it. You wouldn't have let me go."

"You're probably right. There are no words, so let's not rehash the past."

Thea nodded. "Captain Walter James has a nice ring to it." She moved further into the room and sat on the edge of one of the couches. "I'm happy for you."

"Thanks. Still getting used to it. Betty made it look easy, but I gotta say, it's not. Straddling police work and politics is...more than I bargained for. Guess I'm a detective at heart. What happened there?" Walt asked, pointing at Thea's cheek.

"Gunshot. It's just a graze." She seemed to have thawed slightly. "You think your ME will be ready for us?"

Outside the office, Torrez was leaning against the wall with his eyes closed.

"We're headed to the morgue if you'd like to join us," Walt offered.

"Hard pass," Torrez replied, holding up his hands. "One crucifixion is enough for me, thank you. Once you get a confirmed ID, I need to head back to Caligo; I have families to talk to. Police or PI, that part never gets easier."

They made their way from his office to the morgue in silence. Not so long ago, Walt would have described Thea as the one person he couldn't live without, but he *was* living without her. He was even happy with his life, his job, with Fen. And yet...

"It's...strange having you back."

"I'm not back. I won't be here for long. We'll work the case and I'll be out of your hair before you know it," Thea said with a smile that didn't reach her eyes.

Before Walt could say any more, they were at the door to the morgue.

Dr Ella Montgomery was a marked improvement on her predecessor. Friendly and warm, she was a White woman in her mid-forties with stunningly red hair, glasses and a love of pant-suits.

"Captain," she said by way of greeting when Walt pushed open the door.

"Hey, doc. Sorry to keep you waiting. This is Agent Williams; she works for ARC. She'll be liaising on the case."

"Thea Williams. You're a bit of a legend around here. It's a pleasure to meet you."

"Likewise."

"Shall we get started?" Dr Montgomery asked Walt.

The medical examiner led them into the mortuary proper. Adjoining her office, it was a cold, white tiled room that smelled strongly of citrus and hydrogen peroxide. There were drains strategically placed around the room, connected by covered channels that ran alongside each of the three autopsy tables.

Helena Cutter was already lying bare on a silver autopsy table. She had been dead for a few days now, and the smell of decay was not entirely masked by the strong chemicals in the room. Her body was distorted by bloat, with large pinkish and watery blisters in several places. The bar upon which she had been suspended was still present through her shoulders. Her legs were a dark purplish red, the blood having pooled there after her heart had stopped beating.

The medical examiner pulled a tray of instruments up to the table side. "Start recording."

"Recording started," intoned a pleasant, artificial voice.

"Tuesday, January 24th, nine fifty-seven am. Autopsy of Helena Cutter, performed by Dr Ella Montgomery. Police Captain Walter James and Supervisory Special Agent Thea Williams present. Beginning external exam. Obvious signs of trauma to the head, face, neck and shoulders. Samples have been taken and sent to the crime lab. Lacerations present across the chest—superficial in nature. There are clear ligature marks on her wrists and ankles measuring...two inches in height. When did you say she was first reported missing?" Montgomery asked Walt as she examined Helena's fingernails.

"November last year. He must have held her captive. CSIs at the scene said she's been dead for less than a week."

"I'm not so sure about that. It's been a cold winter. If she was in a derelict building, the temperatures we have seen recently have been well below freezing. She could have been dead much longer."

"It's warmer this week," Walt said.

"And that is why she thawed." The doctor nodded, placing a head lamp on her forehead. "Small third-degree burns located on the lips, right cheek and a single burn on the chest."

"The other victims had molten metal poured down their throats," Thea said, watching the doctor with grim interest.

"That could be what has happened here, but it's not what killed her." Montgomery gently opened Helena's mouth and peered down her throat as far as possible. "There is no sign of burning inside her mouth or oesophagus."

"Any idea what stopped him?" Walt asked.

"The pattern of the burning lends itself to hesitation."

"If she's the first victim, that makes sense. And the longer the crime went undiscovered, the more confident the killer could have become with the other victims," Thea said, crossing her arms over her chest. "What did kill her?"

"If I had to guess, I'd say the metal bar in her torso, but judging by the bleeding and the bruising, this wasn't a quick death. She may have been suspended for several days before succumbing to her injuries."

"That's an awful way to go," Walt said, shaking his head.

"I'll need to perform the evisceration and internal examination to tell you for sure..."

"Thanks, doc. We'll leave you to that, I think."

"I'll have more for you by this evening."

"We should fill Drew in," Thea said to Walt. "A pleasure to meet you, Dr Montgomery."

The doctor nodded. They left just as she was preparing to perform the Y incision.

DEATH NOTIFICATION

It was the worst part of police work, telling a victim's family that they were never coming home. Alex was drained, mentally, physically, and emotionally. They had spoken individually to loved ones of those who had died in The Kelpie Clinic, each time telling the same horrific story, and watching the horror of what happened sink in. The families and friends all asked the same question. Why? But Alex had no answers or comfort to give in the face of such reckless hate. Just as no one had been able to give them any after their brother had died. And they weren't finished yet; they had one last visit to make.

There is no better way to be murdered, but Alex had been dreading speaking with Mrs Baker-Singh. The details of the fire were one thing, but what had happened to Ranveer Baker-Singh was abhorrent.

With so much death and destruction, officers with bereavement training were thin on the ground. Alex dearly wished that they didn't have to make this particular call alone, but there was no one to accompany them to Uptown.

They tried hard to keep their face neutral as they knocked on the glossy black door, but families always knew and Idina was no different. She pulled the door wide and the moment she saw Alex's carefully curated expression; she dropped to her knees with a howl so hollow Alex had to fight back tears.

It was one of the worst experiences of their life. Alex had never understood the magnitude of the word desolation until they had witnessed Idina Baker-Singh's grief at the loss of her husband Ranveer.

Alex hadn't been comfortable leaving until Idina had cried herself to sleep, but when they finally covered the poor woman with a blanket, it was nearing midnight. Alex's day was far from over, however.

The Caligo Police Department in Caligo Proper was quiet at night. The CPD didn't employ on-call rooms, allowing officers to go home and rest unless they were called in. If a person was looking to go unnoticed between the hours of midnight and three, were the best time to do it.

Alex gave a cursory glance around the detective's office before setting to work at their console. Looking into Thea's background hadn't yielded the answers they were looking for. There was little to no information about what she had been doing in the months before she transferred from the TPD to ARC. Unfortunately, this was exactly the time Alex wanted to know about. Now, with the revelation that Andrew Torrez was a detective at that time, they finally had a new lead.

January

CALIGO TODAY

Keeping you in the know

Morning Edition

6:45 am - **KELPIE CLINIC FIRE OFFICIALLY CLASSIFIED AS ARSON**

A representative from the Caligo Police Department has confirmed that the fatal fire that claimed 18 lives was set deliberately. Flammable chemicals were found at the scene. CPD is yet to name a suspect.

8:27 am – **LEVI SEWARD FORGIVES GUNMAN AND CONVERTS HIM TO UNA ANIMA**

Appearing on Caligite Socialite, the leader of The Church of the Single Soul shocked viewers by claiming to have converted the young man who tried to kill him.

9:03 am – **BREAKING NEWS – MURDERED JOURNALIST REVEALED TO BE ILLUSIVE 'LALIQUE'**

Police have revealed that Ranveer Baker-Singh, the journalist brutally crucified earlier this week, was the man behind the famed pro-aug activist 'Lalique'. Lalique – Baker-Singh – came to fame within the movement for perpetrating a series of corporate thefts.

9:33 am – **BREAKING NEWS – TRAVIS MERCER DEAD**

CPD and ARC have confirmed in a joint statement that Travis Mercer – the father of the modern augmentation movement - has been found dead. More details to follow.

10:17 am – **BREAKING NEWS – ARC TO LAUNCH INVESTIGATION INTO FALSE TIP SCANDAL**

The Augmentation Regulation Committee has announced that it will be launching a full investigation into the false tip, which led to an illegal raid on the Tiernan Shelter. More details to follow.

10:56 am – **BREAKING NEWS – ANONYMOUS SOURCE POINTS FINGER AT DEPUTY DIRECTOR VARGAS**

The Augmentation Regulation Committee's Deputy Director Natalia Vargas is the latest name to come out of the false tip scandal. An anonymous employee of ARC has told The Tenebrium Times, that Vargas not only knew the tip was false but personally ordered the raid to further her own agenda. More details to follow.

11:43 am – **BREAKING NEWS – UNA ANIMA LINKED TO ILLEGAL 'AUGMENTATION CONVERSION THERAPY'**

The CPD have confirmed that they are investigating reports of 'Augmentation Conversion Therapy' within Una Anima. Witnesses claim that the practises are part of an initiation ritual that requires those with augmentations to carve them out before they are permitted to join the ranks of the church. Una Anima has spoken out accusing CPD and ARC of going on a 'witch hunt' and 'denying their religious freedoms'. More details to follow.

FIRES

There was so much information about Helena Cutter, it was hard to separate the facts from the fiction. She was famous, which meant everything from her hair colour to her childhood was sensationalised. As Thea sat in Walt's office surrounded by articles about the deceased actress turned activist, she felt more like a biographer than an investigator.

"I feel like I know more about her life than I do about my own," Walt said, throwing down a report and rubbing his eyes.

"There's nothing here that links her to the other victims—other than the obvious."

"She's had about as many stalkers as you'd expect an actress to have, but none of them have any links to the others, either. Finding who the next target is will be nearly impossible to predict."

"It's not random, but it is. They're being targeted because they are pro-aug, that's a given, but how are they being chosen further than that? Travis Mercer I get, but why wasn't he first? Or last? And how did the killer find out who Ranveer was?"

"And why kill allies, not augs?"

"We had an arson against an aug clinic, killed eighteen. I don't think it's the same killer, but I think it's stemming from the same place."

It was odd to sit somewhat peacefully with someone who had done irreparable damage to your life. Walt had turned her world upside down more than once. He had been her first real taste of love—her only taste if she was honest with herself—and he had caused her more heartache than she could ever have imagined. He had lied to her and hurt her. He had killed her father, but she had long since forgiven him for his transgressions. She'd had to, to survive. The thing with Walt was that he never acted out of malice, no matter how misplaced his intentions were. He was always trying to do the right thing, and she had not been entirely innocent in their mutual downfall. Leaving Tenebrium had been her way of closing that chapter of her life. She hadn't wished him any ill, but she had hoped never to see him again. It was disquieting to find herself in his company once more.

There was a small ding as a notification popped up on Walt's desk. He stood from the couch he had been sitting on opposite Thea and moved over to check what new information had come to light. Thea watched as he read, his eyebrows drawn down.

"The doc has finished the autopsy," he said, still reading.

"What was the official cause of death?"

"Dehydration combined with exposure. She was alive for roughly five days after they crucified her."

They both sat in silence for a moment, contemplating the brutality of Helena Cutter's death. It was an awful thing.

"So, the first victim we know of is Helena Cutter, the killer showed signs of hesitation, which tracks," Thea said. "The second—Ranveer, the killer took his time. The third was Travis Mercer. His death was just as awful but it was more of a statement – the killer didn't draw attention to what they did to Helena, and didn't seem to care if Ranveer was discovered, but they wanted Mercer found. That is textbook escalation."

"There are plenty anti-aug assholes out there—which hardly narrows the suspect pool."

"Helena Cutter was from Tenebrium, and there was a pretty big time-gap between killings."

"You think the killer might be from here?" Walt said, catching onto her train of thought.

"I think it's a good place to start. We should crosscheck vocal anti-aug proponents in Tenebrium with Una Anima patrons. This has something to do with Levi Seward. I know it."

"Okay, I'll get us a list."

"We also need to compile a list of possible victims, see if any pro-aug voices are getting threats like Ranveer or are already missing."

There was a soft knock at the door.

"Come in," Walt called. "What can I do for you, Sid?" he asked the man who stuck his head around the door.

Sidney Kwan was barely into his thirties, Korean and rather handsome. His glossy dark hair was tousled and his cheekbones were the sort of things you only saw in perfume ads. His light tawny skin was flawless. "Sorry, Captain, I'm actually here for Agent Williams. There was a message for you, left at the front desk."

"Let me guess: Natalia Vargas?"

"I don't know you or Spanish well enough to repeat what she said, but the gist was 'call her'."

"Thank you." Thea pitied anyone who had to bear the wrath of Deputy Director Vargas.

"No problem," Sidney said. "I'm Sid—Sidney, by the way. Detective Kwan."

"Thea. Agent Williams."

"Well, Agent, I don't know what you did to piss off your boss, but she is *mad.*

If you need a place to hide, I'm sure we could sort something out. The TPD has an excellent witness protection program."

Thea laughed. "Thanks, but she's all bark."

"I'm not sure I believe you."

"She bites a little, but I'll survive."

"I hope so. It was nice to meet you, Thea."

Thea watched Sidney leave, her eyes lingering on the closed door for a moment.

"So," Walt said, returning her attention to him, a slight frown on his face.

"Looks like I have fires to put out at home."

"Anything I can help with?"

"I don't think you have any pull in Caligo, but thanks."

"What did you do?" Walt asked shrewdly.

"I may have given her name to the press."

"Ah."

"Send me the list when it's done?"

"You're leaving?"

"For now, yeah. I'll follow-up on my side and let you know anything I find."

"I could—no, you're right. I'll get to work on that list. It was good to see you."

"You, too."

CROSS PURPOSES

Fen wiped a tear from under her eye with the back of her hand and drained her glass of wine. She was sitting on the edge of the bed in her hotel room in Caligo, in the exact spot she had been when she had heard the news.

Ranveer had been a close friend and ally of hers. He had sought her out after an exhibition, and as like-minded as they were, they had made an instant connection. To her, he was a real hero, someone who was willing to risk it all and fight for what they believed in. To have him killed for his beliefs and in such a brutal way was abhorrent.

She knew that many of his detractors would try to paint him as a criminal, but she resolved with herself not to let them. She had taken Agent Williams's words to heart and had done a little digging. A brief detour into the life of Natalia Vargas and her recent augmentations had led her right back to Levi Seward.

Fen hated a riddle she couldn't solve. And Levi Seward was definitely that. She had been sitting in her hotel room in Caligo for hours before the news of Ranveer's death had broken, searching for anything that might explain the mystery of the man; it was exhausting and frustrating work. He was born and raised in Tenebrium City, but there were no records of him after he turned eighteen until two years ago when he formed The Church of the Single Soul. No trace of any previous employment or social media presence. There was nothing on the datastream, or any private archive that could tell her how he came from, seemingly the ether, with no money, and formed a megachurch.

A welcome distraction came in the form of a call from Walt. She shut off the datastream and leant back against the hotel's over-soft pillows.

"Hey, you," she said, keeping her tone light. She wanted to be distracted, not comforted.

"I'm in bed and I was wondering if you would like to join me?" His voice was low and full of suggestion.

"I would love to, but I'm still in Caligo."

"You really know how to leave a guy hanging."

"If you're that hard up, I'm sure you're old enough to know how to finish yourself off."

He let out a crack of laughter that made her smile. "Not quite what I meant."

"I know. I miss you too."

"Ready to tell me about your story?"

She hesitated. "Promise you won't be mad?"

"Why would I be mad?" He sounded instantly suspicious.

Even over her cicada, Fen could hear the rustling of sheets that meant Walt had sat up straighter.

"My story is about Levi Seward."

"What happened to 'It's too dangerous to snoop around Seward and Una Anima'?"

"You're mad."

"I'm not mad, I'm worried. He's a person of interest in a murder case. And you can't print that."

"Three crucifixions. I know."

"Of course you do."

"You sound mad."

"You have an informant in my precinct, and I don't know who it is. I don't love it."

"Maybe I can make it up to you. Did you know that there has been an Una Anima press event at the same time as all three of the murders?"

"What?" She could tell interest was overtaking irritation.

"My...contact got me the approximate times of death and I checked. There has been a broadcast Una Anima event, with Levi Seward front and centre at the time of each killing. Very convenient, don't you think?"

"That's one hell of a coincidence. Like he's been creating very public alibis, or someone is creating them for him. Thank you for telling me, but this conversation isn't over."

"I know."

"When I find out who your informant is—they're fired."

Fen paused, knowing she was on thin ice. "Can I ask you one more thing?"

"Are you seriously trying to pump me for information?"

"I'm hoping that I'm charming enough to pull it off."

"No promises," he said gruffly.

"I got a tip from an ARC agent, and I looked her up. She used to work at the TPD, but huge amounts of her file are redacted. Do you know a Thea Williams? Is she on the level?" There was a long pause. "Walt?"

"You can trust her."

"You know her?"

"I used to. We were...she was my partner back in the day."

"You know you can trust *me*, right?"

"I know and I do. Our jobs just aren't always going to mesh."

"Is this gonna be a problem?"

"Only if we let it. Dinner when you get back?"

"Definitely, but if you don't have any plans right now, I'm sure I could think of something to help you sleep."

"Is that right?" She could hear her favourite sexy smile in his voice.

THE PAST

Two years ago...

It had been over a year since Bastion had lost the lower half of his right leg, yet whenever he awoke, he had to remind himself of his new reality. It could be seconds before he would remember that the limb was no longer there. It could be minutes. On really bad days, he wouldn't remember until he tried to stand, and found himself tumbling to the ground.

To complicate matters, the floor of his claustrophobic cell was covered by half a foot of stagnant water. The bare stone walls were thick with moss and the rusted bars looked out onto yet more concrete. His bed was a cold metal slab, covered by a thin mattress that provided no comfort. Dirt encrusted the tiny round window at the top of the north-most wall. The Pit, the prison level of Colony Six, was several hundred fathoms below the surface of the Atlantic Ocean. Even if his porthole had been clean, he still would have had a view of nothing but blackness.

This had been his home for the last nine months.

"You look like shit."

Bastion hadn't had a single visitor since his trial, so he had taken the sloshing footsteps for the scurrying of rats, but the man leaning casually against the wall outside his cell was no rodent.

Walt was tall, White, and angular. His blue eyes characteristically shrewd as they surveyed Bastion. He had cut his dark hair and looked far better groomed than when Bastion had seen him last. This was not an apathetic, drunken Walt. This Walt was stone cold sober and all the better for it.

"The facilities leave something to be desired, but I'm sure my personal barber will be along shortly." Bastion said, sarcasm mixing with contempt.

"Quite the fall from grace, Bast."

"Did you just come here to gloat?"

Walt didn't say anything; he just watched Bastion as if appraising him.

"You've seen what I've been reduced to. I got my comeuppance. I lost a leg. I'm paying for the things I did, so save me your disappointment and your pity." Bastion grabbed his crutches from where they sat next to his bed. He stood up gingerly and moved to face the back wall, away from Walt.

"I'm not disappointed," Walt said bluntly. "The Gold Legion, the greed, that desperation to be bigger and better than everyone else, that's you through and through. I don't pity you either. You did this to yourself. I don't hate you, not anymore, but I don't pity you, and I'm not here to gloat. I need your help. I was hoping we could be on the same side one last time."

"You want to be brothers again?" Bastion sneered. While not related by blood, the two had grown up together.

"No," Walt said with a wry smile. "We'll never be brothers again. But maybe you can do some good for the people you hurt."

"I can't help anyone. Not now."

"That's not true. I'm leading a task force that's hunting down the remnants of the Gold Legion."

"And none of them would talk?"

"Cults are like that." Walt shrugged. "But I thought, just maybe, you still have a shred of decency left in you."

"What do I get out of it?" Bastion said over his shoulder.

"There's the man I knew. You get out of here for a little while. I can't promise anything better because the powers that be didn't give me anything to bargain with. They aren't offering you a pardon or immunity. But I'm offering you a chance to make amends, and to see the city again. You'll land right back here when we're done, but isn't a last little taste of freedom worth it?"

BASTION

Bastion was panicking. He grabbed a bag from under his bed and began to empty his possessions into it. He didn't have many. No luxurious mansions for him anymore. He was a fugitive. A dangerous criminal by all definitions. He deserved to be in jail; he knew it, and yet, when he and Walt had finished their assignment, and it had been time to return to The Pit, he had fled. He supposed he ought to add coward to the list. But he had been trying to be better.

When Caroline and the other augs had picked him up and brought him to the shelter, given him an augmented leg, given him food and a place to call his own, he had resolved with himself that he would repay their kindness and keep them safe. And he had been. Over the last year or so, he had become a leader of sorts, a pillar in the aug community. A voice of reason, a good man in a storm, a trusted and valued friend.

All that was over now.

Caligo was supposed to be a fresh start; it was just his luck to have run to the same city as Thea. He paused his packing for a moment, wondering if Cora had come with her. She was the only woman he had ever really loved. Or at least he thought so. Their relationship had been so messy, and the circumstances so twisted, it was hard to tell what was real.

"Past caught up with you?"

Bastion started. He turned to see Caroline standing by the door. At barely more than four feet tall, she was not someone who would generally be thought of as threatening, but her stare was one that could make the bravest of hearts falter and her wit was more devastating than any bullet.

"I have to leave," Bastion said. There was no point in lying. Caroline knew he had a past, and an illegal one, but she believed in second chances and never asked for details. "Nothing will come for you or the shelter. I'm not part of a gang or—"

"A cult?" Caroline gave a sly smile. "I was born and raised in Tenebrium, Bast. I knew who you were when you turned up here, hungry and broken."

"Then why did you take me in?"

"I thought about not. I thought about calling the cops, but I'm no saint and I set this shelter up to help people. You being in jail might have given some people a sense of justice or safety, but for me, it's just easier to pretend Tenebrium never happened."

"One of the people I hurt the most is here. And I kinda stick out. It's safer if I leave."

"Well, be safe."

"That's it?"

"Yeah. That's it. I'm not your momma, though I may do a damn good impression of it."

Bastion didn't know what to say. He had expected a fight. He stood stunned, holding a shirt he had been about to stuff into his bag.

"Ahh. You want talked down. You want begged to stay. You want me to tell you that the people here need you? They do, but it's not my job to convince you of that. You need to run? Run. You want to face your problems, and maybe some of your demons, accept that actions have consequences, then stay. I'm not gonna make that decision for you. You're grown."

She turned and left.

It was true; he was grown. Grown enough to have known better. He was sure that if Thea saw him he would end up back in jail or with a bullet between the eyes. He should get out of dodge, but where could he go? He was a wanted man. His face was known throughout both Colony Six and Eleven. The end of the line was approaching far faster than Bastion was ready for, and he had no idea what to do.

SUSPENSION

Caligo had never felt less like home. Returning to Tenebrium had been confusing and a touch sad, but nowhere near as hostile as Caligo was about to become. Thea hadn't spoken to Cora in a couple of days and knew that she should probably check in, but the desire to get the necessary over and done with outweighed her fear of being a bad sister.

It was with a familiar sense of dread that Thea made her way to The Orchard. She had called her team from the shuttle and told them to meet her there. This would not be pleasant.

Like students waiting to be told to enter a classroom, her team was lined up outside her office looking nervous. This was the first time they had come face to face since before the raid.

"This won't take long," Thea said, opening the door and ushering them inside. She flipped a switch on the corner of her desk and the clear glass walls went black; they didn't need an audience for this.

"Thea—" Rosenberg began, but Thea silenced him with a raised finger.

"You were just doing your jobs. You were just following orders. This is on me and Vargas. Except, this isn't the military and the last time I checked, you all have minds of your own. If you don't see how wrong that raid was, I strongly suggest you find a new job. You're more scared of Vargas than you are of Castillo? Fine. But not being afraid of me is a big mistake." Thea paused to let her words sink in. "If I were you, I'd be more worried about the fact every single one of you was willing to terrorise an already oppressed minority to save your own skins. If you had stood down like Castillo ordered you to, the only person facing discipline, as the leader of the team, would have been me—and I was more than prepared to take the hit. If one of you had used the brains you supposedly possess, you could have called me and I would have told you that myself. Instead, I have to find out second-hand. And then, one of you idiots gave my name to the press."

"We're sorry, ma'am." Rosenburg said. "We know it was wrong and we all—"

"Are you their spokesperson now? I promised there would be hell to pay when I called you in and I would hate to set a bad precedent by lying. You're all suspended pending an investigation."

All at once, her team seemed to find their voices.

"Enough," Thea snarled, quieting them again. "I'm nothing if not a woman of my word. Get out of my sight."

It was almost comical the way they filed out, heads hung low, and if Thea hadn't been so angry, she might have laughed.

If she had been hoping for a moment alone to calm herself, she was about to be sorely disappointed.

Castillo showed in the corner of her vision just as her Cicada buzzed.

"Thea," he whispered. "Vargas is trying to pin the raid on me. I've been suspended. She knows you called in the tip to CPD and she knows you gave her up to the press. She's on the warpath, heading your way."

The call ended just as her office door was thrown open. Unlike Thea, Vargas loved to create a scene.

"Deputy Director Vargas, how can I help you?"

"Cut the shit," Vargas snapped, slamming the door behind her. "You suspended your entire team? How dare you? What gives you the right to make that decision?"

"How could you order that raid? You knew it was wrong or you would've clued me in. You begged me to work here. Gave me the whole spiel about changing things and making a difference. Fighting for people in need. What happened to that Natalia? Was it all bullshit?"

"Thea," she stretched out the name imploringly. "It's complicated..."

"It always is, but that's usually just an excuse. Taking money from a shady source is not the same as letting that source use us as a private army to enact their hateful agenda. That was a rousting, designed to create fear, and you know it."

"The city barely gives us enough credits to keep the lights on. We rely on the funding of donors and we do not have the luxury of choosing who those are."

"Don't we? Seward can donate all he wants, but we are not mercenaries."

"You're being naïve."

"I understand that there is nuance here and I understand we need credits to function as an organisation, but we have to draw the line somewhere. He's an extremist."

"You can't just throw accusations like that around. Choose your words carefully."

"Why? Are you worried he'll hear me?"

"Thin ice, Agent Williams," Vargas said through clenched teeth.

"What would you call him? His rhetoric has people boycotting businesses that are run by or support people with augmentations, protestors outside healthcare clinics, people being kicked out of their homes and refused jobs, not to mention the crucifixions and the Kelpie Clinic arson."

"We don't know if any of those things are linked."

"To each other, or to Una Anima? Because it's hardly a leap in either case."

"It is not for you to question how I do my job. I don't need your opinion on who we take credits from, and I certainly don't need your input on what missions I send my teams on."

"But you sent *my* team. It's my name that's out there—"

"And mine, thanks to you. I know you called in the CPD. The raid was averted. You got what you wanted, so why can't you just let this go?"

"I don't get it. Does he have something on you? I've been here three years and you've never interfered once. Or are you skimming off the top?"

"Pull up," Vargas warned. "You are flying dangerous skies."

"Does he throw a little extra your way if you do his bidding?"

"You're suspended."

Thea let out a laugh that was more of a threat. "That shit might fly with Castillo, but not me. I'm not a flatfoot. You can't just suspend me on the spot. You need to call a committee and disciplinary panel. They make that decision—to avoid moments like this, I imagine. Feel free to do all that, but I will tell them my suspicions about you and Seward."

"What do you want?"

"Stay out of my way and let me do my job."

Vargas looked for a moment like she was about to explode, but when she spoke, her voice was professionally measured. "I'd like a progress report on the crucifixion by Friday."

"Yes, Ma'am."

SUBMISSION

Sitting on the edge of their bed, Levi watched as Syed's eyes moved down the page. His eyebrows were drawn together, and his mouth was pressed into a hard line. He was propped up on a mound of silken pillows, glasses perched low on his nose and bare chested.

"What do you think of my speech?" Levi asked enthusiastically, leaning forward to press a quick kiss to Syed's forehead.

"I think you've gone too far, Vi. I think you've been over the line for a while now. Are the rumours true? Are you having people maim themselves?"

"They've gotten too bold. Why should they have things we don't?"

"What don't you have? Look around! What exactly are you missing out on? Careful, Vi. You're starting to believe your own dogma."

Levi didn't respond straight away; he just looked at his husband, drinking him in. Syed Seward was of medium height and slim. Born to Pakistani parents, he had glossy dark hair and rich brown skin. He had a diamond-shaped face and a smattering of dense stubble. His fine lips were turned down into a frown. He'd always been moral, and it was one of the things Levi loved most about him, but it was also the thing that caused the most friction in their marriage.

"Oh, come on, I'm just giving the people what they want." Levi reclined next to Syed on the bed.

"A couple hundred years ago this would be us." Syed pushed the paper back at Levi. "A Muslim and a White Christian. Two men. We'd have been ostracised. Cast out. Shunned. And now you're doing the same thing. Persecuting a minority. And what's worse, you're doing it for money. You don't hate these people; you aren't afraid of them, but you're more than happy to sacrifice them at the altar of your image."

"Careful, my love. Those in glass houses...you may protest, but it's only half-hearted. You like to live in a certain way, and I provide that. Would you like me to disband the church? Change my ways? For you, I will, but then we lose the donors and the sponsors and all of this..." he gestured to the beautiful bedroom in which they sat, as grand as the rest of their mansion house, "...goes with them."

"The way you are manipulating religion is wrong."

"God is God," Levi shrugged. "He doesn't seem to mind."

"My God and your God are not the same. Allah preaches peace and tolerance and that's not what you're doing. You are teaching hate."

"If I'm going to keep you in silk sheets and fine wine, I need to follow the money. People love to see blood spilled in the name of the Lord."

"And that's all right with your conscience, and your God? You used to be a real preacher."

Levi rolled over so he could sprawl across Syed's chest. "You love me. And you love our life. We both know you don't want that to change." Levi brought his lips to Syed's and kissed him deeply. He could feel acquiescence in the kiss and knew he'd won.

"We aren't done here. You can't fuck me into submission."

"Watch me."

MOBSTER LOST

Alex knew they were being followed as they strolled down the wide street that led to their apartment, but they weren't afraid. Marvin Lewis wasn't the sneakiest of fellows. He was skinny, squat, and White. He didn't have a limp, but he walked with a strange swagger that gave the same effect.

"What do you want, Marv?" Alex said, stopping under the dim glow of a tall streetlight.

"Detective, how did ya know it was me?"

"I got eyes on the back of my head."

Marv used his thumb to rub his nose and shrugged his shoulders. "I got info. How much is it worth to ya?"

Alex snorted. "Nothing." They started walking again, but Marv grabbed their shoulder.

"You want to know what I got."

"Then take your hand off me and spill it."

"Gimme a pair of Cs in credits."

Alex let out a crack of laughter. "That's a good one, Marv. You have a good night."

"A Benjamin?"

"No deal."

"Fifty. That's my final offer."

"You can keep your information. I'm not biting."

"You want to hear this." He emphasised every word.

"So start squawking," they said, copying his cadence.

"I deserve compensation for my time."

"Goodnight, Marv."

"Detective, wait! You're one tough elbow."

"Talk or I split."

"There have been fewer button men and box jobs if you follow me. Word is the local family men are scared. The Johnson brothers are shutting up shop."

"Get to the point."

"Mobsters are going missing."

"What?"

"Your trouble boys are going missing. No family is safe. Gone without a trace."

"Nothing has been reported."

"Gangsters don't cry to the coppers, but the various families of Caligo are seven men down."

"What do you want me to do about it? If nothing is reported, I can't investigate. Do you have names?"

"That's all I got for you for free."

"Then we're done here."

Alex wasn't stupid enough to pay a snitch like Marvin. He had already told them everything he knew. They wanted to play coy, so they could investigate in their own time. Any person who was brave enough to target the mafia in Caligo, was either high-up in the establishment or very bad news.

Alex watched Marvin out of sight, then made their way home, with yet another case to add to their already overflowing plate.

EXHIBITION

Walt detested press conferences. The theatre of it all felt distasteful. So much so, that since he had become police captain, he refused to hold them in the usual way. Instead of standing outside the precinct in front of a crowd of rabid newshounds, he sat behind the long desk in the conference room, alone. A small number of officers lingered off to the side, waiting to take notes or funnel questions to him. A single camera hovered in front of him, waiting to broadcast. As a show of trust, Fen stood near the back with the small group of journalists who had been allowed to attend in person.

Their reunion had been passionate, but far too brief for Walt's liking. They hadn't had a chance to talk about her informant, but they would. They couldn't not come to some sort of agreement if either of them wanted their relationship to work. In his mind, they needed to apply the division of church and state to their personal lives lest their differences make the relationship untenable, but now wasn't the time to be worrying about that.

"Techs are saying they can't pick up your mic, Captain," Sid said as he entered through the double doors and walked up to the desk. "They asked me to give you a new one."

"Thanks," Walt said, taking the lapel pin he was offered and attaching it to his jacket.

"No tie?" Sid joked, nodding towards Walt's open collar. He and Sid were something close to friends; they worked well together, and they trusted one another.

"I don't wear 'em. Too much like a noose."

"You really gonna use the 'S' word?" Sid asked quietly.

"It's the truth, and we need people to take the threat seriously. We have no idea how victims are being chosen among the pro-aug movement. We need everyone on high alert."

Sid nodded in agreement, but he still looked worried. "Whenever you're ready."

Walt waited for Sid to take his place with the other officers before nodding to the hovering camera. A little red light appeared on the side that told him he was live.

"Good evening. I am Tenebrium Police Captain Walter James. Thank you to the assembled press, both with us in the room and those watching via stream for joining us. As you will all be aware, the body of actress and activist Helena Cutter was discovered in the Eltham district of the city. I would like to begin by offering my condolences to her family. I would also like to thank the people of the TPD, who have been working tirelessly to bring answers to those she left behind. Their work exemplifies the very best of police field operations and detective work.

It is with great regret that I inform you two other victims have been discovered in Caligo City. We believe these murders were conducted by the same perpetrator and therefore are linked. The victims have been identified as Ranveer Baker-Singh, the prolific journalist and writer, and philanthropist Travis Mercer. For the avoidance of doubt and to answer the question that I know is on everyone's minds, I can confirm that these are abnormal homicides. These murders are, by definition, a series, and we now believe we are dealing with a serial killer.

We are working in conjunction with partner agencies, including the Augmentation Regulation Committee, and have formed a joint task force dedicated to investigating these murders.

We believe that the killer, who remains unknown, is targeting those with links to the augmented community, particularly outspoken allies and would like to take this opportunity to advise caution. This person is dangerous in the extreme. If you or anyone you know notices anything untoward, please report it. If you have any information pertaining to these murders, please call the TPD tip line without delay.

Thank you for your time. I will now take any questions."

"Captain, do you have any idea of the motives for these killings?"

"It's hard to define an exact motive, but we believe the killer is targeting pro-aug allies. Beyond that, we're not sure."

"Is there any truth to the reports that the victims were crucified?"

"Yes, I can confirm that the victims were crucified, in a manner of speaking, but I cannot disclose any more details at this time."

"Do you have any suspects?"

"Not at this time."

"Would you say that the augmented community and its allies are more at risk than the rest of the public?"

"Yes. There is a clear pattern here, however, with serial killings of this nature, there can be adaptation. I would urge everyone, aug, pro-aug, or otherwise, to be vigilant and employ common sense safety."

"What is the timeline for these murders? Has there been an escalation?"

"The first murder took place in November last year, with the two in Caligo being more recent and closer together."

"Do you think the killer is getting bolder?"

"It would appear so."

"Will you be offering extra protections to the augmented community?" Walt had to fight back a smile as he heard Fen's voice. "Will there be more police on the streets?"

"We will be utilising the Onyx Legion as extra security as well as increased police patrols. We would ask that any pro-aug events let the department know so we can attempt to arrange security. I think we have time for one last question."

"Do you think other cities are being targeted?"

"We have victims in Tenebrium and Caligo currently, and while we haven't had reports of any others, we are open to the possibility that the killer might be acting in multiple areas."

Sid waved a hand through the air to tell Walt it was time to wrap up.

"Captain, just one more question. Please. If reports are to be believed, you yourself have an augmented spine."

"Is there a question in there?" Walt sighed. "Yes, I have a biomechanical cage that protects my spinal column in place of vertebrae that were damaged in the line of my duties as a detective. What's your question?"

"I have no skin in the augmented debate, but are people like you, with medically necessary augmentations at the same risk as those who have chosen augmentations for aesthetic or upgrade purposes?"

"Anyone with links to the augmented community is in danger. For the record, the vast majority of augmentations are medically necessary, or quality of life improvements. Less than one percent of those with augmentations have them for things like improved strength, or what you call upgrade purposes. Thank you again for attending. The TPD will keep you updated when we have more information. Goodnight."

Walt stood up and stepped away from the desk. As his eyes re-adjusted to being out of the spotlight, he scanned the crowd for Fen. She wasn't there.

He walked to the end of the room, searching for her. She wasn't with the other press members who were questioning the other officers outside the conference room. Walt had to suppress the slightest flutter of panic as he walked further down the hall in search of her. She couldn't have been taken from the police station and yet she was vocally pro-aug. These were dangerous times for her.

"Fen?" he called as he made his way to the smaller conference room opposite. He could hear a soft voice inside.

He didn't know why he lingered instead of announcing himself, but something, perhaps his many years as a detective, told him to stop and listen. As he pressed his ear to the door, he knew it was Fen.

"It's what Ranveer would have wanted," she was saying, her voice low. "No, it goes ahead as planned. Police would ruin it. It's underground. Secret. We can't have them there. We are not cancelling the exhibition and that's final."

Fen tapped her tragus implant to hang up just as Walt pushed open the door.

"There you are," he said, giving nothing away. "Everything okay?"

"Of course," she smiled widely. "You did great. Do you have more work to do, or can we go?"

"We're good to go." Walt held a hand towards the door, letting Fen exit ahead of him. Something was up, and he was going to find out exactly what.

THREATS

Marielena was buzzed. She'd had a wonderful day. She'd had lunch with Cleo, then spoken about the benefits of augmentations at an event, before joining a couple of friends for drinks to toast the legacy of Lalique. These drinks were what had led to her current, mildly heady, state and were the perfect end to a productive day. Her only regret was that Cleo had to work and would not be coming over that night.

Ever since she had been fitted with her M-Pulse, Marielena loved to walk. She walked whenever she could, and tonight was no different. As she left French 75, the streets of Tenebrium were quieter than usual on this icy winter's evening, but no less alive. The cobbles glittered with a frost that refracted the colours of the hundreds of bright neon lights all around. It was beautiful. Music was everywhere. The sounds of the Slipstream Highway, far above, was a muffled hum by the time it fell on the ears of those on the streets. Couples huddled together against the chill, while others turned their collars up against the cold.

Her apartment wasn't far from the former speakeasy, and all too soon, her nighttime adventure was over. As Marielena stepped onto the stoop of her building, she noticed that the security door had been forced open, which was no mean feat. The door was black metal intricately inlaid with geometric panes of glass, lit from behind. It was supposed to be able to withstand a military incursion and yet the frame was warped and scratched.

Caution was sobering as she stepped inside the elevator and selected her floor. She had meant to call Walt and report the threats she had been receiving, but it hadn't seemed pressing until now. She thoroughly regretted that lapse in judgement as the elevator doors opened onto her landing.

The three globe-shaped lamps that sat between the doors of her apartment and her neighbours had been smashed. Only the emergency light flickered dimly above, casting red shadows through the gloom.

Even where she stood, a single step from the lift, Marielena could see that her front door was ajar, and while she couldn't make out what it said, there was scribbled graffiti on the door.

Fear pushed her to call for help. She stepped back into the elevator and held an arm out to hold the doors open. With the other, she reached for her cicada.

"Hello?" Walt said, answering almost immediately. There was the ghost of a laugh in his voice.

"Walt, it's Marielena. I need your help."

"What's wrong?" he asked, immediately alert. "Are you okay?"

"I think someone has broken into my apartment."

"Are they still there?"

"I don't know. I haven't gone inside, but the door is open and the lights in the hall have been smashed."

"Good. Don't. Go back to the lobby and wait for me. I won't be long."

True to his word, Walt arrived less than fifteen minutes later. For the first time since she had known him, he wasn't wearing a full suit. He was wearing slacks and an open-collared shirt; his shoulder holster had been hastily thrown over the top. He didn't look dishevelled, however, he looked like a man ready to spring into action. It was at times like these that Marielena understood why both Thea and Cleo had fallen for him.

"Are you okay?" He asked, looking her up and down for injuries. Marielena nodded. "Wait here for me."

"No. I'm coming with you."

"They could still be in there. It's not safe."

"You can't stop me. It's my home."

"Fine. Stay behind me." Another mark of favour for Walt in Marielena's eyes. "We're taking the stairs."

Walt pulled out his gun as they entered the stairwell and held it in front of them as they ascended. Even fit and healthy as she now was, there was a lot of stairs. She was panting by the time they were half-way to her floor. Not Walt though, he was nothing but focussed.

As they crested the final set of stairs, Walt put a finger to his lips, ordering silence. He carefully stepped up to the front door and peered in the small gap that the door being ajar had left. Up close, Marielena could finally read the words scrawled in black across its face. It read: "SOULLESS".

Walt carefully nudged the door open with his foot. Even from behind him, Marielena could see that her home had been ransacked. The furniture was destroyed, bookcases had been toppled and pictures had been ripped from the walls. There was broken glass everywhere.

"Why would someone do this?" Marielena whispered, barely holding back tears.

As Walt stepped further into the apartment, they both heard a loud metallic *CLICK* and before Marielena knew what was happening, there was an explosion of force. A visible wave of energy erupted from the place where Walt had stood, throwing him backwards into Marielena and sending them both into the air and over the banister. They tumbled down a flight of stairs before landing painfully in a heap at the bottom.

Marielena's ears were ringing. She was winded and bruised, but otherwise unhurt. Walt had broken her fall with his body.

"Are you okay?" She could tell Walt was shouting, but he sounded far away as if she was hearing him from underwater.

"I'm fine. I think. Are you okay?"

He nodded and used his arms to prop himself upright against the stairwell wall. Marielena's neighbours had come out onto the landing above to see what had happened. She could hear panicked voices.

"Someone, call the police!"

"What was that?"

"Is everyone all right?"

"What's going on?"

Marielena clambered to her feet. "What do we do?" she asked Walt, who was still leaning against the wall.

"Tell them that the police are on their way and that they need to wait inside their apartments if there isn't any dangerous damage or injuries. Go, I'll be right behind you."

"Why can't you get up?"

"The device attached to my spine—the blast must have knocked it out. It's temporary. I'll be fine in a minute." *That must be terrifying,* Marielena thought.

A blue light flashed across Walt's eyes, and Marielena knew a call had come in.

"Captain James here... How many...? Where...? I'm already there. Get teams out there now and take Medicus with you. Keep me updated."

"What is it?" Marielena asked.

"This wasn't the only explosion tonight."

EXES AND SIGNIFICANT OTHERS

"You have to wait here," Thea said, rounding on Torrez.

They were standing just beyond the police cordon outside the apartment building, where he had once lived with Marielena. There was a crowd of tenants being looked after by beat cops, no doubt on Walt's orders. Thea felt strange being back so soon. She hadn't been back to Tenebrium for three years, yet in the last three days she had found herself there twice.

"My name is still on the deed," Torrez said belligerently.

"You're not a cop anymore, and Marielena didn't ask for you. You can't be here. Stay behind the line," Thea said, stepping under the old-fashioned crime scene tape.

"And if I don't? You gonna arrest me, Querida?"

"I know you're worried, but don't push me, Drew."

"We're still married, and it's my home. You have no grounds to stop me."

The elevator ride to Marielena's apartment was unusually frosty as Thea seethed and Torrez glared at the floor. She knew he technically had the right to enter the scene, but she was sure that Marielena wouldn't want to see her estranged husband while already dealing with the night's ordeal.

Two uniformed officers that Thea didn't recognise greeted them as the elevator doors opened.

"Thea Williams, ARC."

"The captain is expecting you, Agent Williams. Who are you?" the officer demanded of Torrez.

"Andrew Torrez. It's my apartment."

"It's fine. He's with me," Thea said reluctantly.

The landing was untouched, except for the broken bulbs that littered the concrete floors with glass, and the debris that had been thrown through Marielena's door. The door itself was hanging off its hinges.

The inside of the apartment was a different story entirely. It was obvious where the device had detonated. There was a small clear space on the floor just beyond the square hall, leading into the living room. Everything out with the small clear patch had been blasted back until it had collided with one of the walls. Broken furniture, books, lamps, pictures, and plants lay in haphazard heaps. Every window on the bottom floor of the apartment had been blown out. Wind whipped the debris around the room. The destruction was immense; Thea doubted much could be saved.

Marielena was standing with Walt near the epicentre. She was wrapped in a blanket. She had a sort of unconcerned expression on her beautiful face that Thea recognised instantly as shock.

"Hi, Marie," Thea said, stepping forward and hugging Marielena. Marielena gripped her as if she was a lifeline; it was almost painful. "Are you okay?"

"I'm fine. I just can't believe this. What is he doing here?" she asked, spotting Torrez over Thea's shoulder.

"I'm sorry. He was there when I got the call."

"It doesn't matter."

"Have you called Cleo? Do you want me to?"

"She's on her way."

Thea nodded and stepped away, gesturing to Walt to join her. "Leave her be," she muttered to Torrez as she passed. Thea led them to the kitchen, which was in far better shape than the living area and the plant room, but still showed signs of the blast, with its cracked tiles and shattered window.

"Are *you* okay?" Thea asked Walt now that they were away from the hubbub of the crime scene and the plethora of police personnel.

"I'll feel it in the morning for sure, but I'm fine." He cracked his neck and stretched his shoulders as if to emphasise the point. "Cleo?" he asked, raising his eyebrows.

Thea gave a tight-lipped smile, but said nothing.

"Good for them," Walt said with obvious sincerity. "Does Torrez know?"

"He's about to."

Walt groaned, clearly thinking the same as Thea. A crime scene was no place for marital drama.

"So, what the hell happened here?" Thea asked after a moment of silence.

"Someone planted a pulse bomb in this apartment and nine others around the city. All the victims were vocal supporters of the augmented community, some were augs themselves. No one's claimed responsibility—yet."

"Any fatalities?"

"One and seven injured."

"Pulse bombs are perfectly capable of causing fatal injuries, but they tend to do more damage to property than people. You think this was a warning?" Thea asked, absently scratching the back of her neck.

"Judging by the size of the device, I don't think the perp cared if the victims lived or died. This was a message."

"Any evidence these are linked to our murders?"

"Too soon to tell." Walt shrugged.

"Levi Seward is in town holding a conference."

"Is he now? I'll send a uniformed officer to check it out."

"Let me."

"Are you sure?" Walt asked, quirking an eyebrow. "You must have better things to do."

"Trust me, I don't." Thea gave a wicked grin.

"Before you go, have you made any progress with the crucifixions?"

"Yes, and no. I checked all the security footage in the areas surrounding the crime scenes, but there was nothing. Either the killer is exceptionally good at blending in, or they are travelling by alternate means—maybe the sewers. I had my team go through all the threatening calls, comments, emails, letters that have been reported and we have people working on most of them now, but none link to the killings. Or none seem to, anyway."

"This killer is so many steps ahead of us there is no way we catch them before they kill again."

"I found one thing. The metal poured down the victim's throats is made from augmentations. The killer melted it down. Our lab is trying to figure out a way to trace where it came from. Until then, I've got people looking into hospital thefts and dumping sites as well as medical waste centres."

"Smart," Walt said approvingly.

"Did you both know?" Torrez said as he stalked into the room with the air of a moody teen.

"About Cleo?" Thea guessed. "Yes. I knew. But it wasn't my secret to tell." Torrez gave a gruff and noncommittal grunt. "You have Joseph, remember?"

"And you?" Torrez shot at Walt, ignoring Thea.

"Not my business," Walt said with a shrug. He returned his attention to Thea. "Let me know what Seward says. I'd love a chance to bring that bastard in."

"C'mon," Thea said to Torrez. "We're going to the Tenebrium branch of Una Anima."

ASSOCIATION

Syed loved to travel. He and his husband had always dreamed of travelling the colonies, and when Levi had become successful, Syed had thought that their shared dream was about to become a reality. Instead, far from seeing the world, he'd had to content himself with musty amphitheatres, conference halls, and gaudy churches. He lived a life of luxury. By all accounts he should be grateful, and yet, there was a bitterness festering inside him.

Levi was loving, attentive, and increasingly absent. He provided in all senses of the word, but he had become so caught up in his own deification that Syed barely recognised him. It was this thought that stuck uncomfortably in his mind as he sat off to the side of the stage like the good little husband he was.

The venue tonight was a gallery. The owner, a snooty young White man whose name Syed had no desire to learn, had commissioned a portrait of Levi that he had unveiled earlier that evening. Now as he listened, with growing resentment, his dear husband was giving a speech about the danger of the 'soulless', as he had taken to calling those with augmentations of late.

He was barely curbing the urge to stand up and walk out when he spotted the agent who had ruined Levi's press conference. She was lurking near the back of the crowd, clearly waiting for an opportunity to corner Levi. Syed had half a mind to let her until he had a better idea.

Syed waited for Levi to finish his speech and before the applause had died down, he slunk off the stage and into the crowd. He had watched carefully where the agent had gone. She had made her way through the 'Staff Only' door that led to the makeshift greenroom. In truth, it was a storage room, but there were so many beautiful and expensive works dotted around that it appeared grander than most high-end dressing rooms.

"I know you," the agent said as she turned to see Syed standing in the doorway. "You're Seward's arm candy."

"I suppose I deserve that. I'm guilty by association." And he felt it. To him, that's what loving his husband meant. To love Levi, in all his wickedness, was to be equally guilty of his crimes. "What do you believe in?"

"Excuse me?" the agent's eyes narrowed in suspicion.

"I'm about to betray my husband, and I'd at least like to know that it's to the right person."

"I believe in justice. I believe that your husband is a liar. A conman. A fake idol peddling hate. He's built an empire out of it. And I will stop him."

"I love my husband," Syed said, because it felt important to make that clear. "But he has become a monster that I don't recognise."

The agent didn't say anything, she just waited. It was clear he had no interest in handholding and it made him respect her more. She wasn't going to coddle someone she saw as a villain.

"I won't hurt him," Syed went on. "But what he's doing is wrong."

"Did he have anything to do with the bombings earlier tonight?"

"No, nothing."

"And you're sure? You two have no secrets?"

"We have several lifetimes worth, but bombings aren't his style."

"Style." The agent's mouth twisted into a smile filled with disdain.

"The attack outside Una Anima, the one in which you were shot defending Levi, was a setup."

"What do you mean? I need details."

"It was staged. Levi has a devout inner circle who will do anything he asks, and he asked it of Joel Curtis. He didn't expect the boy to be firing lead, but the attack was a publicity stunt."

"And you'd testify to that if I could evidence it?"

Syed thought for a long moment. Could he do that to Levi? He found, with some shock, that he could. "Yes," he said quietly.

"And the crucifixions?"

"I think whoever is doing it is spurred on by Levi. But he isn't directly involved. He's a lot of terrible things, but the murders don't serve him. If you can't think of a way that a crime would make him money, assume he had nothing to do with it."

"And if I were to come to you for information in the future, in the name of protecting the vulnerable, would you talk to me?"

"Yes," Syed said again, hanging his head.

THE PAST

Seventeen years ago...

Five months to the day since she had wandered into Bourbon Street casino, Cynthia found herself, once again, in a chauffeured transporter on her way to the home of Vincent Russo, head of the Russo crime family.

Vinny, for his part, was a gracious host. He was kind and considerate. More attentive than her husband had been in years, but still so tangibly dangerous. The blood on his hands was visible, no matter how clean and well-manicured they were. The man had an air of death about him, like he had the power to snuff out life as he saw fit. And he did.

Unusually, for their Thursday meetings, Vinny was waiting on the front steps when the transporter pulled up.

"Cynthia," he beamed, taking her hand and brushing his lips across her knuckles. This was the most he ever touched her. He never made any unwanted advances or lewd comments, though Cynthia knew he desired her. There was a glint in his eye that told her so. "I thought you might be getting bored of the house." 'House' was not the word Cynthia would have used to describe the beautiful mansion. "How would you feel about hitting the town?"

Cynthia thought for a moment. It was so clear that he was giving her a genuine choice, without pressure or fear of consequences, should she decline.

"I don't want to be seen..."

"In my company?" His smile was devilish.

"Out of my husband's."

"I don't think we'll meet anyone you know tonight."

"In that case, where are we going?"

"It's a surprise."

Cynthia had been repulsed by Vinny at first. He had made her skin crawl, but the more time they spent together, the harder it was to define exactly what she thought of him. He was kind, to her, though she knew he was perfectly capable of cruelty. He was sweet, to her, though she had heard him cut with words when displeased. He was gentle with her, though the flecks of blood that stained his cuffs from time to time told stories of brutality and violence. He was...interesting and quick to laugh. He loved art and music and food. He hid nothing from her, even the depths of his own darkness, of which there was plenty.

Her time with Vinny was supposed to have been a hardship born out of necessity. He had paid for the surgery her son so desperately needed and her company was the price. But now, far from a hardship, she enjoyed their meetings. Looked forward to Thursday nights, when, for a few hours at least, she could step out of her own comparatively dull life and experience something more, something thrilling; the life of an honest to God mobster. If she was honest with herself, she loved it.

She loved her son, but she wanted more than being a housewife. Since Vinny had paid for her son's operation, her husband had insisted that she needn't keep her job and once again, like she had been for so long before it, she had found herself listless. But every Thursday night all that went away as she allowed herself to be swept into Vinny's world.

"You're quiet tonight," Vinny observed softly as they sat together in the back of the transporter, soaring high above Tenebrium City. "Is everything all right? If you're having second thoughts, we can go home."

Home.

"No, I was just...thinking about my son." She had almost confided in him. She mentally chastised herself for being so foolish. He was her escapism, but he wasn't her friend, and he definitely wanted something from her.

"How is he?" Vinny asked with the genuine concern he always showed.

"Flourishing, thanks to you."

"I think Dr Cutter would argue he had a hand in that."

"I'm grateful to you both."

"We're nearly here," Vinny said, peering out the tinted side window.

The transporter landed softly on the roof of an impossibly tall building. The view of the city was almost unbelievable. Cynthia could see everything from the SubLevel gates to City Hall. She could see the Pleasure Quarter lit up in red and Eltham glowing white. She could see Jonks zooming around on the Slipstream Highway. It was breath-taking.

Vinny stepped out of the transporter and walked around the side to open Cynthia's door. "City's beautiful, isn't she?" he said, smiling at the wonder on her face.

Cynthia smiled widely and nodded.

The wind whipped her hair as she stepped out onto the roof proper. "Where are we?"

"Motley Tower."

"Playground for the elite." Cynthia shivered in the chill night air, and Vinny took off his coat and wrapped it around her shoulders.

"I own it." He laughed at the look of shock on her face.

Motley Tower, named after the famed artist, was an immense structure that loomed over the Tenebrium Skyline. It was home to shops, bars, casinos, hotels, brothels, theatres and so much more, but it was open only to those with immense wealth. There was even a credit check at the front door; fail and be denied entry.

"C'mon." Vinny held out a hand to Cynthia, who took it without thinking. He led them over to a small elevator. The inside was black and gold, with mirrors on the back wall. Before she could do more than wonder how much the lift alone had cost, they were stopping. It seemed they had only gone down a single floor.

The doors opened into a jungle of plants, trees, and flowers. Wooden pathways were lined with green fronds and beautiful blooms. The chirping of insects and the singing of birds filled the air. It was warm, like the hottest summer.

"This is..." Cynthia was filled with such wonder it robbed her of words.

"The Tenebrium Botanic Gardens, and for tonight, it's all yours."

It was like they had stepped into a rainforest. Vinny led her across a small bridge over a beautiful pond filled with glimmering fish. "Would you like to eat first? Or walk?" he asked.

"Walk, please," she said almost breathlessly. As someone born in the colonies, Cynthia had never seen plants that weren't in pots or surrounded by concrete.

When she'd temporarily had her fill of the flora and fauna, Vinny took her hand again, leading her to the centre of the tropical garden. There, there was a small table covered in the finest linen and set with glimmering tableware. Two wicker seats were positioned at right angles facing a large pool with a small waterfall. Trees lined the edge and their vines hung into the water below. Birds flew across the surface and all manner of aquatic life swam its depths.

"This has been amazing. Thank you so much." Tears of joy trickled down Cynthia's cheeks.

"It's my pleasure."

Cynthia allowed him to pull out her chair before sitting and picking up the small menu card that sat on her empty plate.

"What's Salmon Poke?" she asked.

"It's pronounced poh-kay. It's marinated salmon, with avocado over a brown rice salad. If you'd like something else..."

"No, that sounds delicious."

And it was. When they had finished, they sat in a comfortable silence watching the water.

"Can I ask you something?" Cynthia said quietly. Vinny was very open, but she usually avoided asking him questions for fear of the answers.

"Anything," he said immediately.

"Why me?"

"I don't understand."

"The things you've shown me in our short time together are astonishing. Your world is so much bigger than mine. I feel simple."

Vinny smiled. "You remind me of me. We're both broken, damaged in a way that makes those who aren't look at us with pity or fear. But they're wrong, in your case at least." Cynthia absently touched her prosthetic hand. "You deserve more, and I want to give it to you."

Cynthia considered this as she looked at Vinny. He was sort of handsome. Looking past his scars, and his hulking figure, she could, for the first time, see the man behind the monster.

"I have something else to show you tonight, if you're willing." Something dark passed behind his eyes, but Cynthia didn't shy away.

"Show me."

They stepped back into the elevator, but this time they took it all the way down to the basement. Deep underground, Motley Tower was all concrete offices and storerooms. Nothing of the extravagance above touched the seedy underworld below and that was exactly how it felt to Cynthia—like she had just stepped into the underbelly of Tenebrium.

Vinny stalked through the low, bare corridors, Cynthia following nervously behind. When he stopped, it was in front of a metal door with a keycode lock. Not troubling to hide the digits he pressed from Cynthia, he opened the door.

Inside was what could only be described as a dungeon. Dark and dank, the room was cold and smelled of excrement. Vinny clicked his fingers and painfully bright lights flared into life overhead, allowing Cynthia to see the room in full.

She kept her shocked gasp to herself. Hanging by his shoulders from vicious meat hooks, was a tanned White man with dark hair. Blood oozed from where he had been impaled on the steel hooks. He was shirtless and his body showed signs of merciless beatings. Beside him was a tray of torture instruments. Knives, saws, hammers and plyers, brass knuckles and needles, lighters and ropes.

"This is Barney. He used to be one of my most trusted guys until he turned snitch for the Brigantes. I think I need to make an example of him. What d'you think?"

"I—What?" Cynthia was trembling, but this time it had nothing to do with the cold.

"I'm all of that." Vinny pointed a massive hand to the ceiling. "The gardens, the dinners, the romance, but I'm also this. If you're gonna be part of my life, and I really hope you are—You'll be part of this too. So, what do you think I should do with him? You don't want this? Forget the money. You don't owe me anything. You can go home and you'll never hear from me again, or you can tell me how you think I should deal with this traitor and I'll know you're as in as I am."

"Please...help...me," Barney slurred, stirring for the first time since they had entered the room.

"He betrayed you." Cynthia's voice shook. "If you do nothing, it'll make you look weak. You have to be the monster they think you are."

WONGS

It was oddly disconcerting how much sitting behind her old desk in the TPD felt like home to Thea. With her and Torrez scheduled to take a Jonk early the next morning, it had seemed the obvious choice for a place to research Syed's claims.

The TPD bullpen was quiet. It was late and most of the people surrounding Thea were doing exactly what she was—working.

It wasn't her desk anymore, however, and as it turned out, it now belonged to Sid.

"I can move," Thea said, when Sid expressed his surprise at finding her there.

"No. Stay. We can share." He sat down gracefully opposite her in the seat that, in the past, had so often been occupied by Walt. "What are you working on?" he asked lightly.

"Following up a lead on Levi Seward," Thea said, turning back to the datastream which hovered in the air in front of her. "What about you?"

"Well, the Captain just assigned me to your case, so I guess I'm following up on a lead about Levi Seward."

Thea let out a short laugh. She had only met Sid a handful of times, but he had an easy charm that she enjoyed. "I had a weird conversation with Seward's husband. He said the shooting was a fake."

"Syed, right? Forty-seven, currently a stay-at-home husband. Married for seventeen years. He was a painter, and quite a progressive one. A decade or so ago, he used his platform to speak out against Islamophobia, but he hasn't been active in any kind of activism for years."

"Wow," Thea said, impressed. "You've done your homework."

"You're kind of a legend around here. I wanted to make a good impression." He blushed slightly, but seemed pleased, nonetheless.

"Don't believe everything you hear around the water cooler."

"It's all good things. There's a lot of respect for you here. I know we aren't supposed to talk about the fact the city was taken over by a cult, but I lived through it. The talk around here is that you were the one who cracked the case."

"Captain Charles, Walt and so many other good people were all a part of that."

"The way Walt tells it, it was all you."

"Yeah, well, he's a fan," Thea said nonchalantly, before they strayed any further into dangerous territory.

"Having the Captain as a partner...what was that like?" Sid leaned in conspiratorially.

"Anything in that encyclopaedia brain of yours about Joel Curtis?" Thea said, ignoring the question.

"He attacked Levi Seward, and you arrested him before the charges were dropped. It didn't seem like he had much to do with the case, so I didn't dig." If Sid had found Thea's deflection strange, he gave no sign, he just went right back to business.

"We only had him in custody overnight, so I didn't get much of a chance, either."

"What have you found out now?"

"He's clean. No record prior to the shooting. He's either been duped by Seward or he's just a kid that needed some quick credits."

"Would you call the attack on Seward domestic terrorism?" Sid asked shrewdly.

"If it wasn't faked...there's been a lot of discourse around whether we should call mass shootings or attempted mass shooting terrorism events." Thea pondered this for a moment. "I think I know what you're getting at. Faked or not, it showed the ability to perpetrate organised violence. Like a mass shooting...or a bombing."

"What do you think?" It was clear that Sid was eager to gain her approval. Little did he know, he already had it.

"I think it's going to be difficult to prove. Syed told me it was staged by Seward—he's the mastermind, not the kid."

"We could stake out Una Anima events."

"Can you get some Uni's on that? Seward is still in Tenebrium."

"Sure thing." Sid tapped his Cicada and relayed the order. When he was done, he said, "Can you prove the shooting in Caligo was faked?"

"Not conclusively. The fact no one was hit, other than me, is suspicious. But he was firing real bullets. If someone had been hurt, it would have been a much different story. It will be difficult to convince a jury unless Curtis confesses. Plus, the charges were dropped. We'd need new and very strong evidence to get them reinstated."

"Man, there are so many layers to this case." Sid ran his hands through his glossy hair. "Are you hungry?" he asked, catching Thea off guard. "I'm hungry and there's this amazing noodle bar around the corner."

"Wongs?" Thea asked in surprise.

"Yeah. You wanna go?"

She had done all she could in the TPD. There were no more answers to be found tonight.

"Sure."

Wongs was just as she remembered it. Dimly lit and authentic. It had a cosy and casual atmosphere that bordered on intimate. It was why Thea and Walt had chosen to eat there so often after a hard day's work. Tonight, however, she wasn't thinking about Walt.

Sid was fun, smart and witty, not to mention handsome. The conversation flowed easily between talking about work and more personal topics. He was quick to laugh and had a way about him that put Thea instantly at ease. It was long after midnight when they parted for the evening and when Sid leaned in for a chaste goodnight kiss, Thea didn't push him away.

RED HANDED

"Where have you been?" Detective Fry demanded when Alex got to their desk. "I've been calling you for hours."

"I'm sorry. I had a late night."

The Caligo Police Department was much like any other, overfunded and understaffed. The detective's bullpen was a high-ceilinged room, with pale stone walls and archways, some ten feet up, that framed the grilled windows. The desks were dark wood and set up in two rows of eight, with matching round backed chairs. The floors were chequered, with large tiles alternating between black and off-white. There were short staircases at either end, surrounded by wooden railings, that led to the elevators. Pendant lights hung from the ceiling, interspersed with clear glass screens that showed the city's many news networks.

Alex's desk was right in the centre, a position they lamented. They took off their coat and flopped into their chair, holding their head in their hands. It had been a late night, but that had nothing to do with police work. Alex was more determined than ever to find out what really happened in Tenebrium three years ago, but their investigation was stalled. The city had done an extremely thorough job of covering up the mess left by the Gold Legion, but Alex was not put off that easily.

"Don't just sit there," Fry railed. "We got a match on the print from the bottle of accelerant we found at the Kelpie Clinic."

"What?" All tiredness forgotten, Alex sat up straight, ready and alert.

"We know who set the fire. You wanna come arrest him, or just sit there doing nothing?"

Guilt itched at Alex as they followed Fry to the transporter bay. They had been letting their personal agenda get in the way of doing their job. A job that used to mean the world to them.

Seamus Denver lived in a rundown apartment a stone's throw from Caligo's industrial district—The Forge. Like all buildings near Caligo's manufacturing hub, its face was blackened with the accumulated dirt and pollution synonymous with industry. The air near The Forge was thicker. It clung to the back of Alex's throat and seemed to get stuck in their lungs. Living in such conditions was definitely not a choice, more a by-product of a system that favoured the rich and punished the poor. Life expectancy in homes near The Forge, was nearly half that of those who lived in the Diamond Ward.

"Seamus Denver," Alex said to the rough iron slab that was Mr Denver's front door. "This is the police. Open up."

"Come in, Officer," a calm and measured voice called.

Alex and Fry nodded to one another, then Fry pushed open the door.

Mr Denver's apartment was a tiny studio. The living room, kitchen, bedroom and bathroom were all in the same square space, the kitchen and bathroom partially partitioned by wooden screens.

Seamus Denver was a middle-aged White man, with dark hair that was greying at the sides and prematurely deep wrinkles around his eyes. He sat in a threadbare armchair in front of an old-fashioned television set that must have been some two-hundred years old. Alex was amazed it still worked. On the sofa, which sat at the end of the bed, a slender Japanese woman perched clutching a handkerchief; she looked ill.

"What can I do for you,

Officers?" Seamus asked as if they were old friends.

"We have reason to believe that you were involved in the arson of The Kelpie Clinic that resulted in eighteen deaths," Alex said sternly.

"That's right." Seamus nodded. "Those augmented freaks have the devil in them and the only way to purge that kind of evil is with fire." Mrs Denver let out a sob. "Don't worry, my darling, they can't arrest me for doing God's work."

"Actually, I can. Seamus Denver, you are under arrest for the arson of the Kelpie Clinic and the murder of the eighteen individuals trapped within. You have the right to remain silent. You have the right to an attorney. If you cannot afford one, one will be appointed to you by the Caligo Criminal Court. You will be transported back to the CPD, where you will be detained and questioned. Do you understand?"

"God will punish the wicked," was his only reply.

SAUDADE

When Thea arrived back in Caligo the next day, it was to mixed news. Alex called to inform her they had caught the arsonist who burned down The Kelpie Clinic, but the tensions in the city were rising and there had been several acts of vandalism and violence committed against augmented individuals and aug owned businesses. On top of this, Thea's team were still suspended, which meant that if there were any call-outs assigned to her, she would have to go alone.

There was an obvious shift to the air in the city; a tension that hung over the streets like an invisible mist. It was clear that the citizens were on edge. People moved through their daily lives with mistrust and fear. Thea had experienced this sort of situation before and knew it was only a matter of time before the city erupted, because tensions cannot, and will not stay bottled up forever.

She spent her day following up on as many of the anti-aug incidents as she could. She took statement after statement, followed up on lead after lead. She arrested two thugs who had been boasting loudly about how they had given a café owner with a prosthetic eye 'The Broderick'.

When evening came, she was more than happy to join Torrez in a drink to unwind.

Thea had just changed into her loungewear when the doorbell rang.

"Where's Cora?" Torrez asked as Thea ushered him inside her apartment.

"Night shift. She was not pleased."

"You look tired, Querida." Torrez placed the paper bag he had been carrying on her sideboard and took off his long, dark coat.

"I am. Oooh, very nice," she said, approvingly inspecting the bag's contents. As was his custom, Torrez had brought with him a bottle of top shelf tequila.

Thea poured them both healthy measures before the pair settled themselves onto the sofa. They chatted for a while, and it was comfortable enough, but Thea could tell there was something more on Torrez's mind. She may have been tired, but he seemed sad, and that was more important.

"What's wrong?" she asked, though she had a pretty good idea.

"I'm sorry about before. I behaved like an asshole."

"Yup." Thea gave him a friendly punch on the arm.

"Marielena has moved on. I knew she would eventually. It's been three years, for Christ's sake, but it still sucks."

"What about Joseph? Haven't you moved on? You two seem so happy."

"He's the perfect man. He's wonderful, and he loves me so much. He's smart and sweet and funny. The sex is amazing...He can do things with his tongue that would make your eyes water, but I don't love him. I want to. You have no idea how much I want to, but I don't. At least not how he deserves."

"You still love Marielena?"

Torrez nodded, his eyes glassy. Thea leaned forward and pulled him into a hug. He clung to her.

"I'm not being fair to Joseph," Torrez said after a moment, gently releasing the embrace.

"No."

"But it's just so comfortable and yet so damn lonely."

"You're a romantic, Drew. And I get that you're trying to be a better man. You turned yourself around. You don't cheat but letting him think you love him is almost worse."

"You think I should end it?"

"That's not for me to say."

"I've been in love twice in my life. Salvador and Marielena. Real, big love. I know how that feels and this isn't it. We could probably spend the rest of our lives together happily enough, but I want more. I want to feel that spark, that fire."

"Joseph deserves to be loved the way you loved Marielena, and he thinks he has that with you."

"You're right, but I...I'm scared of being alone. Of ending up alone."

"You won't. There is someone out there for you. Besides, you'll always have me."

Torrez discarded his glass on the coffee table and sat up straighter. He looked Thea dead in the eye and leaned quickly forward. She could tell what he was going to do before it happened, but she made no efforts to stop it. Softly, he pressed his lips to hers as if testing the waters. Then he slipped a hand into her hair. She felt his lips part, and then his tongue met hers. They both kept the kiss going for several long seconds before Thea gently pulled away.

They looked at each other for a moment. "What're you doing, Drew? We both know you don't want me," Thea said gently.

"No. But, God, I wish I did. Think how much easier both our lives would be if we just fell in love with each other."

"It would be great, but I don't think it's on the cards."

"Me neither. You are the most important person in my life. You're my best friend, my person. I love you. I would die for you, but I'm not *in* love with you."

"Rude."

Torrez let out a chuckle and as the sound faded away, they lapsed into silence. Thea supped at her barely touched drink.

"Can I ask you something?" Torrez asked, draining his glass.

"Of course."

"I've never known two people more drawn to each other than you and Walt. How did you leave him? Where did you find the strength?" He sounded so earnest it was sad.

"I didn't leave him. I fled," Thea said with a self-deprecating laugh. "I ran away to another city. I knew if I stayed, we'd end up together and I didn't want that."

"Why not?"

"We hurt each other so much. We bring out the worst in each other. If I had stayed, we wouldn't have healed. We would have gotten lost in each other like we always did, and he would never have stayed sober. I never would have been able to come to terms with everything that happened. It would have exploded, and we would have made each other miserable. And we would have done it over and over again, probably for the rest of our lives."

"Did you ever ask Walt to leave Cleo?"

"Never. Not once."

"Why not?"

"Because I knew he wouldn't. I knew it wasn't right."

"But how did you know?"

"The same way that you already know what you're doing to Joseph isn't right."

Torrez nodded thoughtfully. "Was it hard seeing him again? Walt?"

"Yes, and no. I don't really know how I feel about it. It feels...weird, like going back in time. Everything's changed, but nothing has. Working together has been almost too easy."

"Do you still love him?"

Thea didn't answer. She didn't need to.

"He's everything you wanted him to be three years ago. Maybe..."

"No, Drew," Thea said flatly.

"I just don't want you to be lonely."

"I'm not lonely. I'm happy being on my own. I like my life."

"But don't you wish you had someone to come home to?"

"I'm not sad and lonely because I'm single. I'm not sad at all. I don't need a partner right now. I've been dating. It's been fun. Nothing has stuck, and that's fine."

"I'm sorry. You're right."

"I actually went on a date yesterday. I think. Sort of. Maybe."

"Well, spill," Torrez said, brightening at once. He had always been a sucker for gossip.

"He's a detective in the TPD."

"Oh, Querida, I've had some bad ideas in my time..."

"I know. I didn't plan it."

"I guess you have a type. You like him?"

"I dunno yet. We were working the case, and he asked me if I wanted food. I didn't think anything of it, but we ended up chatting for hours in this tiny little restaurant."

"What's his name?"

"Sydney. Sid."

"That's not a hot name."

"What's a 'hot name'?" Thea asked, bemused.

"Andrew...Thea...Mateo," he said with a wink.

"My boss? Really?" Thea screwed up her face trying to imagine AD Castillo romantically. She couldn't see it.

"Oh yeah, he has 'daddy' written all over him."

SCOOPED

"You *have* to tell me where you get your leads," Jimmy said, reading Fen's article over her shoulder.

Jimmy, a tall Black man with a short afro, was sitting next to Fen at her desk in The Tenebrium Times press room. She had asked him to read her latest article on the pro-aug crucifixions. So far, he seemed impressed.

"How did you find out that he calls himself 'The Zealot'? That's a phenomenal scoop. Catchy too, it'll be everywhere come tomorrow morning's news cycle."

"A lady must keep her secrets," Fen said slyly.

"But a good friend would share."

"I guess we aren't friends then." Fen picked up her bag from the back of her chair as she stood and slung it over her shoulder.

"I'm hurt," Jimmy said, but it was clear he was anything but.

"And I have a date."

"You kids have fun," Jimmy called as Fen made her way to the exit. "I'll see that this is printed tonight."

"Thanks."

Both she and Walt had been busy over the last two days and hadn't had a chance to see each other. Their dinner date tonight was, in her opinion, way overdue. She felt silly for missing him after such a short amount of time. They had spoken and exchanged messages, but they were getting to the stage where that wasn't enough for her. She was equal parts excited and apprehensive; it had been a long time since she had connected with someone so deeply.

Her happy musings about their future together kept her busy all the way to the docking junction. The nearest junction, where a Tenebite could call for a Jonckheere transporter, was only a block away from The Tenebrium Times offices, but it wasn't in the best area; it was hidden away down a short alley lined with dumpsters, where the streetlights didn't quite reach.

The docking junction itself was a short silver pillar, around two feet tall, with a small screen on its flat top and there was already a man standing next to it. Fen hesitated at the mouth of the alley, instantly suspicious. The man was slight and hummed to himself with his hands in his pockets, but that was not what gave her pause. He had covered his face with a gold mask that reflected the alley back at her. It was creepy.

Fen checked her watch. If she didn't get a Jonk soon, she was going to be late. Swallowing her misgivings, she made her way to the docking station and pushed the button marked 'CALL RIDE'.

The man nodded at her when she came close, but other than that paid her no mind and Fen began to relax. Maybe it was just an odd fashion statement. They waited just over five minutes before a pleasant female voice emitted from the pillar.

"Customer number one, your Jonk will arrive within three minutes. Customer two, your Jonk will arrive in twenty minutes."

"Damn," Fen muttered.

"Somewhere to be?" the man asked pleasantly, speaking for the first time. His voice was warm and friendly.

"I have a date."

"Where are you headed? Maybe we can share," he offered.

"Apotheon."

"That's near the Pleasure Quarter, right? I have to pass over it to get home. If you want to share, it's no trouble."

"Are you sure?" Fen was hesitant.

"Of course, I wouldn't want anyone standing out in this cold."

Against her better judgement, Fen nodded in agreement and gave thanks. Before she had finished speaking, a transporter landed neatly in front of them. It was yellow, with round doors and an aerodynamic fastback body. When resting on the street, Jonks looked like relics from the past, based on the cars that were popular in the long-forgotten Gatsby era.

"Ladies first," the man said as the Jonk door opened with a mechanical hiss.

Fen stepped inside. The warmth washed over her as she took up the farthest seat, grateful to be out of the grasp of Tenebrium's bitter winter.

The man respectfully settled himself in the seat farthest from Fen and turned to look out the window. They had been in the air for around five minutes, both politely ignoring the other, when a rustling made her turn to look at the man.

He fished a small round disc, similar to a chocolate coin in size, and pressed it against the door. Nothing happened for a moment, then there was a click that told Fen he had just engaged the central locking system.

"What are you doing?" she asked, panic already threatening to overwhelm her. The man in the mask ignored her.

He pulled a set of pliers from his coat this time and tinkered under the dashboard. An alarm sounded, causing Fen to jump but was silenced almost immediately, then the man input a new destination. The small blue screen under the windscreen changed from 'Tenebrium Industrial District – with one stop', to 'Caligo Proper'.

As what was happening sunk in, Fen frantically tried the doors, but they wouldn't budge. Not that it would have done her much good. They were hundreds of feet above the city.

"Who are you? What do you want?" she all but screamed.

"I'm sorry, Miss Yeoh, but you won't be making your date."

NEW GOD

Caligo City had a problem with the mob. This meant it had a rather large illegal weapons and drug trade to contend with, as well as illegal gambling rackets and an exorbitant amount of fraud and counterfeiting.

Around five years ago, a mobster by the name of Marco Barone had been caught on racketeering charges. To avoid an all-out war between the CPD and the Conti Family, the then Police Captail, Harry Galinski, offered Barone a chance to hand himself in. Barone accepted and presented himself the next morning for questioning. When he sat down with detectives, however, he pulled out a long blade he had been concealing in his sleeve and proceeded to gut the detectives, earning himself the nickname 'Mack'.

It was because of this that the CPD interrogation room, as Alex knew it now, looked as it did. It was a large, bare white room, with a small cage similar to what shark divers used. There were no desks or chairs, just the cage and two-way mirrors on all sides.

Today, the cage held Seamus Denver. He stared blandly at his own reflection as Alex paced around the perimeter.

"Are you ready to talk yet?" they asked, stopping in front of Denver. "We have your fingerprints and footage of you fleeing the scene."

"I wore a mask. The video proves nothing."

"But you confessed when we arrested you and again just now. I already know you did it. What I want to know is why? What makes a working-class man, with no priors, commit mass murder?"

"Caligo used to be a God-fearing place, but these augs have brought the devil into our midst."

"How? I'm really asking."

"Someone like you wouldn't understand." Denver sneered. "You are unenlightened. They no longer have souls. They steal our jobs and they are a danger to our children with their perverted agendas. To accept them is to accept the fall of mankind. It is God's will that we cast them out."

"I thought God preached forgiveness and salvation."

"Our Gods are no longer the same."

"I understand that you hate them, but you killed eighteen people. Children. You burned them alive. It is a sight that I will never be able to forget. And you don't seem bothered. It's unthinkable to me."

"I have already found salvation."

There was a knock at the door and a White man wearing an expensive suit entered a moment later without waiting to be admitted.

"Mr Denver, I'm your lawyer Simon Howe. I will be representing you on behalf of an anonymous party. I'd like to have a chat with my client. This interview is over."

"Just tell me why?" Alex said to Denver, ignoring the lawyer.

"Levi Seward is God."

JILTED?

Apotheon was a spectacle of gold and terracotta. The restaurant was hidden down a dark and cobbled street on the seedy outskirts of the Pleasure Quarter. Its entrance looked like the back exit of a particularly low-rent nightclub, but the interior was a thing of beauty.

The walls were covered in ruddy clay and painted with glimmering frescoes from Greek mythology. The tables and chairs were made from pale wood and topped with deep blue marble.

"Do you have a reservation, sir?" the Maître d' asked with a wide smile as Walt entered.

"Yes, it should be under 'Yeoh'."

"Right this way, sir. You are the first of your party to arrive."

The Maître d' led Walt to a secluded corner, where the tables were surrounded by plant encrusted trellises. Midnight blue curtains hung for diners who wanted more intimate experiences.

The Maître d' closed the curtains as Walt sat down. The tabletop was a mosaic that depicted an alternate legend where Medusa was victorious over Perseus.

Fen had said the restaurant was 'nice', but Apotheon was downright fancy, perhaps too fancy for Walt.

Fen was already five minutes late. It wasn't like her, but Walt wasn't worried. Perhaps she was caught up at work. At fifteen minutes, he thought she would have called, but again, perhaps something big was happening in the news world. At thirty minutes late, he called her.

"Hi this is Fen, leave a message."

He called again.

"Hi this is Fen, leave a message."

It was only half an hour. If someone had called the precinct to report someone missing after thirty minutes, they would have been told to stop wasting police time, and yet, an odd sensation in Walt's gut told him that something wasn't right.

"Would you like to order or are you still waiting for the rest of your party?" the Maître d' said, popping their head around the curtain.

"Still waiting."

"As you wish."

Another fifteen minutes passed, and Walt could wait no longer. He knew it was an abuse of power, but his heart was ruling his head.

"Hey, this is dispatch, whaddya need?"

"Put me through to the Chief Editor of The Tenebrium Times."

"Sure thing, Captain."

Walt tapped his foot impatiently as he waited to be connected.

"This is Dean Samuel, Editor in Chief, The Tenebrium Times. How may I help you, Captain James?"

"I need to know the whereabouts of one of your reporters, Fen Yeoh," Walt said without preamble.

The editor made a surprised little noise over the cicada. "I don't keep tabs on my reporters...give me a moment." Walt could hear the unmistakable sounds of a man getting out of a leather chair, then swift foot falls and the opening of a door. "Jimmy? Have you seen Fen this evening?" There was a pause. "What time did she leave?" Another pause. "Are you still there, Captain?"

"Yes, I'm here."

"I'm afraid she left several hours ago."

Walt hung up without so much as a goodbye and raced from the restaurant. He cursed himself for not listening to his gut sooner. He had known something was wrong. Worry flooded him as he made his way out into the street. He ran to the nearest docking junction and thrust his badge against the scanner on the side. There was a soft *beep.* Less than thirty seconds later a Jonk was landing beside him and thirty seconds after that he was on his way to Fen's apartment.

When he arrived, he hammered on the door, but there was no reply. He pulled the key she had given him out of his pocket and shoved it into the lock with shaking hands. The apartment was dark and empty; not a thing out of place.

Walt slammed the door behind him and sprinted back to the Jonk he had left waiting on the roof. Maybe, just maybe, he had misunderstood their evening plans, and she was waiting at his home. He knew in his heart of hearts she wasn't there, but he had to check.

As he stood in the centre of his living room, front door still flung wide, he was not surprised to find himself alone.

Fen was missing.

Fen was missing.

She was a pro-aug journalist and there was a serial killer out there looking for people just like her. He had no leads, no means of finding the killer. The investigation was stalling, and he had nothing that would help him find Fen. Allowing panic to cloud his judgement, Walt called the one person he trusted more than any other.

"Thea, I need your help."

HOLOSUITE

"Can't you just come here?" Walt railed through Thea's Cicada, the worry in his voice clear.

"Sure, just give me three hours while I hop a shuttle," Thea said, only half paying attention. "Or I could just help you now."

"What good is me being in Virtual Evidence?"

Virtual Evidence was the TPD's virtual reality suite. It allowed officers to replay any footage captured on their ocular implants in real time as if they were there again. It was an invaluable tool that had been instrumental in the solving of innumerable crimes.

"It's just to allow you to come here. I just sent a code to your index. Hold it to the VR panel."

A moment later, a holographic version of Walt appeared next to Thea. He was wearing a full tuxedo, the only thing missing was the bow tie. "This is amazing," he said, looking around the room.

The Orchard was one of the few places in the colonies that had invested in a full Holosuite. It was the upgraded version of virtual reality and allowed the controller to create a private metaverse that anyone with access to VR technology could be invited into. This small metaverse allowed investigators to collaborate and interact as if they were in the same room.

The Orchard's metaverse took the shape of a large library. Hugely tall bookshelves lined the walls below a domed ceiling painted with frescoes inspired by ancient Egypt. In the middle of the room, instead of tables, there were six obelisks that were only just taller than Thea.

"This job comes with toys."

Tentatively, Walt reached out a hand and touched one of the bookcases. "I can feel this!" he exclaimed.

"You can interact with anything here, except other people," she added when he reached for her.

"Explain the wonders of modern technology to me later."

"Okay, when did you last speak to Fen?"

"Uhm...around three-thirty."

Moving over to the nearest obelisk, Thea set to work. Moments later, she had a wealth of information at her fingertips.

"Right, so, she called you at three-twenty-three. The call lasted eighteen seconds."

"She was just confirming our date. Fen and I are..."

"Former detective, current investigator. Don't worry, I'd already put that one together." It was odd to think of Walt with someone else, but now definitely wasn't the time to examine those feelings any further. "Okay, looks like she hasn't made any other calls, though she has a few more missed ones from you."

"That's not a good sign, is it?"

Thea didn't reply. "I think a streetcam caught her, but it was nearly three hours ago; I have some footage here..."

The room changed around them in a whirl of colour; the library disappeared into blackness and then the room reformed into a Tenebrium street in the evening. As if from a rooftop, Thea and Walt watched Fen half run down the street in a stunning red evening gown, the beads and tasselling glinting in the light from the streetlamps.

The scene shifted as Fen turned a corner, and then again, finally resting on a dead-end alley. Thea let out a little gasp of shock and Walt swore loudly beside her. Fen was standing at a docking junction next to a man in a gold mask. Thea had seen one just like it before.

"The Gold Legion soldier who tried to arrest me in the subway tunnels. He wore that mask."

"Is it him?" Walt was shaking with rage. "Is it the same person?"

"I can't tell. I never saw his face."

They watched in silence as Fen waited for her Jonk. She chatted with the masked man, but the footage had no audio, so Thea and Walt had no idea what words were exchanged. A few minutes later, a Jonk landed and both Fen and the masked man got inside.

Thea quickly dismissed the footage and entered the Jonk's registration tag into the terminal. "The Jonk was supposed to fly to The Quadrant," Thea said, reading the proffered information. "But a few minutes into the journey, it went dark."

"I should have searched for her sooner. She could already be dead."

"We don't know that."

"There's a serial killer out there targeting pro-aug allies and Fen is missing. That's not a coincidence." Walt was on the edge of a very dark precipice.

"You're probably right. But the killer has a pattern. They need to take her somewhere. They make the crosses themselves. We have time. Stop thinking like a lover and start thinking like a cop."

Walt took a long steadying breath, then said, "Can you track her using her Cicada?"

Thea paused. "That's very illegal, but yes, the holosuite is capable. Halo?"

"Yes, SSA Williams, how may I help you today?" a sweet, musical and almost childlike voice filled the air.

"I need the last location known of Fen Yeoh, Colonial ID number four-two-eight-two-F-Y-X-S."

"This action is restricted."

"Director's override. Mateo Castillo."

"Password?"

"Serena."

"Fen Yeoh was last detected on Zadkine Street at the corner of Lozowick."

"That's in Caligo," Thea said in surprise.

"I'm on my way," Walt said before disappearing.

BREAKTHROUGH

The ghoul screeched and snarled as it hurled itself against the glass of its cell. No more lucid than it had been a day ago. Cleo sighed, another round of experiments a failure.

Her lab at MedTech's Tenebrium branch was impressive. It was a lab she could only have dreamed of running when she first qualified, but now, its impossibly white walls, state-of-the-art equipment, vast amount of space and innumerable resources at her disposal just made her feel like more of a failure.

She stepped out from behind her wide minimalist desk where she had been taking notes on her test subjects' behaviour and crossed to the cell. She looked sadly at the ghoul. It had been a young woman once. Its long dark hair was irreparably matted, and black spittle flecked its face as it continued to bite and snap at Cleo through the glass.

Cleo and her team tried their best to treat ghouls like the people they once were, to keep them clean and feed them properly, but the only thing ghouls would eat was flesh. This meant that more often than not, they looked like fiendish monsters.

"I'm sorry," Cleo said sadly as the ghoul hurled itself at the glass separating them. "I'm trying my best, but I don't know how to help you."

"So...rr...yy." The rasping drawl was barely recognisable as speech, yet the ghoul had spoken.

"Computer," Cleo called to the air excitedly. "What stage of degeneration is Subject Seven in?"

"Subject Seven is in stage five."

"She shouldn't be able to speak. She shouldn't be able to speak!" Cleo punched the air in triumph. "Computer, transfer all the data for the latest test round and serum to my terminal, as well as device schematics."

CAPTIVE AUDIENCE

Fen's ears were ringing, and her head felt fuzzy, like her brain was filled with water. She was cold and something warm was dribbling down her neck. She opened her eyes, blinking slowly as she tried to clear the fog in her mind. She was lying on a damp metal floor that seemed to list from side to side. A pungent odour wrinkled her nose; the air was filled with the smell of mould and rust and something familiar...maybe salt?

The room was dark. The only light came from the dim glow of an emergency exit sign. Fen got shakily to her feet and felt her way around the room. Just like the floors, the walls were rough iron, with huge octagonal bolts joining the panels together. It struck her in an instant where she must be. She was on a ship.

Fen brought a hand to her ear, searching for her tragus. She let out a yelp of pain. The warm substance on her neck was blood oozing slowly from where her implant used to be. Her Cicada had been cut out.

Visions of the man in a gold mask came back to her, of the Jonk ride where she had been kidnapped. She remembered she was supposed to be meeting Walt for dinner and hope swelled inside her, pushing away some of the fear that was unfurling in her chest. She wouldn't have shown up for dinner, and Walt would be looking for her.

Walt was looking for her.

She followed the red exit sign to the door. It was a bulkhead door, shut fast with a locking wheel. Fen tried with all her might, but she couldn't turn it. Alone in the dark, all exits barred, panic was starting to creep in.

"Hello? Is there anyone there?" she shouted, her words echoing back at her around the room.

There was the sound of static for a moment, then a loud voice boomed over an intercom. "Be patient, sinner. You will face your judgement soon enough."

THE WRONG PLACE

Zadkine Street was right in the heart of Caligo's Dock Ward. Even though the city topped the colony it was perched upon, it was home to a huge cargo lift, which took goods from the topside, Caligo, right to the docks thousands of feet below on the ocean's surface. It made shipping, import and export much easier than in other cities like Tenebrium, but also allowed for a varied trade in illegal goods to come into the city by sea. Piracy was alive and well in 2429, and the city's criminal element took full advantage.

The night was crisp and foggy as Thea pounded the streets. She had uploaded a map of the Dock Ward to her ocular implant and was carefully following it to the place where Fen's cicada had registered last.

There was nothing there when Thea arrived at her destination. It was a street corner like the many others in the city; surrounded by tall buildings and alight with neon.

Standing at the corner of the block, Thea felt like she was at a crossroads. There were four paths, four directions, four choices. The detective and the cynic in her told her to go west. The streets there became narrower and darker. If she were going to carry out nefarious deeds, she would want to do it where she was less likely to be discovered.

It wasn't long before she came to the mouth of a dark snicket. She peered down it, as she had the several others before it and noticed something tiny flashing on the ground. She made her way to the end and knelt to get a closer look.

Sitting in a small pool of blood was a tiny metal device that Thea knew to be a Cicada. She scanned it with her ocular implant and her worst suspicions were confirmed at once. It was Fen's. The kidnapper had carved out the only thing that could help track her. It was a worryingly clever move, and it didn't bode well for the reporter.

Thea was so caught up in her gruesome discovery, she hadn't heard the footsteps approaching from behind until it was too late. She made to stand, but something hard was pressed to the back of her head. The clicking sound of a revolver hammer being cocked told her it was a gun.

"Stay right where you are." The voice was drawling and lazy. It had a gruff quality, like its owner chain-smoked cigars. "You fucked up, little lady. This is Barone territory."

Out of the corner of her eye, Thea could see the shadows of two men in flat caps standing behind her. "If you're going to threaten someone, you shouldn't put the gun right to their head. It makes it really easy to do this."

Thea turned lightning fast and grabbed the barrel of the gun. She stood, so that there were only mere inches between their bodies and hit the button on her chest. Her aegis of gold burst forth with a flare of glimmering light, slamming what she now saw to be a mobster against the alley wall and leaving her holding his gun by the barrel. She flipped it deftly in her hand and raised it to point at the other mobster. Everything had happened so quickly that he hadn't had time to react. He just stood slack-jawed off to one side.

"You mobsters are just attacking people in the street now? It's not exactly good for business."

"Dangerous times," the mobster muttered.

"You know anything about this?" Thea pointed to the small pool of blood on the ground at her feet. "You see a woman down here? Couple of hours ago. Dark hair? Red dress? She would have been in distress."

"You a cop or somethin'? No, I didn't see nothin'."

"Get out of here," Thea said, gesturing with the gun. The mobster didn't need to be told twice. He turned on his heel and ran.

Returning to the matter at hand, Thea slipped an evidence bag from her pocket and used it to carefully pick up the severed Cicada before replacing it in her pocket and using her own to call Walt.

"What did you find?" he said, answering on the first ring.

"The kidnapper cut her cicada out. I found it in an alley." He was a cop, he could handle the truth.

"Bastard," Walt spat.

"How far away are you? We're going to need to ask around, and this is Barone territory. I could use the back-up."

"I just got to the city. I'll be there soon."

ANOTHER LIFE

By the time Mateo found himself outside Natalia Vargas's office, he was still trying to remember if he had told his daughter he loved her when he kissed her goodbye. He decided that even if he had, he should tell her again when he got home.

It was late, but Mateo wasn't surprised to find that Deputy Director Vargas was still working. He was, however, surprised to find her crying. The door to her office was ajar and he could hear the soft sobbing emanating from inside.

He knocked gently on the door and let himself in.

"What are you doing here?" Natalia asked, hastily drying her eyes.

"I thought if Thea refused to be suspended, I could do the same. I want to come back."

"Fine. Your suspension is lifted. Now, go."

"You know, friends talk to each other."

"Please, just leave me alone, Matty." The plea in her eyes was a desperate one.

"There's the Nat I used to know. I knew she was hiding in there somewhere." Mateo moved further into the room and took up the seat on the other side of her desk. "Talk to me. Forget about Deputy Director Vargas and AD Castillo, let's just be Matty and Nat. Maybe I can help."

Tears continued to fall as Vargas looked at Mateo with indecision clear behind her violet eyes. "I'm in trouble," she said finally.

"What kind of trouble?"

"The kind that will destroy me and everything I have built," she sobbed.

"What did you do?"

"I can't..."

"What you can't do is deal with this alone. What did you do?"

"I made a deal. A terrible, stupid deal." She gave him a piercing look and finally Mateo understood.

"Your eyes..."

"He paid for them."

"Who?"

"My diagnosis would have been the end of my career, but the surgery costs so many credits and the augmentation needed to correct it completely... I would never have been able to afford it."

"Tell me you didn't. Who paid? Who do you owe?"

"Levi Seward."

Mateo let out a groan. "No, no, no..."

"It was just supposed to be favours here and there. Small things, and at first, it was, but now he wants me to use ARCs people to disband the pro-aug protests in the city and ignore the anti-aug riots and violence."

"You can't."

"But if I don't it's over for me."

"If you do, people will die. You have to tell him no and let the chips fall where they may."

"Is that what you would do? Risk everything, risk your family, your daughter?"

"That's the difference. I always put her first. I never would have made that deal. You let ego and ambition guide you, but it's not too late to do what's right."

"This has to stay between us, no matter what I decide." She was regaining some of her usual authority.

"I won't share what you've told me in confidence, but if you try to do what he asked, I will stand in your way," Mateo said, finding some confidence of his own.

"After all this time, we still understand each other."

"And we still never come down on the same side."

THE BAD PART OF TOWN

Thea leaned against a lamppost as she watched the Jonk slowly descend. It landed smoothly on the dark cobbled street with a low hum. The warm air emanating from the bottom was welcome on the cold night, and Thea stepped closer to enjoy it briefly. With a hiss, the round door closest to her raised up to allow Walt to step out. He was still wearing his tux, though he had unbuttoned his shirt at the collar and dispensed with the waistcoat. Worry creased his brow.

"She was definitely here," Thea said. She knew him well enough to know that this was not the time for small talk. "We're going to have to do some old-school canvassing."

"Fine, let's knock on some doors."

"It's not that simple. This is the bad part of town. This is mob turf. We're no use to Fen if we get ourselves killed."

"Businesses near where you found her implant then."

At this late hour, the only premises that were open were bars, clubs, casinos, and brothels. The Dock Ward was low on entertainment venues; its only nightclub happened to back on to the alley where Thea had been attacked. The club was a dingy, seedy affair, and unsurprisingly, no one had seen or heard a thing.

The next two bars they visited nearby were also a bust. Walt exuded tension, straining the silence between them. Thea wondered how his sobriety was faring in the face of Fen's disappearance.

"I met Fen a few days ago, here in Caligo," Thea said, trying to take his mind off his worry as they looked for the next venue.

"I know."

"She cornered me in an elevator trying to get a statement on Levi Seward."

Walt gave a little laugh that lightened his expression for just a moment. "Yeah, that sounds like her."

"I like her. She seems...driven."

"You have no idea."

Walt stopped at the door of a brothel named 'Lucky Ladies'. It looked like a members only joint, with its subtle signage and heavy metal door. It was probably only for high-ranking members of the Barone family.

A flap in the door opened at eye height, and a pair of brown eyes appeared, looking over them both with obvious suspicion. Thea thought they were a man's, though it was difficult to tell.

"What do you want?"

"We're looking for a woman. Pretty, with dark hair. She came through here a little while ago." Thea held up her badge. "I'm not a cop. I'm an ARC agent. I don't care about the family business and what it's up to."

"We haven't seen anything on the streets, *Agent*." He said the last word with contempt.

"But your fancy security cameras might have," Thea nodded to the ever-swiveling camera above the door. "I can come back with a warrant if you want, but I doubt you can clean out that quickly. Or you could avoid things getting nasty and let me check your cams. Do that, I'll forget I was ever here."

"Cops don't do well around these parts."

"Like I said, I'm not a cop."

"Wait here. I need to talk to the boss." The flap slammed shut.

Walt slumped down on the curb and put his hands in his hair. Thea dropped down beside him.

"I know you're worried, but we'll find her." She made to put a reassuring hand on his back, then thought better of it.

"If it isn't already too late." He sniffed.

"It's not. I don't know how I know, but I do."

Walt nodded with gritted teeth. Thea watched the muscle in his jaw flex.

"You really care about her," she said.

"It's not like it was with you and me, but yeah, I do," Walt made eye contact for the briefest moment before returning his eyes to the ground.

"Good, because we made each other miserable."

"Not all the time," he said softly.

"No, not all the time."

Before they could say anything else, there was a metallic scraping that told them the man at the flap had returned.

"The boss extends her hospitality, but if you try anything..."

"Yeah, yeah, you'll give us cement boots," Walt said with supreme indifference.

The inside of Lucky Ladies was a cliché. A haze of smoke hung over the place. It was so thick it was almost comical. Money and drugs were strewn haphazardly on the tabletops next to glasses and bottles of liquor. The walls and curtains were red velvet. Wait staff, bartenders, and dancers alike were all dressed in barely more than bikinis. Some served drinks, others sat with mobster's arms around their shoulders in dingy booths, while others still danced on poles and small stages.

"This way," said the man who had operated the door flap. He looked much as Thea had expected. He was White, with dark eyes and heavy brows. He wore a tweed waistcoat. The shirt underneath had its sleeves rolled up as if he was perpetually ready for a fistfight. He was formidable, but not enough to give Thea nor Walt pause. "Name's Joey. You'd do well to remember that, because if you try anything with the Boss, it'll be me who comes for you."

"Duly noted," Thea said with as much disinterest as she could muster.

They were led across the main entertainment space to a narrow corridor lined with doors. Red neon lights, coupled with the obvious sounds of sexual relations, left no illusions as to what the rooms hidden within were used for.

Joey pointed them to a room right at the end of the corridor. The door was nicer and cleaner than the others.

"The Boss is waiting for you. Don't fuck around."

The Boss, as it turned out, was an impressive woman in a red suit. Everything from her pin curls to her lipstick was immaculate. She was White and in her mid-sixties. She was attractive, though years of smoking had exaggerated the lines on her face.

"Welcome," she said, waving an airy hand holding a cigarette. Her voice was low and rasping.

"Where's Ray?" Thea asked with narrowed eyes. To her knowledge, the head of the Barone Crime Family was a man named Raymond who went by 'The Shark' or 'Sharky'.

"Dead," the Boss said bluntly.

"My condolences," Walt said, without missing a beat.

"Save it. My husband was a weasel, but he left me an empire, so, God bless his rat-bastard heart. I'm Denise Barone, and you are?"

"I'm Thea, and this is my associate, Walter."

"I dated a Walter once. Wasn't nearly as pretty as you, though." The look Denise gave Walt was nothing short of indecent.

"We're looking for someone—" Thea began.

"And you think one of my boys has something to do with it?"

"No, Ma'am. We know her disappearance has nothing to do with the Barone Family. We'd just like to use your cameras if it's not too much trouble."

"Well, ain't you a sweet-talker? They teach you that in agent school?"

If she wanted to play rough, Thea was more than happy to oblige. "Just trying to keep things civil. I can threaten you if you'd like."

"This ain't a charity. What I'd like is something in return. Information and make it good."

Thea thought for a moment, then said, "The CPD are planning to raid one of your warehouses. I don't know which one."

"When?" That had gotten her attention.

"Delivery day," Thea said smoothly.

"Wait here." Denise got out of her chair. Walt yelped as she passed, and Thea looked just in time to see her hand leave his backside. She sashayed from the room, closing the door behind her.

"You just gave up a police operation. Are you crazy?" Walt said as soon as it was clear they were alone.

"No, I didn't. I made it up. I'm not a cop anymore. I have no idea what organised crime is chasing down in this city. She doesn't need to know that."

Walt grinned, impressed. Not a moment later, Denise returned holding a small device. She held it to her Index as she retook her seat.

"All right," she said, all business. "What are we looking for?"

"Wait," Walt said. "A blind tip is enough for you to just give us the info?"

"Use your head, kid. I don't want law enforcement snooping around my completely legitimate businesses. The quicker you find your missing person, the quicker we can part ways for good. Shame," she added with a wink.

Denise tapped her Index, and several images sprang to life in the air between them.

"We're looking for a kidnap victim. Female, dark hair, wearing a red dress. We know she was in the alley behind Shakers club."

Denise set to work sifting through the camera feeds. Clearly, the Barones had eyes all over the Dock Ward.

"That her?"

Denise swiped a hand through the air and dismissed all the video feeds except for one. She enlarged the video with a gesture like she was stretching chewing gum. It showed a yard full of shipping containers, lit by floodlights that were attached to cranes. A beautiful woman in a red dress was being carried over a man's shoulder. It was clear she was bleeding and unconscious.

"Yeah," Thea muttered, watching Walt out of the corner of her eye.

"I'll kill him," Walt snarled.

"True love is a beautiful thing." Denise moved to another feed. "Looks like she was loaded into a container and put on the freight line."

"What does that mean?" Walt asked, his voice sharp.

"Means she might already be on the water." The look of horror on Walt's face seemed to tickle Denise. "The freight line takes cargo containers—like the one that your girl's in—and transports them to the dock lift. The lift takes the containers all the way down to sea level. To be loaded onto boats. She might not even be on the colony anymore."

"That was only a few hours ago. They might not have shipped out yet," Thea reassured.

"Hold on a second," Denise said, raising a hand for quiet. A little blue light flashed at the corner of her eye, telling Thea she had received a call through her Cicada. "Interesting."

"We need to leave," Thea whispered to Walt.

"Captain James," Denise's voice was loud, and even though she had merely said his name, the threat was clear. "Police Captain Walter James. You brought a cop into my house, Little Miss Agent."

"I don't care about your business. I'm not even a cop on this colony. I just want—"

"Your girl. Too bad. You've seen too much. You ain't leaving, not while your heart's still beating."

The door behind them opened and two huge men entered. Both were comically large. One bald and one with a shock of red hair.

Bald lunged for Walt, who put his head low and threw the man over his shoulder. The mobster landed with a heavy crash on Denise's desk. Red advanced on

Thea. She kicked the chair that was between them into his path, it clattered against his shins, and he crashed to the ground.

"Let's go!" Thea yelled, jumping over the felled redhead.

They ran out into the narrow corridor, but more heavies were making their way up towards them. Just behind Thea, Walt kicked open the nearest door and pulled her by the arm inside. Together, they slammed it shut and held it fast with their shoulders.

Thea looked around the room they had burst into. The wallpaper was peeling and there was a threadbare bed off to one side. A young Black woman in a negligee sat at a vanity mirror, cleaning lipstick from her face that had clearly been smudged by enthusiastic kissing. Beside the vanity was a small window.

"Sorry," Thea said, because there wasn't really anything else to say as the door barely held on under the onslaught of blows from the other side.

"You get used to it." The young woman shrugged and went back to removing her makeup.

"It's not gonna hold," Walt said as a particularly forceful blow pushed them both back for a moment.

"Window. On the count of three?"

"One," Walt said.

"Two," Thea said.

"Three," they said together. Both sprinted to the window. Thea got there first and clambered through, followed by Walt, just as the door was smashed from its hinges and Denise's henchmen flooded the room.

They had come out onto a fire escape two stories up. A quick glance over the edge of the rusted railings told Thea that up was the only option; there were yet more henchmen waiting for them on the street below.

Mercifully, the building was only five floors, which meant she and Walt didn't have far to climb. When they finally reached the roof, Thea did a quick scan of the surrounding area. They were in a bad spot all right. At nearly sixty feet tall, the building was dwarfed by its neighbours. Exit to another rooftop was impossible, but reaching street level without injury wasn't possible either.

"Do you think you could reach that balcony?" Thea asked, pointing to the south, where she could see a rundown terrace haphazardly attached to the side of a cramped apartment building.

"Probably," Walt said with a groan. He had always been scared of heights.

"Then go," Thea said, moving to the western edge of the building.

"What about you?"

"You need to find Fen, but you can't do that with Barone's cronies chasing you. I'll draw them off."

"Hell no! No way. I'm not leaving you here."

"Stow your hero complex. Your girlfriend needs you way more than I do." He shook his head mulishly. "We don't have time for this. Go!"

It was clear Walt hated her plan, but as the mobsters crested the roof, the time for arguing was over. With a roar of frustration mixed with fear, Walt ran for the edge of the building and leapt across. Thea watched long enough to see him land safely before turning to face the mobsters.

"Nowhere to run," Joey said, cracking his knuckles as he advanced on Thea. "Nowhere smart."

Thea turned on her heel, and just like Walt, sprinted to the edge of the building. Aiming for a window several feet below, she jumped from the roof, firing her gun as she went.

THE DISTILLERY

The window shattered when Thea struck it. Glass followed her as she tumbled into the building next to Lucky Ladies, forming a bed for her to land on. She felt the slivers slice the skin on her hands and knees, but she had no time to worry about such petty injuries. With a not insignificant effort, Thea got to her feet and peered out the window she had come through. The Barones had decided not to follow her, or at least not from the rooftop.

Taking a moment to catch her breath, Thea looked at her new surroundings. It appeared to be a warehouse of some sort. The smell of oak and honey told her it was probably a distillery. The room she had landed in had lockers and a kitchen unit; it was a staff room. Most likely, the warehouse was owned by the Barones. She couldn't afford to linger, having no desire to tangle any further with Caligo's mob, and she needed to get to Walt and Fen.

Limping slightly as she shook off the impact of her crash landing, Thea hurried from the room and into a hallway lined with posters of Denise. Apparently, at one point in her life, the head of the Barone Crime Family had been a lounge singer. Thea wondered idly if these had been put up by her late husband as a tribute of sorts, or if Denise was exceptionally vain. The third option was that her underlings were uncomfortably devoted to their leader.

The first door she encountered was marked 'Fermentation', but no sooner than Thea reached out a hand for the handle, a voice behind her called, "Who the hell are you? You can't be here."

A security guard was standing just beyond a gate at the far end of the hall, baton in hand. He was Indian and cresting fifty, with a glistening bald pate. He wore a dull grey jumpsuit emblazoned with the words, 'Technicolour Private Security – Marshall Davis'.

"Working late," Thea invented wildly. She knew the lie was transparent, but it gave her a moment to think. She couldn't stay in this building, no matter how dangerous the street was, and her quickest exit was in all likelihood through the secure gate and its guard.

"Don't fuck with me, lady. Who are you?"

"I'm really sorry about this, Marshall."

Thea darted forwards, intending to snatch the keycard that was clipped neatly to Marshall's breast pocket, but he was faster than she had imagined. He dodged out of reach and launched an immediate counterattack. He slung a telegraphed jab, that Thea dodged easily. She slipped to the outside, so they were almost shoulder to shoulder, and threw her own uppercut under Marshall's outstretched arm. Her fist connected painfully with his chin, and with the other hand, Thea grabbed the front of his overalls and spun him so that his chest hit the card reader that activated the gate. There was a pleasant little *beep,* and the gate slid open.

Thea ran through and slammed it shut before Marshall had time to recover. She reached through the bars and grabbed the keycard from his chest, thinking that it might come in handy.

The corridor she now found herself in was lined with windows. On her right was a testing lab, used to check the alcohol content and purity of the wash before it was used to distil whiskey. To her left was a bottling plant some twenty feet below. Hugely tall vats, surrounded by carousels and packing equipment filled the warehouse proper.

Thea made her way cautiously down the corridor, stopping when she heard voices. Two technicians were drinking cups of coffee in the testing lab. They spotted Thea just as she spotted them. All three looked at the door that separated them, then back to each other. As one, they all ran for the door.

Thea was faster, however. She slammed the keycard she had stolen from Marshall into the wall reader, locking the door just as the technicians reached it. She was sure they had their own keycards, but any advantage, no matter how small, was precious.

She had no time to celebrate. A door at the far end of the corridor was blasted open. Emerging over the threshold were six men in waistcoats and flat caps. The Barones had caught up with her. The closest mobster raised his gun and fired a shot. Just as he did, Thea brought her hand to the button on her chest. The golden shield erupted forth just as the pulse round collided with it. This contact shattered the shield instantly and caused a blast that threw Thea off her feet.

For the second time that night, Thea was hurtling through a glass window. She landed painfully on a metal catwalk that ran around the warehouse, linking the office and lab spaces with the bottling plant and allowing access to the tops of the vats.

This time the mobsters followed her. Scrambling to her feet, Thea sprinted along the metal walkway to yet another gate at the end. Once again, she scanned the stolen key card and slid the gate aside. She was just through it when one of the mobsters caught up with her. He thrust an arm into the gap to stop Thea from pulling the gate closed behind her.

Mercilessly, Thea rammed the metal gate into the mobster's arm, again and again, but he refused to move. Still holding onto the gate, she grabbed his tie and yanked. The sound of his forehead colliding with the wrought bars echoed like a gong. The mobster instinctually pulled back to clutch his head, allowing Thea to shut and lock the gate, trapping the mobster and his comrades on the catwalk.

Thea cursed loudly as she looked over the edge down into the bottling plant. A group of ten or so Barones had gathered and were waiting eagerly to greet her.

"Fuck."

If Thea followed the catwalk down onto the factory floor, she would be running right into a fight she couldn't possibly win. Seeing no other option, she vaulted over the railing, landing on the carousel that transferred boxes and bottles around the room. The mobsters she had trapped followed suit, dangling from the railing and shimmying until they could pull themselves up on the other side of the gate.

"Nowhere to run," one of the henchmen shouted.

She was in another bad spot, all right. She sincerely hoped it had been worth it, and Walt had found Fen. The alternative was unthinkable. Thea ran along the carousel, careful not to skid on the rollers that allowed heavy items to be transported. The mobsters following weren't as agile as she was. They slipped and skidded on the black plastic tubes.

When she reached the apex of the carousel, she was standing between two gargantuan vats and surrounded by wooden boxes that rested on a stationary conveyor. They were filled with newly bottled whiskey.

It was a terrible plan, but it was the only one she had.

Thea grabbed bottle after bottle and threw them onto the floor far below. The mobsters yelped and jumped out of the way as Thea created a pool of whiskey on the warehouse floor.

Usually, she detested Torrez's habit of smoking, particularly when he did it in her home. Today, however, she was grateful. He had left his lighter on her sofa after their last meeting, and Thea had tucked it into her pocket to give to him when next she saw him. She pulled the silver Zippo from her pocket and flipped it open. She ran her thumb over the flint roller and it ignited at once. Without hesitating, Thea let the lighter slip from her grip. It seemed to fall in slow motion, down, down, down towards the flammable pool. When it struck the ground, there was a fractional pause before flames burst to life, sending a blast of heat into the air that reached even Thea high above.

"You can chase me and burn to death, or you can save yourselves and get out of here," she yelled as the flames spread. It wouldn't be long before they caught more bottles or even the vats. She hoped to a God she didn't believe in that the Barones hadn't skimped on fire suppression, or the bottling plant was likely to explode.

The mobsters on the conveyor and the factory floor took one look at the fire and ran. Relieved, Thea made her way back to the catwalk. Just as she set foot on the stairs, there was a *whoosh* from above and then a deluge of water poured from the large pipes in the ceiling.

Cut, battered, bruised, and soaked to her skin, Thea made her way to the fire exit and out of the distillery. She had made an enemy of the Barones that night and would have a lot of explaining to do when she returned to The Orchard.

THE DOCKS

Walt's knees were still protesting vociferously as he ran down the long and narrow bystreet. He had landed badly on the balcony when he'd jumped from the roof of Lucky Ladies and was paying for it now.

He hated that he had left Thea with the Barone cronies. He knew she was perfectly capable of taking care of herself, yet every instinct he possessed, every bone in his body, told him to go back. To make sure she was safe. To protect her from the slew of mobsters. But those very same instincts told him that Fen needed him too, needed him more, and it had been Thea who told him to go. *Stow your hero complex,* she had said. No one saw through him quite like Thea.

Walt pushed his warring emotions aside and pressed on. His heart pounded in his chest as his feet slapped the cobblestones. A stitch was growing in his side, but he couldn't stop. Fen's life depended on it. In his peripheral vision he could see that he too was being followed, but he paid the men no mind.

He burst forth from the mouth of the bystreet into a labyrinth of shipping containers. All large and rectangular made of weathering steel, they were a myriad of dark colours, marked with various logos and warnings. There was a row of shabby warehouses, two of which Walt now stood between, placed on a sort of concrete promenade. In front of each warehouse, was a long metal runway complete with conveyor belts and cranes to allow for the movement of complex and heavy goods. Signage all around told him he had found the 'Caligo Docks'.

All was quiet, far too quiet, considering he was in mob territory and the matriarch of the family had called for his head. The moment he realised he had walked into the trap, it was sprung. Mobsters flooded the docks, scurrying from the gaps between the shipping containers and warehouses like rats.

"Cops in this town aren't stupid enough to come here. You a rookie or somethin'?" Joey stepped forward from between his fellows.

"Yeah, that's me," Walt replied blandly as he counted his foes and tried to calculate a way to get out of this situation alive. "A rookie in his forties. I'm a late bloomer."

"I hope you're a better cop than you are a comedian."

"Jury's still out on that one."

No grand plans came to Walt. No tactical strokes of genius that could make up for the fact he was vastly outnumbered occurred to him. Taking thinking out of the picture, Walt turned and ran. He sprinted down the nearest container-made street. He could hear the mobsters shouting threats as they chased after him, but he didn't let up. Finally, when he thought his lungs might give out, he broke free of the maze and was faced with a gargantuan lift shaft.

Open to the swirling and ever-present winds at the edge of the city, the shaft seemed to shiver slightly. It was made of black metal bars and was large enough to take at least ten of the huge metal containers. There was no top, just a metal plate that served as the floor of the lift. There were no handrails either—it clearly wasn't designed to transport passengers.

The controls were simple. Hanging next to the entrance was a remote with two buttons: one for up, and one for down. Without delay, Walt stepped inside, pushed the button, and the lift began to descend.

The mobsters could do nothing but watch as the heavy gate closed and Walt slowly dropped out of sight. Joey stood at the edge of the shaft with a grin, looking down. "We already caught your girl."

A trill of fear caught in Walt's chest. "You're lying. If you'd caught her, she'd be dead."

"She's gonna wish she was." And with that, he turned and stepped out of view.

Thea was smarter than the lot of them put together, Walt told himself. She had faced far worse odds and came out on top. She was fine. She had to be fine. He had to worry about Fen and Fen alone.

The dock lift shuddered and trundled, deafeningly loud, as it made its way down through the colony itself. It was an odd sensory overload. Like he had entered a subway tunnel with no lights; it was pitch black. The tiny dot he could see high above was the only remnant of the lights from the dock. The oppressive darkness coupled with the cacophony of heavy machinery, and the roaring wind that chilled him to the bone, made him feel like he was enduring some sort of deprivation torture.

Just when the effect was becoming truly maddening, it was over. With a popping sound, like a bottle being uncorked, the lift broke free of the tunnel. Walt let out a strangled yell. The view was both beautiful and terrifying. He was in the air, hundreds of thousands of feet above sea level and surrounded by clouds. The air was thin, and the pressure made his ears pop painfully. The moon cast an eerie glow, and Walt realised it was the first time in years he had truly seen it. Tenebrium was encapsulated by yellow smog. All light, whether daylight or moonlight, was false. It was a once in a lifetime experience.

Setting his acrophobia aside, Walt moved over to the edge of the platform and peered over. He regretted his daring immediately. His fear of heights gripped him anew, and he staggered back, breathing heavily.

Even at the astronomical speed the cargo lift was moving, it wasn't a quick journey. Walt moved to the centre of the platform and sat down, crossing his legs. He closed his eyes and focussed on steadying himself, on Fen, and the extremely dangerous situation he was walking into. He hoped Thea had made her escape, but more than anything, he wished she were there beside him. There wasn't a single person he would rather accompany him into a deadly face-off with a serial killer.

The cargo lift began to shudder and shake, then it began to tilt and sway. Before he could brace himself, Walt had slid along the course floor, slamming his back into the metal bars that formed the lift shaft. The shaking became more violent, and Walt worried that the Barones had done something to the lift, but when he straightened up to look, he realised he was almost at sea level.

Looking out over the edge, Walt could see the true docks. It was the exact mirror image of the docks above, except there were long piers and wharfs surrounded by true blue water. The smell of salt tingled in his nose as he watched with amazement, sea birds flying around some of the boats moored offshore. And the boats! There were small yachts and dinghies as well as huge freighters all bobbing on the smoothly undulating water.

Just as the lift came to its final resting place, Walt realised he was once again caught. Either the Barones owned the docks at this end too, or they had a faster way of getting to sea level. Whatever the truth, they were there now.

How long had it been since he had realised Fen was missing? How long had it taken him to get to Caligo? How long had they searched the Dock Ward? How long had he spent running from Mobsters? How long did Fen have left?

"Look," Walt said, stepping out onto the pier as soon as the lift came to a halt. "I don't have time for this. I don't care about your shady dealings. There's a serial killer using your docks, and they have taken someone I love. I just want to find her. So, let's just call it a night before things get messy."

"And if there was one of us and five of you, that might be convincing, but you're one copper and I got me some orders from the top." The man who had spoken was a stereotype with a bowler hat and cigar.

"You were warned."

Walt ran up the pier and jumped onto one of the small boats, knowing that anyone who tried to follow him would likely end up in the water. The boat rocked with his weight, but he managed to stay upright.

As he had predicted, the mobsters followed. One fell straight into the water and began to yell that he couldn't swim. Another, who carried a lead pipe, was more agile than Walt had predicted and landed beside him without throwing them both overboard. The mobster raised the pipe and swung it hard at Walt's head, but Walt absorbed the blow with his forearm, bringing it up to protect his head and allowing the pipe to land flush with the full length of it. He would be feeling it for days, but it was better than a broken arm or worse, a cracked skull.

With his free hand, he grabbed the pipe and thrust it back at its wielder. The man let go to avoid being struck in the face, allowing Walt to take hold of it and swing it back at its original owner. It collided with the man's temple, knocking him out cold. Walt caught him before he fell into the water and dragged him back onto the small boat. No one needed to die tonight.

Walt sprang from one boat to another, avoiding the rest of the mobsters who had run along the nearest wharf. Quickly realising he would be caught if he set foot on shore, he dived into the water.

The freezing waves were a shock to his system. He shivered uncontrollably as he struck out for the nearest freighter. He swam as fast as he could, every breath of icy air a knife to his lungs. Finally reaching the anchor chain, he climbed with numb fingers, but as he did so, he could see the remaining mobsters running up the gang-plank onto the deck.

Soaking and with aching arms, Walt clambered onto the deck to face the three remaining mobsters. He cursed as he realised that his gun wasn't in its holster. He must have lost it as he swam. With no other options available to him, Walt took up a boxing stance and waited for the mobsters to come to him.

The first to reach him swung a heavy haymaker that Walt slipped underneath easily, following up with a punch to the solar plexus, which sent the man reeling back. At the same time, one of the other mobsters grabbed a small wooden crate and hurtled it at Walt. He only just got his arms over his face in time, and it shattered on impact, showering him in splintered wood. Temporarily blinded as he protected his eyes, Walt didn't see the push kick that followed the crate. It hit him squarely in the stomach, sending in hurtling backwards and crashing to the ground.

The man who had thrown the crate was upon him in seconds. He kicked and stomped on Walt's prone form in a merciless onslaught. As he raised his leg to strike again, Walt rolled away and the man's foot came down hard on the deck. Walt sprang forwards, catching the man off guard and taking him down to the ground. They rolled back and forth wrestling on the slick deck before Walt managed to subdue him. He mounted the mobster, straddling his chest and unleashed a torrent of blows, stopping only when the man lost consciousness.

Panting, Walt got to his feet to face the other two mobsters who had been patiently waiting their turn.

The cigar smoker struck first. He fainted to the right with a hook that Walt weaved underneath leaving his head unguarded. The smoker landed a devastating straight on Walt's face. Walt felt blood explode from his nose as his eyes watered, blurring his vision. The mobster pressed his advantage, and another heavy blow collided with Walt's cheek. Still reeling, Walt felt hands grab his shoulders before, finally, a knee was buried in his stomach, sending him back to the ground.

Instead of trying to get to his feet, he lurched forward and caught the mobster by the knees, bringing him to the deck with a substantial clatter. Wasting no time, his hands found the mobster's neck, and he squeezed.

The remaining Barone, who Walt had momentarily forgotten about, kicked Walt in the side, throwing him off his companion. Walt used the momentum to roll away and get quickly to his feet. He charged forwards, spearing the man who had kicked him and launching him overboard, before turning back to the cigar smoker, who was still coughing and clutching his throat. Walt grabbed him by the back of the collar and dragged him over to the freighter's railings. He pulled his handcuffs from his belt and secured the cigar smoker there. His protests were feeble.

Walt quickly disembarked. He was a little unsteady on his feet from the multiple blows to the head, but he shook off the dizziness as he ran to the furthest end of the dock. There, there was a sort of ship graveyard, filled with derelict and rusting vessels, some were half sunken, and others floated like ghosts creaking eerily in the moonlight. Fen had to be on one of these, he just had to find the right one.

YOU KNOW MY NAME

The heat from the furnace was sweltering, and little sparks burned Fen's skin as they flickered out into the boiler room.

"Who are you?" She whimpered. Sweat was dripping down her back as she sat bound to the broken metal chair, her hands behind her back. The man in the gold mask ignored her. He just kept throwing scrap metal into the flames of the furnace.

"Who are you?" she asked again, her voice more forceful.

"You already know," he said, in a rough voice that was warped by the dry air. It was the first time he has spoken since she had heard his voice over the intercom.

"I don't know what you mean," she said, twisting in her restraints to keep sight of him as he moved behind her to the pile of disused augmentation parts, then back to the furnace.

"You call me The Zealot. I like that. It's fitting." He sounded young, not child-like, but younger than Fen. "That's who I am."

"If you're going to kill me, let me see your face. I should at least get to look my killer in the eyes." The fear was making her bold.

"Are you trying to make an emotional connection? Are you hoping if I see you as a person, I won't kill you? I know who you are, Fen Yeoh. You've seen my face before and once was enough."

"What do you—"

"How did you know that I went by 'The Zealot'?" he overrode her.

"The threats you made under that username—you carved one into Ranveer's chest." Tears for her friend came to her eyes, mingled with tears for her and their shared fate.

"You make these grand statements with your writing and your art. You convince people that augs are nothing to fear, but what about those who force it on their children?"

"Augmentations can't be given to children unless they are life-saving measures or provide significant quality of life benefits. That they are is just another lie people like you tell to justify their hatred." Her voice shook, but she willed him to see that she meant every word.

"It was forced upon me as a child by my parents. They thought they were making me better, but all they have done is succeeded in damning me." His voice was fierce and dangerous, laced with vengeful bloodlust.

"I'm sure they were trying to do what's right." Fen grabbed onto the thread like it was a lifeline. The longer she kept him talking, the longer she stayed alive.

"I would have taken any ailment, any illness or disability over the godless fate they have condemned me to." He grabbed more metal scraps and hurled them into the flames, which billowed forth and licked at the bare skin of Fen's arm; she cried out in pain.

"I don't believe you're soulless or damned. I think you're lost and confused," Fen said through sobs.

"I was, but then Levi found me. He showed me my path and my fate. I may be damned, but that doesn't mean I can't do God's work."

"Seward is a fraud. All he cares about is money. I don't know what he is to you, but I know he doesn't care about you."

"Liar," he lunged for Fen and grabbed the back of her chair. He dragged her so that her face was inches from the flames and held her there. She screamed and cried as she could feel her skin burn, but he didn't relent. "I will gild your blasphemous tongue soon enough."

"No! Please!" The hot air strangled Fen's words, but The Zealot dragged her back from the flames, regardless.

"If you truly believed what you say, you'd be willing to burn for your cause like I am. You'll get your chance soon enough."

THE PAST

Seventeen years ago...

Vinny made Cynthia feel empowered. Powerful in her own right. Alive. The way Vinny's men took orders from her, the way they afforded her the same respect as they did him, and the way they averted their eyes when they saw her gave her a trill of excitement like she had never experienced in her mundane life. It was getting easier and easier to say goodbye to her husband every Thursday night, and easier still to forget about him entirely when she was in Vinny's company.

The hulking brute of a man who had violence dripping from his pores was sweet and kind to her, and he had awakened something inside her. He had lit a fire in her soul that she wouldn't have quenched for anyone. Cynthia was even getting a taste for violence. Not the pain it caused or the gore of it all, but the manipulation it allowed. Violence was a show of strength, and finally, it was one she understood. Vinny earned respect whenever he could, but took it in the form of fear when that was impossible. He rewarded loyalty and punished a lack of it with brutal efficiency. He was an invisible king, a rough hand in the dark that guided high-society life. Being rich afforded stature, but being a mobster, a gangster, a mafioso, a family man, that was where the real power lay.

And yet, there was still the elephant in the room. It had been four months since the night she had signed Barney's death warrant and agreed that she was his. She had told Vinny countless times that she knew he had freed her from their agreement and that she came back by choice every time, but their relationship had gone no further in romantic terms and Cynthia had surprised herself by being disappointed.

She had come to think of him as quite beautiful. A delicate instrument capable of both great acts of monstrousness and Herculean acts of kindness. A curious creature that she wanted for her own, but he was hesitant. The unwillingness she had shown in the beginning still worried him. He was open with his want of her, his care for her, but he never pushed or pressed. He never made salacious comments or seedy innuendos; it made her want him more.

On this particular Thursday night, Cynthia was at his mansion, waiting for him to come home. Usually, he would take her with him when he did business on these days, but this time he had refused. If he thought it was too dangerous, she trusted him.

It was already late, and she should have gone home hours ago, but she was determined to see Vinny, to convince him of her feelings before she returned to her humdrum life as a housewife.

She didn't have to wait long.

The impressive grandfather clock had just chimed one in the morning when she heard the front doors open. She made her way quickly to the foyer, still wearing the long crimson evening gown Vinny had bought her for their dinner.

She could hear hushed voices from the doorway and quick footsteps.

"What happened?" she demanded upon seeing Vinny.

He was slumped and limping, two of his men half carrying him into the house. There was blood all over his suit and his face was covered in cuts and bruises. His blinded eye was swollen shut.

"Told you it was dangerous," he joked feebly. "What are you still doing here?"

"Take him up to his room and bring me a Medicus Kit. Then leave us," she ignored his question and addressed the men holding him.

When they hesitated, Vinny snarled, "Do as she says!" Cynthia was glad to see some of his strength returning already.

Ten minutes later, Vinny was leaning against the headboard in his ridiculously large bedroom. Everything was white, black, and gold. The bed was wide enough for a dozen people to sleep comfortably, and the carpet was thick and fluffy. There was a gently smouldering fire in the hearth that faced the bed.

Vinny winced as Cynthia gently took off his coat.

"What happened?" she repeated now that they were alone.

"No more Brigantes," he murmured, closing his eyes in pain. "We took 'em out. All of 'em. Their turf and their drug business are mine. Ours," he amended, absently squeezing her hand. He went quiet for a moment and Cynthia carefully unbuttoned his waistcoat and pulled it from his shoulders, quickly followed by his shirt.

"Oh my god," she exclaimed. "You've been stabbed!"

There was a thin and bloody knife wound just under his right pectoral; dry blood coated his stomach and the surrounding area while the fresh still oozed if he moved too sharply.

"It's shallow, don't worry about it." He sounded tired.

"I think your ribs are broken, too."

"I'm just bruised." Vinny's mouth curled into a small smile; he liked that she cared.

"Let me sew that up, at least."

"No," he said firmly. "I'm dirty and covered in blood. Everything aches. I want to take a soak in the tub, but if you sew it up, I can't."

"You can't just leave it open."

"I know," he laughed a little, and dark blood spurted lethargically from the wound. "Get the scissors from the Medicus Kit and put them in the fire. We'll cauterise it."

"I don't think I can." It was one thing to understand pain as a motivator, but another thing entirely to inflict it herself.

"I'm no stranger to a little pain," he said, as if he had read her mind. "Please."

The last word was her undoing. With shaking hands, she rifled through the Medicus Kit for a pair of stainless steel scissors. At Vinny's gentle urging, she took them over to the fireplace. She gripped the scissors between the fire tongs and held them into the flame. When the metal glowed orange, she carried them carefully back to the bed. Her prosthetic hand made it difficult to grip the long and heavy tongs, and she nearly dropped them on the way.

"Are you sure?" she all but whispered.

"Do it." His massive hands gripped the sheets in apprehension.

Cynthia's breath came in short, almost panicked gasps as she slowly moved the red-hot metal towards Vinny's skin. There was a searing sound as they made contact, and Vinny let out a strangled howl of pain.

"Fuck me!" he yelled.

As quickly as she had touched the burning hot scissors to the wound, she pulled them back. Where the knife slit had been, there was now an angry red burn, the skin knitted together by the heat. She felt an odd sense of accomplishment and something else that she couldn't quite explain.

"Thank you," he said breathlessly. "Are you all right?"

She nodded, her face flushed.

"It's okay if you liked it a little. I liked it too." The same flush was mirrored in his cheeks.

She didn't know what to say. She just held his gaze. Something dark and covetous seemed to pass behind his eyes.

"Shall I run you that bath?"

He inclined his head slowly, as if he wasn't sure if the comment was as loaded as it had sounded. In all honesty, Cynthia wasn't sure either.

The bathroom was a wonder in white marble, and the tub was more like a small pool. She secured the plug and then turned one of the golden taps. Water came out in a jet that would have the bath filled in no time. On the counter, there were several bottles of expensive looking bubble bath. She picked the liquid that was deep red and rose scented and poured a generous measure into the bath. As soon as it touched the steaming water, it effervesced and filled the air with a heavenly floral scent. The bath was full in a surprisingly short amount of time. Cynthia would have loved to soak in it herself.

"It's ready. Do you want me to turn my back while you get in?"

"Not unless you want to," came the reply from the doorway.

When Cynthia turned, Vinny was already completely naked. His body was beautiful. Scarred, but lean and strong. Without his clothes, he no longer seemed hulking. There was a grace to him as he walked across the floor, even with the limp his night's activities had given him. Cynthia drank him in, not troubling to hide the fact she was staring.

He let out a groan of contentment as he sank beneath the surface, letting the warm water soothe him. He shut his eyes and seemed at peace.

Cynthia took a washcloth from the side and soaked it in the water before she began to softly dab the cuts on his face, cleaning away the blood. The red bubble bath had been a good idea. When his face was clean, she moved to his chest. He brought up a hand to clasp hers for a moment, holding it still against his breastbone. She could feel his heart beating. After a few seconds, he let go without a word and she continued to bathe away the blood.

Vinny's eyes were still shut when she had finished. Finding her courage at last, Cynthia did the thing she had been longing to do for months. Still on her knees beside the tub in a magnificent ball gown, she leant forward and pressed her lips to his. He opened his eyes and pulled back ever so slightly.

"You don't have to," he said, his eyes searching her face.

"But I want to." She kissed him again and again. Soft, chaste kisses that willed him to kiss her back. After what felt like an eternity, he surged forward and captured her face in his hands, crushing his lips to hers and sloshing water all over the floor. The kiss was feverish, like he was going to let loose all his pent-up desire at once. The thought was thrilling. She wrapped her arms around him, pulling him close, not caring that the water was soaking her.

"You're hurt," she said breathlessly. It was her turn to pull back. She wanted him, but she wasn't sure he was in any state to be intimate.

In one smooth motion, he lifted her over the edge of the tub and into the water with him, dress and all. "Then you'll just have to be gentle with me," he said, taking one of her hands and guiding it down beneath the bubbles.

That was the first night she didn't return home to her husband and son, but it wasn't the last.

THE FITZGERALD

"Alex," Thea whispered as soon as the call was answered.

"Everything okay, Tee?"

"Are you at the station?"

"Yeah, we're still interrogating the arsonist—you will love what he's come out with. He—"

"Alex," Thea cut them off. "I need you to get every officer you have to The Dock Ward."

"That's mob territory. It's well known that they have a 'kill on sight policy' when it comes to cops."

"The Zealot is here, the serial killer. He kidnapped a journalist, and I'm on his tail, but I pissed off the Barones and they are everywhere. They're out for blood. I can't find this guy with mobsters on every corner."

"You need to get out of there, Thea. I'm coming to—"

"No," Thea cut them off. "I'm not leaving. He already has his next victim."

"Goddammit. If we're gonna take a run at the Barones, we'll need everyone. How am I supposed to convince my captain to sign off on this?"

"Tell him the truth. You take back the Dock Ward you get a big win and I save a life and catch a serial killer. It's a good deal."

"You don't know Captain Takahashi. He's old school."

"Then he'll understand risk and reward. Even if you don't run the mob off, taking a shot at the Barones shows nerve."

"I'll try. No promises. Don't get killed."

Thea hung up, sure that if anyone could convince their captain, it would be Alex.

She peaked out from the dead-end alley she had been taking cover in. There were mobsters everywhere. Whether they were searching for her or just on high-alert she couldn't tell, but either way, there were far too many of them for her to get to the freight lift without a fight. Thea was no stranger to fisticuffs in the line of her duties, but she thought it best to avoid it when the odds were fifty to one.

Her heart gave an uncomfortable jolt as the buzz from her Cicada startled her.

"It's me," said the familiar voice of Walt. Relief flooded through her. "Are you okay?"

"I'm alive, but I'm pretty pinned down. Are you ok? Did you find Fen?"

"I'm fine. There's part of the dock where the decommissioned vessels are left to rust. He has to be hiding her there, but there are so many of them." Worry was creeping into his voice again.

"We'll find her, just keep looking. I'll be there as soon as I can."

"Be safe."

If they were too late to save Fen, it would destroy Walt, and Thea would lose the best chance she had to catch The Zealot. She couldn't cower in an alley while she waited for backup that might never come. Her plan was a reckless one, but it was the only one she had.

She sneaked carefully out of the alley she stood in. Caligo was never truly dark. Whether it be the neon lights on every building, the towering streetlamps, the trams on rails over every part of the city or the Slipstream Highway alight with Jonks, total darkness was impossible, but, like all cities, shady back alleys and secluded corners provided havens for those wishing to go unseen. Tonight, that included Thea.

Keeping to the shadows as much as she could and ducking out of sight when any of Denise's men got close, Thea crept through the streets until she found a building whose fire escape backed into an alley. As quietly as she could, she climbed to the top of the seven-story building.

For the third time in thirty minutes, she touched her hand to her tragus to activate her Cicada.

"Thea?" the voice of Assistant Director Mateo Castillo sounded tired.

"Can you send a tactical transporter to my location?"

"Why?"

"I'm working my serial killer case."

"The Zealot? Do you need backup?"

"Yes. I'm trying to get the CPD to take a run at the Barones so that we are clear to find the killer."

"He's in The Dock Ward?"

"Yes. Can I have a transporter?"

"It's already on its way. I'll send everyone we have with it."

"Thanks, Sir."

True to Castillo's word, the transporter arrived in a matter of minutes, bringing with it the attentions of the mobsters searching the streets for trouble. Thea had only just climbed into the sturdy black vehicle when they crested the rooftop, and the transporter was taking gunfire before it had even taken flight. Thankfully, tactical transporters were bulletproof and the mobsters' guns had no effect. Unfortunately, they had a clear line of sight on her destination and would be able to follow her to it.

Thea disengaged the autopilot as soon as she sat down in the driver's seat of the transporter. Moments later, a steering wheel erupted from the dashboard. She made a beeline for the freight lift, but as she hovered over it, she saw that the area was surrounded by yet more Barones. Walt must have made quite the exit. There was no way that she could land the Jonk in the lift. It would be far too delicate a manoeuvre, and if she tried to land on the docks, she would be overwhelmed by mobsters in no time. Her only option, should she still want to make good on her promises to Walt, was not a safe one.

Jonks, or at least the kinds that were taxis or tactical vehicles, were powered by the city they were linked to. A special long-distance kind of transporter shuttle was needed to travel off colony. While she would technically still be on the same colony, the docks proper were at sea level and there was no guarantee that the Jonk wouldn't lose power and simply drop from the sky when she got too far away from Caligo itself, but she couldn't see any other way to get where she needed to.

Flying low and scattering the mobsters on the dock, Thea waited until she was next to the freight lift, then brought the Jonk into a complete nosedive. It quickly gained speed and soon she was vertical. Moments into the descent, the Jonk started to vibrate and warning messages flashed on the dashboard and windscreen. A few seconds after that, the Jonk lost power completely and Thea was free-falling. She could do nothing but brace herself and hope for the best as the Jonk plummeted towards the water.

The water was getting closer and closer; it was almost like it was rising to meet her. The time for screaming was long since over as the Jonk hit the water. Thea expected the impact to be the end of her, but the Jonk breached the surface, taking her several meters below the waves. She had no time to comprehend this new problem when the air inside the Jonk sent it zooming back to the surface; it bounced out of the water before landing for a final time on the surface.

Breathing heavily, Thea stayed seated. She couldn't make her hands release their death-grip on the steering wheel. She had survived. She had no idea how, but she had. Shock held her like she had been petrified by a gorgon.

"Move," she told herself out loud. "Stand up."

Finally, her body complied with her commands. She was understandably shaky. And now she had a new problem. The Jonk was floating because it was a sealed capsule, but the doors were on the sides. As soon as she opened them, water would flood in and the Jonk would sink. The doors also opened from the bottom up; she would need to wait for it to be open enough for her to get through, which would be once the Jonk was fully submerged. It was a daunting prospect.

What had she been thinking? She thought she had put this kind of stupid recklessness behind her. A few days back in Walt's company and she was already in a ridiculously dangerous situation. What was it about proximity to that man that made her court chaos?

Her musings weren't getting her anywhere, and if she waited much longer, the tide might pull her out to sea. She ditched her jacket, not wanting anything to impede her swim, then, taking a final steadying breath, pushed the button to open the Jonk door.

The water rushed in, immediately soaking her feet as the door rose. It was knee deep in seconds and the Jonk was well and truly sinking. Thea was treading ice-cold water long before she was ready. She was waiting until the last moment to take a deep breath and nearly missed her chance, only just managing to take a gulp of oxygen before the water covered her head. The Jonk was fully submerged before the door had opened completely.

It was oddly like being in space as she floated in the sinking Jonk surrounded by neon lights and looking out into complete blackness. Thea quickly pushed out of the transporter and kicked for the surface with almost panicked ferocity. When her head breached the surface, she took in long drags of air even though she couldn't have been holding her breath for longer than twenty seconds.

She treaded water, taking full advantage of the darkness. Thea could see activity on the shore but had no way of knowing if they were friend or foe. Her instincts told her foe. Glancing to her right, she saw the rusting and abandoned ships Walt had mentioned.

One of the vessels that was sitting furthest from the docks had a trickle of steam coming from it. It probably wasn't noticeable to someone standing on the docks, but Thea would have bet any amount of money that was where The Zealot was hiding Fen.

It was a large and long ship that looked more like a cruise liner than a freighter. The closer she swam to it, she realised that was exactly what it was. Words painted on the side told her it was called 'The Fitzgerald'.

GHOST SHIP

The eerie creaks as the ship was buffeted by the waves were haunting. It was like something unnatural had taken hold of The Fitzgerald. The top deck was covered in moss and white residue caused by the salty air. The deck chairs lay bent and broken. The Olympic sized pool was filled with black sludge. Rust had eaten away at every metal surface.

Thea pulled out her gun and tapped the button on the side to ignite her flashlight. The singular beam only added to her sense of foreboding. The ship was so large, the pale light seemed weak, barely able to light what was in front of her.

Pushing aside her misgivings, Thea moved quickly and quietly along the deck. Knowing the sort of things The Zealot liked to do, she was sure she would find him in the boiler room.

She wondered idly how The Fitzgerald had come to be abandoned here. The inside was dusty in the extreme, but otherwise untouched. It was creepy, like everyone on board had just vanished. In reality, it had most likely been abandoned here by the company who ran it, sans passengers and crew, but it didn't feel that way as Thea moved through deserted corridor after deserted corridor, echoing stairwell after echoing stairwell. The ship seemed truly abandoned, but as she got deeper into the bowels of the lower decks, she heard a hum.

Low at first, but getting louder and louder, it was like a guiding hand showing her the way. The beautiful, panelled walls and crystal chandeliers became bare iron corridors as she got closer to her goal.

Faded signs painted on the walls told her that the boiler room was down a final set of stairs at the end of the passageway she stood in.

The steps were narrow and there was a bulkhead door with a wheel-lock at the bottom. If The Zealot was inside, there was no way for her to sneak in unnoticed.

Counting herself down from three, Thea turned the wheel. It gave a loud screech with every rotation as metal ground against metal. With a final noisy *clunk*, the door swung wide.

A blast of searing air burst from the room. It was so hot that Thea's eyes watered immediately. The room itself was a metal cavern, awash with the amber glow from the open furnace. There was a haze of smoke that had Thea coughing as she stepped into the room.

Near the furnace was a metal chair. Tied to that chair was a dark-haired woman. She was very much alive.

"Fen," Thea said, running forward and untying the ropes that bound her. "Are you all right? Where is he?" Fen's face was red, and her skin peeling slightly, like she'd had a terrible sunburn. There were smaller contact burns on the arm closest to the furnace and her hair on that side was slightly singed. Drawn cruelly in marker, there were crosses on her palms; no doubt marking the spot where The Zealot would have driven nails had he been given the time.

Fen didn't reply to Thea's question. As soon as she was free, she threw her arms around Thea's neck and began to sob. Thea wrapped her arms around her for the briefest moment, then pulled her to her feet. They weren't safe yet.

"Fen," Thea said again, pulling away to hold her by the shoulders. "Where is he? How long has he been gone?"

"You...you're that agent." She was having a hard time focussing and Thea could hardly blame her with what she had been through, but Thea needed her to regain her wits so they could escape.

"Fen," Thea said more forcefully. "I'm Thea. We've met before. I'm a friend of Walt's. I know this is hard for you, but I need you to focus. Do you know where the man who took you is?"

She blinked, seeming to find herself. "No. He's been gone for a while. An hour maybe."

"Okay," Thea said, taking her gently by the arm and pulling her towards the door.

"But he has cameras." Her voice was stronger now as she pointed at the camera in the room. "He must have access to the ship's control room. He knows you're here."

"But it also means he's far away. The control room is on the top deck. A ship this size—he'll never catch us in time."

Fen was still wearing her evening dress and a pair of stiletto heels. Having left her jacket in the Jonk, she had nothing that might make Fen feel less exposed, but she did have something that could make her safer. Thea stopped her at the foot of the stairs.

"Lose the heels."

"What?"

"We need to be fast."

Nodding once, Fen leant down and undid the buckles on her sandals, then kicked them off.

"Now, take this and put it under your dress." Thea pulled a kite shaped object from beneath her shirt. It was a dull sand dollar gold. "Put it against your breastbone. If you get into a tight spot, press the button on the centre and it creates a shield. Do you understand?"

"What about you?"

Thea didn't reply. She took Fen by the hand and led her up the stairs.

The Fitzgerald felt even more like a ghost ship now that Thea knew The Zealot could be watching them.

They were several decks above the boiler room and back onto the passenger decks when they came across the entertainment deck. They must have taken a wrong turn somewhere because Thea hadn't passed it on her way down.

It was similar to a mall, except instead of shops, the outlets were casinos, bars, restaurants, theatres and nightclubs. The floors were a chequered black and white marble and the walls a pale mint green. Each venue had tall columns framing the entrance.

Thea motioned to Fen to stop for a moment. It was time to call Walt. No sooner had she brought her hand to her Cicada when a sharp keening sound in her ear had her grunting in pain.

"What's wrong?" Fen asked, startled.

"He's using a jammer to block coms."

Before she could say anything more, the ship began to shudder. Soft vibrations ran through the floor.

"Are we moving?"

"No," Thea said slowly. "I don't think so." The shuddering became more intense and lights overhead flickered to life, followed by music all around. They could hear holographic croupiers calling them to the tables, as flickering theatre masters performed monologues from the plays the ship had hosted. After the silence and the gloom they had experienced until now, it was jarring; almost overwhelming.

They had no time to readjust however, gates made of translucent red light were taking shape in every doorway.

"Run!" Thea yelled, grabbing Fen by the hand and all but dragging her to the nearest one. They missed it by moments.

"Can't we just push through?"

"Not unless you want to take a hundred-thousand volts. They're security gates."

They were quickly running out of options. Thea dragged Fen to the nearest open gate. She activated the shield she had given Fen and then shoved her through the doorway. Fen made it through to the other side just as the gate took form between them.

Thea turned to see the last few gates spring to life, trapping her on the entertainment deck.

"Go!" she shouted as Fen stood motionless, watching her.

"I can't just leave you here! You saved my life!"

"Yes, you can. I'll be fine. Walt is here somewhere. Find him. Go!" she said again when it looked like Fen was about to argue.

Looking conflicted, Fen turned and made her way out of sight.

Thea waited. She didn't search for an exit; she didn't panic, she just stood where she was. She had seen enough during her time in law enforcement to know when she was playing a game. Sure enough, moments later, the flickering red gate in front of the casino disappeared. It was the only path forward.

HAVEN

Fen's feet ached, her legs burned, and her lungs felt like they were filled with sandpaper. She hadn't stopped running since she had left the entertainment deck. All she wanted to do was to find Walt and get the hell off the ship.

When she finally broke through onto the top deck, and felt the cold sea air wash over her, the antithesis to the hellscape that was the boiler room, she felt like someone had opened a floodgate inside her. She dropped to her knees and cried. Sobs wracked her body as she truly felt how afraid she was and how close to a terrible tortuous death she had come.

The adrenaline that had been fuelling her was fading, and she realised how tired she was. She barely had the energy to haul herself to her feet.

"You don't look like an agent or a cop."

Fen hadn't noticed the man lurking on the deck. He was almost completely concealed by shadow. She couldn't make out any of his features, yet he still had an unmistakable air of danger about him.

"A lady alone out here could get into trouble." His voice made her skin crawl. "You can run if you want," he said, predicting her plan. "I love to chase."

"Why don't you chase me?" a familiar voice from behind the man said.

There was the muffled sound of a fist colliding with a face, and then the unmistakable sound of a body falling to the ground.

Fen let out a cry of relief as Walt stepped out of the shadows and into the moonlight. She stumbled towards him as he ran to meet her. He pulled her into his arms as soon as she reached him. He was soaking wet, but she didn't care.

"Thank God," he said, kissing the top of her head.

She couldn't find words to express the relief that washed over her. She clung to him as if he was a lifeline. "Please get me out of here," she sobbed against his chest.

Fen didn't have to tell him she could barely stand. He scooped her into his arms and walked her to the edge of the deck.

"Thea—" but her words were drowned out as the air was filled with the sound of sirens and red and blue flashing lights broke through the blackness of the night. Fen clutched Walt so tight he groaned. A spotlight burst into life above them, and a Caligo Police transporter moved through the air to hover beside them.

The door opened, and a tall Black person with gold earrings stood just inside.

"I'm Detective Alex Wyndham. You Captain James?"

"Yeah, that's me." Walt said.

"Thea sent me. Need a ride?"

Fen passed out inside the Jonk, cradled in Walt's lap. She awoke only when he nudged her to tell her they had arrived at the Caligo Police Department. In a blur, she allowed him to lead her through the station to the detective's bullpen. Walt kissed her on the top of the head as he sat her in a chair and wrapped a blanket around her, then moved off to the side to speak to the detective who had brought them to the precinct.

She hardly took in their words as they spoke in hushed tones nearby.

"We dealt a real blow to the Barones tonight. You catch your serial killer?"

"I don't know. Fen's in shock. I don't want to question her until tomorrow. She needs rest. Is Thea back yet?"

"No. I haven't heard from her. I'd hoped you'd know where she is."

"When's the last time she checked in?" Even through her daze, Fen could hear the new sharp edge to his voice. It brought her back to herself slightly.

"When she called in the cavalry," the detective was saying. "I'll try her now." There was a pause. "Straight to voicemail."

"Dammit!" Walt slammed both his fists down on the detective's desk. "Anything could have happened while we've been fucking about here."

"Thea..." Fen mumbled, trying to fight through the fog in her brain. "Thea..."

"Fen," Walt said, kneeling in front of her so he could match her eyeline. "Do you know where Thea is?"

"He has her."

"The Zealot?" His face went pale. "On the ship?"

Fen nodded groggily.

Walt let out a roar of anger. "Alex, contact your teams searching The Fitzgerald, maybe they've already found her."

Fen wanted to be worried about Thea, but she was just so tired. She let sleep claim her as she watched Walt sweep from the room.

THE SOULLESS AND THE DAMNED

In Thea's experience, serial killers loved to chase the high that murder made them feel. They lacked remorse and guilt. They were impulsive and needed control above all else. They were predators, and they loved to play games.

Separating Thea from Fen, trapping her alone and attempting to funnel her where he wanted, was all a form of control for The Zealot. Thea's best chance against him was to not play his game. To try to unsettle him and throw him off. To make him feel weak and out of control.

She waited where Fen had left her, testing The Zealot's patience. The door to the casino remained the only exit without a red gate, but Thea ignored it. Within minutes, a ragged voice came through the tannoy system. "Move."

"No." Thea responded immediately, but she stretched the word almost lazily. She looked directly into the nearest camera, goading him.

"Get in the fucking casino!"

"Why? I know you're a killer. Why would I do what you want?" It was dangerous to provoke a man who crucified his victims, but it was equally dangerous to walk into a trap of his making.

Thea could hear the low buzzing hum that told her the tannoy channel was still open, but The Zealot didn't reply.

She knew she was being watched as she walked over to the door Fen had escaped through. She examined the frame around the red barrier. If these translucent gates were anything like the ones in The Orchard lock-up, they relied on a circuit created by conductor pins. If any one of the pins was damaged, it would disrupt the circuit and the gate. If more than one pin was tampered with, it should cause the gate to disappear.

She pulled her gun from her holster and took aim at the top corner of the door frame. She fired a single shot. It struck right on target and the gate flickered. She fired at the pin again.

"Stop!" The Zealot's voice over the intercom was slightly manic. Thea ignored it. She took aim at one of the bottom conductor pins and aimed true. The red light flickered and then dispersed.

"If you take a single step through that door, I'll sink this ship."

Again, Thea ignored him.

It took all her self-control to walk, not run. The moment she stepped into the corridor, the lights went out and she was plunged into darkness. While the flashlight attached to her pistol would provide a better view for her, it would also make her easier for The Zealot to find on his cameras. She tapped her index, blinked, then opened her eyes to a world of black and green. She was sure The Zealot wouldn't have banked on her Seer having night vision. Now able to see again, she continued her ascent.

The control room was nearer the stern of the boat, overlooking the pool. If Thea were to make her escape that way, she may come face to face with The Zealot in an environment he was far more familiar with. Instead, three decks below the top, she exited the stairwell and headed towards the aft of the ship.

Once on the lower deck proper, she was faced with a set of tall double doors. It was hard with the green hue to make out much detail about her surroundings other than the long carpet that led to the portal. She pushed the doors wide and found herself in what must have been a magnificent ballroom. Even with the night vision, she could see the gleaming floor and the several crystal chandeliers hanging from the ceiling.

Later, she wouldn't be able to explain how she knew, but in that moment, standing in that cavernous room, the darkness pressing in on her, she felt in her gut that she wasn't alone.

"You're here, aren't you?" she said quietly. "Show yourself."

From the shadows to her left, a man stepped into view. He was lean and of medium height. His face was covered by an eerily familiar gold mask.

"Hail Khrysos," she said bitterly, searching for a reaction.

"Should that mean something to me?" In person, his voice sounded less harsh, younger.

"I guess not. What do you want?"

"I want you to understand." He circled her. Thea matched his movements, ensuring he was never able to get behind her and keeping her gun raised.

"Understand what?"

"They made me what I am. I didn't choose this."

"Who? What didn't you choose?" Thea said, trying to sound empathetic.

"I am not a sinner."

"I believe you."

"Do you think I'm stupid?" he shouted suddenly. "You're trained to empathise. You're told to find a bond, appear sympathetic. You can't manipulate me."

"I'm not trying to. You want me to understand, I want to understand."

"We have one soul, and if that soul is tarnished or damaged, we are damned. I have accepted my damnation, but I will end those who tarnish others."

"What do you want with me?"

"You protect the soulless and the damned. You freed a sinner. You have blackened your own soul."

Thea prepared for an attack. Instead, The Zealot moved back into the darkness out with her field of vision. She held still, listening hard, but she heard nothing; not a footstep or a breath, not the rustle of clothing or the squeak of a shoe.

Seemingly from nowhere, he pounced from behind. Before Thea knew what was happening, a looped chain was around her neck and she was hauled off her feet. Her gun clattered to the ground as she instinctively brought her hands up to grip the chain above her head.

The Zealot dragged her easily across the waxed wooden floor. Thea used the slickness of the dancefloor and swung her legs around to collide with his. The Zealot fell to the ground. His grasp on the chain was momentarily slackened and Thea yanked hard, pulling it from his clutches. She scrambled to her feet to face The Zealot as he did the same.

He reached for her with almost clawed hands, like he wanted to scratch out her eyes. Thea used the length of chain to trap one of his hands. She pulled him close so she could elbow him in the face, but with the golden mask, she wasn't sure how effective it had been. She didn't wait to find out. She raised her knee and buried it in his stomach. The Zealot dropped to the ground.

As he fell, he grabbed Thea's ankle and pulled her down with him. He clambered up her body, so he was on top of her, the length of his body pressing her into the floor. His hands found her neck and squeezed.

Thea couldn't breathe. She could feel the pressure building in the tiny blood vessels in her eyes. She jerked onto her side, causing him to fall onto the floor next to her. As his head hit the hardwood, there was a cracking sound like porcelain breaking. Through her slowly blurring vision, Thea saw a crack down the centre of the mask. She reached for it and The Zealot immediately grabbed her outstretched hand, crushing her fingers in his.

"Thea Williams. Agent Williams. If you are here, call out."

The Zealot released Thea at once. As she coughed and spluttered, gasping for breath, he scrambled to his feet and ran off into the darkness.

Thea lay where he had left her for a moment, raggedly dragging air back into her lungs, staring at the ceiling. Then, as if nothing had happened, she got to her feet, found her gun where she had dropped it a few meters away, and left the ballroom heading towards the voice.

She heard more muffled shouts as she ascended the stairs following the sound of her own name as it was called over and over again. She walked towards them, too tired to run and too sore to shout. As she exited the final stairwell and opened the door that led to the top deck, she was blinded by many bright flashlights.

She held up a hand to allow her to see the holders. Walt, Alex, and a troop of CPD officers she didn't know were standing there wide eyed.

Walt ran forward and pulled her into a bone breaking hug. "Thank God," he said, resting his cheek against her hair.

"Thanks for the rescue."

"Shut up," he said with a half laugh that she felt in his chest. This was the first time they had made physical contact since their reunion. Something forgotten that

Thea had thought was long buried stirred as he held her and, afraid to wake it fully, Thea stepped back.

"Is Fen okay?"

"She's in shock, but she's alive. Thanks to you."

"We got the Barones," Alex said, stepping forward and pulling Thea into a hug of their own. "Not Denise, but all of her capos and a hell of a lot of her foot soldiers. I'm really glad you aren't dead. Did I mention that?"

"Congratulations. And thanks."

"You go missing again; I'll kick your ass."

"Are there any ARC agents here yet? Have your officers search the ship. The Zealot can't have gone far."

"Yes, and yes. They're already looking. Your chariot awaits," Alex said, pointing to a small transporter that was hovering just above the deck.

"I'm not leaving until we find him."

DEFINITELY ME

Torrez was tired of chasing adulterers. It was boring and trite. Petty, selfish people, behaving like teenagers with no regard for the feelings of their loved ones. Idiots living for the thrill. Fools who were ruled by their sexual desires. He would have loved to be able to judge them, but in truth, when he was married to Marielena, he had been worse than any spouse he had outed as a private investigator.

He hadn't had an affair; he hadn't fallen in love with a person who was married and felt guilt like Thea had with Walt. No, he had gone out on the prowl every night he could, looking for a lover from dusk until dawn. He had revelled in it. He'd had no emotional connection to any of them. It had always been physical only. It had made him feel powerful, like he had status, but he had been fooling himself. It made him more witless than any of his cheating foils. He had loved her, he still did, so why had he behaved so terribly? The question played on a constant loop in his head. Why had he tested their marriage so often? It was like he wanted to see how far he could push before their relationship finally broke, not realising that when it did, it would be irreparable.

The mascara blackened tears of his last client still wet his lapel as he opened the door of his apartment. As usual, around dinnertime, Joseph was standing in the kitchen. Naked but for a white apron and cooking dinner. He didn't notice Torrez enter as he danced to the loud music that emanated from the Gramophone while he stirred his latest concoction. It smelled heavenly. Torrez could have watched his muscled form move forever. The sight of the man's bare skin sent electricity flowing through Torrez's body as he remembered the sex they'd had on the dining table that morning. It had been rough, primal, and phenomenal. Just the sight of Joseph had him ready to go another round. But that was just his problem. He was still driven by desire.

Giving himself a mental cold shower, Torrez walked to the gramophone and turned it down, so it was more like pleasant background noise.

Joseph turned to look at him. A wide smile broke across his beautiful face. "Hey, babe," he said, turning off the cooktop. "Sit your ass down, I made Gram Gram's gumbo."

"My favourite," Torrez said without enthusiasm.

"Okay, what's up with you, sourpuss?" The man was a barometer for Torrez's emotions. He knew instantly when something was amiss.

"Nothing." Torrez shrugged and sat down at the dining table.

"I'll take that bull with a side of shit," Joseph said, abandoning the plates he had been ladling gumbo onto and crossing his arms like he meant business. "You haven't been right for days. Is it work? I know those murders really shook you. Is it Thea? Did you two have a fight? Or are you wallowing in self-doubt again?"

Torrez often thought that Joseph was wasted as a tattoo artist. His work was unparalleled, his skill with both a brush and a needle belonged in an art gallery, but he had a shrewd mind and a real gift for seeing the heart of a problem; he would have made a great detective if he had been so inclined.

"I want more."

"More like what? I know we talked about getting married, but we can't until you get a divorce. This queen is ready, but the ball's in your court with that one." Torrez could tell that Joseph knew marriage wasn't on his mind.

"You are amazing—"

"Here we go. Every time you have a crisis, you think the problem is us."

"Please, listen to me, Joss. You are the perfect partner. You are supportive and loving and when I'm with you, I feel loved in a way that I didn't know was possible."

"So, what's the problem? Why can I feel you slipping away from me?"

"Every moment I'm not touching you feels like a moment wasted, but I don't love you. Not the way you love me. And that's not fair to either of us. I want fire, and I want that for you, too."

"You love to fuck me, but you don't love me. Real nice, Drew."

"I didn't mean it like that..."

"We've been together for nearly three years. You've told me you loved me every day since we moved in together. Now you're saying it was all a lie? Every time I told you I loved you and you said it back, you didn't mean it? You were, what? Trying to be nice?"

"It's not that simple. You are everything I ever wanted. I want so badly to love you—"

"Oh sure, fake it till you make it, baby," Joseph brandished the words like a whip.

"I'm sorry."

"You don't get to say sorry. Sorry is for when you say, 'I don't love you anymore'. No amount of sorrys can make up for, 'I never loved you and I've been lying about it for three years'."

"I could spend the rest of my life with you and I'd be happy, really happy. I care about you so much, but I have been in love. Real love and it's more. It's more than what we have."

"You can leave now." It was like shutters had closed behind his eyes. "You're leaving me, so leave."

"Joss..."

"You were supposed to be 'the one'. You talked about true love and soulmates, and I told you you were crazy. You said you would change my mind and make me see things your way and now that I do, now that I can't imagine my life without you, now that I tell people you are my soulmate, you tell me, that it was all a lie? That you never loved me. Get the fuck out of here, Drew, and don't come back."

Joseph vented his frustration by grabbing one of the plates from the counter and smashingit against the wall, sending gumbo and broken china flying through the air.

What could he say? Torrez stood up and left the apartment feeling more alone than he ever had in his life.

CHIPARUS

Walt was on edge. He was twitchy, unable to sit still. That was the thing about being an addict. Even now that he was sober, he was never free of the cravings and the night's exertions had them at the forefront of his mind.

"How much would you kill for a glass of bourbon right now?" Fen said, her eyes on the fingers he was drumming on the table between them.

Walt laughed uncomfortably. "You read my mind." He had always been open with Fen about his struggles with alcohol, and he was glad that they could talk about it candidly. It made it easier to ask for help when he needed it. "I'll be okay," he added when she continued to look concerned.

The Witness Room of the Caligo Police Department was much like an Interrogation Room, except there was no two-way mirror and the table was wooden rather than cold metal. There were no loops for handcuffs, and the seats were comfortable armchairs. A water cooler stood in the corner.

"Are you sure you're ready to do this?" Walt asked Fen. The shock had worn off, and she was much more herself, but Walt couldn't ignore the angry surface burns on her face or the blisters on her arms and bruises at her wrists. Her feet were bloodied from her run through the abandoned cruise ship. "The sooner we do this, the sooner you can take me home."

Walt nodded and leaned forward to press record on the audio device that sat between them. He had pulled some strings to get his fellow captain to allow him to conduct the interview. "Police Captain Walter James of the Tenebrium Police Department. Witness interview of Fen Yeoh. Tell me in your own words, what happened?"

Fen told Walt how she had been abducted and imprisoned. She told him of the horrors of the boiler room and how Thea had rescued her, then stayed behind so she could escape. Walt let her talk, resolutely silent throughout, but he couldn't help grinding his teeth as she explained how The Zealot had held her face to the heat of the fire.

"Is there anything you can tell me about the man who abducted you that might help us identify him?"

"He wore a gold mask the whole time, so I didn't see his face. He seemed like he was in his twenties, maybe. He was under six feet tall, maybe five-ten? He's white, I think. It was hard to tell in the light, but the hair on his arms and hands was light. He might be fair-haired."

"Did the suspect say anything to you that you think could be important? Anything about the murders? Or anything that might help us find him or his next victim?"

"He said that I'd seen his face once before, but nothing about him seemed familiar. He preached about Levi Seward, said that he was a God. I didn't recognise his voice. He's a native English speaker with no accent."

"Do you know of any reason he would have targeted you?"

"I'm pro-aug. I think that's why he targeted me."

Fen couldn't look him in the eye and Walt paused the tape.

"What aren't you telling me?" He knew a liar when he saw one.

"I've been lying to you."

Walt leant back in his chair and crossed his arms. "What about?"

"Ranveer Baker-Singh was a friend of mine. I knew that he was Lalique. We met at an underground art show focussed on aug allyship. I think I was targeted because The Zealot has been following my articles about him and my investigations into Levi Seward. Somehow, he discovered that I'm Chiparus."

"The artist?"

"Yes." She looked mildly surprised that he knew of her work.

Walt didn't know what to say. He just watched Fen as he tried to process this shocking new information.

"Please say something."

"I don't know what to say. I thought I knew you. That's quite the lie."

"You do know me. Can you honestly say that this doesn't fit?"

"Oh, so I'm just an idiot for not guessing?"

"Of course not."

"If his wife hadn't told us about his alter ego, would you have said anything? You wouldn't, would you? You would have withheld information from the investigation." Walt shook his head. "Reporters."

"I get that you're a little pissed."

Walt was about to retort, then he remembered what she had been through. He got to his feet and came around the table to kneel in front of her. He took both her hands in his. "You nearly died. We can have this fight later." He leaned in and placed a gentle kiss on her lips.

"The thought of you got me through today. I knew you'd come for me."

"And I always will." He kissed her again. "Are you ready to finish the interview?"

"Yes, and I promise I won't hold anything back."

"I know."

VANISHED

Thea, the CPD, and the teams from ARC had searched The Fitzgerald top to bottom, but they had found no trace of The Zealot. Either there were secret compartments on the cruise ship that they were yet to find, or he had somehow slipped past them.

"He's not here. Not anymore." Thea said to Alex as they stood together in the now fully lit ballroom. The only signs that the beautiful room had ever seen use were the scuff marks on the floor from her altercation with The Zealot.

"You'll catch him next time," Alex said, putting a reassuring hand on Thea's shoulder. "You should go home. You've been through a lot today. Let the uni's do the final sweep."

"I'll leave soon," Thea said, giving Alex's hand a gentle squeeze.

"I have to co-ordinate with my guys about the Barones."

"Have fun."

"Oh, I will." Alex winked and left.

Thea paced the room with her hands in her pockets lamenting the lost opportunity to catch a dangerous killer. She had saved Fen, and that was no small thing, but The Zealot would kill again.

"Boss?" a soft voice called from the door.

Thea turned to see Billy Rosenburg, dressed in casual slacks, standing just inside the ballroom. He looked strained and uncharacteristically scruffy.

"You shouldn't be here," Thea said with no real conviction.

"I heard you were in trouble..." He shrugged. "I want to help."

"You did the crime, you gotta do the time. There'll be time to talk about it later."

"I know I disappointed you. We all did. And I'm sorry." He looked lost.

"It's not about me. Disappointing me is nothing compared to the harm you could have done if it weren't for the CPD."

"If it weren't for you. I knew that raid was wrong and I did it anyway. We deserve the suspension. I lie awake at night thinking about it and I'm ashamed. Thing is, I've been a soldier my whole life. You're taught to follow orders."

"Here's an order for you: it's time to start thinking for yourself." She gave him a small, reassuring smile.

"Yes, Ma'am."

Evening **CALIGO TODAY** Edition

Latest news and bulletin updates

CPD DEALS A MORTAL BLOW TO ORGANISED CRIME

Raymond Barone was a name that sent shivers down the spines of law enforcement. A family man with a brutal reputation who built an empire with the blood of his enemies. His sudden death, two years ago, led many to hope that the finest days of the Barone family were over. That the power vacuum his death would create could lead to the kind of infighting that destroyed organised crime rings. But instead, a new leader rose through the ranks. His wife Denise: smarter, more business savvy and more blood thirsty still, she single-handedly took over The Dock Ward claiming import and export by sea as hers alone. So complete was her grasp on the region that even the CPD feared to go anywhere near The Dock Ward—until last night.

In a coordinated sting, the proportions of which Caligo has never seen, police officers, led by Detective Alex Wyndham stormed the proverbial keep and won. Officers arrested a total of eighty-seven members of the prolific crime family all of whom face long custodial sentences if found guilty. While the leader of the crime family remains at large…

[MORE ON PAGE 7]

THE ZEALOT

A reporter at the Tenebrium Times has exclusively revealed that the serial killer plaguing our city has his very own title. In an exclusive to her own paper, Fen Yeoh Ranveer Baker-Singh before he met his grisly end. There have been unconfirmed reports that Ms Yeoh has now been targeted by this so-called 'Zealot'. revealed that law enforcement are referring to the killer as 'The Zealot.' This is due both to the use of biblical themes in his kills and the username used to threaten Whether this is related to the exclusive, or her personal pro-aug leanings is yet to be disclosed by the police…

[MORE ON PAGE 4]

SHOCKING DISCOVERY ABOARD THE FITZGERALD

While searching for the killer who styles himself the zealot, CPD officers and ARC agents made a startling discovery in the bowels of *The Fitzgerald* – an abandoned cruise ship sat rusting on the sea level dock. The body of an unidentified male has reportedly been discovered in a walk-in freezer. No cause of death has been released and no word on whether this is another victim of the serial killer or just a gruesome coincidence.

[MORE ON PAGE 15]

MISSING MOBSTERS

An anonymous tip given to this paper has claimed that several of Caligo's mobsters are missing. Do we have a vigilante on our hands? Are they a hero or a villain? Information is sparse at the moment, however, the source claims that there have been victims in all the major families, prompting them to believe that no one involved in organized crime is safe.

[MORE ON PAGE 20]

SUBJECT NUMBER SEVEN

Cleo hadn't left the lab in days. She felt reinvigorated. Finally, she could see redemption. She would never stop feeling guilty for her part in creating the ghouls, but if she could help them now, it would go some way to making amends.

Subject Seven had shown limited progress since the first breakthrough, but it was still progress. While still prone to the violent outbursts that were typical of all ghouls, particularly those who had been in the rabid state for the longest, the periods in between seemed calmer somehow. Like for a brief time, Subject Seven was experiencing peace.

Cleo had taken to calling her 'Sarah'. Sarah could mimic, much in the way a raven would, but the only word she ever said without Cleo's gentle nudging was 'Sarah'. Cleo wondered if it was the subject's name, or perhaps that of a family member or partner. Unfortunately, it was too common a name to allow Cleo to identify her. Even narrowing the search by race and rough age provided far too many results, and the effects of the SubLevel had most likely rendered Sarah unrecognisable. Still, Cleo had several of her team devoted to the attempt on the off chance they could bring some comfort to her family.

"Computer, begin audio log."

"Recording."

"Dr Cleo James continuing previous notes. The initial success with the current cocktail has been replicated in other subjects, however, no further gains in terms of higher brain function have been recorded. I can only conclude that while the cocktail is a good base for progress, it still requires alteration and experimentation."

Cleo rose from her desk and moved over to the glass holding cell to sit cross-legged in front of Sarah. She did this most days when she wanted to observe behaviour or just to think. Today, Sarah paid her no mind. She stood like a statue, staring at the ceiling as if she could see something beyond the painted concrete and silver metal of the ventilation system.

"I needed Quietus to stop my regression. But I was able to create synthetic endocrine glands that are capable of producing the drug as if it's a hormone and after extensive hormone therapy they were successfully introduced into my body and now my body makes its own supply of Quietus." Cleo knew Sarah couldn't understand her, but she found talking to her helped her sort through her muddy thoughts. "What if we could do the same thing with the new compound? But it contains Styxx. It could make things worse."

"Sarah die," the ghoul said, dropping to her hands and knees and crawling towards Cleo like a curious toddler.

"That's what I'm worried about."

THE PAST

Seventeen years ago...

The velvet of her dress felt like silk against her skin and the heavy weight of diamonds around her neck felt like power. It was getting harder and harder to leave Vinny each night and easier and easier to return to him.

Derrick didn't look up as she entered the living room. He sat, as had been his custom for the last few months, in front of the television with a home-brewed liquor in hand.

"It's not Thursday," he mumbled, his eyes still on the flickering screen.

"I know," Cynthia said simply.

"You're still going back to him, then?"

Cynthia didn't answer. What was there to say? She was going out most nights with another man and her husband knew it. It was strange. At first, it was a duty they both understood. It was for their son. But now, she went because she wanted to. There had been guilt at first, but that had long since disappeared in the warmth of Vinny's embrace.

"Make sure you kiss Georgie goodnight before you go. He won't sleep if you don't. Daddy just isn't the same as mommy." Derrick took a long draught from the glass held loosely in his hand. He was distant now, rarely glanced at her and never touched her. She didn't blame him. She didn't miss him. He would have been the perfect husband if her only ambition was to be a mother, but her ambition stretched far beyond that. She loved her son dearly and resented her husband in his attempts to turn her into a homemaker. Their marriage was over, and they both knew it. In truth, it had been over long before Vinny.

"I will," she said, crossing to her son's room.

George was already tucked up in bed. Really, he was too old to be tucked in, but he didn't care. She felt a pang of guilt; it was probably because she wasn't around as much. More than if she had a full time job, but not the amount he was used to and often not at bedtime.

"Are you going out again, Mom?" he asked, twisting his fingers.

"I am." She smiled with closed lips and sat down on the edge of the bed to stroke his hair.

"Is it that man? Dad says you've found another man and that you love him more than you love us."

"You shouldn't listen to Daddy when he's drunk."

"Do you have to go?" he asked, the smallest hint of a quiver in his bottom lip.

"Do you want to come with me?"

"I get to stay up late?" George's eyes were alight with excitement.

"Just this once."

"What the hell do you think you're doing?" Derrick demanded ten minutes later when she and her son stood, now fully dressed, at the front door.

"You're drunk. I'm taking him with me."

"Why? So he can watch you fuck that scumbag?"

"Go wait in the hall, baby," Cynthia said to George, giving him a gentle nudge towards the door. When they were alone again, she rounded on Derrick. "You do not speak to me like that, especially not in front of our son."

"Oh, I'm sorry. I should show you respect while I sit here night after night taking care of our son, while you're off spreading your legs for a mobster? He waits up for you, sits by the door some nights."

"I'm not a good wife, but I am a good mother. I take care of our son."

"When you're here. I saw that fucker on the news. Implicated in a murder. You think you can pal around with someone who's covered in shit and not stink yourself? You think his enemies won't use you or our son? I'm not rich. I'm not dangerous, but I love you. Leave him. Come home for good."

"To what? Life as a glorified maid? I have dreams, aspirations. I am more capable than you've ever cared to notice. I don't want to be a housewife. I never did. But you wanted the perfect wife, and you didn't care how hard you had to push to force me into that mould. I won't do it anymore." It was like a weight had been lifted. Ten years of resentment were finally off her chest.

"You can work if you want."

She laughed bitterly. "Thank you for the permission."

"I'll be better. I'll try to stop drinking and I'll be here more. Come home."

"I can't."

"I know the hospital bills are paid."

"I can't because I don't love you anymore."

Derrick blanched and all the defiance and anger left his face. His features crumpled like she'd struck him.

"George is waiting for me," she said, and she turned and left. She heard him let out a soft sob as she shut the door.

If Vinny's guards were surprised to see Cynthia's son, they didn't let on. They nodded deferentially and opened the door for her to enter the mansion as usual.

"He's waiting for you in the dining room," the nearest man said.

"Thank you."

Cynthia ushered George inside. He was uncharacteristically quiet.

"You okay, sweetie?"

"Is this a bad man's house? Dad says he's a bad man."

"No, this is the house of mommy's friend. I think you'll like him, and I know he'll like you."

"Does he have ice cream?"

"I'm sure he does."

Cynthia reached down and took George's hand. His tiny fingers gripped hers like a vice. He did the same thing every time, like she was a lifeline, and every time it made her heart swell in her chest.

She knocked gently on the dining room door. "Vinny, I've brought someone with me. I hope that's okay?"

She heard the scraping of a chair on wood and then light footfalls before the door was opened to reveal Vinny. His smile quickly turned to shock as he looked down at George.

"Hi." He lent forward as if meaning to give her a kiss, but straightened, seeming to think better of it. "And hello there, young man. I'm Vinny." Vinny knelt down from his considerable height and held a hand out to George.

George turned to look up at Cynthia, who nodded encouragingly. George shook Vinny's hand. "You look scary. What happened to your face?" The question was asked with the innocence of a child and carried no malice.

"George!" Cynthia reproached half-heartedly. Vinny was terrifying if you didn't know him.

"They told me I could either be a giant or I could be handsome, so I decided to be a giant." Vinny smiled at George, who giggled slightly.

"You're plenty handsome," Cynthia said quietly.

"You're plenty biased," he murmured back, reaching out and giving her hand a squeeze.

"Mom said you have ice cream."

"She was right," Vinny said to George. "Is it okay if I give him some?" he asked Cynthia. She nodded. "Let's go, kiddo."

As it turned out, Vinny was great with kids and George enjoyed the mobster's company, but as Cynthia watched them laugh and play on the dining room floor, she couldn't help but think about what Derrick had said. Vinny's lifestyle—her lifestyle now—was dangerous. She had been targeted already. Could she really be with Vinny and protect her child?

MOLTEN MOBSTER

CPD's morgue was in the precinct's basement. It was a dark place with bare brick walls that were somewhat juxtaposed with the white tile floor and gleaming silver equipment. It smelled strongly of formaldehyde and decay. Air fresheners dangled from every available surface, but rather than masking the unpleasant odours, they more added to their pungency.

"Our fridges have been down since last night," the medical examiner explained as Thea entered. "Supposedly someone is coming to fix it, but hell if I know when they will arrive."

"That's ripe," Thea said, grabbing a mask from the side and holding it over her nose and mouth.

"I'd say you get used to it, but I'd be lying. Dr Oliver Das." The medical examiner extended a hand to Thea.

"Agent Williams," she said, giving it a brief shake.

Dr Das was handsome, Indian, and well-muscled, with a glossy moustache and hazel eyes that stood out brightly against his warm brown skin. He had an air of professional confidence that elicited immediate respect.

"Alex said you had something for me?" Thea asked.

"They'll be here in a moment. In the meantime, and I mean no disrespect, but you look like shit. Can I see to a couple of those cuts?"

That settled it, Thea thought. They were definitely going to get on.

She hadn't had the chance to get a good look at herself since returning from The Fitzgerald, but with her foray in the whiskey factory, the Jonk crash and the subsequent swim coupled with her tussle with a serial killer, Thea had no problem accepting she looked worse for wear. More than this, everything hurt. She was tired, her head ached, and her body had taken several beatings. She gladly accepted the Doctor's offer of aid.

Oliver set to work cleaning the various cuts on her arms, neck, and face. Thea could have fallen asleep under his gentle ministrations, but she forced herself to stay alert. While the doctor was applying butterfly stitches to the last of the cuts on her elbow, Alex came bounding through the morgue doors.

They looked positively buoyant. Triumphant. They had a glow about them that Thea knew well. They had achieved an impressive victory tonight.

"Congratulations," Thea said with a smile. "Just wait 'til it hits newsstands tomorrow. 'Detective Wyndham strikes mortal blow to the Barone crime family'."

"It never would have happened without you."

"I made a suggestion—you did the work. This win is all yours."

"If you two are done congratulating yourselves, we have pressing matters to attend to."

"I love it when you get pushy," Alex said slyly. Oliver rolled his eyes. "All right, let's tell Tee what we found."

Oliver wheeled one of the several occupied dissection tables into the centre of the room. On it was a body covered with a white sheet. The only thing Thea could see were its toes. The closer she stepped to it, the clearer it was the cadaver was accounting in no small part for the stench in the room.

"This one is not pretty." And with no further ado, he pulled back the sheet to reveal the head and shoulders of the deceased.

The body appeared to be that of a man. It was hard to tell his age, but his hair was greying at the temples. He had been White in life, though his skin had now taken on a reddish and blotchy hue. Some sort of furry white fungus was growing across his face and his eyes were sunken, still intact but cloudy and sightless. His mouth was mangled, his top lip almost entirely ripped away, and his jaw was detached from the skull. Only fleshy tendrils loosely held it to the face. His teeth were smashed and broken, and his tongue had been eaten away, probably by rodents.

"Where did you find him?" Thea asked, unconsciously screwing up her face against the gruesome sight.

"On The Fitzgerald. We searched that thing top to bottom, but we found no sign of your serial killer. We found him." Alex nodded to the cadaver. "Stuffed into the walk-in freezer in the ship's kitchen. It wasn't on, so it didn't provide any preservation, but I doubt that was a concern."

"Who was he?"

"Calvin Schultz. Reported missing yesterday."

"But he's been dead about two weeks, right?"

"Give or take," Oliver confirmed.

"He's part of the Vollero family."

"How did he die? He doesn't look like he's been crucified."

"Come and see for yourself."

Oliver pulled the sheet back further to show the chest and abdomen of Calvin Schultz. A small metal frame was placed over the large open incision in the stomach. Clearly, Oliver had already started the autopsy.

Thea moved closer to examine the viscera. "What the hell?" There was a clump of metal that had formed itself to several of the corpse's organs.

"The damage to the face was caused by some sort of machinery that was forced down his throat used to funnel molten hot metal directly into the victim's stomach, burning him from the inside out. It would have been excruciating. He would have felt his organs burst and bleed into one another before he died. I can't think of many worse ways to go."

"I don't think it's too much of a stretch to classify him as a Zealot victim. But why this guy? Was he pro-aug?"

"I couldn't find anything that says he was anti-aug," Alex shrugged. "But he wasn't pro-aug in the way we would expect to draw the attention of The Zealot."

They went quiet for a moment, each contemplating this new development.

"Why isn't he killing augs?" Thea asked, looking from Alex to Oliver.

"What do you mean?" Alex quirked their head to the side.

"He hates augs, that's clear, so why is he killing allies, and not augs themselves?"

"I'm not following."

"He spouted Una Anima dogma at me. He hates augs, but he's only killing allies. I think he's augmented. I think he's been twisted up by Levi Seward into regretting his augmentations. He truly believes he's damned and now he's taking out his anger on those who support augmentations. Who say that they are medically beneficial. Necessary."

"He has to be one of Levi Seward's people."

Thea nodded. "I've said that from the start. But I'd go further. I bet Reverend Seward knows who he is. Maybe he doesn't know he's a killer, but he'll know him. He spoke almost like he loved Seward. We need to get a list of Seward's inner circle."

"How? He'll block that with everything he has. I already tried."

"The DA here is a fence sitter, but the DA in Tenebrium is an old friend."

THE FOREST OF INFORMATION

Cora's office was exactly the same as that of every other in the ARC Information Centre. Around the size of a single bed, with screens covering every surface. The only furniture was a brown leather recliner and attached headset.

Cora climbed into the Info Rig and strapped herself in, then placed the headset over her eyes. She was immediately transported to a dense rainforest, the likes of which no longer existed on the earth's surface. Greenery covered the forest floor and hugely tall trees soared to the sky, their leaves and vines creating a canopy that made it impossible to tell whether it was day or night. The chirps and buzz of insects could be heard all around, the squawks of birds and howls of animals formed a cacophony, completed by the sounds of rushing water in the distance.

To anyone unaware, it was an intimidating and isolating sight, but to Cora it was home, because she could see it for what it really was. Every leaf, every branch, every bug, and every bit of bark was a piece of information waiting to be collected or sifted through.

Cora made her way through the trees until the fern-covered paths turned to rocky banks. She broke through the tree line to see an impossibly deep river with crystalline blue waters. She knelt at the river's edge and cupped her hands in the water, reflected back at her wasn't her own face, but that of Bastion.

"Find him," she told the water.

Something troubled the water. It shifted and splashed, even though the rainforest was calm. Slowly, the water drained away and Cora knew when it returned, it would bring with it the information she sought.

DANGEROUS LIAISONS

Torrez lay in the darkness on Thea's couch. Cora had let him in before she left for work and he hadn't moved since.

He was miserable. As a hopeless romantic, the end of any relationship was devastating. He knew he'd done the right thing; to have continued as they were, stringing Joseph along, was cruel, but the problem was—Torrez was genuinely going to miss him. He might not have loved him in an undying way, but he did care about the man. And now, he found himself exactly as he feared he would—alone.

A soft scraping noise put his personal woes on the back-burner and awoke the detective inside him. The metal-on-metal sound was coming from the front door. Someone was picking the lock.

Torrez got silently to his feet and crept to the sideboard where he knew Thea kept a gun. He pulled it out, then moved to stand in front of the door. If he startled the felon, they might get away, but if he let them get inside, he could question them.

Either Thea had phenomenally good locks or this would-be burglar was inexperienced. It was taking them an inordinate amount of time to get past the door. The adrenaline was fading from Torrez and he was growing impatient.

Finally, the door creaked open. Before the intruder had time to see Torrez and before, he had them by the throat and pushed up against the wall next to the door.

With his free hand, Torrez hit the light switch.

"You?" he said in surprise when he realised he had his hand around the neck of Thea's friend Alex. "Why are you breaking in?"

They looked just as surprised as Torrez. "I was looking for Thea, but you'll do," and Alex shoved his hand roughly away and pulled him down into a fierce kiss.

"Wait," Torrez said, pulling back. "You and Thea?"

"Never, but I'm wired and there's a first time for everything." Torrez wasn't sure if he believed them. There was definitely an intensity, but he couldn't tell if it was from being caught in the act or not.

"You wanna help me scratch that itch, or are we bidding each other goodnight?"

Desire had always been Torrez's weakness. Alex was both beautiful and handsome, a delicious blend of both. He was miserable and had felt lonely long before he parted ways with Joseph. Who was he to deny himself comfort when it was offered so willingly?

Torrez threw the gun to the side and recaptured Alex's lips.

THE PAST

Three years ago...

Tenebrium's dead lined the streets. The hospitals were full of the living or soon to be deceased, and no one had time to worry about the already departed. Those who had died in what the news outlets were already calling 'The Battle of Medicorum' were laid in long rows along the Eltham District's Main Street.

No one could tell Alex what had happened in the city. They hadn't known anything was wrong until they had received a call to tell them that David was missing presumed dead. They had gotten the first transporter they could and arrived to find Tenebrium on fire.

Their brother had been part of the Onyx Legion, a paramilitary unit under the command of Tenebrium's District Attorney. They didn't know why there had been a battle, what it had been fought over, and where their brother was.

Alex allowed the tears to flow freely down their face as they took in the extent of the destruction. They looked at corpse after corpse, praying every time that it wasn't David. Praying every time that it was.

They felt alone and yet one with the other families in the same position, bonded in grief. They watched as, time and time again, a family found their loved one dead and collapsed to the ground. It was the thing they feared most and yet the not knowing was almost worse.

As the artificial sun dimmed, the law enforcement co-ordinating the identification told everyone still looking for loved ones to come back tomorrow. Tenebrium had truly fallen from grace. At a loss, Alex found the first open bar and decided to hunker down until first light.

The flashing lights and loud music did nothing to temper the sombre atmosphere inside and Alex could tell that they were not the only one waiting to restart their search as soon as they were allowed back into Eltham.

"Who died?"

Alex turned on their bar stool to see a squat White man sink into the seat to their right. He had a ruddy and jowly face. His hair was dark and curly, with a shining bald pate at his crown.

"You lose your tact in all the chaos?" Alex said with disdain.

"Nah, I just don't see the point in bullshitting."

"I'm looking for my brother. I don't know if he's dead. You?"

"The Name's Damian O'Malley. I think I'm looking for you."

"Cute, but it's time for you to fuck off."

"Not like that, and definitely not you. No one's talking, right? Won't tell you what went down?"

"But you know, right?"

"I do."

"And you'll tell me for the low low price of...?"

"I don't want anything but to share the truth. The people who burned you burned me."

"I haven't been burned, not yet."

"Fine, the people who burned your brother. I don't know him. He could be dead, and if he is I can tell you who's responsible." Damien positively brimmed with malintent, but he was the only person offering answers. How could Alex refuse?

"Let me tell you a tale of two TPD detectives and how they single-handedly fucked Tenebrium."

THE DISTRICT ATTORNEY

When Thea got home late that night, she wasn't surprised to find a shirtless Torrez on her couch. Cora had called and warned her that he would be moving in for a while. What did surprise her was that Alex was draped over him. Both were asleep. Deciding that what she didn't know couldn't hurt her, Thea showered and went to bed.

She slept for hours. Her exertions in The Dock Ward had taken their toll. When she awoke, however, she felt refreshed, if still a tad achy.

She waited until midday to call Jian Zhao, hoping to catch him between meetings. Zhao had been yet another victim of her father, Tenebrium's previous DA. Harold Williams had threatened Zhao's family and forced him to do his bidding.

"Thea!" She could hear the delight in his voice. "It's wonderful to hear from you. How's life in Caligo?"

"Not as different as I'd hoped," she joked. "How are you?"

"I can't complain and wouldn't dream of doing so without a cocktail in my hand. But you didn't call to catch up, did you?"

"I wondered if I have enough credit with you to ask for a favour?"

"After everything we went through together and everything you did for Tenebrium, you will always have credit with me."

"And you with me."

"I never doubted it. So, what can I do for you?"

"I'm investigating Una Anima, specifically Levi Seward."

"Good," Zhao said with clear dislike. "That man is no preacher, he's a general. His disciples are soldiers in a war that everyone can see coming, but precious few seem willing to take steps to avoid."

"Red tape is a killer."

"Indeed."

"I was wondering if you could get me a list of his closest associates, his inner circle, and some background on them."

"No problem. He'll fight me and he'll lose."

"You are nothing like my father."

"A compliment I never tire of hearing. I'll send you the info as soon as I have it. And Thea? Don't be a stranger. I know you and Tenebrium have history, but there are people here who care about you."

"Thank you," Thea said warmly.

"Next time you are in town, I insist we go to dinner."

"It's a done deal. I'll see you soon."

"I'll hold you to that."

He hung up.

Thea took a moment to collect her wits before getting ready to face the day. Once she had washed and dressed, she made her way tentatively into the living room, hoping that Torrez and Alex had bid each other farewell and she would not have to make morning after small talk.

Augur by DataSteam©

BROWSING HISTORY

TODAY

CLEAR BROWSING DATA / REMOVE SELECTED ITEMS

USERNAME: Zealot
NETWORK: Error: Unknown/Untraceable

SEARCH HISTORY

- Encripted://DataStream/Search/Police+Captain+Walter+James
- Encripted://DataStream/Search/Results=TenebriumToday.SC11/TPD-Captain-Warns-of-Serial-killer
- Encripted://DataStream/Search/Results=Idolons.SC11/Disgraced-Detective-Now-Police-Captain
- Encripted://DataStream/Search/Results=AugArtificer.SC7/TPD-Captain-Augmented-After-Workplace-Spinal-Injury
- Encripted://DataStream/Search/Results=TenebriumTimes.TNB/Another-Win-For-New-Captain-Walter-James
- Encripted://DataStream/Search/Results=ColonyCaller.SC6/TPD-Detective-Sentenced-To-Death-For-The-Murder-of-District-Attorney
- Encripted://DataStream/PeopleFinder.TNB/Walter+James
- Encripted://DataStream/PeopleFinder.TNB/Results=Walter+James/ContactDetails
- Encripted://DataStream/PeopleFinder.TNB/Results=Walter+James/PersonalDetails
- Encripted://DataStream/Search/Results=Voyuer.CGO/TPD-Captain-And-The-Truths-He-Won't-Tell-you
- Encripted://DataStream/Search/Results=OubierArchive.789/The-Gold-Legion

Page 1 of 260

CHOICES

Mateo watched the Una Anima march from the window in his office in disgust. Legions of Levi Seward supporters flanked by ARC agents made their way through the streets of Caligo. Many held signs scrawled with anti-aug slurs, while some carried crude dolls, clearly intended to be people with augmentations, nailed to crosses.

Seward walked at the front of the procession, a grin plastered across his smug and entitled face. He carried no signs, as if distancing himself from his followers, but on top of his usual black suit and collar was a light golden cloak; a clear sign that he was the Master of Ceremonies.

There would be blood on the streets of Caligo before the day was done. Mateo could feel it in his bones.

Incensed, Mateo stormed through the halls searching for Deputy Director Vargas.

"Have you looked outside?" he demanded when he found her in the executive staff room making herself an artisan coffee.

"Excuse me?" Vargas said, turning away from the AD she had been chatting to.

"Have you noticed the parade of bigots marching outside ARC, carrying hate symbols and being protected by our agents?"

The staff room was small, with only seven or so other Executives dotted around, but the silence could have filled an auditorium.

"Follow me, Assistant Director." Her voice was icy.

It was hard to tell who was angrier as they walked in silence back to Natalia's office.

"Children create scenes when they are displeased," Natalia hissed, slamming the door behind them. "Are you a child now, Mateo?"

"I'm not afraid of you, Nat. I warned you what would happen if you went through with this."

"And what exactly is going to happen? What are you going to do?" There was a dangerous glint in her eye. "I have the support of the Directors. They don't even know who you are."

Mateo ignored the slight. "This agency is supposed to be unbiased. We are supposed to protect people; we aren't supposed to throw our weight behind bigots. They have dolls on crosses out there for fuck's sake. People are dying and it's only the beginning. You think The Zealot is going to be the only one, with people like Seward stoking the fires of hate? And what about the people who harm themselves because they're told they're damned because they have augmentations, or the people who are too afraid to get augmentations that they desperately need because they fear discrimination and violence? Those are the people we are supposed to be helping, people like you! Without your augmentation, you wouldn't have been able to continue as Deputy Director. You think that because you hide up here in your ivory tower that they won't come for you too? They think people with augmentations are less than human."

"I am protecting them. I'm keeping the march in line."

"Bullshit! Protecting them would have been posting agents outside aug businesses on the routes, putting out PSA's to warn people of the dangers. Asking the Mayor to prohibit the march in the first place. You didn't do any of those things. You didn't even consider it because all you care about is yourself. You are on your way to becoming Director someday, and what a sad day that will be for justice in Caligo. I may be a nobody, invisible to upper management, but at least I know what I stand for.

I'm taking a team out there to ensure those with augmentations are safe. The longer this march goes on, the more likely there will be violence on the streets."

"Don't you dare. We don't want the agency to look fractured."

"You mean 'fair'. You don't want it to seem like we're trying to protect everyone, not just those capable of donating."

"If you do this, Mateo..." Vargas warned.

"I recorded our conversation a few nights ago. I didn't mean to, but I was on the clock and my Seer did it automatically. If you try to stop me, I will give it to the board. How popular do you think you'll be, then?"

"You fool!" Vargas hissed. "They are in his pockets as much as I am! They won't care, they'll just get rid of you and cover it up."

"We'll see. I hope it doesn't come to it, but if it does, I'm willing to roll the dice —are you?"

JUDY'S BEST

Miss Cilla Cone was the proud owner of the drag bar, Judy's Best. It was a café by day, and one of Caligo's hottest comedy venues by night. She was delighted to showcase the art of drag, but more than this, all the drag artists who worked for her had augmentations in some form or another. As a group, they went by the name Metallic Soul.

Usually, Judy's was busy from dusk until dawn, but not today. Today, Cilla had opened the venue more as a form of resistance than because she actually expected to have any customers. Judy's was empty but for the staff, who sat together in one of the window booths watching the Una Anima procession.

Cilla wanted her staff and other augs to know that she wasn't scared of people like Levi Seward, and that, if they needed it, Judy's would always be a safe place.

"It's getting rowdy out there," said a beautiful drag queen named Roxy Wilde. She wasn't wrong. The march had become more like a wave. Una Anima members were peeling away from the main group to target aug-run businesses.

"I think it's time for y'all to head home. Use the back exit. Go quick now," Cilla said firmly. She was willing to take a stand, but it wasn't fair to force her staff to. She had just seen the last of them out when she heard a thunderous crash from the front of the shop.

She ran back into the main café to find that a trashcan had been thrown through the café's front window and two men had come through after it.

"Get out of my café," Cilla said loudly. "That's the only time I'll ask nice."

"You think 'cause you got metal legs that I'm scared of you?" The man who had spoken was White and skinny, with over-long thinning hair and a scraggly beard. His friend was of a similar design, though taller.

"I don't expect anyone to be scared of me, but heels and wig or not, I will toss you out on your ass."

"You're a freak. A godless, soulless freak," the man spat.

"And then some," Cilla said with a smirk. "Last chance."

Both men began to overturn tables and smash chairs. Skinny picked up the mug that had been Cilla's and hurled it at the bottle rack, smashing most of the optics.

Cilla picked up a chair of her own and brought it crashing down on Skinny's side. She grabbed him by the collar, dragged him over to the window and tossed him out the way he came. "You can walk out on your own through the door or follow your buddy through the window. The choice is yours."

The little bell above the door tinkled as the door was opened from the outside to emit an ARC agent clad head to toe in black. "There a problem here?" they asked.

"Yes. These two men vandalised my business and threatened me."

"Well, seeing as the only one to use violence against another person was you, how about we call it quits? I'll clear these two out and you can go back to your day."

"That's your idea of justice now, is it? I have the right to defend myself and my property."

"And you did that. So, let's call it a draw and go our separate ways. I got a lot more calls to attend."

"And heaven forbid you actually do your job. Fine, go. I don't know why I expected anything else from an agency in the pocket of Levi Seward."

CONNECTIONS

Walt had decided to stay in Caligo to be closer to the investigation, and he'd brought Sid with him. Thea was happy to see the detective, but as they sat around her living room with Torrez and Alex, she couldn't help but feel awkward.

"How many missing mobsters are there?" Thea asked Alex.

"Four that we know of, not including Calvin Schultz," they said. "Not one from the same family, either. I got the tip a while back from a local snitch, but with no reports, I didn't really have anything to go on."

"Mobsters and pro-aug allies – particularly ones with a media presence. What's the connection?" Walt asked.

"I don't get it either," Sid shrugged.

"I've got Zhao working on a list of Seward's known associates. Hopefully, that will narrow the pool," Thea said.

"We've been working on potential victims, but the list is a long one," said Sid, shaking his head.

"I've put a protection detail on Marielena," Walt said to Torrez who nodded his thanks. "As far as I can tell, the bombings have no connection to The Zealot other than Levi Seward's influence."

"There are so many pieces that just don't fit." The frustration in Alex's voice was mirrored in them all.

"Torrez," Thea said. "Do you think you could get in touch with any of your old mob contacts and see if they know anything?"

"I can try, but after what happened with Dill Kelly, I dunno how happy they will be to see me."

"Alex, can you dig into the victims? We need to know everything about them. Fen and Ranveer knew each other personally. That's a connection. There must be others."

"What are you gonna do?" Walt asked.

"I'm going to take a run at Levi Seward. He may not be killing anyone with his own hands, but he might as well be, and I have no doubt that the killer is someone close to him."

"Be careful," Walt murmured.

Before Thea could say anything else, her Cicada buzzed. "'Scuse me a second."

She moved away from the group into the kitchen.

"Agent Williams."

"Thea." AD Castillo's voice sounded stressed. "I need you to come in now. I know you had quite the ordeal yesterday, but a mob of Una Anima supporters has broken away from the march and is causing havoc downtown."

"I'll be there soon."

"Duty calls?" Torrez had followed Thea into the kitchen. "Can we have a quick word before you go?"

"If it really is quick."

"About Alex..."

"You're both adults, but if you mess them around, I'll end you."

"Have you and they ever...?"

"What? No. Why?"

"It's nothing." Torrez looked pensive, but Thea didn't have time to find out why.

"I have to go," she said, stepping back into the living room. "Feel free to use this place as a hub. I'll be back when I can."

"Thea," Sid called, standing up to join her at the door. "I'll walk you out."

He waited until they were standing next to the elevator to speak. "I know this is terrible timing, but it always is in our line of work," Sid paused, waiting for her to say something. When she didn't, he continued. "I'd like to take you out on a date."

"Another one?" she smiled.

"We haven't been on a date. The noodle place was two colleagues having dinner after a hard shift."

"You kissed me."

"Yeah...that was great. Still not a date though. But you and me at a restaurant tomorrow around eight—that could be a date. There could even be more kissing."

"Sure." Thea liked Sid, and she had enjoyed their kiss. She wasn't sure if it was truly romantic yet, but she enjoyed his company and was willing to find out if that relationship could develop.

"Great," he said with an endearing grin.

"I really have to go," Thea said, grinning back as she stepped into the lift. "See you later."

"See you."

She saw him fist pump the air just before the doors closed. She snorted, then, pushing their date out of her mind, made her way to the Orchard.

WE DON'T WANT YOUR HELP

"How the hell was this march even allowed?" Thea demanded, as she and AD Castillo stood at one of the incident bays in the Investigation Wing. They were surrounded by news feeds and incident reports that hovered in the air.

"Behold, Caligo's idea of freedom of speech," Mateo said with clear contempt.

"Seward is long gone," Thea said, examining live footage of the march. "We have one death reported, and multiple injuries, but who knows what the actual numbers are? I don't think we can have a plan here; I think we just need to get out on the streets."

"Where do you want us?"

Thea had been so engrossed in watching the march, she hadn't noticed Billy Rosenberg and the rest of her team join them. They all looked bright-eyed and alert, though slightly scruffy. Billy had let his moustache grow into a stubble beard. Clearly, suspension hadn't agreed with them. *Good,* Thea thought. Perhaps they would think twice about doing someone else's dirty work in the future.

"With me," she said. There would be time to talk about what had transpired between them, but it wasn't now. The bottom line was she trusted them, and she knew they trusted her. That was enough.

"We'll meet you in the Mission Hub in ten," Billy said to Thea. "Let's suit up," he added to the rest of the team.

Thea watched them go before turning to Castillo. "C'mon," she said with a nod. "We'd better gear up too."

"I think I might be of more use here." He couldn't quite meet her eye.

"Okay." Thea shrugged. She didn't have time to press the issue.

"I know you think I'm spineless," he said matter-of-factly.

"I never said that."

"No, but I can tell you think I'm weak. What is it you say when you're displeased? 'You're no Betty Charles'. The Tenebrium Police Commissioner is a fine woman, so I won't take that too harshly. Thing is, I've done more rebelling in the last few days than I've done in the last twenty years." He paused. "My wife was a wonderful woman—"

"Why are you telling me this?" Thea interjected, but Castillo continued as if she hadn't spoken.

"She was an amazing person, but we were better as friends than we ever were as a couple. We divorced when my daughter was two and bought apartments right next door so that she would never be without either of us. She remarried a couple years later. His name was Phil, and he was great. She loved him. My daughter loved him, and he sure adored her. He and I would even watch the game together on Sundays, but my ex-wife, she got sick. Cancer."

"I'm sorry."

"It took her quick. My daughter lost her mother and Phil. He couldn't cope. He just sort of faded away. He's alive, out there somewhere, but he's gone. My daughter is ten now and I'm all she has. This thing needs to be done, but think about what you have to lose before you dive in headfirst."

"I know the risks. It's not in my nature to be a bystander."

"You're brave and I respect the hell out of you for that, but you're reckless too. I read your report on The Fitzgerald, and I watched your Seer footage. I can't argue with the results, but you were careless with your life. Why isn't my business, but your safety is. Don't put yourself in harm's way if you don't have to."

Thea held his gaze, willing him to know she understood what he was telling her.

"You can manage the response from here. We'll call if we need you."

"Be safe."

The transporter journey to The Entertainment District was a tense one. Thea didn't like the idea of facing off against the violent faction of Una Anima, but even more than this, she didn't want to be on the opposite side to her colleagues, some of whom she had considered friends.

The transporter hovered over Delorme Square, the very centre of the district, where concerts and fairs were frequently held. There was a rabble of bodies screaming and fighting, chasing those unfortunate enough to have found themselves on the street.

"Land here," Thea ordered.

"Are you sure, Boss?" Sarina asked, looking down at the crowd directly below. She was the team's resident tech expert. Short, Iranian, and extremely candid, Thea enjoyed her no nonsense attitude. She had tattoos on her face and neck, as well as several glimmering piercings.

"They'll move."

"They'd better."

As Thea had predicted, when Sarina set the transporter on a downward trajectory, those in the landing zone scattered with shouts of anger.

"As soon as the doors open, break up as many fights as you can and get people to safety. If you can avoid it, don't engage with other ARC operatives. If you can't avoid it, do what you gotta do."

As the transporter doors rose, the team spread out and made their way into the crowd. It was chaos. The Una Anima supporters attacked anyone who they suspected of being augmented or an ally. If there had been resistance, it has long since dissipated to be replaced by running and hiding.

Thea stopped two young women kicking an elderly man with a silver plate affixed to his face. She pulled a teenager out of a crashed Jonk and she stopped a group of robed men attempting to break into an artisan coffee shop advertising the artwork of the famed pro-aug sculptor Chiparus.

It felt like the violence was never ending as she moved from crisis to crisis. She made no attempts to arrest anyone; that would come later. When the streets were cleared, she could review what her ocular implant had recorded, and she planned to at length.

As Thea ran towards a man carrying a hammer, someone grabbed her arm. She turned to see Haytham, the SSA who occupied the office next door to hers.

"What are you doing? Vargas said we weren't to get involved."

"You have your orders. I have mine." Thea quickly shrugged him off. She had lost sight of the hammer-wielding man, but saw Miss Cilla Cone trying to pull the shutters down on her café, Judy's Best.

"Here," Thea said, taking hold of the other side of the shutter.

"Thank—No. No. I don't want your help."

"Cilla—"

"One of your agents saw two men break into my café today and did nothing. I watched countless agents wearing your badge look on as augs were assaulted, beaten, their businesses ransacked, their livelihoods destroyed and you want to come here and play good cop?"

"My team is trying to help as best we can."

"You'll forgive me if I don't believe you, Miss Thea. I don't want to see you around Judy's anymore." A cry of pain broke the tension. "I don't want your help, but it sounds like someone else might need it."

Thea said nothing. She just turned and headed in the direction of the cry.

CALIGO TODAY

Keeping you in the know

NEWS BULLETIN

➢ 08:04 – Police and city officials have confirmed that the planned Una Anima march will continue as scheduled despite calls for it to be cancelled.

➢ 08:07 – Una Anima announces that leader Levi Seward will march with his followers.

➢ 08:38 – Fatal Jonk crash kills four.

➢ 09:45 – Actor, Jotaro Carmine, 45, will retire after production wraps on his latest film, 'Given Heart'.

➢ 10:01 – Businesses owned and operated by those with augmentations and their allies in The Entertainment District will remain closed today.

➢ 10:03 – Atmosphere in the city centre tense as the city prepares for the Una Anima march.

➢ 11:34 – Levi Seward spotted leaving The Church of the Single Soul as the highly anticipated march begins.

➢ 11:45 – ARC agents join the UA march to protect the church's followers.

➢ 11:50 – A group of Una Anima followers have broken away from the main procession and set fire to an aug-owned clothing store.

➢ 12:13 – Brawling in the city centre as the UA march continues.

➢ 12:47 – Multiple assaults and rioting reported at the UA march.

➢ 13:05 – Levi Seward has left the march as his followers continue to perpetrate violence.

➢ 14:35 – 1 dead, and at least 50 injured as The Entertainment District is gripped by anti-aug violence. Police are urging citizens to avoid the area.

➢ 14:59 – In a shock turn of events, ARC agents have stepped in to ease tensions in The Entertainment District.

➢ 15:07 – Religious leaders across Caligo condemn Una Anima and call for an end to the violence.

➢ 15:14 – ARC vs. ARC – Agents from the Augmented Regulation Committee are reportedly operating on both sides of the rioting in The Entertainment District.

➢ 14:26 – Death toll rises to 3. Hospitals and medical centres struggling to cope with influx of patients. No end to the violence in sight.

THE PAST

Sixteen years ago...

The letter sat between them on the dark wood coffee table. Its vulgar threats were not the first Cynthia had received, but they were the most personal. The image of her sleeping in her bed in the spare room was unsettling. The picture of her son outside his school was downright chilling.

"They think they can get to me through you?" Vinny sounded affronted.

"They can."

"They will die for the thought."

"The Lucianos won't be the only ones thinking this. We've been too bold."

"Too bold? If I want to take the woman I love out on the town, to the theatre, to restaurants, to the fucking moon—I will. We may be criminals, but we're supposed to be gentlemen, or at least pretend to be. You don't go after kids, that's rule one. And you do not go after what's mine, not if you want to live. Deano will die for this." Vinny cracked his knuckles as he seethed. The bloodlust in him was like a fire behind his eyes. Usually, she loved it. He was never more beautiful than when he was in a towering rage. Now, it looked to her like the end.

"It's time, isn't it?"

"Time for what?" He said, softening instantly.

"Your enemies are my enemies. I accept that, but my son shouldn't have to."

"I should never have forced you into this. I'm sorry."

"You didn't force me into anything."

"Yes, I did. You were vulnerable, and I took advantage because I wanted you."

"The only thing you forced me into was dinner. You gave me the chance to walk away time after time, and I never did. You are the best thing that has ever happened to me. You make me feel strong. You make me feel loved. You make me feel powerful. You are the love of my life."

"I love you more than anything. I'd give up my empire for you in a heartbeat, but that wouldn't get rid of the enemies I've made. It would just mean that I couldn't protect you."

"I didn't want to be a mom. I didn't want kids and I know without a shadow of a doubt if I hadn't fallen pregnant with George, I'd still feel that way and I'd be happy. But I am a mom. The love I have for him—there are no words. There is nothing I wouldn't do to protect him."

"You have to go. It's okay. I understand," Vinny said with glassy eyes.

"What would that achieve? Leaving you wouldn't make a difference. I'm not some moll. I don't sit at home in my feathers and pearls eating Turkish Delight and waiting for you to come back so I can clean the blood off your shirts. I have blood on my hands, and I wouldn't have it any other way. If I leave you, I'm just unprotected and so is my son."

"What do we do? Bring him here? We could make up a room for him, have a teacher come here."

"That's no life for a child. I chose this. He didn't."

"How do I make this better? What do you want me to do? I'll kill them all. Every last one of them. I'd destroy the world to keep you safe."

"You aren't the problem. I am. His father is sober now. I think he should stay with him and I should stay here. Permanently. I've made my bed."

"Yesterday I would have given anything to have you with me day and night."

"This is how it has to be. I've made my choice. Actions have consequences. He knows I love him and we can furnish Derrick with the money he needs to give George a good life. When he's older, he'll understand and maybe we can reconnect. I thrive in the darkness, but I don't want this life for my child."

"Are you sure?"

Cynthia meant to say yes, to tell him that it would be fine, that she loved him and that he was enough for her. Instead, she dropped to her knees on the floor and began to sob.

THE LIES WE TELL EACH OTHER

Walt sat in the semi-darkness with his back pressed against the hotel room headboard and Fen encased in his arms. It had taken her a long time to fall asleep and when she finally had; he hadn't wanted to wake her, even to turn on a lamp. Instead, he stared peacefully out the window, absently watching the infomercials flickering on the billboard that covered the face of the building across the street.

He was more grateful that he had words to express, that Fen was safe and that he was able to hold her. He didn't know what he would have done if they had been too late. Fen was quickly becoming the most important person in his life. When searching The Dock Ward, he had realised that he loved her.

The realisation was heartening, but he couldn't ignore the problems in their relationship. She had lied to him, interfered in a murder investigation. She had a mole in his office and frequently published information that the TPD wanted to keep quiet. And then there was Thea. His relationship with Fen was far from simple, but it was infinitely less complicated than that of himself and Thea.

They had done so much damage to each other, and yet, when he had seen her for the first time in years, he had felt elated. Her presence was confusing. It stirred emotions he had tried so long to bury and reminded him of the man he had been. The struggling addict. The liar, the cheater, the drunk. The man he never wanted to be again. He wished she had never come back. He wished she had never left.

He loved the woman in his arms, her head resting on his chest; for now, that was all that mattered.

Fen stirred. She yawned and opened her eyes, twisting slightly to look up at him.

"Hi," Walt said softly. Fen still looked tired. It would take a while for the hollow behind her eyes to fade. Her cheeks were peeling, and the skin was still red where it had been burned. Fluid filled yellow blisters had formed on her arm and shoulder.

"We need to talk," she said firmly.

"It can wait." Walt kissed her softly.

"No, it can't."

"Where are we going?" Walt asked as he sat in the back of a Jonk with Fen.

"I lied to you."

"I know. You've been through a lot. We don't have to do this now."

"Look, you rode in on a white horse and I'd be lying if I said that didn't make a girl a little weak at the knees, but I'm okay. I...care about you and I want things to be right between us and they can't be until I tell you everything. We're nearly there. Have a little faith."

"Faith's hard for a cop."

Fen smiled weakly. They spent the rest of the journey in comfortable silence. Walt didn't know Caligo well, but he could tell the area they were traversing was run down. Clearly residential, the buildings looked like factories and warehouses that had been repurposed as housing.

Eventually, the Jonk made its descent, landing on the roof of a tall factory building. The faded signs on the side told Walt it had once made clothing.

Fen still limped slightly as she stepped out of the Jonk. Her shoeless run through the ship had cut her feet badly. Even her uncharacteristic trainers were clearly not providing complete comfort. Nevertheless, she stretched and walked over to the edge of the building. She let out a happy sigh as she looked out over the city.

Walt lingered further back, letting her enjoy the moment of freedom.

"Come join me," she said, turning back and holding out a hand to him.

"I'm fine here," Walt said, examining his shoes.

"You don't like heights?" She quirked her head to the side as if trying to fit this in with her understanding of him.

"Terrified of 'em."

"Really? How did I not know that?"

"We're still getting to know each other." Walt shrugged.

"I guess we are. You don't let it stop you." She gestured to the view.

"I try not to, but if they can be avoided..."

"Let's go inside." She stepped away from the edge and he gladly took the hand she offered him.

Even though the garment factory had been converted into low rent housing, the halls were still rather more industrial than residential. The walls and floors were bare concrete, and the doors that led to each individual apartment were reminiscent of those found in cold storage.

"This is bleak," Walt muttered.

"On the outside. C'mon." Fen picked up her pace. She led him to the far side of the building. There were fewer apartments here and more of what looked like storage spaces. Fen led him around a final bend. There, he was faced with a huge, red metal sliding door.

"You ready?"

"Lead on."

Fen pulled the door wide and stepped back to allow Walt to enter first. The room was a large studio space with a concrete floor and impressive floor to ceiling windows. There were piles of metal and discarded augmentations next to bags of plaster and clay. Dotted around the room on plinths were beautiful sculptures made of metal.

"These are beautiful," Walt said, looking at the nearest sculpture. It depicted two lovers embracing.

"This has been my studio since I was a teenager."

"So...when you were going out of town for stories, you were coming here?"

"Sometimes."

Walt nodded and continued to admire the various pieces around the room.

"My mother was...troubled. She hurt herself a lot. She was sweet and kind, and I couldn't have asked for a better mother. She loved me and supported me no matter what, no matter how hard she was struggling, but sometimes things would get too much for her. Augmentations couldn't fix her mind, but they could repair a lot of the damage she did to her body. Augmentations are the reason my mother is still alive. She got help. She's doing a lot better now. That could never have happened without augmentations."

"This had to have been a few years ago. How could you afford it?"

"Deduced like a true detective," she smiled sadly. "I used my skill as a sculptor to help those in need get black market augmentations. I made casts for the body parts, things like that. Or fashioned pieces that would allow ill-fitting augmentations to function better. Augmentations mean something to me. They are important and they are beautiful."

"I can see that, and I think I'm starting to get it."

"There was nothing going on between Ranveer and I romantically. He was a dear friend who just wanted to help people."

"I never thought there was. We have a lot to work through, but inside our relationship, when it's just you and I, no cops and reporters, I trust you."

Fen let out a sigh that was almost a sob.

"What's wrong?" Walt took a step towards her, but she stepped back.

"I don't want you to hate me."

"Impossible."

"It's not. I'm about to ruin everything." She paused, as if bracing herself against a tidal wave. "You are my mole in the TPD."

Walt blinked, not quite comprehending. "What?"

"My mole in the TPD, how I know things I shouldn't. It's you." She looked afraid, not of him, but of his reaction.

"How...? I don't understand."

"We didn't meet by chance at that press conference. I went there looking for you. I knew you were single, and I thought you seemed lonely. Damaged. I thought it would be easy. You were kind, and I thought you liked me. But then you kept saying 'no'. I could tell you wanted to, but there was something holding you back. So, I pushed until you gave in."

"I don't think I wanna hear this."

"The first time we slept together, I waited for you to fall asleep and then I twinned your Index with mine. I have access to your calls, your messages, your emails...everything. That's how I get my information. You are my mole."

Walt couldn't take the information in. He just stood there, staring blankly at her.

"I'm so sorry." Fen was crying now.

Walt laughed. There was nothing funny, but he couldn't stop. "You were literally pumping me for information."

"At first!" It was almost a shriek. "I could have left and never came back after the first time, but I didn't. It was good, we were good, and I didn't want to give that up."

"Well, thank you so fucking much. I'm glad you enjoyed the services we provide here." It was such an intimate betrayal.

"It's not like that. You were just supposed to be a mark. A way to get information. But when I got to know you, I realised how smart you were, how brave, how sexy, how—"

"Damaged?" He cut in bitterly. "You're not wrong."

"Stop! You're twisting my words. It was supposed to be a one-night stand for information, but we had such a good time I realised I actually liked you. I wanted to see you again. It was real after that."

"You used me. That's the only thing that's real."

"I fell in love with you! That's the truth. We started out as a lie, but not anymore. We are real." She closed the distance between them and took one of his hands. She pressed it to her heart with both of hers as tears flowed down her face. "This is real. I love you. I'm sorry. I'm so sorry."

Walt let her hold him there. "After you decided you loved me, did you get rid of the tap?"

Fen didn't reply, she just clutched his hand tighter.

"Did you get rid of the tap?"

"No." It was barely more than a whisper.

"When did you use it last?"

"Please, Walt..."

"When did you use it last?" He said again, the hard edge to his voice turning cold.

"The day I was kidnapped, before I headed out for our date."

Walt wrenched himself free of her with a grim smile.

"That's not love. You don't do that to someone you love. You've been spying on me for months. Lying, breaking my trust. Invading my privacy. It's an unspeakable violation."

"I was trying to do what's right. I never set out to betray you. I was only planning to get a little info about Una Anima and then deactivate the link. But we ended up together, and it felt like a wasted opportunity. I felt guilty, but the longer I did it, the smaller it seemed."

"I'm the fucking Police Captain!" he roared. "Do you know how serious this is for both of us? Did you even think about that?"

"Of course I did. I just thought it was worth the risk. Are you happy now?"

"Happy? The woman I love is a liar who used me for my position. If I report it, she goes to jail and if I don't and get caught, we both do. I'm single and out of a job, so, no, I'm not happy."

"I never wanted to hurt you."

"That doesn't really matter now, does it?" No rift could repair the gigantic rift between them. Walt was angry and hurt, his chest ached and more than anything, he was desperate to drink. He wanted to drown his sorrows in a bottle of bourbon.

Walt shook his head and made his way to the door. Fen reached for him, but she stood badly on her injured feet. She fell, and he turned back. Walt stooped down and took her in his arms.

"Let's get you out of here." He carried her back to the roof. She sobbed softly the whole time. He said nothing. He offered her no words of comfort because he had none. He didn't see how they could come back from this.

The Jonk ride back to the hotel was filled with more silence. Neither of them spoke again until he laid her gently on the bed in their shared hotel room.

"This is over, isn't it?" she asked, her voice distant.

"Yes." He turned and left.

PLUS ÇA CHANGE

The last few days had been the worst since Thea had moved to Caligo. The events that had unfolded had tainted her view of the city forever. Once a haven from the horrors of Tenebrium, she was now having trouble distinguishing one from the other. Perhaps Cleo had been right; maybe the world and the colonies were all broken. It was a bleak thought.

It had been a long day, and she ached all over. She was exhausted and covered in cuts and scrapes from the riot. Thea was sitting at her desk, trying to summon the will to stand up and make her way home when she saw him. Walt was walking towards her office. There was something off about his movements, he seemed twitchy, on edge.

He could see her watching him through the glass and didn't bother to knock when he reached the door. He looked awful as he dropped into the seat opposite. His face was drawn and his eyes were red. There was a subtle sheen across his forehead.

"Are you drunk?" Thea asked bluntly. She had seen him like this before.

"No," he smiled in a pained sort of way. "But I wish to God I was."

"What happened?"

When he had finished telling her about the implosion of his relationship with Fen, Thea could hardly blame him for being a mess. He may want to drink, but in the past he would have been drunk already. That meant something.

"I'm sorry," Thea said, knowing that it offered little comfort. "I can tell you care about her, and it sure seems like she cares about you. Are you sure it's over?"

"Are we the kind of friends who give relationship advice?"

"Apparently." Thea shrugged.

"I don't know. I'm so mad," he said, running a hand through his hair. "I wouldn't even know where to start. How did you do it?"

"Do what?"

"Forgive me...for all the crap I pulled?"

Thea gave a short laugh. "I don't think rehashing our past is going to help you fix your current relationship."

"You're right. I'm sorry. I shouldn't be talking to you about this, but I don't know anyone else in the city. And Torrez and I definitely don't do relationship advice."

There was an awkward pause, then Thea said, "I did it because I loved you. Because hating you hurt me. Do you love Fen?"

Something seemed to pass between them as they looked at each other, the echo of a long dormant spark. Walt dropped his eyes to the floor as he said, "Yes."

"Does she love you?"

"She said she does."

"Do you believe her?"

"Before today, I would have, without a doubt."

"Walt, we've all done terrible things to the people we love. You and I know that better than most. I'm not making excuses for what she did, but if you want her in your life, you have to at least try to forgive her."

"When did you become so sage?"

"I like her. I think she's good for you."

Walt drew his brows down for a fraction of a second as if he didn't like what she had said, but it was so brief, Thea wasn't sure if she had imagined it or not.

"Fen's is the first person I've dated since..." Walt smiled awkwardly. "In a while. I had no desire to be with anyone, but she wore me down and I was so glad she did —until today. Now, I'm starting to think I was better off alone."

"You don't do so well alone," Thea said quietly.

"I think that was part of my problem. But I've been alone. I got sober alone. Strained as it is." He gave a short, self-deprecating laugh. "I really thought I'd found something."

"Then make it work. Fight for her."

"She said she went after me because she thought I was an easy mark. She said I seemed lonely and damaged."

"Ouch."

Walt chuckled darkly.

"You need to work out what really needs fixing. Your heart, or your pride. You got played and it's okay to be pissed, but don't let your ego ruin a good thing."

"That's good advice."

"I know." Thea yawned. "It's getting late."

"Will you sit with me for a little while longer? The only thing waiting for me in my hotel room is the minibar. I need a sober buddy."

"Fine, but you're gonna help me with my paperwork."

"Deal."

She threw him a glass tablet and couldn't help but smile as he leaned back in his chair, put his feet up on her desk and set to work.

INTERROGATION ROMANCE

Alex had no regrets when it came to the night they had spent with Torrez. They had been attracted to him from the moment they met. He was handsome and funny. Thea liked him, which, to Alex, was a strong recommendation. All of this was nice and made what they were about to do both easier and harder.

Alex gave themself one final check over as they stood in the hallway. They had donned a casual yet romantic outfit. A loose white shirt unbuttoned to the breastbone and dark trousers, with a velvet stripe down the side. Their shoes were gleaming and pointed with a low heel. Satisfied with their appearance, they knocked.

Torrez opened the door. He looked good. He hadn't bothered to slick back his hair, instead; it sat like a crown of dark curls around his head. His five o'clock shadow had grown into stubble over the last couple of days. It was sexy.

"Hey," he said with an easy smile.

"Drink?" Alex asked, showing Torrez the bottle they had brought.

"Come in." There was a dark glint in Torrez's eye that told Alex they were off to a good start. He had enjoyed their last encounter, too. They had been worried that he would see through their lies, and realise that they had been trying to break into the apartment. If it had been anyone else, Torrez probably would have, but Alex was a known friend of Thea's. It had worked in their favour. They had been impatient and reckless. The idea that Thea would have information about their brother just lying around was ludicrous, but the not knowing was driving Alex crazy. They knew nothing about their brother's death other than what a shady figure in a bar had told them.

When they had first set out to befriend Thea, they had believed that she had caused the death of their brother, but now, knowing her, Alex was sure there was more to the story. But Thea refused to talk about Tenebrium, and there was a tiny part of Alex that worried the unknown Damien might have been telling the truth.

Alex pulled off their coat and hung it over a chair as they did whenever they visited Thea's apartment. "Where's Thea?"

"Work."

"And Cora?"

"Same."

"I guess we're alone then."

"Looks like."

Alex knew their way around Thea's kitchen having been there many times before. They pulled two glasses out of the cupboard and proceeded to fill them with the tequila they had brought.

"I had fun last time," Alex said, handing Torrez a glass and then moving over to the couch. They sat down and waited for him to follow suit. "I was hoping maybe we could get to know each other. See if my moment of madness could be the start of something."

"I'd like that." Torrez settled himself comfortably at the other end of the sofa.

"Before we go any further, you are single, right? Because I don't want to get in the middle of anything."

"My boyfriend and I broke up. It was recent."

"Rebound alert."

Torrez laughed, but didn't say any more. Perhaps he wasn't sure if he was rebounding or not. Alex supposed it didn't really matter. The fact they liked him was a bonus, but it was neither here nor there—they had something to accomplish.

"Where do we start?" Torrez asked, taking a sip of his drink, completely at ease.

"I'm Alex. I'm a CPD detective..." They laughed softly. "I dunno. Tell me about your family."

Torrez thought for a moment. "My grandparents on both sides are from Mexico. My parents were born on the surface, but they moved to the colonies as soon as they could. My mother died when I was eight and I was raised by my dad. He lives with my mother's mother now. He takes care of her."

"Are you close?"

"We used to be. It's been a long time since we've talked. I made some poor decisions, did some bad things. I didn't want to see his disappointment, so I just stopped calling."

"That's sad."

"And you?"

"I don't know anything about my birth parents, but my adoptive family were amazing. Still are. I'm really close to my mom. She's my rock. She never married. Romance wasn't for her, but motherhood was her calling. I had a brother by blood and I have a lot of adopted siblings. Holidays are crazy."

"What happened to your brother?"

"Have you ever been married?" Alex changed tack at lightning speed.

"Uh...yeah. We're separated."

"Bad break-up?"

"Very. It's my fault.You?"

"Nope. Not for me, I don't think. I have no problem with commitment and I get why other people do it, but I've never felt like I needed it or wanted it. Have you always been a PI?"

"I used to be a detective. That's how I met Thea."

"So you worked at the TPD?"

"Yup. What about you? Did you dream of polyester?"

"I fell into it to be honest. I wanted a steady job, and it seemed as good a place as any. But I really found myself on the force. I love helping people. Being able to protect people and bring closure to families makes it all worth it."

Torrez nodded his approval.

"Were you involved in the incident?" they asked, keeping their tone casual.

"What incident?" Torrez was instantly suspicious.

"At Medicorum. The one Thea dodges a mile around every time I bring it up."

"We're not supposed to talk about it."

"That's a yes. Why is Thea so cagey about it?"

"She lost a lot back then. But it's not my story to tell."

"So tell me your side. What happened in Tenebrium? The people want to know."

"I can't talk about it," Torrez said seriously.

There was something about the way he said it that told Alex not to push. "Fine. Boring, but fine. Have you eaten? I could really go some takeout."

They would get their answers, but they had to be smart about it.

CHAOS IN CALIGO

For the second time that week, Thea had come home to find Alex and Torrez asleep on her couch. Her friends were adults. Whatever they did together was their own business, but she wished they wouldn't do it in her living room, especially when she and Cora had a spare bedroom.

She wasn't home long enough to point this out to them, however; she had to shower and head straight back to work.

Lack of sleep was becoming a regular theme, and she was starting to feel the effects. She felt sluggish and her eyes stung, but she ignored her body's demands and headed to the Investigation Wing.

She had never seen it so busy, but she wasn't surprised. On the tram ride over, she had seen the mess the Entertainment District was in. She had pulled her team back because they were exhausted and she didn't want to risk them getting hurt, but the work was far from finished.

Witnessing the small-scale rebellion she had led with the help of AD Castillo seemed to have heartened the other SSAs. Entirely ignoring the directives from Vargas to stand down, the majority of Thea's peers were using their teams to protect the targeted augs; it went a long way to restoring her faith in ARC.

"Miss Tee," Roe, a tall Black woman and a Supervisory Special Agent like Thea, called as soon as Thea set foot in the common area. "Welcome to the madhouse. We're working on rotation to keep everyone fresh and safe. Castillo's orders; no exceptions."

"Catch me up," Thea said, making her way towards Roe, who stood surrounded by screens and files.

"Your team has just been out in the field, you're tired and probably more than a little battered. Which means you are running HQ. Field the incoming reports, send teams where they need to go, keep everyone in the loop. My team is out next. When we return, you have ten hours to go home, get some food and sleep, then you are back into rotation as one of the active teams on the street. You following?"

"Sounds good. How long are we expected to run like this?"

"Until the dangers have passed."

"Roger that. Be safe out there."

"Yes, ma'am."

Thea watched as Roe and her team of agents left, then took up her place as the head of the operation for the next ten hours.

It was invigorating to feel like a force for good again. Thea directed teams, took reports, prioritised incidents, co-ordinated with the police and ensured that ARC helped as many people as possible. Feeling like she was back on the right side of things didn't blind Thea to the realities of Caligo, however. The city was aflame, tensions that had been brewing under the surface had boiled over and now there was chaos, with no end in sight.

"You look tired," AD Castillo said, coming to stand beside Thea as she watched over the many screens and camera feeds, monitoring the teams in the field.

"This system was genius," Thea said, ignoring the well-meaning slight.

"I'm not AD for nothing."

"We don't have enough people to keep this up for long. I want to take another run at Seward."

"Are you asking for permission?" Castillo queried with a raised eyebrow. "It's not like you."

"I guess I am."

"Do it. We have five reported casualties, and that's five too many. Countless injured. And don't let Vargas catch you."

"I haven't seen her in days."

"Keep it that way, and that *is* an order."

"Yes, sir."

Thea debriefed Castillo so that he could run the mission hub in her absence and excused herself into her office.

"ARC Information Centre," a familiar voice answered on the first ring.

"Cora, hey, can you put me through to Syed Seward?"

"Sure. How are you holding up?"

"I'm all right. You?"

"It's chaos down here, too." There was a pause and Thea knew her sister was trying to locate Syed. "All right, I've got his details. You ready?"

"Patch me through."

There was another pause, and then Thea heard a click.

"Syed Seward, with whom am I speaking?"

"Thank you for taking my call. I'm SSA Thea Williams, we met—"

"I remember you, Miss Williams. What do you want?"

"I would like to meet with your husband and I was hoping you could arrange it."

"Call his office."

"He won't agree to meet with me and you know it."

"Then I suppose you won't be meeting with him."

"You told me he faked the attempt on his life—"

"Is that a threat?" he sounded outraged.

"No, not at all. Your secret is safe, but I think you told me that because you don't like what his followers are doing any more than I do. They aren't going to stop; they think he's a god. He's the only one who can end this."

"He won't meet with you."

"Mr Seward—"

"He will not meet with you, but he and I will be dining at Moderne tonight after six."

The line went dead.

Moderne was an extremely expensive restaurant. Reservations were nearly impossible to get and the dress code was absolute. Thea was not one for drama, but there was something satisfying about slipping on a red velvet dress and entering the lobby.

Inside, Moderne was psychotropic and pretentious. There were mirrors everywhere, and any non-reflective surface was covered with black and white geometric patterns. A blonde, White man in a white suit stood behind the reception desk, his face painted to match the patterns in the décor. It was hard to look at him.

"Do you have a reservation, ma'am?"

"Yes, I do." Thea slipped her badge from her clutch bag and slid it across the counter.

"Oh, I see," the man said, eyeing the badge with concern. "Agent Williams, I do hope you aren't planning to make a scene."

"I wouldn't dream of it."

Thea gave the man a winning smile and headed into the dining area.

The dining area was much the same as reception, except for the addition of tables, chairs and booths. The tabletops were made from bright green leaves preserved in glass and the seats were bamboo, with green velvet cushions. The entirety of the ceiling was one huge screen that depicted the goings on of the gleaming chrome kitchen.

The deep crimson of her dress stood out against the monochrome of her surroundings, and several heads turned as Thea entered. She spotted Levi and Syed immediately.

It surprised her that they weren't at a private table, or a secluded and expensive booth. They sat at a small table off to the side. Absent of his usual audience, Seward looked different. His smile was easy and his gaze loving as he chatted happily with his husband. The fact that he was in love didn't change the things he had done or Thea's plans, however.

She walked between the tables, ignoring the eyes that followed her, and pulled a seat from an empty table nearby. She dragged it a couple of feet before adding it to Levi's table and dropping elegantly down into it.

"I'm sorry Ma'am, you are very beautiful, but I promise you, you are barking up the wrong tree."

Thea let out a little laugh. "Do you often get propositioned by strangers, Preacher?"

Recognition dawned on Levi's face. "Agent Williams. I didn't recognise you without your gun."

"It's in my purse." She shook her clutch bag gently and placed it on the table. She wasn't threatening him, but she was more than happy to make him uncomfortable. Meetings like these were power struggles, and she was determined to keep the upper hand. Throwing her opponent off-kilter was the first step.

"I'm in the middle of dinner with my beloved husband. Please leave."

"No. You and I are going to have a little chat."

"I'll call security."

"You do that," Thea responded smoothly. "I'm an officer of the law. They can't throw me out of a public place."

"Not even if you are disturbing a most valued patron?"

"If you were most valued, wouldn't you be in one of the VIP booths?" That nettled him, and Thea was glad. "You can talk to me here or we can make this official and I'll take you down to The Orchard for questioning."

"You have nothing to hold me on."

"Have you looked outside?"

"Vi," Syed said softly, speaking for the first time. "Just talk to her."

"You don't seem surprised to see her, husband mine. Did you have something to do with this?"

"I—"

"How else would she have known we were here?"

"You're going too far, Levi. I love you, but the things you are doing aren't right."

Levi held his husband's gaze. It seemed to Thea like some unspoken conversation was happening between them, the kind that can only happen when you know someone inside out.

"Fine," Levi grunted, looking away from his husband at last. "What do you want?"

"You're a fraud."

"Not a good start, Agent."

"You don't believe the hate you're peddling. This is about money for you. Do you deny it?"

Levi said nothing.

"You're twisting religion and stoking a culture war that has already killed. Do you truly believe that people with augmentations are damned? Soulless? Less human?"

"My followers—"

"I'm not interested in the company line. Do you believe what you preach?"

"He doesn't," Syed said before Levi could answer.

"Syed!" Levi snapped.

"You don't. All you care about is money." Syed looked defiant.

"All I care about is providing for you."

"Not like this. Not anymore." The look on Syed's face was nothing short of fierce. "Tell her the truth. Tell her the truth or I will leave you. I love you and I have loved the life you have cultivated for us, but when you touch me, all I can feel is the blood on your hands. The faces of those you have hurt haunt me when I'm alone in the vast house you paid for with their sorrows. This was never supposed to be us, Vi. Tell her."

"Fine," Levi said, turning back to Thea a muscle twitching in his jaw. "No, I don't really hate augs. But Bigotry sells. Hate is a billion-credit industry."

"The attack outside your church was staged."

"It seems my husband has loose lips." Syed's face showed no regret. "What do you want from me?"

"I want you to tell the truth. I want you to tell your followers that you have lied to them. That you don't have a link to God, and that you don't believe augs are soulless."

"Out of the question. Absolutely ridiculous. I'd be ruined. We'd be ruined." He turned to his husband. "You may have found your morals, but will they keep you warm at night when we're on the streets?"

"Then tell them God has spoken to you," Thea said loudly. "And he wants all augs to be saved. I don't care how you do it, but look outside. There is violence on the streets, a serial killer who thinks you are God. People are dying. Is that really less important to you than credits?"

There was a pregnant pause.

"You disgust me," Thea snarled. She couldn't help herself. "You are offering augs up as a sacrifice in exchange for gold. If being rich is really more important to you than their lives?"

"You want the truth? Here it is. Yes, yes, it is more important to me. I don't care about the pitiless scrabbling around at my feet. I am a god. I may not be divine, but I am worshipped, and that means more to me than all the augs in Caligo. I may disgust you, but history will remember me."

"As a villain."

"Is it more important to you than me?" Syed asked. Tears streamed down his face. He looked like he had seen a ghost.

Levi looked at Thea, then back to his husband.

"Is it?" Syed demanded.

"You are the only thing in this world I care about."

"Then do it for me."

"Or you'll leave me?"

"Yes."

"I will be undone. I'll never forgive you."

"I can live with that."

"You wouldn't."

"You are a monster," Syed said quietly, but there was nothing but love in his voice. "I already knew that. I knew it when I met you. I knew it when I married you. I could see the devil on your face and I loved you, anyway. I have made my deal. I sold my soul to be with you and I would do it again. But you've gone too far,

Vi. Your legacy is a bloody one that I don't want to be a part of. Do what she asks. Call off your followers. Maybe you will be ruined, but we'll be together."

"And if I don't?"

"I will leave you. I will not be party to the deaths of the innocent. I have buried my head in the sand for too long. No longer."

"You are turning on me? You'd leave me? Me? The man who provides for you, puts food on the table, gives you your every desire, the man who puts you above all others, the man who loves you more than life?"

"I need you to love me more than money."

"Well, Agent Williams, you have destroyed my marriage and my career. Are we done here?"

"Not quite. The serial killer styling himself as 'The Zealot' took a friend of mine. We were able to save her, but he spoke about you. Not like a follower, like he knew you personally. Is there anyone in your circle, inner or otherwise, who you think is capable of murder? Has anyone been acting strangely?"

Levi looked at his husband for a moment, then back to Thea. "Daniel Muller. You met him at the church. He's unhinged and capable of great brutality and he's not the only one. But if I had to put money on a person, it would be him."

"Red hair?"

Levi nodded curtly. "I have answered your questions. Please leave."

"I want your word you will address your followers."

"Would you trust it if I gave it?"

"Vi," Syed said softly.

"You will be the death of me, but there is no life without you. I'll do it. If this ends me," Levi hissed, rounding on Thea. "I will drag you down to the depths with me."

"See you in Hell."

THE MISSING FACE

Walt felt like there was a maelstrom inside his head. The last few days had been stressful, and it was when he was stressed that Walt struggled with his sobriety most.

He found himself twitchy and on edge in a way he hadn't been in a long time. He had called his sponsor and gone to an Alcoholics Anonymous meeting; it had helped, but it wasn't a cure. Confused and alone once more, giving into the sweet and blissful embrace of bourbon-induced oblivion was an attractive proposition.

Something Torrez had said after he had found Fen was rattling around in his head.

You have an entire police force at your disposal, and who do you call in a pinch? Thea.

Why had he called her? Why, in his hour of need, had she been the first person he thought of? Why had he gone to her when he was struggling with his sobriety? Why had he asked her for relationship advice? He loved Fen; he had been entirely focussed on finding her, and yet it was like something had been shaken loose inside his head. A door he had thought locked had creaked open when he wasn't looking and now, he couldn't close it.

There was a knock at the hotel room door. Walt was still in the same hotel as Fen, but he had switched rooms and floors. She had tried to contact him, but he wasn't ready to talk to her. He was still far too angry. If he wanted to make things work, and he wasn't sure if he did, he would need to be levelheaded when they hashed it out.

"Captain. Walt? Sir, it's me, Sid."

"Come in."

Sid opened the door and entered the hotel room. He took in Walt, who was sitting fully dressed on the bed, and the empty takeout containers on the writing desk. Walt had a suspicion he was looking for booze. He must have looked rough.

"What is it?" Walt asked, irritation bleeding into his voice.

"I have a message for you. It's from Fen."

"You are swimming in dangerous waters, my friend."

"I have no desire to get involved in the personal relationships of any of my friends...or my boss. But I think it has to do with The Zealot. She wants you to meet with her at her studio."

"Let's go."

"Is there any chance that isn't an order?"

"If it's about the case, we should both go. Personal problems aside, there is a serial killer on the loose."

"I have a Jonk waiting at the docking bay."

Fen was standing in front of the vast windows in her studio when they arrived. She looked much more herself. The burns on her face and arms were healing, and she seemed more relaxed, if a little sad.

"Miss Yeoh," said Walt brusquely, putting his hands in his pockets.

"Thank you for coming, Captain." It was an obvious reminder to watch his tone with her, relationship in tatters or not. Walt could feel the heat coming from Sid, who looked like he wished for nothing more than to melt into a puddle on the floor.

"You've been ignoring my calls," Fen said.

"I'm here in an official capacity only."

"Fine. Let's get to it, then." She was as stubborn as he was. It was one of the things Walt loved about her. "When The Zealot had me, he said I had seen his face. I had no idea what he meant when we did our interview, but yesterday I noticed that the latch on one of the windows is broken."

"Someone has been here?" The detective inside Walt took over at once. "When? Is there anything missing?"

"Yes. I have a lot of old pieces mounted in the back. There is an empty spot."

"What was in it?"

"The cast of a face."

"You think it's his face?"

"It's the only reason I can think that he would have said I had seen him before and why someone would steal an old cast. There are thousands of credits worth of artwork and equipment here. A thief would take that unless it was the face that needed hiding."

"Can you draw us a sketch?"

"No, sorry. It was with the casts I made for black-market augmentations years ago. I have no idea what it looks like. I don't keep inventory. If the thief had taken the plinth, I'd never have noticed it was gone. It has to be the cast of a face because it was with other casts, but like I said, I don't know which one. It's something I haven't done or looked at in years."

"Sid, see if Thea can get a team here. Fen, do you have any old sketches or material that you might have used to create the cast?"

"No problem," Sid said, stepping away to make the call.

"Maybe. Probably, but this place holds twenty years' worth of work. It's going to take a while to sort through and then identify who I've drawn."

"It's a lead. Thank you for letting us know." Walt was careful to keep a businesslike tone.

"Maybe while we work, you and I can talk," Fen said, taking a step closer and lowering her voice.

"I'm still too mad." Walt couldn't meet her eyes. "I don't want to say anything I'll regret. I need time."

"Teams are en route." Sid said, re-joining them. "Looks like I know how my evening is going to go."

"Oh, did you have better plans than trying to solve a serial murder case, detective?" Walt joked half-heartedly, trying to ease some of the tension he felt. He understood. Police work perpetually interfered with the personal lives of those who carried it out.

"I had a date. We've rescheduled."

"Anyone we know?" Fen asked with a smile that didn't reach her eyes.

"Uhh...Thea. Agent Williams." Sid mumbled, smiling bashfully.

Walt felt something uncomfortable twist in his stomach. "That's great," he said mechanically.

THE FALL

"You can do this," Syed said, straightening Levi's tie.

"All my years, scrabbling, struggling, building a legacy. Today I lose it all because I can't live without you." Levi stared at their reflection in the dressing room mirror. In less than five minutes, he was going to stand on the steps of the church he built and tear it all down. He felt numb.

"You never have to." Syed kissed him softly.

"Murders didn't change my mind," Levi said, cupping Syed's face with both his hands. "Discriminatory laws, talk of a culture war, hate crimes...I don't care about any of that. I can't empathise with these people. I don't give a damn about their suffering. I could see them bleeding at my feet and I wouldn't be compelled to lift a finger to help them."

"I don't believe that."

"Then you don't have the measure of me at all." Levi let his hands slip to his husband's neck. "I am a wretched bastard. I make no apologies for it. I care about nothing and no one except you. You are my weakness, Sy." It would be so easy to turn his gentle caress into a stranglehold. To take Syed's throat in his hands and squeeze the life from him. With his husband dead, he could keep his empire, he would be invincible. It was a tempting thought. He would be all powerful, a god among men, but he would be hollow. Empty. Syed was his life.

"I like to think that I'm your conscience."

"You're my heart, black as it may be." Levi slipped his arms around Syed's waist and kissed him again.

"Are you ready?"

"No."

"I meant it. I can't live like this."

"That damned agent has turned my husband against me. She'll pay for that."

"All she did was remind me what it's like to fight for what you believe in. I believe in tolerance and acceptance, in celebrating our differences. Maybe now you can find something to believe in."

"I can't believe I'm doing this."

"Come on, they're waiting for you, Vi."

The crowd assembled on the steps of Una Anima was one of the biggest Levi had ever seen. *What fools,* he thought. They probably imagined that he was going to claim the recent violence in Caligo was a sign from God that they were righteous. Little did they know he was going to expose them for the bigots they were. Not that he judged. He had built an empire on the credits of the small-minded and the scared, the stupid and the ignorant. They would have preferred God-fearing, he was sure. God-fearing was such a strange phrase. Why should those who believe themselves devout fear their God? It didn't matter now; they were in for a rude awakening.

The thought of what he was about to do filled him with a sort of perverse joy. If he was going to have the ultimate fall from grace, he would at least do it in style. Perhaps he could make another small fortune telling the press and talk show hosts how he fooled the city of Caligo. Maybe he could switch off his maniacal mind and enjoy some quiet time with his husband before the wolves came scratching at the door. Maybe.

"People of Caligo, of the press, of law enforcement, devout Una Anima followers and doubters, those with augmentations and those without. You have been lied to."

There were a few shouts of, "Amen," from the crowd.

"I have lied to you. I'm not sorry, but that doesn't make it any less true. The fact is, you're all idiots and I'm the colony's best conman. I don't have a link to God. Nothing divine has ever communicated with me. I know nothing about what does or does not damage a soul, and there are no new commandments. Not now, not ever. Not from me."

Silence followed his little pronouncement.

"I don't hate augs," Levi said with a wide smile. There was something cathartic about tearing yourself down before your enemies had the chance. "I don't care what anyone does to their body. People wear glasses and get pacemakers. Why would all of those things be acceptable but not augmentations? Fear and stupidity have made me a rich and happy man. You are all fools. Why am I telling you this? Because Agent Thea Williams, the agent who saved me from an assassination attempt that I set up, turned my husband against me. He said he'd leave me if I didn't tell y'all the truth. So put down your torches and pitchforks, call off your crusades. It's all lies. You have been conned. Swindled. Duped. Hustled. Thank you, Caligo, and I mean that from the bottom of my heart. Thank you for every hate-soaked credit. You can read all about how I fooled the world and built an empire on lies in my memoir, 'The Preacher Who Sleeps on Silk Sheets', coming this fall.

I'm sure Miss Williams would have liked something more heartfelt. 'Stop the persecution in the name of justice and what's right, fluffy bunnies and rainbows', but that's her job. Church is closed. Find a new God, or try to reconcile with the old one."

Without waiting for a reaction, Levi turned on his heel and walked back inside his church for the last time. Syed was waiting inside.

The flutter in his chest and the smile he couldn't remove from his face was exactly the reason he would never hurt Syed, and the reason that his husband was the one person he would do anything for.

"You don't do things by half, do you? You could have at least pretended to care about the damage you've caused."

"I did what you asked. What more do you want?"

"Right now, nothing. Let's go home."

SINKING SHIP

Mateo felt like a leader for the first time in years as he stood in The Orchard's Mission Hub. He had stepped up, picked his side and because of it, he felt more alive than he had in years.

His newfound clarity and rebellious spirit could never make him abandon his fatherly duties, however. It wasn't ideal, but Serena was asleep on a bed he had made up in his office. He had kissed her good night and tucked her in as always, before returning to the mission hub.

Every agent who wasn't out on the field was gathered to watch the fall of Levi Seward. It was elegantly inelegant, the way he tore down everything he had built. It felt like ARC was holding its breath. Seward removing himself as one of the major players in the anti-aug tensions was a good thing, but the immediate aftermath was likely to be messy.

"All right, back to work, everyone," Mateo said as the broadcast ended. "Be prepared for it to get rough out there."

"And what about in here?"

Mateo hadn't noticed Vargas standing off to the side, watching the broadcast with everyone else in the Investigation Wing.

"You must be pleased. You're off the hook."

"Careful, Matty. Don't push me."

"He's worried he's going broke, and he called due?" Vargas didn't need to answer. The look on her face was enough. "Sucks to be you. I guess being spineless has paid off for me."

"You will help me get out of this or—"

"Or what? You pay him or he tells everyone you're corrupt. Those are your two options. Last time I checked, you're a little more flush than a single father."

"I will beg you if that's what it takes. He pays me monthly. If I default on the payments, repo will take my hardware. They will take my eyes, Mateo."

"All the better to see the damage you've done."

"You're not that cold. Take your pot-shots, make your jibes. Tell me that I am despicable and a disgrace to ARC, but you will help me. I know you."

"Even if I wanted to, I don't know how."

"Help me build a case against Seward."

"That's sort of the whole agency's job at the moment."

"We need to make our own case, things that they don't know. We need leverage to make a deal." She sounded desperate and panicked. It wasn't a good colour on her.

"So...you are willing to let him escape justice to save yourself. You might know me, but I don't know you at all."

"He will go to jail. He will see justice, anyway. Maybe if we uncover one of his darker secrets, he will help me."

"What if he really does lose it all? I'm sure he had plenty of skeletons hiding in his closet, but what if you blackmail him and he doesn't have the money to pay? What will you do then?"

"We can't let that happen."

"I will not help him avoid justice just so he can afford to pay you," Mateo said in disbelief.

"Then what am I supposed to do? I need my eyes. Surely you understand that." She was crying now, and not even pretending to hide it. Those nearby couldn't hear the conversation, but they were watching with interest, nonetheless.

"I won't help you help him—"

"Please, Matty. Please. Repo don't care, they remove augs carelessly. They aren't surgeons. They will destroy the socket ports, and I'll never be able to see again."

"But," Mateo said pointedly, "I will help you steal from him."

"What?"

"Everything we do, we do through you. I want no attachment to this. Nothing that can come back on me and jeopardise my job and my daughter. If this goes sideways, you take the fall and the blame. I need to stay clean."

"Yes. Yes, of course. Thank you so much. Where do we start?"

"You've been out of the investigation game too long. We start by asking the info team to get us a list of his accounts and assets. We will need to take multiple small amounts so he doesn't notice until it's too late. Hopefully, he'll be in jail and unable to do anything about it by the time anyone notices the money is missing."

"You found your backbone."

"Don't make me regret it."

ROMANCE INTERRUPTED

Thea wasn't one to fuss over her appearance. Her life didn't allow it. She followed the same pattern before her date with Sid. The red dress she had worn to Moderne had gotten a positive response, so she decided to wear it again.

"Does Walt know you're going on a date with his second in command?" Torrez said from Thea's bedroom doorway, watching as she put on a pair of earrings.

"What?" she asked, adding a necklace.

"Sid is Walt's guy. His right-hand man. You didn't know?"

"I knew they worked together."

"And you didn't think that would be a problem?"

"Why should it be? The past is...in the past."

"Sure it is."

"Walt has a girlfriend."

"That he does. He also had a wife."

"Stop it. Stop trying to ruin my night." She met his eyes in the mirror over her dresser.

"I would never, Querida. Not another word about Walt."

"Maybe we should be talking about you and Alex. Do I need to give you 'the talk'?"

"The one about having sex on your couch? Or the 'hurt them and I kill you' talk?"

"You have a bedroom here. Use it."

"Understood."

"I know you—"

"Here it comes."

"—And I love you, Drew, but you're a romantic. You tend not to think with your head, and you just broke up with Joseph. Alex is my friend. Don't use them to rebound."

"It's not like that. They came onto me. Actually, they were looking for you, but I was a reasonable substitute. We're just having fun. No strings, no attachments, no rebounding. I promise."

"You're describing you. You're not describing Alex. They aren't a casual sex person. They get attached and they fall easily."

"I have to trust what they've told me. No strings, we agreed. We're just getting to know each other." Torrez checked his watch.

"You're both adults, but please be careful."

"Worry less about me, Querida, and more about your date. It's nearly seven, you better run."

Cross Road Blues was a faux speakeasy and restaurant on the outskirts of the entertainment district. It reminded Thea of French 75 in Tenebrium with its bare brick walls and scrubbed wooden tables. It was in the basement of a large hotel, which only served to further its prohibition aesthetic.

"I've never been here before," Thea said to Sid as they slid into a booth.

"Me neither." He seemed rather pleased with his choice of venue. He looked handsome in his fitted sweater and pressed slacks. His dark hair was tousled and his eyes bright.

They ordered some drinks and watched the jazz band play in comfortable silence.

"I have a confession to make," Sid said, turning back to Thea. "I'm bad at dates. I can't do small talk. It's awkward and I feel like an idiot. I blabber nonsense. See? This is a prime example of the blabbering and the nonsense."

"You had plenty to say last time."

"That wasn't small talk. We were talking about horrific murders. We were talking about work. That doesn't count."

"It doesn't?"

"What the hell do you do on dates?" He said, feigning outrage. "No, it doesn't count. Definitely not."

"I guess I'm not so good at dating, either."

His smile made her smile.

"Well, then, we need to find a way to ease the tension. To get through the awkward pre-dinner phase."

"What do you suggest?" He had piqued her curiosity.

His eyes came to rest on her mouth. "Can I…kiss you again?"

Thea nodded and Sid leant forward. She did too, meeting him halfway. His lips were soft and smooth. The kiss was gentle at first, like he was enjoying exploring and then rougher as his tongue met hers.

"Tensions eased?" she asked when they parted.

"Not exactly, no." A kind of static passed between them. "How about this? A quick fire round. Tell me the worst thing that ever happened to you. Go!"

Thea laughed, caught off guard. She couldn't help it. His energy was infectious. "You first."

"I was born in Tenebrium—"

"Me too."

"Well, that covers that one. Not much tops a cult—"

BOOM.

An explosion outside shook Cross Road Blues, causing the chandeliers and bottles to tinkle. The power of the blast had little bits of dust falling onto the tabletops.

"What was that?" was echoed from table to table.

"Was that a bomb?" Another mirrored chorus.

The band stopped playing and conversations were cut off mid-sentence as the bar held its breath as one, waiting for another blast. When it didn't come, Thea got to her feet. She pulled her badge from her clutch purse and held it over her head.

"I need everybody to stay calm," she called, and all eyes turned to her. "And stay here. We don't know what that was and until we do, stay put, where it's safe." There was muttering at that, but Thea didn't stop. She moved over to the bar and beckoned to the bartender, who came over at once. "Keep everyone here, offer free coffees and softs. Food if you have it. Put it on a tab for ARC. And Call CPD."

"Yes, Ma'am." The bartender nodded and set to work.

"Want privileges?" Thea asked Sid, who had followed her to the bar. He nodded. "You got it. You can represent ARC in Caligo."

"This is because of Seward, right?"

"I'd put money on it."

There was a crowd gathered outside when Thea and Sid emerged onto the street. The sounds of screaming filled the air, mingling with smoke and ash.

"Out of the way," Thea said, pushing her way through the sea of people to glimpse what they were looking at. "ARC. Get out of the way." When she finally broke free, she was horrified by what she saw.

Fire had engulfed the ground floor of the building opposite Cross Road Blues, but it wasn't stopping there. The flames were moving up and up, licking the walls as they crept towards the sky, consuming story after story. More than this, the flames were starting to invade the neighbouring buildings. Those inside rushed out onto the street from the fire escapes, doors and windows.

"Call the fire department and liaise with police," Thea told Sid. "Everybody shut up and get back!" she bellowed at the crowd. "Be quiet!"

Thea had only just heard it. The smallest of voices almost drowned out by the panic. She could hear it now, however. Someone was calling for help, from the small bakery where the fire had originated. "There's someone in there!" a voice in the crowd cried.

"No," Sid said, grabbing Thea's arm as she made towards the burning building. "It's too dangerous."

"That's not how this job works."

The door to The Metal Spoon Bakery was shut fast. She thought about breaking the large front window, but that much oxygen flooding in could cause a secondary explosion. She had only one choice.

She raised her right leg, dress be damned, and kicked the door. It was thrown open and, as predicted, a surge of flames erupted forth. Thea pulled the shawl from her shoulder and pressed it to her face, then stepped inside, Sid right behind her.

The interior was so hot that her vision immediately blurred. A haze of orange flames engulfed nearly everything in sight. "Hello?" Thea called. The smoke was already getting to her lungs. She coughed through the shawl.

"Is someone there? Please help me!" It was coming from a room to her left. The initial explosion had pushed some tables and chairs from the bakery's waiting area against the door.

"Help me with this," Thea said to Sid, who came to her side immediately. The metal and wood were almost too hot to touch, but Thea ignored the pain in her hands as they tried in vain to clear the way. "The door's stuck!" the voice cried.

"On three?"

Sid nodded.

Together, they threw their shoulders into the door. It had been jammed but not locked, and it burst open. A young East Asian woman with pin curls, glasses and a pink apron was huddled next to the sink in what was clearly the staff bathroom.

Sid was coughing, his eyes were streaming, and he was starting to seem dizzy.

"Get out of here. We're right behind you." Thea said, giving him a gentle push. Reluctantly, he ran for the door.

"I was making cupcakes and then this thing came through the window and the next thing I knew, the bakery was on fire."

"Come on," Thea said, grabbing her by the arm and dragging her back out into the street.

"I was just making cupcakes."

The fire department had arrived while Thea and Sid were inside and were preparing to douse the flames and send fighters in to rescue any others who were stuck. Sid was already speaking with them.

BOOM.

There was another explosion. Thea and the woman were thrown to the ground as the bakery succumbed fully to the flames.

"Are you okay?" Thea said, reaching out to the woman where she lay next to her.

"You saved my life. Thank you. Thank you so much." A Medicus approached to treat the women for smoke inhalation.

"You could have been killed," said Sid, holding out a hand to help Thea to her feet. She couldn't quite tell if it was a reproach or a shocked statement of fact.

"We need to speak to the police. I think this was a firebombing."

THE PAST

Ten years ago...

The private dining area at Deveraux was exquisite. Everything was copper and gold with Ancient Egyptian designs painted in black on the walls and hieroglyphics carved into the tabletops.

Cynthia sipped at her champagne, watching Harry Monroe gorge himself on the food that Vinny had paid for.

"I'm glad Vinny finally saw sense," Harry said, gnawing on a pork rib. He was small and Black, with a short high-top fade and a love of green suits. His high-cheekbones and long lashes gave him an elegant quality. He was dapper, if overconfident. "We're stronger together and that means sharing profits. We earned our cut."

"You certainly did," Cynthia said, sweetly.

"I gotta say, if I was Vinny, I wouldn't leave a beautiful dame like you all on her lonesome. There are dangerous men here." He winked.

"I'm sure I'm safe with you."

His replying laugh had a definite undertone Cynthia pretended not to hear. "That you are."

"How about a toast to new friends?" Cynthia raised her glass, and Harry followed suit.

"To new friends." Harry took a long drag from his champagne flute.

There was a thump from downstairs in the main restaurant area. Harry looked towards the sound, but shrugged and went back to his meal. "I hope your boy is playing nice with my boys."

Cynthia gave a winning smile. "Oh, I'm sure he is."

A gunshot sounded somewhere underneath them, and then another, followed by strangled cries, shouts of anger, thuds, bangs, crashes and more gunshots.

"That son of a bitch!" Harry jumped to his feet. He stumbled slightly, like he'd stood up too quickly, but he shook it off. "That Frankenstein looking mother fucker thinks he can cross me? Do you think it will still seem like a good idea when he comes up here to find your brains scattered across the wall?" Harry pulled the gun from his belt and levelled it at Cynthia's head.

Cynthia looked at Harry with as much disdain as she could muster, then pointedly drew her eyes away. She took another sip of champagne, then leant back in her chair, unconcerned.

"You are a dumb bitch if you think I won't blow you away because you're a woman. Maybe I'll have some fun with you first." There was a faint sheen of sweat forming on his forehead.

"You seem to be having trouble holding your gun," Cynthia remarked with supreme indifference. It was true. Harry's hand shook as he struggled to keep the gun aloft. He gave a little cough, then started to wheeze as if struggling to catch his breath.

"What did you do to me?" He could barely get the words out as he dropped to his knees.

"Men like you always underestimate women. You thought you were safe in my company because you don't see me as a threat. You thought that you had the power. That is the last mistake you'll ever make."

Harry slumped to the side, blood oozing from his eye sockets as a thick white froth formed in his mouth. He spluttered and convulsed, his eyes wide and panicked, before he finally stilled.

Cynthia stooped to collect his watch and his gun before exiting onto the mezzanine. The restaurant below was awash with blood. Bodies littered the floor, tables and chairs were overturned and standing amidst the chaos as if he were death himself, was Vinny.

Cynthia cleared her throat and held out the watch for him to see. Vinny smiled widely. Harry was the third of Vinny's enemies whom she had killed. They never suspected her, which made her the perfect assassin. She would cut off the head of the snake, while Vinny and his men would go after the subordinates. It was a winning strategy that had ensured they were all but unchallenged in Tenebrium City. The Kelly Family and the Conti Family were the only real competition left, and they had come to tentative truces.

"You're awfully quiet tonight," Vinny said, taking her chin in his hand as they were chauffeured in a Jonk back to their home. "Are you okay?" He stroked a thumb over her cheek.

"George would have started high school today, and I missed it, just like I've missed his last six birthdays."

"I know you don't want this life for him, but you can still go back. We have enough money. We could set you up in another city, hell, another colony. No-one would know who you are, and you'd be safe."

"But then I'd lose you and I don't think I'd survive that. I will see him again.

When he's grown. When he's old enough to choose. If he wants to join us then, he can. Here." Cynthia handed Vinny the watch.

"I'll add it to my collection."

THE OLD GUARD

Tenebrium City would always feel like home to Torrez. He had loved there, lost there, and been disgraced there, but that didn't matter—it was in his blood.

The night air was crisp and cool. It was never dark in Tenebrium, not truly. The ever-present neon lights flashed and glowed on all sides, covering every face in a rainbow of colour. Torrez felt more like himself than he had in a long time as he sauntered down Bellamy Avenue, cigarillo in hand.

Bellamy Avenue was part of the unofficial mob district in the Pleasure Quarter. It wasn't shady or dangerous, however, unless you were looking for trouble. It was a tourist trap filled with eateries. The average joe on the street would have no idea it was run by the mob, and that was just how Tenebrium's mafia liked it. They kept to the shadows these days and kept any bloodshed between the families. Just like that, many of their previously illicit businesses became legitimate overnight. Restaurants, it seemed, were just as lucrative as crime.

The restaurant Torrez was looking for was one he knew all too well, having frequented it as vice detective. Deco, the onetime haunt of Dill Kelly, looked as it always did. Tall gold Corinthian pillars framed the entrance leading into the chequered floor of the refectory.

The dining room was buzzing with activity. The tables were full, and the staff were rushed off their feet. Dill Kelly's death had not been the end of his legendary restaurant, it seemed. Yet, Torrez saw no signs of the old guard. There were no guns lurking under jackets, or brass knuckles pooching pockets.

"Excuse me," Torrez said to the nearest server, a White person with a septum piercing. "If I told you I was a friend of Dill Kelly, what would you say?"

"I'd say you're probably looking for Mr Chang. He's in the kitchen."

"Thank you."

Torrez walked casually between the tables to the back of the restaurant, where a set of double doors stood. He pushed through them in the large stainless-steel kitchen. Chefs bustled, taking orders from servers, plating food and cooking the plethora of Italian-style delights that Deco had to offer, all under the watchful eye of the head chef.

'Chang' was embroidered into the front of his chef's whites, and Torrez wasn't surprised to find that the man he sought was the man in charge. Mr Chang was of medium height and build, with a slight belly. He was young, Chinese and bald under his chef's hat from what Torrez could tell. He was every bit the master of his craft; the way he cooked and controlled the kitchen was nothing short of genius.

"Could I have a word with you, Chef?" Torrez called over the many counters.

"If you make it quick. Follow me."

The chef led Torrez into a small office off the kitchen. There were shelves of high-end ingredients crammed in beside the basic desk.

"I'm Andrew Torrez. I used to be a vice detective with the TPD, and I knew the old owner well."

"Harland Chang. New owner and stepson of the man you killed."

"You're Ari." An uncomfortable chill filled the air between them.

"Yeah. My baby brother never got to meet his father because of you."

Torrez didn't know what to say. He couldn't say he was sorry; it would be a lie. Dill was a dangerous criminal in league with the Gold Legion. He was directly and indirectly responsible for the deaths of hundreds, if not thousands, of people. He had tortured Torrez mercilessly, an experience that still gave him nightmares and when Torrez had killed him, it had been in self-defence. The hulking man had come to his home planning to hang Torrez from the pipes in his kitchen and drain him like a pig in an abattoir.

"I'm not here to rehash the past. Family men have been going missing in Tenebrium and Caligo. You know anything about it?"

"Yeah, but they aren't coming for the Kellys. So, why should I care if some whack job is taking out the competition?" Torrez could tell that Harland was more bothered by the murders than his bravado portrayed, but he could hardly blame him for not wanting to talk to the man who had murdered his father.

"Why are the Kellys safe?"

"Because we don't have any old Russos."

"No one does. There aren't any Russos anymore."

"The Family is defunct, but plenty of its members survived and joined other families. Just not ours."

"Why the Russos? What's so special about them?"

"Before my time. Mom would know more. Maybe you should talk to her."

"You gonna tell her I'm comin'?"

"Yup."

"Give her time to decide how to kill me?"

"If that's what she wants, but you're gonna have to roll the dice on that one. She's the only one around here who remembers the Russos. They were dad's cousins by marriage. They were close before business got in the way."

"I bet there are plenty other people who remember the Russos."

"You're right, there are, but trust me, this is the warmest reception you're gonna get."

"Why are you helping me? Why aren't you trying to kill me yourself?"

"You don't seem the type to stage a coup. He was trying to kill you when you killed him, right? My dad."

"Yeah."

"That's how it goes in the life."

"That's how it goes in the life." Torrez nodded. He thanked Harland and left, hoping that his mother would be as understanding as her son.

He sincerely doubted it.

GHOST

ARC and the CPD had set up a makeshift mission hub inside Cross Road Blues. The entire venue had been converted into a field office in minutes. Terminals were installed on tabletops and law enforcement personnel took the place of customers.

Thea, thanks to Alex, had changed out of her dress and into the same black tactical gear her team wore on missions. It reminded her uncomfortably of the armour favoured by the Onyx Legion.

"I know you're all tired," Thea said to the assembled agents and police. Sid and Alex stood side by side in the back. "I know it's been a long day, but it's not over yet. An Una Anima affiliated group calling themselves 'The Soulful Elite' has claimed responsibility for the firebombing of The Metal Spoon bakery. CPD officers raided a suspected hideout and found empty containers and supplies to make at least four more explosive devices. We have to assume that these bombs are out in the city as we speak. This is it, people. We are on high alert. These anti-aug attacks are officially being labelled as stochastic domestic terrorism and going forward, we will be treating them as such.

CPD, will be running damage control and triage centres. Officers, you will be ensuring the welfare of victims and co-ordinating search and rescue with the Fire Department and Medicus; you will be reporting to Detective Wyndham or myself. ARC Teams, you be evacuating potential target sites, or you will be out in the city carrying out tactical raids—we have to find these bombs. We were lucky this evening, property damage only, no casualties. I'd like to keep it that way. You will report to your SSA, who will have your individual mission details, if you find anything you report to me. Any questions?"

"Are we sure this is anti aug? I'm not arguing that those folks are unfairly targeted. I just want to be sure we're looking in the right places. Thousands of people could die here," said a CPD officer with shaggy brown hair and a robust beard.

“We’re sure. Following Levi Seward’s statement, the group made several threats on the datastream. The members have managed to remain anonymous, but several videos have been circulating, claiming responsibility and promising more violence. Tech teams have verified the authenticity and analysts agree they are credible. Anyone else?” Thea waited for a moment. “All right then. You know what to do. Move out. Alpha Team,” she called to Billy and the others, “We head out in fifteen, rest up while you can.”

“What do you want me to do?” Sid pushed to the front as the various teams set about their various assignments.

“Can you liaise with Alex and the CPD. We need all hands on deck.” She was glad he was there to help.

“CPD it is. Be careful out there.”

“You too.”

An hour later, Thea and her team had evacuated a charity augmentation clinic, and a high-end medical centre that offered augmentation. Now, they were on the way to the Tiernan Shelter.

Thea was nervous. After her team’s unprovoked raid on the place, she was worried that the residents wouldn’t want their help or worse, wouldn’t believe that they were in danger, but they had to try. The shelter had been identified as a prime target, due to The Soulful Elite’s many references to it in recent social media updates.

“Stay out here,” Thea said to her team as they stood on the street in front of the shelter. “Check in regularly and report anything suspicious. Watch the perimeter.”

“You can’t go in alone,” Billy said with concern. “It could be dangerous.”

“You victimised these people. They aren’t going to want to see any of you. I wasn’t there; they might listen to me. You’ll be close by if I need you. That’s an order,” she added when Billy looked as though he was going to argue.

Thea turned away from him and stepped up to the entrance. She pushed the door open and stepped inside. It was late, and she wasn’t surprised to see that many people slept on pallets or piles of blankets on the floor. Only a blonde, White woman with Achondroplasia and a metal arm appeared to be awake. She was reading by the light of a tiny lamp at one of the long canteen style tables.

The room she had entered was clearly a refectory. If people were sleeping there, the shelter must have been direly overcrowded. It made her heart ache.

“Excuse me,” Thea whispered.

“Christ!” The woman started.

“Sorry, are you the...leader here?” Thea tiptoed between the sleeping bodies.

“I suppose I am. Who are you? You’re dressed like a soldier...” She let the sentence hang, but her meaning was plain.

“I’m from ARC, but this isn’t a raid, I swear it. Did you hear about the bombing earlier in the evening?”

“No, but I saw The Soulful Elite bleating on the datastream. Is it true? Are they coming for us?”

“We have reason to believe that this shelter might be the target of another bombing. We need to evacuate now. We have rest centres set up, with food, clothing, beds—You'll be safe there."

"All right, I'll wake them."

"Hold on," Thea said as a call came through her cicada.

"Boss, an unmarked Jonk just landed across the street." Billy was speaking quietly. It was clear he was watching the Jonk and didn't want to be heard. "They're getting out. Shit, it's them. Thea, it's them. Get the hell out of there."

"They're here," Thea said to the woman. "Up! Everybody, get up!"

The sleepers were jolted awake, and began to scramble towards the exit, grabbing their belongings as they did so.

"Do you have more rooms? Are there more people here?"

"Yes, in the back and upstairs. I'll go—"

"No, you get everyone out down here. I'll go."

Thea sprinted towards the door the woman had indicated. It led to a short corridor with six doors, a staircase and fire exit at the end. She ducked into each of the rooms and woke the occupants, then headed for the upper floors.

"You need to evacuate. Everybody up and out." Thea banged on doors and pushed through any that were open. "Outside, now—you are in very real danger." People flooded the landing, running for the stairs.

SMASH

Thea turned just in time to see a heavy metal box come hurtling through one of the windows. It skidded to a halt at her feet, resting against her right boot.

"Is that a bomb?" a teenaged boy asked, stopping at the top of the stairs.

"Yup. Get out of here, kid."

"But—"

"Go!"

The boy ran down the stairs, keeping his eyes on Thea until he was out of sight.

"Is there anyone else here?" Thea shouted. She waited a fraction of a moment. No response. She knelt down and examined the outer shell of the device. It was a plain black lunch box. Praying to Gods she didn't believe in, she flipped the small latch and opened it.

Inside was a small metal device that glowed red around the edge. A tiny timer was ticking down from twelve.

Thea straightened up and bounded for the stairs. She was glad that she encountered no one as she ran down into the corridor, back into the refectory, heading for the exit. She had only just put a foot on the street when the bomb went off. She hadn't fully registered what the sound meant when the wave of energy that followed sent her flying through the air. She landed painfully on the cobbles. Her head throbbed and her ears rang. Hands pulled her to her feet. She could see that Billy was talking to her, but she couldn't make out his words. It was like there was cotton in her ears.

As the ringing cleared, she heard the cries of the blonde woman, "Bast! Where is Bastion? Has anyone seen Bastion?"

"Bastion?" Thea repeated. It couldn't be.

She looked up at the shelter. It was a blaze. The fire in the upper floor was already making its way down the stairs.

There was a crash from above and Thea saw a first-floor window being smashed. Then a tall and well-muscled Black man clambered out. He coughed, pushing his long locs from his face.

"Bastion!" the blonde cried out in relief.

Bastion lowered himself from the balcony, then let go falling the seven or so feet to land deftly on the sidewalk.

"Can't get rid of me that easily, Caroline," he said, smiling as if he had just done nothing more taxing than opening a window.

"Bastion," Thea said. Her voice seemed to carry over the shouts of the shelter goers and the roar of the fire.

The smile slipped from Bastion's face. Their eyes met and for a moment, it was like everything else faded away. They stood there staring, both as shocked as the other. Then he turned on his heel and ran. Those from the shelter called his name in concern, but he didn't stop.

Thea made to go after him, but Billy kept his firm grip on her arm.

"You're bleeding. You need to get that cut on your forehead seen too. Who is that guy?"

Thea was still feeling discombobulated, but she pulled herself free of the helping hands.

"Did you catch any of the suspects?"

"No, they threw the bomb and fled."

"Get everyone from the shelter to the rest centres."

"We're supposed to be off rotation. You need to eat. You need to sleep. You need medical attention."

"Get them to the rest centre. Eat, rest. I'll be back."

Billy yelled after her, but Thea ignored him as she set off after Bastion.

The Legacy of Levi Seward

Stochastic Terrorism refers to political or media figures overtly demonising a person and/or group in such a way that it inspires others to commit a violent act against the target of the speech.

Bigotry is an ever-present problem that has cut a bloody path through history, and it still has a strong foothold in our society today. Whether it be racism, sexism, queerphobia or inmutationphobia, the effect it has on marginalised groups cannot be overstated. But I am not here to talk about historical bigotry, though there are innumerable examples of it.

It has never been more dangerous to be part of the augmented community. Acts of hatred are being perpetuated against Augs on a daily basis. Levi Seward did not invent bigotry; but people like him are why it continues to flourish.

Since Una Anima made its debut in 2426, hate crimes against those in the augmented community have risen by 86% [*The Mercer Papers, 2429]*. Those who are affiliated with Una Anima or similar organisations are 50% more likely to perpetrate hate speech against members of the aug community [*Dr Amber Stevens, UCL, 2429]*, and those who take in hateful media (media that perpetuates bigotry and biased opinions) are 90% more likely to commit violent crimes against the object of their intolerance [*Pipeline of Hate by Isadora Grey, 2427]*.

Una Anima has been trying to start a culture war for three years and this week it succeeded. Five people were killed in a riot that was sanctioned by authorities. Aug-owned businesses have been vandalised and members of the community had been attacked in the streets. There have been multiple instances of bombings. I myself was a victim of one, and there is a serial killer targeting those who dare to speak out against these hateful acts.

No matter what commentators will say, this is not surprising. This outpouring of violence was easily predicted by anyone paying even the slightest bit of attention.

Levi Seward may have thrown in the towel, but the ball he started rolling shows no sign of slowing down. He has been the acceptable face of their hatred, but the bigots don't need him anymore. The fact he has stepped down as their idol changes little if the church still continues to function. It won't be long before they find their new hateful messiah. Make no mistake, this has nothing to do with religion. That's just the latest cover story.

Levi Seward started a war. His legacy is rooted in the blood and trauma of the augmented community. I cannot find the words to express my anger at the revelation that he did it all for money. It's just more evidence that we as a community are seen as less than human.

I planned to say more, to talk at length about my personal experience with anti-aug violence, but honestly, I'm too tired. It's too close to home.

To my friends and family in the aug community, and the allies who stand with us: be safe and have hope; hate never wins in the end.

GHOSTED

Blood still trickled from the cut above her eyebrow, Thea wiped it away before it could drip into her eye as she jogged hazily through the streets of Caligo.

How was Bastion there?

He was supposed to be in jail on Colony Six. Was he there for Cora? Was he trying to restart the Gold Legion in Caligo? Her mind was spinning.

Memories were flooding her consciousness and all of them were unpleasant. She remembered confiding in Bastion when she couldn't talk to Walt. Trusting him when she felt so alone. Falling into bed with him in a most vulnerable moment and believing that he could provide solace. Being attacked by Bastion, realising that he had betrayed her, discovering that he had kidnapped her sister, and that he was in league with the Gold Legion was a betrayal that had left a lasting mark on her, and it was that which drove her now.

There was no doubt that Thea had a concussion, but had she harboured some lingering uncertainty, it was washed away when she doubled over for the second time to vomit on the pavement. Billy had been right. She was exhausted and in no fit state to be scouring the city for a dangerous escaped criminal, but both ARC and the CPD were stretched thin; there was no one available to search if she didn't. She needed help, and there was only one person who would understand how dangerous Bastion was.

Walt.

FLAMES

Hate was all Alex could see. It was everywhere. It was in the burns being treated by Medicus, in the cries of the injured and the worried shouts of those whose homes and businesses were ablaze. Only a person consumed by hatred could inflict that sort of suffering and feel righteous.

It must be a miserable life, Alex thought, being so twisted. They would have felt sorry for the arsonists if they too, weren't succumbing to a burning hatred of their own. As sure as the nightmare they would have tonight about the smouldering mass of bodies in the ruins of The Kelpie Clinic, Alex was determined to catch every single member of The Soulful Elite and their Una Anima co-conspirators.

"Are you okay?" Sid placed a hand on their shoulder causing Alex to jump. "Sorry, I didn't mean to startle you." They hadn't noticed him join them in the make-shift interview room on the street outside Cross Road Blues.

"It's fine. I was just...having a moment. Folks keep saying 'we got lucky'. No one died, and that's a goddamn miracle, but lives have been destroyed here. How long is the city gonna fund the rest centres for? It won't be forever. And once the hubbub dies down and we move onto other cases, what happens to the people who are homeless now? What happens to the people who have lost everything they own?"

"I don't know, but right now we are doing good work. We need to focus on that."

"Yeah," Alex said noncommittally.

"I've taken about sixty statements; most people didn't see anything. A few have reported hearing a group of men talking about how they think Levi Seward's statement was coerced. And another couple heard someone shout 'die soulless metal freaks'."

"Nothing we didn't know then."

"Excuse me, Detectives?" An ARC agent in the same black tactical gear Thea had left in had joined them in the interview tent.

"Sorry, I don't think I caught your name," Alex said, rubbing their hand over their short hair.

"Havers, Simon Havers." Simon was lean and White with sharp features and the look of someone who had seen combat. Alex guessed he used to be a soldier. There was something in the way he held himself, or maybe it was just the body armour and assault rifle he was holding.

"Do you have a report?"

"There has been a detonation at one of the target sites."

"Fuck!" Alex slammed their hand down on the plastic tabletop. "Any casualties?"

"None, property damage only but...SSA Williams—"

"Is Thea okay?" Sid's tone was sharp.

"She... well, she was clear of the actual blast, but she was caught in the shock-wave. She hit her head pretty bad."

"Where is she?"

"She recognised one of the augs at the shelter. He ran off when he saw her and she ran off after him. Nobody's heard from her since and she isn't answering any calls."

"Don't go running off," Alex said, as Sid started to move away. "We have work to do here. Thea's a big girl. She's on the hunt—it's what she does. I wouldn't answer if I was chasing a perp. We have to assume she's fine until we know she isn't. She doesn't need a hero, and she definitely doesn't need rescuing."

"I'll keep you posted if we get any new reports," Simon said, turning to leave.

"Thanks. Can you send in the next interviewee? And ask ARC to let me know when they find Thea."

UNCHANGED

Thea's head was starting to clear as she walked along the long corridor that led to Fen's studio. She had a concussion; she was exhausted. She should be resting before her next mission and running off after Bastion had been stupid. And yet, she was still going to tell Walt and hope that he would help her find the man.

Thea had forgotten that there were forensic teams scouring the place, trying to find evidence of the missing bust. Many sets of eyes turned to her as she threw the sliding door wide.

"Any luck?" She asked the nearest crime scene tech.

"Not yet, ma'am, but there is a lot to go through."

"Where's Walt?"

"In the back room with Miss Yeoh."

The back room was clearly for storage. Old pieces, or perhaps pieces Fen had fallen out of love with, were stacked neatly against the wall. There was a library's worth of sketchbooks on various shelves around the room. Fen and Walt were kneeling on the floor, going through them in silence. Thea could tell by the set of his shoulders, even with his back to her, that he was still angry.

Walt turned to look at her, alerted by the sound of her footsteps. His expression softened instantly into one of concern. "Are you okay? You're bleeding."

"I'm fine—"

"I heard about the bombings." He got to his feet.

"I was at a suspected target site and it was hit—"

"Jesus, have you been to a Medicus?" He moved over to her, taking her face in his hands to examine the cut on her forehead.

"Walt," Thea said sharply, batting him away impatiently. "I got caught in the shockwave, that's all. I'm fine, but Bastion was there."

"In Caligo?" His reaction wasn't what Thea was expecting. There was no outrage or sign that this was a revelation. He sounded curious rather than shocked. "You saw him? You sure?"

"He looked me dead in the face, then ran off. How is this possible?"

Walt crossed his arms, avoiding her gaze. "He escaped over a year ago." His voice was low, as if he thought this would soften the blow.

"You knew?"

"I got Zhao to agree to putting him in my custody so he could help me round up the rest of the Gold Legion—"

"You idiot."

Walt ignored this. "The deal was he would help in exchange for a last taste of freedom before he started his life sentence. He helped. We rounded up a lot of those who would have otherwise escaped justice, but when it was time to go back, he bolted. We looked for a while, but I had other cases and..." he ended with a guilty shrug.

"Why didn't you tell me?"

Walt said nothing.

"Why didn't you tell me?" Thea said again, her voice shaking slightly.

"Would you have taken my call?"

"You almost had me fooled, but you never change." It was like every lie he had ever told was coming back to her, like she could finally see him again.

"I'm the Police Captain. It was my decision." There was defiance in every word. "If you're so interested in what happened to the remnants of the Gold Legion, where have you been for the last three years? You didn't even stay for his sentencing."

"Maybe this isn't the place to have this conversation," Fen said, reminding Thea she was there.

Thea felt a flush in her cheeks. She had forgotten that she had a job to do. She had, for a moment, forgotten everything but Walt. Some things never changed.

"I should go see a Medicus and then I need to get back," Thea said, as if she hadn't been arguing moments before.

"What are you going to do?" Walt asked bluntly.

"I'm going to find him."

"I'll come with you."

"No," Thea said a little too sharply, "You stay here and keep working The Zealot case."

MRS KELLY

"Andrew Torrez, here to see Virginia Kelly," Torrez said into the intercom. There was no reply, but the soft *buzz* told him he was permitted to enter.

Dillard Kelly's penthouse was exactly as Torrez remembered it: extravagant and irritatingly classy; the opposite of it's deceased owner. Domed ceilings and mother-of-pearl floors with frescoes on the curved walls and the kind of rugs that made Torrez wish he was barefoot.

"Virginia?" Torrez called tentatively as he stepped out of the elevator into the main area. Again, there was no response. Torrez took a few steps further into the room.

BANG.

A bullet whizzed past Torrez and embedded itself in the beautiful wooden panelling behind him. Virginia had stepped through the arch that led into the kitchen, gun raised, eyes alight with danger.

She fired again, and again she missed. Torrez dived behind the long white sofa as bullets continued to fill the air.

"Virginia," Torrez yelled from his hiding place. "You aren't a killer. Stop this!"

"You came into my home. You ate at my table. You did business with us. You laughed with us!" Her words were punctuated by more shots. "I was eight months pregnant as I stood at my husband's graveside."

"You want me to say that I'm sorry. That I'd give him back to you if I could, but I can't. I'm not going to lie to you."

"Have you ever tried to care for a baby while you grieve your husband?" More shots.

"He was trying to kill me. He threatened my wife! You know who Dill was. You can't seriously have expected to live a fairytale life together."

"It was never a fairytale, but he loved me and I loved him."

"That doesn't change who he was."

More shots.

"He was your friend!"

"He was an informant. He was my partner in crime. He was a man who tortured and threatened me, but he was never my friend. Men like him don't have friends."

"Like you're so different?" A vase exploded nearby, showering Torrez with shattered porcelain. "You think you're better than him?"

"I was worse because I pretended I wasn't like him. That I was better. That I was on the right side of things. I betrayed my friends, and I treated my wife like crap. I'm not sorry that I killed him, but I'm not better than him."

There was a long stretch of silence.

"For now, that's enough." Torrez heard the metallic clunk of a gun landing on a wooden floor. "What do you want?"

"Harland sent me. Someone's killing Russos." Torrez remained where he was on the ground, huddled behind the couch.

"Coffee? I just brewed a pot."

When Torrez chanced a glance over the top, he saw Virginia's back retreating further into the penthouse. He took a moment to gather his wits, then stood and followed her.

The kitchen was a deep emerald green with white fittings and fixtures. A toddler with dark hair and round, rosy cheeks sat in a booster seat eating carrot sticks from a plastic plate. The toddler seemed completely unperturbed by the ruckus moments before. The thought was troubling.

"I named him Dill after his father. I'd introduce you, but...well. Hanji?" she called over her shoulder.

Moments later, a Japanese man in a pressed suit appeared in the kitchen. "Yes, Mrs Kelly?"

"Could you take Dill to the playroom, please?"

"Of course." Dill reached eagerly for Hanji, who scooped him up and left the room, making silly faces for the child's amusement.

Now that they were alone, Torrez got a proper look at Virginia Kelly as they sat on opposite sides of the kitchen island. She was slight and very pretty in a striking sort of way. Chinese, with long dark hair, streaked with flecks of silver.

Mrs Kelly pulled a pot of coffee from the stove and poured herself a cup, and then Torrez. "Milk? Sugar?"

"Both."

When the cup was handed to him, Torrez eyed it suspiciously, but took a sip nonetheless. He suppressed a satisfied sigh; it was good coffee.

"How's Marielena?" Her tone was icy.

"We're separated. She wants a divorce, but I..." He didn't finish.

"Shame." Virginia didn't sound remotely sympathetic.

Torrez smiled stiffly.

"So," she went on. "What do you want to know about the Russos?"

"Someone is killing them. I want to know why. Tell me anything you can remember."

"Don't you have fancy records for things like this?"

"There was a fire at the TPD. Destroyed the archive. They're still trying to rebuild, but they lost a lot of information."

"Let me see." She sipped at her coffee thoughtfully. "Back in the day, they were led by Vincent Russo, though we called him Vinny. He was a cousin to Dill by marriage—his first marriage. They were more like brothers."

"Until?" Torrez could hear the reminiscent tone in her voice that told him something had changed between Dill and the unknown Vinny.

"Business got in the way. Vinny started taking out other families, whole families, mind you. He never came after Dill, but his enemies were fair game."

"Why?"

"Beats me. He was always a loner. Lonely on account of his looks. Tall and broad. He was just too big. He scared people. He lost an eye when he was young—his old man had a funny idea of what acceptable discipline was. People used to call him 'Lurch' or 'Cyclops'. 'Monster'. 'Freak'. He didn't have much luck with the ladies. Then he met her. Cynthia. Some tomato from the Poor Quarter with ideas of grandeur."

"What does the dame have to do with it?"

"Vinny might not have been pretty, but he was smart. Real smart. He was a force to be reckoned with in the underworld. Got a real reputation for being a beast. Brutal. But he always knew how to keep the delicate balance intact. Kept things in his favour, but never enough to spark a war. That changed after he met Cynthia. We figured he was under the thumb. Wanted to impress her. She was beautiful, see. Movie star beautiful. Not the kinda dame anyone expected Vin to end up with. I met her a couple of times in the later years of their relationship. He looked at her like he could see the divine in her eyes. Together, they were downright vicious. In love like I've never seen two people, but dangerous."

"You think someone from the old families could be holding a grudge?"

"Maybe, but the Russos got theirs, as you know. Most went to jail or were killed. The others changed loyalties. Doesn't make sense to kill them now." Viginia looked thoughtful as she sipped her coffee. "Vinny took Cynthia from a husband. He harassed them for a while after she left him. Maybe he's still bitter."

"Do you know where either of them are now?"

"Vinny's dead. God knows about Cynthia. She did enough bad with her own hands she might be in the clink. What they had was the real deal, but it was always gonna end in the ground or in the big house. We lost contact long before the law got involved and it wasn't in our interests to dig too deeply."

"And the remaining Russos?"

"Like I said, no idea. Anyone who escaped jail was either low level or a snitch. We didn't take anything to do with them. I can't imagine what any of those small timers could have done in their own right. If someone's killing Russos, it's probably about Vinny. He made more enemies than all the families today have put together. He had fingers in all the pies. Wouldn't be surprised if he was with the Gold Legion in the early days."

Torrez's eyes widened slightly in shock.

"What?" Virginia said defiantly. "Am I just supposed to pretend I don't know anything? Like nothing happened? The rest of the city might be content to forget it, but I'm not. Those Gold Legion bastards got my husband killed."

Torrez didn't have the heart or the nerve to tell Virginia any differently. She may have known about her husband's business interests, but she didn't seem to know how entwined he was with the Gold Legion, and Torrez had no desire to tell her. It seemed that even Dill had realised that the Gold Legion might have harmed her if they feared she knew about their plans.

"Thank you for your time, and the coffee," Torrez said, getting to his feet.

"If I ever see you again, I'll kill you."

"Fair enough."

Outside on the street, Torrez thought over what Mrs Kelly and Harland had told him. He was missing something. While interesting, he couldn't see the link between what was happening in Caligo and a defunct crime family in Tenebrium. What would link mobsters and pro-aug allies? Why, after the Russo family had been defunct for nearly a decade, would someone suddenly start seeking out the last remaining remnants and killing them?

He had to find out what had happened to Vinny Russo. Perhaps the Zealot was trying to draw him out. But why? What was the connection? On the journey back to Caligo, Torrez did as much digging as he could into where the remnants of the Russo family ended up.

THE PAST

Ten years ago...

Cynthia had known she was being followed for several blocks now. What she didn't know was if her would-be pursuer was friend or foe. Her instincts told her foe.

Cynthia could handle herself in a tight spot, but she didn't want to get into an altercation with an unknown quantity. If she kept up her current pace, she would be off the street and into the restaurant before they could catch up with her, if they wanted to be discreet. If they picked up the pace and ran after her, all bets were off.

Cynthia cursed herself as she tried to keep a surreptitious eye on them. Why had she not gone straight to the restaurant with Vinny? Why had she stopped at the damn night market?

As if from nowhere, a hand grabbed her by the arm and dragged her into a nearby alley. A handkerchief was placed over her mouth as she was forced into its depths. She tried to scream but the muffled sound would never make its way back to the street to be heard over the music and the endless noisescape that was Tenebrium City.

She tried to twist in the grip of her attacker to get a good look at them, but their hold on her was too strong. At the end of the alley, she saw a White man in a sharp tweed suit waiting for her. He leaned casually against a closed dumpster, smoking a cigarette. In the darkness, the soft orange glow whenever he took a drag was the only light.

"Apologies for the nasty business, Mrs Russo, but I was hoping to have a word with you."

The person who had grabbed her pushed her forward slightly, pulling her purse from her shoulder as they did so. She cursed herself again for not keeping her gun in her pocket.

"Who are you?"

"My name is Kenneth Russell. I'm an investigator with the District Attorney's office."

"What do you want?" Cynthia squinted through the darkness, but she couldn't get a clear view of the man's face.

"Congratulations on your wedding. Though, seeing as you're still married to Derrick Wayland, it's just for show."

Cynthia said nothing. She stood up straight, holding her head high. Fear was twisting in her gut, but she wasn't going to show it outwardly.

"That husband of yours is a piece of work. Hard to pin down."

He was trying to engage her in conversation, perhaps to see if she would let something slip, but all he would get from her was stoney silence.

"But we're closing in," he went on with a sigh. "I've come to offer you a deal. You pass information to me and my agents and when we come knocking on your door and believe me, we will. You won't serve any jail time."

"You have nothing, or you wouldn't need a snitch. And when you knock on my door, if that day ever comes, you'll be met with two law-abiding citizens and you can't prove otherwise."

"We'll see." She could hear the smile in his voice. "Take some time. Think about it. I'm offering you an out. I'll find you in a few days. Tell me your answer then."

"You won't find me."

With a confidence she didn't feel, Cynthia turned away from Russell and strode from the alley. She had to force herself not to run. Walking at a smart pace, she made her way to Deco, but she didn't breathe easy until she stepped inside and saw Vinny waiting for her at their favourite table.

"Are you all right?" he said as she sat down. He must have seen how flustered she was.

Quickly and quietly, she recounted her meeting with Kenneth Russell.

"Don't worry about it," he said, waving an airy hand. "Our operation is airtight. He's fishing. If he had anything on us, he would have come after me. Not you."

"Are you sure?" There was something in his face that made her suspect he wasn't telling her the whole truth.

"Of course."

"You promised never to lie to me. We're a team."

"One of our boys is missing. He was on a routine scout and he hasn't reported back."

"Do you think the DA's office has him?"

"Better that than one of our rivals."

"What was he doing?"

"Looking into augmentations. Word is they'll be big game soon. There was no job to go wrong, which means he's just been nabbed. The other boys are looking for him, but that's enough shop talk. It's date night. It's supposed to be about us."

"Are we moving into augmentations, or were you thinking for yourself?"

Vinny sighed exaggeratedly, but it was clear he wasn't really annoyed. "Just something I'm investigating. Might not be worth it."

"Would you ever consider it?" she asked, moving away from business talk.

"Would you?"

"I don't know. Not everyone, not even most people, but some people look and I wish they wouldn't." She touched her remaining hand to her prosthesis absently.

"I have appearances to keep up." Vinny indicated his eye. "But if you didn't like it, if you wanted me to, I'd get it fixed."

"I love you the way you are. Do you wish I had two hands for you to hold?"

"The thought never crossed my mind."

PARTNERS

Walt and Fen had been working in silence for hours. Guilt and anger were clouding his mind, and he was finding it hard to concentrate on the sketchbooks he was examining.

"You've been staring at that drawing for nearly twenty minutes."

"It's really good," Walt said, setting the picture aside.

"Do you wanna talk about it?" Fen asked.

"About what?" he replied distractedly.

"Bastion."

"No, thanks. It's a very long story."

"We've got time."

Walt sighed and shook his head, then picked up another sketch book.

"It's okay, you can talk to me. I won't think it means anything. I know we're over."

"I don't," Walt said, making eye contact for the first time. "I'm angry, I have a right to be, but..." He let the sentence hang, unsure of how it was supposed to end.

Fen closed the book she was holding and reached for another.

"We don't really know each other. That occurred to me today. I know I lied to you and I'm sorry. I hope you'll let me make it up to you. But I realised I don't know you. Not the way I want to because you don't let me in."

"Let you in? I've never lied to you."

"No, you don't lie. You just don't talk."

"What aren't I saying?"

"You're open about the here and the now, but whenever I ask about your past, you shut down."

"What d'you wanna know?

"What happened between you and Thea?"

"No," he said bluntly.

"You said you were partners."

"We were."

"You talk to all your old colleagues like that?"

"Drop it."

"See!"

"I told you I'm divorced. I told you I'm an alcoholic. What else is there?"

"Why did you get divorced?"

"It's complicated."

"That's not an answer. You know about my parents and my exes, my hobbies. I know nothing. Did you fall out of love? Did she cheat on you? Did you have an affair?"

"Yes." Walt almost growled the word.

"I never thought of you as a cheater." Her eyes widened in surprise, but Walt couldn't tell if it was that he'd answered the question or what he had admitted in doing so.

"Neither did I," he said blandly.

"Why did you drink? Why did you stop? How long were you and Thea together? Don't look at me like that. It's obvious you two have history."

"What's the point of all these questions?"

"On the surface, you seem open and honest, but I'm a journalist; I can tell that you're hiding something."

"Is that why you didn't get rid of the tap?"

"It's part of it."

"What could I possibly be hiding from you? You've had access to everything."

"You're the mystery guy and I like that, but I have fallen in love with you. If we stand any chance of making this work, I need to know it's real."

"It's real. I have things in my past I don't want to talk about. Things I'm ashamed of. I love you, but I haven't forgiven you and I don't know if I'll be able to. If we find a way back to each other..." he let the sentence hang, not wanting to make promises he wouldn't keep. How would he ever be able to explain Thea? How could he tell Fen how he had murdered a man and nearly hanged for it? How would she look at him when she learned who he was three years ago? If she saw the coward and the cheater, the addict, and the liar.

"Boss?"

Sid's voice in the main studio sent a wave of green anger through Walt. The feeling had nothing to do with his conversation with Fen and that was another problem.

"What?" Walt called, making his way out to meet Sid.

As Sid gave Walt his report, jealousy unfurled, unbidden, in his chest. Unwanted, but undeniable.

"I'm going to head back out to help the CPD, unless you need me here?" Walt had only half-hearted what Sid had said about the bombings in the city.

"Sure, but before you go," Walt hesitated, his better nature fighting against his worst. "We're working a case here. It's unprofessional to start a romantic relationship with a colleague in a partner agency."

"Are you saying I need to stop dating Thea?" Sid looked genuinely surprised.

Walt folded his arms over his chest. “Until the case is over, yes.”

It was a petty, small thing to have done and yet, it soothed the newly awakened monster in his chest.

Looking crestfallen, Sid nodded and left. When Walt turned away from the door and saw Fen watching him. She must have followed him unnoticed into the studio proper. She had a look on her face that told him she had heard what he had done and that it had confirmed her suspicions about Walt and his former partner.

“It’s not what you think.” That was the first real lie he’d told her.

“I found more sketchbooks. Let’s get back to work.”

CARE(FUL)

Marielena had spent every night since the attack on her apartment staying with Cleo. The beautiful apartment was starting to feel dangerously like home. Not only did it mean that she and Cleo were able to spend more time together, but it was free from reminders of Torrez.

Marielena didn't feel like she had to earn her keep, but that didn't stop her from delighting in cooking. Before her illness, she had loved to cook, and she relished it anew now that she was able to do it again.

Tonight, she had created a Mexican feast of discada, tacos, frijoles puercos, chile en nogada and aguachile. She knew it was a ridiculous amount of food, but she couldn't help herself. She had gotten carried away, and enjoyed every minute of it. They would be eating leftovers for days.

She had just finished setting the table when she heard the front door open and close.

"Mi amor," she called happily. "Dinner's ready."

"How very Agnieszka Louise of you," Cleo joked, but as she appeared in the dining room, her smile seemed a little strained.

"And yet she has a show on the kitchen network and I don't." Marielena gave Cleo a lingering kiss on the lips, then went back into the kitchen. She quickly brought out each of the dishes she had made and laid them on the table. A feast for two.

"This looks incredible. It must have taken you hours."

"Are you okay?"

"It's nothing like what's happening in Caligo, but I saw some of the violence on the streets from the Jonk on my way home. Una Anima loyalists broke into Dr Sinclair's pharmacy and beat him."

"That's awful...but there's something else, right?"

"I read your article."

"And you didn't like it?"

"No, of course I liked it. You have a gift for words and I agree with everything you said, but...it's dangerous. You're here because someone attacked you in your home. Maybe you should—"

"Stop? Keep quiet and don't draw attention to myself?" Marielena bristled.

"You're twisting my words." Cleo placed a soothing hand on hers. "I only just found you, and I don't want to lose you."

Marielena softened. "I know you're scared, so am I, but augmentations changed my life. We wouldn't be together if I hadn't got my implant."

"Yes, we would," Cleo contradicted with a small smile.

"Maybe we would. But that doesn't change the fact that augmentations helped me, and they help other people. The more of us who stand up and say no to this violence and bigotry, this ignorance—they can't ignore us all. We're a community. I won't censor myself out of fear."

"I don't want you to. I'm proud of you and your work, so proud. But the thought of you getting hurt scares me so much I can't bear it."

"I love you too."

PROJECTION

Thea was still in a towering rage when she returned home. Bastion was free and roaming around Caligo city and Walt had known about it. It was the last in a very long list of grievances that she had convinced herself didn't matter anymore. But if that was true, why was she so angry?

"Are you okay?" Torrez asked from the kitchen where he had been making a coffee, unnoticed by Thea, so consumed as she was in her thoughts of Walt, Bastion, Cora and Tenebrium.

"Is Cora here?" she asked roughly, throwing her jacket on the nearest chair.

"You're bleeding!" Torrez rushed out of the kitchen to inspect the damage.

Thea was sure she looked awful, but she didn't care. "There was an explosion," she muttered absently.

"Querida, you need to sit down and tell me what happened. Have you seen a doctor?"

Thea ignored him as she continued to pace, too wired to slow down.

"Querida." Torrez grabbed her by the shoulders. "Sit." He guided her gently but firmly to the couch. She sat reluctantly. "What happened?" he pressed. It was rare to see Torrez so serious, and it was perhaps this that allowed her to gather her thoughts.

"Is Cora here?" she said slowly and clearly.

"No, she's still at work. You're worrying me."

"The bombings in the city, they're anti-aug. But the violence and chaos are so widespread now, we have no idea what could be hit next. So, my team and others like it have been evacuating potential targets before anyone could be hurt. I went to the Tiernan Clinic, and it was hit. I got everyone out just before the bomb went off, but I got caught in an aftershock. I hit my head, but I'm fine. Woozy, but fine."

"I'm glad you're safe." Torrez pulled her into a hug, but he must have been able to feel the tension in her body, because he said, "That's not all, is it?"

"Bastion was there."

"He's supposed to be in jail."

"He escaped. Over a year ago."

"Does Walt know?"

"That's where I just came from. He knew, and he didn't try to find him. He didn't call to warn me or Cora."

"Hijo de puta."

"Cora is still messed up over Bastion. Walt knew he was out and did nothing."

There was a charged silence. Thea was mad at everyone, mad at Torrez, though she had no reason to be. He was and had always been the one person she could count on. Seeing Bastion had been like stepping back into the past. It had brought back old memories and unsealed old wounds, or perhaps it had just reminded her they were still there, ignored, but unhealed, nonetheless.

"I'm due back out in the field in six hours. I'm going to shower and go to sleep. I'm just tired."

"Are you sure you don't need Medicus?"

"I'm sure. I'm fine, Drew." She squeezed his hand and stood.

"Thea," he called just as she got to the door of her bedroom. His tone was hesitant.

"Don't start," Thea said on a long exhale. Tiredness had fully taken hold now, bringing with it a dull headache.

"This isn't starting. Walt is an asshole. But he's always been an asshole, and you've always loved him, anyway. You still do. It's why none of your dates have amounted to more. The spark between you two is obvious. Be pissed, feel your feelings, give him what for and then—"

"Do you really not get it?"

"I get you're scared, but I don't understand why."

"Walt is an all-consuming fire that will burn your life to the ground if you let it. But he didn't just burn me. He destroyed me. We destroyed each other. We left each other's lives in ruins. He killed my father—"

"I know you don't blame him for that."

"Being with him made me question everything. It changed me in ways I hate. I compromised everything—my morals, my beliefs because I was so desperate to be with him. There is nothing I want less than to go back to being the person I was when I was with him. I lied, I cheated, I hurt people, I crossed lines that can't be uncrossed."

"Cleo forgave you."

"That's not the point. I closed that door, and I'm finally back on my feet. I've put myself back together. I have a job that I love and a place in this city that makes me feel like I have purpose again, like I might actually be one of the good guys. I'm happy."

"You don't seem it right now."

"Being happy isn't about being happy all the time. I've had a long, hard day. I get to be sad. That doesn't mean I'll be sad forever."

"All I want is for you to be happy. You seem lonely."

"I'm not lonely. And I'm definitely not lonely because I'm single. You're a romantic and I know you're struggling with losing Marielena and now Joseph and I'm sorry but stop projecting your problems onto me."

"Call me whatever you like. Romantic. Childish. An idiot. What if he is the love of your life?"

"Can you hear yourself?"

"What if you're missing your chance?" There was a desperation to his words.

"I mean it, Drew. Stop. You want some unfiltered truth? This is about Marielena, and we both know it. You didn't miss your shot. You treated her badly and you're going to have to come to terms with that. She's moved on. You have to, too. Stop torturing yourself with what ifs. I am not the one who's sad and I am not the one who's lonely." She may have been in the right, but she had gone too far and she knew it.

"You don't get to talk to me about Marielena. Not after you lied about her and Cleo. You are supposed to be loyal to me first. You want to bust Walt's balls over Bastion? You're no better. You should have told me."

"Oh, well, I'm sorry. You forgot to tell me that you got me in the divorce. And it's not the same, not even close."

Torrez ignored the jibe. "And I broke up with Joseph because you told me to. If I'm lonely it's because of you. We were happy."

Thea let out an angry sort of exhale. "No, you weren't! And you'll never be happy until you let go of Marielena. Grow up, learn from your mistakes and move on."

"You haven't. Or you wouldn't be so angry."

"I'm not you. Stop projecting your insecurities onto me. It hurts me. Okay? It hurts me."

"You never get over the ones who break you."

"I'm not having this conversation again."

Thea left a watery-eyed Torrez and got into the shower. When her head finally hit the pillow, it was a while before she could quiet her mind enough to sleep, and all too soon, it was time to go back to work.

WITHOUT A TRACE

In the days that followed, Thea had little time to worry about Torrez, Walt, or Bastion. Seemingly scared into hiding by the large ARC and CPD presence, there was no trace of The Soulful Elite and no further bombings. There was, however, still a large amount of tension and plenty of small and violent outbursts to keep Thea and her team busy.

Things were neither simple nor easy at the re-homing centres, either. Conditions in the centres were excellent. Thea and Alex had gone to great lengths to ensure it was so, but it wasn't home and it wasn't permanent. Some were afraid to leave, as the conditions waiting for them were invariably worse. Some were starting to wonder if the centres were a palatable precursor to camps, and that at some point in the not-too-distant future, they would stop being optional. Thea, for her part, didn't blame anyone for subscribing to either school of thought. The centres would last while the threat did, but they wouldn't be funded forever. There was the very real chance that the establishment could withdraw funding at any point and those who desperately needed the shelter they provided would be abandoned. She also didn't think it was too far of a stretch to think that they might be turned to a nefarious purpose if the chance arose. All she could do was try her best to ensure neither worst-case scenario happened. For now, while the threat of more bombings was very real, for better or worse, the centres were needed.

It was nearly a week later when Thea had her first bit of free time. She and her team had all but been forced by AD Castillo to take a couple of days off to recuperate from the constant field missions. He was right that they needed a break, but it didn't mean Thea was going to take one.

Away from the front lines of the tensions in the city, she took the opportunity to search for Bastion. She felt guilty having not yet told Cora that he was free, but she was worried about what it would do to her sister. To anyone who wasn't in her inner circle, Cora seemed completely recovered from her ordeal in Tenebrium.

When she laughed and joked, worked and performed her day-to-day duties with an easy sort of grace, it was almost too easy to forget that she suffered from nightmares and significant PTSD. She was coping heroically, but it didn't mean that she couldn't backslide if the right pressures were exerted and it was this Thea feared most. She would never forget the frightened child that Cora had regressed to while in the psychiatric ward, prone to bouts of childlike wonder and dark anger. It was this memory that eased her heavy conscience.

Thea had kept her inquiries about Bastion subtle. He could have gone underground and joined with a criminal element, but she thought it more likely he was hiding amongst the augmented community. From what she had gathered from speaking to the former residents of Tiernan, he was well-liked and well-respected. Someone they trusted and turned to when they needed help. This didn't surprise her. Bastion had been Walt's best friend, more like a brother and someone she would have described as open and honest, reliable, until his true nature had been revealed. She would have loved to believe he had turned over a new leaf, but a cynicism born and raised in Tenebrium City made her doubt it.

And so what if he had turned over a new leaf? Repented his cultish and murderous ways. Did that mean that he had a clean slate? That he got to walk free while his victims and their families had to deal with the aftermath? Thea believed in rehabilitation, but there was a part of her, somewhere between her love for her sister and her own wounded pride that wanted to see him punished. It was a thought she struggled with and one that made her feel shame. After all, prison wasn't supposed to be punishment; it was supposed to keep those on the outside safe while reforming those within. Could a cult following murderer be redeemed? The cycle of questions in her mind was endless.

She walked through the unofficial augmented district. It was just a street in The Entertainment District that happened to have exclusively aug-owned businesses along it. It was a safe space and a haven of sorts. Today, however, it was barren. Shutters were down and businesses were closed. She would find no answers here. And even if she did find someone to speak to, would they tell her anything? The last couple weeks had gone some small way to redeeming the reputation of ARC with the augmented community, but quite rightly, many were still suspicious and many more were outright hostile.

As she turned out of the street, pondering where next to take her investigations, she wasn't at all surprised to see Walt walking towards her. He had been calling her for days, but she had ignored him. Any official lines of investigation were to be funnelled through Castillo, which gave her the perfect excuse to avoid him. She couldn't avoid him now unless she planned to turn on her heel and run.

"I'm sorry," he said when they were about five feet apart in the deserted street, surrounded by towering buildings.

"Are you? I don't even know why I was surprised."

"I should have told you."

"Yeah, you should." This was one of the moments she feared: when it was just her and him, and nothing but his empty apologies; she had fallen for it so many times before. Walt said nothing, however. He just waited, as if expecting her to say something more. "What?" she said, a little sharply.

"I hate that you think I haven't changed." He took a step towards her.

"My opinion shouldn't matter to you anymore." She stepped back.

"Don't bullshit with me. You know it matters. You saw me at my worst, at my lowest, and you know how much I hated who I became. I'm not the guy I was when we first met, but I'm not the guy I was when you left, either. I fought damn hard to get sober, to be better and I am. I'm reliable. I do my job. I'm the Police Captain, for fuck's sake. I'm steady." He was almost challenging her to disagree.

"If you really are all better now, why does it matter what I think?"

"Because you know me, just like I know you."

"But you don't know me. Not anymore. You don't know anything about me or my life—"

"You left!"

"Three years. Three years and the first thing you did was lie to me."

"That's not fair. What was I supposed to say? Hey, nice to see you. Thanks for ditching me without so much as a word, oh and by the way—Bastion's out."

"You're unbelievable."

"Thea—"

"He slept with her while he held her captive. Did you know that? He slept with her while he was sleeping with me."

Walt paled. "I didn't know."

"Cora thinks she was in love with him, but I think he's not capable of it. He took advantage of her at best. He tried to kill me, he tried to kill you. He kidnapped Cleo. He was part of the cult that nearly razed Tenebrium to the ground."

"After you left—"

"Don't you dare try to pin this on me."

"Cleo was gone. You were gone, and I was struggling to stay sober. I was alone. He was the closest thing to family I had left. It was stupid, but he did help people. If I had known about Cora—"

"You wouldn't have done anything differently," Thea said, holding up a hand. A call had come through her Cicada, and worried that there had been another bombing, she answered. But it wasn't work.

"Sid?" She was surprised he had called. She had tried to contact him, but he was ignoring her much as she had been Walt.

She looked up at Walt, who was still standing in front of her, frozen.

"I've been ignoring you." Sid sounded guilty and a little flustered.

"I've noticed."

"I'm sorry, it was just...I didn't want to but...The captain told me to stop seeing you. He said that it's unprofessional to date someone at a cooperating agency while we're still working on a case. It makes for conflicts of interest that can have evidence thrown out, but I like you. I don't want to end things."

"Is that what he said?" She was looking Walt directly in the eyes. His expression told her he knew exactly what Sid was saying.

"He's right. We have to stop seeing each other until the case is over, but afterwards we can do whatever we—" But Thea didn't hear the end of the sentence; she hung up and rounded on Walt.

"You're pathetic," she spat at him. "I can't believe you. You get to move on, but I don't? You have Fen and I'm supposed to have no one?"

"Is Sid the new love of your life?" He sneered.

"Oh, fuck you."

"Why don't you care?"

"Excuse me?" She didn't understand.

"About Fen. You aren't fazed. I'm not—I don't still—I tell you I love someone...I would care. I would feel something."

"You've always had someone else, or are you forgetting Cleo? You were never mine, but you seem damn intent on making sure I'm never anyone else's. If you really love her—"

"Don't. You don't get to go there. I love her." His voice was fierce.

"Then why are you here? Go be happy, go fix your relationship and leave me alone. I'm over it. You should be too."

"Why did you come back? My life was going great without you—and then you appear, and everything falls apart."

"You were pissed I left and now you're pissed that I came back?"

"You...I've moved on, I love Fen but..."

"If I can't have you, no one can?"

"No, of course not. I want you to be happy. I just didn't expect..."

"It's the addict in you. It's making you think you want things you don't. You still think that you can do whatever you want and a simple 'sorry' will make it okay. You used to do it with 'I love you'. You would say it like it fixed everything. Because you think it's enough. Because you're still arrogant. Because you think being a drunk was your only problem. Because you're you. Congratulations, you're the hero again. Everyone's favourite captain and you think that being the good guy makes up for all the shitty little things you do to get there. Well, it doesn't. You aren't the hero in my story, and if you had any respect for me, you would have stayed out of my personal life. You haven't changed, but I have. Go home. Tenebrium needs you. I don't."

She had meant to hurt him, and it had worked. The look on his face made that clear. She was glad he had no retort. She just left him standing there wishing, not for the first time, that it would be the last time she saw him.

THE PAST

Ten years ago...

The oppressive weight of Vinny's body on top of hers made the pleasure more acute. Every thrust he made drew a moan from her lips. Cynthia curled her fingers around the bars of the headboard and wrapped her legs tightly around his waist, pulling him deeper.

Vinny's face was buried in her wet hair, his forehead resting on her shoulder, but it didn't muffle the sound of her name as it rolled off his tongue like a prayer.

They had started the seduction in the large bathtub; it was Cynthia's favourite place to conduct their passionate trysts. It reminded her of the first time; when they had both given in. Acquiesced to each other and how they hadn't been apart since. The bath oil still clung to their skin, making it smooth and slick. She could get lost in Vinny forever.

He cried out her name one last time, and she followed him over the edge into a bliss so complete she never wanted it to end.

Breathing heavily, he let his full weight press down upon her for only a moment before he rolled onto his side and pulled her in close. He nuzzled her neck with sweet kisses.

"Again," Cynthia said.

"You're insatiable." He laughed in a low rumble, his breathing still not back to normal. "I'll need a minute or two. How about I run us another bath and we see where the night takes us?"

"Yes." She kissed him fiercely and deeply.

"Yes." He repeated with a sated smile. He pressed his lips to her forehead, then got to his feet. She drank in his body as if it was the first time she had seen it. Cynthia was certain she would never tire of looking at it. At him.

A loud, melodic chime brought an irritated grunt to Vinny's lips. The doorbell had been rung. "Who the hell is calling at this hour?"

"Whoever it is can wait. We're busy."

Vinny smiled, but picked his boxers up from the floor and slipped them on, nonetheless. She watched with an exaggerated pout as he made his way out onto the landing, closing the door behind him.

Minutes ticked by and Cynthia was starting to worry that Vinny wouldn't be coming back anytime soon, having been drawn into some kind of business. As the afterglow faded and she started to feel the chill in the air, she sighed and covered her naked body with a silk dressing gown, resigning herself to the fact that date night was over.

She was idly browsing her shelves for a book to occupy her time when she heard the first shot. It was quickly followed by several more. Then there were shouts and yells, thunderous footsteps and then nothing.

Cynthia froze for a fraction of a second, then dived for the dresser. She pulled a pistol from inside and was about to rush from the room when the door was thrown open. Vinny was standing there, blood pouring from a bullet wound in his upper chest near his left shoulder.

"Vin! Are you all right?"

He disregarded the question. "They're here. They've come at last."

"The Kellys?"

"The pigs. The idiots watching the doors opened fire. There's at least one dead cop downstairs and they are coming for blood. There's no getting out of this now. I'm going away."

"No!" Cynthia shrieked. "No. I am not finished with you yet. You don't get to leave me."

"I don't want to. I would do anything not to have to, but it's the end of the road, baby."

"We shoot our way out. We go on the run. I don't need an empire, I just need you." She pulled on a pair of trousers.

"There's too many of them and I'm not risking your life. I won't do it."

"This can't be our end." Tears fell unbidden down her cheeks. She wiped them roughly away.

"It isn't, it's just mine."

"No," she spat. "I won't do it."

"We talked about this. You promised."

"I won't betray you."

"You aren't. They have me dead to rights. We knew this day would come and now they can add cop killer to the bill. I'm going down, but I refuse to take you with me."

"They'll get nothing from me."

"Baby. Cynthia," he implored. "You promised me on the life of your son."

"I can't," she sobbed, but they both knew she would.

"Save yourself. Tell them everything you know in return for your freedom. Make a deal. Be free. Go find your son. Be happy."

"There is no happy without you."

There were more shots, but they sounded closer now.

"I love you." She could barely get the words out.

"This was the best dream." He grabbed her and dragged her into his arms, kissing her like he knew he would never see her again.

The shots were right outside the door, and Cynthia could hear what was being shouted now.

"TPD, put down your weapons and surrender! Come out with your hands up."

"I gotta go, baby."

She dug her nails into his arms, trying to hold him in place, but she could have no more stopped him than she could a wave. He wrestled himself gently free, and she collapsed to the floor.

"I love you." He gave her one final look, as if he was trying to burn her face into his memory, then raised his hands and walked towards the landing. "All right! All right. That's enough boys. Put down your guns. I'm coming out. I surrender."

Cynthia pulled herself to her feet and staggered, distraught, to the landing. She peered over, her vision blurred by tears, and watched in a haze as Vinny, still bleeding and wearing only a pair of monogrammed boxers, was handcuffed and escorted out through the front doors.

"Mrs Russo."

Cynthia jumped. She hadn't noticed Kenneth Russell standing as he had in the alleyway, leaning against a wall and smoking. He looked entirely unruffled. She could see him properly now. He was handsome in a roguish sort of way, but more than this, he was smug. Everything from his sharp eyes to his subtle smile made her want to claw his face off.

"You did this," she spat. She wasn't stupid enough to attack him, but it took all she had not to.

"Are you ready to talk? I bet you've got some stories."

The next morning the papers read, 'Gangster's Moll Tells All!'

DAWNING

Walt sat alone in his hotel room, staring at the minibar. No matter how hard he tried to forget it was there, his eyes somehow found it.

Guilt had always been the driving force behind his desire to drink and he was currently steeped in it. The urge to drink, to lose himself at the bottom of a bottle, was stronger than it had been in years. He wouldn't drink, but that tantalising notion he could was enough to drive him crazy. It would be so easy to walk the five steps over to the small fridge; to open the door and grab every one of the tiny little bottles hidden inside. He wouldn't drink, but he could. Walt took perverse pleasure in his own discomfort.

His lie of omission about Bastion was one thing, but what he had done to Sid was petty and small. Bad habits had abounded since he had stepped out of that lift and seen Thea again. Was she right? Was she so intertwined with his alcoholism that it was playing tricks on him, or was the burning in his chest something completely different?

He loved Fen. He knew it. The thought of her made him smile. Her proximity made his skin tingle. He had been terrified when he had thought he might lose her. But then, he felt all those things about Thea, too. He had pretended he didn't, locked the memories of her in a tiny box inside his head. He had gotten so good at not thinking about her that he had almost convinced himself he didn't care about her anymore, but he couldn't pretend now as he sat contemplating giving in to the addict inside.

It dawned on him dully that it was possible to be in love with two people at once. He had always thought that was for people like Torrez, not him, not someone steady. But then again, he had never imagined himself a cheater or a drunk, and he was undeniably both.

He had been a fool, thinking he could be around Thea and not feel anything. He didn't know how to deal with this new revelation. There was no choice to be made. She had left him and made it clear they were over. Walt and Thea, as a couple, was a thing of the past.

He loved Fen, but he wasn't sure if he could forgive her. Perhaps alone was how he should remain.

His love life was in tatters with no solution in sight, but one thing he did know was that he wasn't going back to Tenebrium and abandoning the case. The Zealot had made it personal when he attacked Fen, and Walt, having an augmentation himself, wasn't about to leave the community to its fate.

Purpose was the only thing that allowed him to get to his feet and walk past the minibar without opening it.

MOTHER DEAREST

As Thea stood on the doorstep of the beautiful townhouse, she wished more than anything that she and her mother had a better relationship. She would have loved to be able to tell Athena about her worries and fears, and seek comfort as she had been able to in the past, but what was broken between them couldn't easily be repaired.

It was odd to think that after her husband's death, Athena had followed Cora and Thea to Caligo, to be closer to her daughters. Thea could count on one hand the number of times she had seen her mother in the last three years.

Athena gave a little start when she opened her door and saw that it was Thea who had come to call.

"Can I come in?" Thea asked when her mother just stared at her, her mouth slightly slack.

"No," Athena said quickly, but she seemed to regret it.

"Fine. Shall we sit?" Thea indicated the wicker bench under the front window. She didn't wait for an answer this time. She walked resolutely over to it and sat. Athena followed slowly behind.

"I'm glad you came." Thea was surprised to see that her mother's eyes were overbright.

"Cora needs her mother."

"And you?"

"Not for a while now."

Athena nodded sadly. "Is Cora all right?"

"Do you remember Bastion?"

"Hardly a man I could forget."

"He isn't in jail. He hasn't been for nearly two years. He escaped, and he's here in Caligo."

"Does Cora know?"

"No. I was hoping you'd be there when I tell her. She'll want her mom."

"All right."

"She's on her way home now. I have a transporter waiting, unless you want to travel separately?"

"No, I'd like that."

The Jonk ride to the apartment Thea shared with her sister was predictably silent. It was probably for the best, Thea reasoned. Any conversations attempted with her mother usually led to arguments. All too soon, they were arriving at the Jonk dock in her building. Thea had no desire to prolong her time alone with her mother, but the prospect of telling her sister something that might shatter her delicate recovery was far less appealing still.

"Should we call her therapist?" Athena asked quietly as they walked down the corridor outside the apartment.

"That would be an invasion of her privacy. If she wants them, she'll call."

"What if she has another break?"

"She won't," Thea said firmly, trying to convince herself as much as her mother.

Cora was in the kitchen when they arrived, humming a jaunty tune as she stirred a pot of chilli. Torrez, an apron on top of his shirt, was chopping vegetables next to her.

"I have never heard that song in my life," he said with a laugh.

Cora continued to hum. "Sure you have. It's in all those adverts for that hair regrowth stuff."

"Nope, still drawing a blank."

"Thea," she said upon spotting her twin. "You've heard—Mom?" she looked in shock from Thea to Athena. "Did hell freeze over?"

"I'm going to go...somewhere else," Torrez said, grabbing a glass of wine from the counter and making a swift exit. Thea could hardly blame him. They hadn't addressed the argument they'd had and a family feud was something no bystander wanted to get caught up in.

"Should we move this to the living room?" Athena asked.

"Okay," Cora said, her brows knitted with suspicion. "What's going on? What's happened? You're both looking at me like I'm a bomb."

"It's Bastion."

"Thea!" her mother chastised.

"What about him?" There was something off about Cora's demeanour.

"He's here," Thea said simply.

"I know." Cora said with equal simplicity.

Thea's brain had a sort of short. It took her a moment to process what her sister was saying. "What?"

"Looks like we didn't need Mom here after all. I'm not going to flip out or crumble."

"Cora, I don't understand," Athena said, voicing what Thea felt.

"My therapist said that I had unresolved issues around my relationship with Bastion. I loved him, but it was more complicated than that. She said that knowing what happened to him might give the closure I needed. That's why I took the job at

ARC. To look for him. I found out he'd lost a leg in the fight with Walt. That he went to jail and then escaped. I tracked him to Caligo."

"You've spoken to him," Thea said. It wasn't a question.

"Don't be silly, Thea—"

"She's right, Mom, I have. We've been talking."

"Where is he?" Thea tried valiantly to keep her voice level.

"I'm not gonna tell you."

"Cora, you could be charged with harbouring a fugitive."

"By who? Are you gonna turn me in?" Thea hadn't seen this side of Cora since before her disappearance.

"If you get caught, I lose my job too. Did you even think about that?"

"I'm sorry, but I won't tell you."

"He kidnapped you; he held you against your will. He was telling you he loved you while sleeping with me. Do you see how messed up that is?"

"You're one to talk. You were sleeping with him to get back at Walt."

"No, I really wasn't. And what does that have to do with anything? He killed people, Cora. He had a hand in Dad's death. He tried to kill me."

"He's changed."

"They never change."

"He has. He helps people now."

"That doesn't matter, even if he has—he killed people. A lot of people. He was sentenced to life in prison. He should serve that sentence." Thea turned from Cora and raised her hand to her Cicada.

"Who are you calling?" Cora demanded trying to pull Thea's hand away.

"Walt."

Athena let out a scoff that sounded like a hiss. "You still turn to that man."

"Oh, unclench. He's the captain of the Tenebrium Police Department."

"They hire murderers now?" Athena asked nastily.

"Please, Thea." Cora had lost her bravado. She grabbed Thea by the forearm and squeezed. "Please, don't do this. I just need a little more time. He's helping me work through things. You can turn him in, but just not yet."

"You don't know what you're asking."

"I do and it's awful and unfair and I'm sorry. I know I should hate him for what he did in Tenebrium, for what he did to you, but I don't. I just don't. I don't feel like his victim. He was the only thing that kept me sane. My problems came from the Morpheus chip, not my time with him."

"He held you captive."

"He never locked the door."

A horrible numbness came over Thea. "You could have left?" Cora nodded, and Thea felt her heart evaporate in her chest. "I searched for you for two years. I was the only one."

"I knew that there would be consequences for us all if I left. The Gold Legion was powerful. I stayed to keep us all safe, to protect us, and I fell in love."

"You could have let me know you were alive. Mom held a memorial," Thea said, reminding herself that Athena was there. She turned to her. She was standing with her arms wrapped around herself, silent tears streaking her face.

"I'm sorry. I had no choice. Bastion is as much a victim as I am."

"The hell he is."

"Please Thea, I have never asked you for anything."

"I can't just forget."

"You've spent our lives saving me from myself—"

"I thought we were past that."

"We are. I'm all put back together now, but there is one missing piece. I need to untangle my thoughts about Bastion, and I can't do that without him. Please, Thea. I'm begging you. For me, please." Cora's watery eyes met Thea's. It was like looking into a mirror and yet Thea saw nothing of herself in her twin. Outwardly, they were identical, but inwardly, they were built completely differently. "Please," Cora said again.

There wasn't another person in the world who could have made such a request of Thea. Cora wasn't anyone, though. She was the one person Thea couldn't live without.

"Fine. I won't tell anyone, but when you're done with him, and I need you to promise me, you will be done with him, convince him to turn himself in."

"I promise. I will. He will."

A pervasive sense of unease was unfurling in Thea's stomach. This was a bad call, the wrong choice, and she knew it. She had just read Walt the riot act for doing the same thing. This was wrong, but she couldn't bear to cause her sister more pain.

"I need...to...go." Athena said shakily. She turned on her heel and left the apartment. Neither Thea nor her sister tried to stop her.

"Do you think she'll ever forgive me?" Cora asked her twin.

"I don't know."

"Will you?"

WHERE DO WE GO FROM HERE?

The streets of Caligo would bear the scars of the anti-aug rebellion for some years to come. It was still ongoing, with violent attacks occurring on a daily basis, but it was only one of the many worries that plagued Thea's mind.

She hadn't heard so much as a whisper about The Zealot since she and Walt had rescued Fen, but the silence was unsettling. Serial killers were known to disappear, but having met him, she would have bet money that he was on a path to escalation. This meant that either he was going to kill soon, or he already had, and they hadn't found the victim yet. Neither thought was comforting.

There was only one thing to do when an investigator hit a wall in their investigation: go back to the beginning and examine everything for missed clues. Thea summoned everyone who had been involved in the case so far to The Orchard.

The meeting room she had reserved was comfortable and private. It had dark carpets and wood-panelled walls. It looked much more like the TPD she was used to than the usual metal, glass, and stone of ARC HQ.

The first to join her at the long, glossy table was Sid.

"I was hoping we'd get a chance to talk," he said, sitting down opposite.

"It's fine. We don't need to."

"But I want to. I know this is new and that a couple of kisses aren't a promise of anything more, but I like you. I really like you. And once the case is done, I'd like to pick up where we left off."

"This had nothing to do with the case. I bet there are plenty of couples in your precinct back home. I used to date Walt. That's why he said what he said. Your captain is petty."

Sid's face fell ever so slightly. "I never knew...was it serious?"

"Yes. Very. And now it's very done. But you work with him—for him. You're friends. There is too much history. It's a bad idea."

"I'm not asking for any kind of commitment. I just...I'd like to date you. I'd like to keep dating you when this is over."

"It's too complicated. I like you too, but there is no 'after the case' for us."

"If I ask again, I'm pushing, and I don't want to be that guy, but this sucks."

"Look, this isn't the time. Maybe we can talk after..."

"It's okay. You don't have to."

Sid looked more upset than Thea had expected. She didn't have long to linger on what might have been, however. Torrez and Alex joined them moments later, followed by Walt himself. Putting their personal baggage aside, Thea had called him and was glad to find he hadn't taken her up on her offer to leave Caligo and abandon the case. As Walt sat down on the other side of the table, Sid's eyes seemed to bore through him. Walt noticed.

"Are you all right?"

"Yeah, Boss. Just eager to get to work."

"All right then," Thea said before anyone could say anything else. "Thank you for coming. I know you're all busy, and we're all exhausted, but there is a serial killer out there biding his time and I want him found. I've compiled everything we have," she nodded to the files flickering on the screen behind her and the many glass tablets sitting on the table in front of them. "We're going back to the drawing board. We must have missed something. Pick a file, start reading."

"Did you hear from Zhao? About Seward's inner circle?" Walt asked, not quite meeting her eye. Both were pretending their argument had never happened.

"Yeah, that's where I'm starting. I'll run backgrounds on them all and see if anything flags."

"What about the name he gave you? Muller?"

"He has alibis. They all checked out."

Over two hours later, everyone in the room was feeling thoroughly deflated. They still had a lot of data to go through, but they hadn't uncovered anything new, and the tiredness that came from pouring over document after document was setting in.

"Has anyone found anything about Helena Cutter's husband?" Torrez said, raising his hand like he was in class.

"Uh...nope," Alex said, quickly checking through their notes. "I don't think we interviewed him."

"We didn't," Walt said, looking to Sid for confirmation. Sid shook his head.

"I don't think we did either," Thea said, quickly pulling up the communication records attached to the case. "Nope, nothing. Who did the death notification? Who claimed her body?"

"CPD called him, according to this." Alex indicated a holographic form that hung in the air in front of them. "No response."

"He was abusive," Torrez said. "They were in the process of divorcing when she went missing."

"He should have been the prime suspect." Thea turned to Walt.

"He was, but he had a solid alibi. He was in surgery. Over ten witnesses and footage from the hospital in Caligo. He wasn't in Tenebrium. We followed him for a while after too, to make sure he hadn't stashed her somewhere, but he never left the city. He never did anything other than go to work. Sad life."

"Couldn't have happened to a nicer guy," Torrez toasted the unknown Dr Cutter with his coffee. "He was a real bastard. Being alone wasn't even close to all he deserved."

"Maybe he'll be able to shed some light on Helena's life. I'll have someone track him down. There has to be a deeper link between these victims. The Zealot hates people who support augmentations, that's clear. Fen knew Ranveer, but the others..."

"We think he's augmented," Alex said, and those around the table nodded in agreement.

"I've asked Cleo to get me a list of those who have been augmented in the last twenty years, but it will take her some time," Walt said. "Those records are closely guarded. Could take the TPD years to get through all the red tape and we've asked Zhao for enough."

"That's a dangerous ask," Thea said. "Cleo's been through enough. We shouldn't involve her any more than we need to."

"Cleo?" Sid asked.

"My ex-wife."

"I didn't know you were married. Learning a lot about you today."

"Okay," Thea said, cutting through any brimming tensions. "If we go with the profile, we're looking for someone twenty-five to thirty-five, though Fen said he seemed young, and I'd agree. White, male and with an augmentation that predates Levi Seward."

"It's not much," Alex said, rubbing their hand over their short hair.

"No, but it's a start."

TEST

He didn't understand. He couldn't comprehend. He had watched Levi's speech over and over, so much so that he had every single word memorised and even so, it didn't make sense to him. Levi was his guiding light; he showed him the way. Levi couldn't be lying. It must be a trick. It wasn't possible that Una Anima was not the true path for those who sought redemption.

What if it wasn't a trick, but a test? What if Levi was testing his followers? Yes, that made more sense, he reasoned. Levi was testing their devotion. But then, why was Levi ignoring his calls? Why had he called him a freak?

He had been caught in this Ouroboros-like cycle for what felt like days. Levi couldn't have lied to him, because if Levi had lied, he would have to die.

He thought back to his life as a teenager. His father had long since sequestered himself to a life of channel surfing and booze. He wasn't abusive, but sometimes neglect and indifference were just as hurtful as a clenched fist. He had been aimless; he had no aspirations after finishing high school and hadn't known what he wanted to do with his life. That was when he had met Levi. The father figure he had always longed for. A strong man he could idolise. Levi had plans, dreams, goals and when they had met, all of those ambitions became his. Levi had given him purpose, honed him into the instrument that he was.

If he could just get in touch with Levi, he could tell him about all the things he had done for Una Anima. He could tell Levi that he was The Zealot and that he had done it all for him, for his mission, for the greater plan. Yes, that was what he would do. He would go to Levi's house and be welcomed like the prodigal son. Levi would commend him for the lengths he was willing to go to. He would congratulate him and shower him with praise, for he had truly spread the message. He had ensured that everyone saw what would happen to those who spoke false. Those who lied and preached that augmentations were nothing more than medical advancements. To those who encouraged others to damage their souls. Pedalling damnation in the name of false freedoms was the most grievous sin. To damn another was unforgivable.

It had been so long since he had spilled blood for the cause, but he wouldn't have to wait much longer. He had his eyes on a target and when the perfect moment arose, he would strike.

THE PICTURE

Fen hadn't left her studio in days. She had set up a sleeping bag in the storage space and had been having food delivered. She was determined to find the missing piece of the Zealot puzzle, and she was getting close. She had narrowed it down to fifty drawings. With every other sketch or sculpture she had identified the subject, but not these remaining few.

The CPD officers helping with the search had long since gone home for the night. Darkness pressed against the windows of the huge space, but Fen paid it, and her body's desire to sleep, no mind. She had laid the sketches out in a tiered circle with a tall ladder in the centre. It was atop that ladder that she stood, peering down at the images, willing herself to remember. The remaining sculptures had been set up in a ring around the drawings, waiting to be matched. The drawing without the sculpture would be the match. The problem was that many of the sculptures had not been completed, as they hadn't needed to be. Only the part that needed augmented would need to be sculpted. Any drawings she had done of faces had been for her.

Though they thought The Zealot was male, she couldn't sort by gender, because those in the pictures might not identify as they did when they were drawn. That didn't matter to Fen. She had far more nuanced ways of telling people apart: she had an artist's eye. It was specific facial features that she was looking for. That one beautiful something all faces have that makes them unique. If she could spot it in the drawings, it would help her remember the person and the sculpture she had created for them.

Like a hawk searching for prey, she scanned the pieces below her until finally, she saw the missing piece. There was a drawing of a young, sandy-haired boy with no accompanying sculpture. He was seven at the most. His eyes were shut like he was sleeping. He looked peaceful and content, happy and sweet even. It was hard to ratify in her mind this childlike innocence with the monster she knew he had become.

She jumped down from the ladder, spraining her ankle slightly, but she didn't care. She picked up the image and stared at it, searching for anything that might jog her memory. She hadn't dealt with many children that young. And then it hit her. He hadn't been sleeping; the boy was blind. The picture she held had been drawn for his mother, but she had never come back to collect it.

The boy had been in an accident, and she had taken a cast of his face to help the doctors install ocular implants. Expensive ones, if she remembered correctly, that would have served the boy into adult life. The mother had had a benefactor of some kind, Fen hadn't asked who – it wasn't her business. None of that mattered now. She had found The Zealot. She had finally found him. The kind-faced boy on the paper in her hands would grow up to be a killer.

DETAILS

Torrez had never been to Alex's apartment before, but it was exactly how he had imagined it. A haven for plants, with books everywhere. The couches were huge, squishy and velvet. The floors were hardwood and covered in thick, fluffy rugs.

When he had arrived, the small dining table was set for two and a delicious meal was cooking in the kitchen. It had been exquisite. And now as they sat on the couch together, glasses of wine in hand, in front of a holographic fire that Torrez was projecting using his index, he found, to his great surprise, there wasn't a place on earth he would rather be.

"I don't want to have sex tonight," Torrez said. He inwardly cursed himself. That had not come out at all as he meant.

"Has the spark gone out already?" Alex joked.

"No. Not at all. No." Torrez put his glass down on the table and turned to face Alex straight on. "This was just supposed to be a casual hook-up, and it's been great, but...well, I like you. I'd like to just talk to you, laugh with you, maybe see if we can actually be something out of the bedroom."

"This wasn't supposed to get serious...and you just broke up with someone."

"You're right. Ignore me. It's the wine!" Torrez said, hiding his disappointment. He leaned forward to try to capture Alex in a kiss. They pressed a finger to his lips, halting him in his tracks.

"This wasn't supposed to get serious, but that doesn't mean I'm not happy it might."

"Thank, God," Torrez said, relaxing with a laugh.

"I worried you for a minute there, huh?"

"Maybe a little."

"I want to take things slow. I like you, and that's enough for now, but I'm not stupid enough to be someone's rebound."

"I won't lie to you. I still have complicated feelings when it comes to my ex-wife, but I'm in this for real."

Alex turned themselves so they could rest with their back against Torrez's chest.

"What's the deal with Thea and the cop from Tenebrium?" they asked after a moment of quiet. "The Captain, I mean. Things seemed real awkward today."

Torrez snorted. "It's a long story, and it's not mine to tell."

"They were a thing, though, right? He's 'the' guy."

"Yeah, he's 'the' guy. It was big, and it was messy, and it really isn't my story to tell."

"He still loves her. That's obvious, but Tee is harder to read."

"My lips are sealed."

"She keeps things so close to the chest. I adore the dame, but it's hard to be her friend sometimes."

"No, it's not. I've never met a kinder, more loyal person in my life. She's my person. Once she loves someone, she'll fight to the death for them. She'd fight for you. I hope you know that."

"I do. It's just hard to get to know her. I tell her everything."

"What do you think you don't know? I know I've known her a lot longer, but she's pretty open."

"What's the deal with Tenebrium?"

"What's with all the questions?"

"You want to get to know me? I'm nosy. So, spill."

"We can't talk about it."

"So you were there when...whatever happened." Alex was pushing in a way that made Torrez suspicious.

"Why do you really want to know?" Torrez sat up straighter, creating some distance between them. "I used to be a detective; I know when I'm part of an interrogation."

"I just want to get to know my friends and my...special friend." They gave a flirty smile, but Torrez held his ground.

"Nice try. You want me to spill, but you're awfully cagey yourself."

"I told you, I'm nosey." The act was slipping, and they had a slightly desperate air about them.

"I have no interest in bullshit. I've dealt too much of it out not to recognise it when I see it."

Torrez clambered awkwardly out of the embrace and stood.

"Wait," Alex said, watching Torrez search for his jacket. They sounded almost panicked now.

"Why?"

"My brother died in Tenebrium." The words came out in a rush. "At Medicorum and all the files are sealed. Today should have been his thirtieth birthday, and I don't know what happened to him."

"I'm sorry." Torrez felt some of the ice forming in his chest subside.

"A creep in a bar told me Thea killed him. I hadn't met her then. She was just this faceless villain to me. When I heard she was here, I made sure to meet her. I was going to question her, but we became friends, real friends, and now I'm afraid of the answer. What if she really did kill him? Is that possible? I know there was a fight. What if he was on the wrong side? What if she was? I've been investigating. Snooping, really. Trying to find as much about what happened in those weeks as I can. Please, I have to know what happened to David."

Torrez put his hands on his hips and looked towards the door, then back to Alex. They had lied; it was true, but he understood.

"Who was he with?" Torrez said finally.

"What?"

"Gold Legion, Onyx Legion, TPD?"

"He was an Onyx Legion soldier."

Torrez nodded slowly, wondering how much he could say. "There was a coup in the city. Meticulously planned and carried out by a cult of the rich who called themselves the 'Gold Legion'. They took over the Onyx Legion and used them as foot soldiers when they waged war on the city. Thea's dad was one of them. It was real hard for her." It felt crazy to say it out loud, but it was what happened. Their city had been besieged by a cult. "People died. A lot of them. Her father included. You know about the ghouls right? That was all them. Their first attempt at eradicating the poor. It's...there is so much more to this. But the gist is, we fought—me and Thea and Walt—for our city. It was bloody and people died. The government covered it up because they didn't want the world to know that they let Tenebrium get taken over by a cult. Served us all with gag orders."

"Please, sit back down."

Torrez did as he was bidden. "It's hard to know how to explain. We all lost a lot. Thea, more than most."

"I'm sorry I lied, but I need to know."

"I'll tell you what I can, but you should talk to Thea."

"I'm afraid of what she'll say. What if he was a villain?"

CURSED KNOWLEDGE

All the ghouls that were used as test subjects had small rooms, akin to student dorms, instead of cells. They couldn't be allowed to roam freely as all were still prone to violent outbursts, but Cleo felt it was important to treat them with dignity. To treat them like the people she was trying to turn them back into.

She'd had the most progress with the ghoul she was calling 'Sarah'. Sarah said the name so often that Cleo decided it was probably hers.

Today, Cleo and Sarah were sitting in leather armchairs in a corner of her office come lab. Sarah was relaxed today, she seemed peaceful. If Cleo couldn't provide them their humanity, she could at least give them peace. That being said, she was far from giving up on a cure.

The mixture of drugs and an augmentation device similar to the M-Pulse that Marielena was fitted with had, so far, proven the most effective. Sarah had undergone the procedure four days ago and was recovering well.

"Sarah," Cleo said gently. Sarah turned to look at her serenely. "It's time for your first dose of the new formula. Do you mind if I give you an injection?"

Sarah extended her arm. Cleo hadn't restrained Sarah; she was hoping that it would no longer be necessary, but hoping for the best outcome; didn't mean she wasn't still wary.

As gently as she could, Cleo pressed the needle to Sarah's skin and depressed the plunger.

Nothing happened right away. Cleo sat back down in her chair. "Begin recording," she called in a clear voice.

"Recording," intoned the pleasant voice of the lab's mainframe.

Sarah was breathing heavily now and blinking rapidly.

"Are you all right?"

"Remembering," Sarah ground out.

"Sarah, can you tell me anything about yourself? Can you tell me your name?"

"Not Sarah. I'm not Sarah. I'm...Isobelle."

"Isobelle who?" Cleo could barely contain her excitement.

"Sarah...daughter." Isobelle let out a snarling wail and fell to the ground, her body wracked with sobs of pure desolation. "Take it away. Take them away!" she screamed.

"Take what away? What's wrong?"

"My memories, I don't want them! Take them away!" Her voice was clearer now, she seemed to truly know who she was, but she was panicked. "I remember. Make it stop, please make it stop!"

"I can't," Cleo said shakily, all excitement gone. "But the drugs will wear off."

Sarah lunged forward, the red veins so common in other ghouls, still pulsing under her wild eyes. She grabbed the front of Cleo's blouse and pulled her in so close their noses almost touched.

"I killed her. Sarah. I killed her. I took the drug and I turned, and I tore her apart. She was screaming 'Mommy, no!' the whole time but I didn't stop. I just kept tearing. I couldn't stop. I couldn't stop. Why didn't I stop? Why did you do this to me?" Sarah let out a dismal howl and slumped against Cleo; she had fainted. The return of her memories had been too much for her, as had the trauma that came with them.

Shakily, tears rolling down her face, Cleo half-carried, half-dragged Isobelle back to the armchair and placed her in it. The terrible evil she had inflicted in helping create the drug Styxx had never been more apparent and in that moment, Cleo had never felt more monstrous. The ghoul slumbering inside her was nothing compared to the woman who had destroyed so many lives.

WINNOWING

George had never been to Levi's house before; the preacher hadn't allowed it. He'd been exceptionally strict about it, saying he liked to keep his business and his personal life separate. Church and state he called it.

The house was almost a palace. It was huge to the point of excess and fit for a king. It was all glass, with very few patches of brick or metal. Ultra-modern and ultra-classy. It wasn't to his homier tastes, but it was beautiful.

George had expected there to be guards, but he could see none. Even if there were guards hidden away, he doubted they would stop a true believer.

He made his way leisurely to the front door. It was unlocked, so he let himself in. The interior was as it had appeared from the outside, a marble cavern. Music played softly emanating from the direction of the kitchen. Soft voices and the tinkling of laughter mixed in with it.

"You go to the cellar and get more wine. I'm going to take a quick shower. You better be ready for me when I get back."

Syed stepped into view. The preacher's husband was wearing pale slacks and a striped jumper. He carried a half-drunk glass of red wine in a relaxed hand. Syed didn't spot George at first. He was still looking over his shoulder towards the kitchen, but as he turned to look where he was going, he gave a small yelp of surprise.

"You," he said warily. "What're you doing here?"

"I came to speak to Levi."

"He has nothing to say to anyone from Una Anima."

"That's not for you to say. You can't keep him from me."

"I think he made himself perfectly clear in his speech. He's done with all of you. Whatever anger you feel is understandable, but you aren't going to hurt him. I won't let you."

"Why would I be angry? The speech was lies. I know he doesn't mean any of it. Someone forced him to say it. I'm here to help. To show him we are still faithful. To help him get out from under whoever is threatening him."

"George, I need you to listen, to really hear me. No one made him say it. He said it because it was the right thing to do. It's the truth. People with augmentations were getting hurt because of his preachings. He doesn't believe any of it. He doesn't have a link to God. No one does. God listens, but he does not speak."

"My God is not your God."

"No god speaks to his disciples. Yours or mine. That is why we have faith. People like you, people with augmentations, you aren't damned."

"Does the preacher know that he is living with a Judas?"

"You need to leave."

"Are you going to make me?"

"I told him we needed security," Syed mumbled to himself. "Vi," he called loudly. "Levi!"

George sprang forward. He wrestled Syed into a chokehold and dragged the man over to a slim door under the impressive staircase. Syed pulled at the arm around his throat, kicked and attempted to scream but it did no good. George had him whether he liked it or not. With one hand, he pulled open the door. As he thought, it was a small cupboard. He forced Syed in and slammed the door shut. He used a heavy end table to barricade it.

Surely the man would be calling his husband from inside; he only had moments to catch Levi.

He had been right. Less than thirty seconds later, Levi sprinted into the kitchen from what must have been a basement. Fury made his usually handsome face blotchy and contorted.

"Where is he?" he demanded. "What have you done to my husband?"

"Nothing. He's in there." George nodded towards the cupboard.

Levi went pale. "You didn't...?" He sounded scared; it didn't suit him.

"I didn't hurt him, if that's what you mean. He didn't want to let us talk so I put him in there. He's fine though. I wouldn't hurt him. I know how much he means to you."

"Open the door and let me see him. Please." George had never heard Levi sound anything other than commanding, it was unnerving to hear him sound so nervous.

"Fine." George shrugged. He shoved the table aside and opened the door. Syed was sitting with his knees to his chest. He looked shaken, but otherwise unharmed. "Happy?" George asked petulantly, closing the door back over again.

"You can't just leave him in there."

"He wouldn't let us talk, so he stays in there until we're done. If he's out here and he gets in our way...you know I can't always master my temper."

"What do you want?" It was an order. This was the Levi he had followed.

"Will you sit with me?"

"All right." There was something off about the preacher, but Geroge couldn't tell what it was.

"Lead the way."

Levi turned and made his way back into the kitchen.

But what if the preacher tried to run? As soon as the thought occurred to him, George picked up a lamp from the nearby table and brought it down on the back of Levi's head. He slumped to the ground, dazed. George picked him up in a fireman's carry and made his way into the kitchen.

The room was large enough to cook for a whole restaurant. There was a marble island in the centre that doubled as a dining table. Two places had been set at the top corner.

George set Levi down in one of the tall chairs. He was already starting to rouse. George grabbed two dish towels and tore them into strips, then quickly used them to tie Levi to the chair.

"What...do you...want?" Levi asked blearily.

"To talk. You've been avoiding me. You've abandoned your flock. Why?"

"I thought you'd all be angry with me." He gave a strained smile.

"Some are, but they aren't the true faithful. There are plenty like me who know you didn't mean what you said, and I'm going to help you show everyone that you were forced to tell those lies."

"It wasn't a lie. I did it all for money."

"No. That's not true. You are our link to God."

"I don't even believe in God. Not anymore."

"No. No. No." It felt like his brain was glitching; shorting out. He couldn't process what the preacher was saying. It didn't make any sense.

"Calm down. It's all gonna be okay."

"But I killed them for you."

"I thought it might have been you. I hoped it wasn't, but when they released the names of the victims...You killed anyone linked to your surgery as a boy. Someone will figure it out eventually."

"They are the worst kind of sinner. They say that augmentations are safe, but they are lying. They are damning anyone foolish enough to listen to them."

"They aren't lying. They aren't damned and neither were you."

"I don't believe you. You wouldn't lie to me. You rescued me from a life of damnation. You took me off the street!"

"You were an easy mark. An impressionable kid I could bend to my will. I knew I needed loyal followers if I was going to make the church work. I needed people who could convince others. That's what I saw in you."

"You're lying!" George bellowed.

"I was then, but I'm not now. You can stop this. I'll help you. Properly this time. I care about you. That wasn't a lie."

"But the church was?"

"Yes."

"They've gotten to you. Corrupted your mind. Turned you from the path but I'll help you regain your faith. I will save you from damnation."

"You're not listening to me. You can stop now. I made it all up. The whole thing."

"I'd hoped you were stronger than this, but it's okay. I'll help you find your faith again."

The excitement was starting to build up inside George. He was going to get his hands dirty for the greater good. He was a true warrior for God. The first soldier of Una Anima. He cleansed souls by spilling blood, and it was time to give the almighty another offering.

Levi seemed to see the change come over him. He had been nervous before but collected. Now he was sweating. His eyes darted all around as he struggled against his restraints.

"You don't have to do this! I've told you the truth! You're free."

"I was already free, but you have been burdened with doubts and I am going to wash them away."

"Stop, whatever you're doing. Stop!" Levi was panicking now. It excited George like nothing else in life ever could. A tiny part of him would feel shame afterwards, but right now he was savouring the moment. "You were right! I lied! They forced me to. That agent forced me to. Those with augmentations are damned and it's up to us to remind them."

"I knew it. I knew you would not desert me. But you still strayed. You let yourself be turned from the light. You need to show penance."

"I will. I will. I will kneel before God and beg his forgiveness."

"Good. Do it now. Beg for his forgiveness."

"I'm tied up."

George picked up an empty bottle of wine from the counter and brought it down on the smooth edge; it shattered into jagged pieces. He picked up the largest ones and used it to cut Levi's restraints. "On your knees now."

Levi stumbled forward and dropped down into a prayer position. "Dear God, I have failed you. I have shied away from your teachings and the link you opened before me. I beg for your forgiveness, and I pledge that should you, in your infinite wisdom, give me another chance, I will serve you with a holy vengeance like no other servant before you."

Beautiful words, George thought, but there was still blood to be paid. He grabbed Levi by the hair and wrenched his head back. He took the piece of glass that he was still holding and slipped it into his mouth. Levi began to struggle. He tried to shout but the glass was holding his tongue in place. In one swift motion, George pulled the glass to the side, slicing the left side of Levi's face from mouth to ear. Levi screamed in pain, tears streaking his face and mingling with the waterfall of blood that fell to the floor around him.

The preacher brought his hands up to try and wrestle the glass from George, but he batted Levi's hands away easily. In another swift motion, he sliced the right side of Levi's face, then stepped back to admire his work.

Levi was screaming in agony and sobbing at the same time. His jaw, barely still attached to his face. He was trying to speak but his words were too slurred to make out.

"You have paid what you owed and can rejoin the proper path."

Levi slumped forward into the pool of his own blood. It soaked his clothes as his writhing grew slower until he stilled. Perhaps George had cut too deeply. If it was Levi's time to die, that was God's will. It wasn't George's fault. It was those who tempted Levi, who forced him to lie. They would pay for Levi's death. His blood was on their hands—not George's.

He caught a glimpse of red and blue flashing lights as the police Syed had surely called arrived on the property, but they didn't see him as he slunk through the back door and off into the night.

THE STRANGE CASE OF LEVI SEWARD
By Anthony Oubier

***Author's Note**: I do not condone the things Levi Seward did, nor do I seek to once again turn him into an eidolon or a martyr, however, sinners can be just as interesting as saints. I believe that it is important to study these people and learn from their mistakes. For the avoidance of doubt, I stand firmly with the augmented community.*

A fascinating man by all standards. Complex and flawed. Greedy, amoral, cold-hearted, cruel in some ways and yet charismatic in the extreme. Levi Seward, the man who captured the heart of Caligo, is a biographer's dream, and yet his past is unclear, the official records having been destroyed by the man who killed him. The events that brought Levi Seward to the forefront of the anti-augmentation movement are shrouded in shadow and hearsay.

What I present to you here is the story of a man pieced together by talking to those who knew him. I cannot guarantee that it does not contain embellishments borne by love or hatred of that man, but I can promise that I have done my best to separate the fact from the fiction.

Levi Seward was born in Tenebrium City on May 13th, 2377, to a mother who was an engineer and a father who owned a bakery, having been removed from the priesthood. I have not been able to find any definitive answer as to why Levi Sr had his clerical status revoked, but rumours, and I have to stress that they are rumours, suggested inappropriate behaviour with members of his congregation.

According to teachers and fellow students who witnessed the young Levi Seward throughout his school career, he was a good student. Above average, certainly, but never the top of the class. He showed an aptitude for debating and was accomplished enough physically to join both the swim team and the wrestling team. He finished high school with scores that earned him a place at Tenebrium Central University.

While at TCU, Seward studied theology and marketing, taking a minor in both occultism and theatre studies. It was in his college years that he met his future husband Syed Hussain, who was attending TCU on a sociology scholarship. The soon-to-be Syed Seward would spend his post-college years as an artist and political activist.

Seward graduated with honours and began working for Tenebrium Central News as a broadcast intern. This is where the story takes a mysterious turn. Seward was fired when it was discovered that he was tapping the communication appliances of his colleagues. I have yet to find a concrete reason as to why; when I made inquiries at TCN they refused to comment. However, a close personal friend of the preacher has told me that at the TCN Christmas party there was an incident between a senior anchor and one of the other interns. A hazing of sorts that landed the intern in hospital with a life altering injury. I have been able to find records of the injury; an Emergency Room intake form of a man in his early twenties, who lost several fingers when his hand was forced into a blender in a drunken game of 'chicken' which seems to confirm their account.

Seward, my source claims, had uncovered a plot to get the intern fired and deny the incident in order to preserve the careers of those involved. He was caught snooping and fired quickly after, or so his friend claims. No charges were ever brought in relation to the incident.

After his surprising dismissal, Seward disappeared from record until 2405, when it was announced that acclaimed activist Syed Hussain had married his college sweetheart in a private ceremony.

What Seward did between 2405-2414 is hard to define. He is noted as a contributor on several of his husband's papers during that time, and held a number of short-term jobs, including a secretarial position on Senator Richard Howell's first campaign for election as Tenebrium's Mayor. To an outsider it appeared that Seward, bright and capable enough, was struggling to find his place in the world.

Friends have stated that he seemed happy; content in his role as husband to a much more acclaimed man. One thing we do know for sure is that the marriage remained strong. It wasn't until 2415 that Seward gained a small amount of notoriety in his own right, when it was reported on Church Watch that 'Disgraced Priest's Son Joins the Clergy'.

Little is known about this time. Seward didn't make waves and from what I could gather was generally well-liked by the congregation. The first whispers of his ability to elicit cult-like devotion, however, were heard in 2422 when the city of Caligo was overtaken by rumours of an underground preacher engaging groups of disenfranchised and homeless youths. Some of his earliest followers had since gone on record to say that, while he never pretended not to be a priest, his sermons tended to shy away from religion in favour of more general advice for self-betterment. He quickly gained a following online and it wasn't long before he was accepting donations. Soon after, he moved his sermons from the streets to take the format of live streams and by 2425, he was well established as a life coach.

No matter how hard I have tried, no matter how many of his inner circle I have interviewed, I cannot find a shred of evidence to explain what happened to Seward between mid-2425 and early 2426. He disappeared from public view as well-liked and forward-thinking life coach, resurfacing eight months later as the founder of an anti-aug church.

Una Anima, formed in March of 2426, was the driving force behind the anti-aug tensions that overtook the city of Caligo in 2429 and Levi Seward was the figurehead, worshipped as a god among mere men. He preached hate and intolerance all the while profiting handsomely.

I have delved into the depths of the preacher's life, leaving no stone unturned. I have spoken to anyone who had even the slightest link to the man and yet, the biggest question around his life remains unanswered.

When did the turn happen? When did a man who cared about injustice become one of the greatest perpetrators of it in the history of Caligo? What could have caused such a shocking change in attitude?

Maybe there was no change. Maybe he merely chose to stop pretending. Seward died before anyone could truly investigate his motives and as such we will never know.

What I do know is that the time Levi Seward spent at the forefront of the augmented debate was one of the darkest periods in Caligo's history. Many lives were lost and many more destroyed. If nothing else, his life and rise to power is a cautionary tale about the deification of public figures and the corrupting influence of power and wealth.

THIEF

"That can't be. It doesn't make sense."

"What doesn't make sense?" Natalia said, fear lacing her voice.

In Mateo's office, it had taken the ARCs systems less than five seconds to show Levi Seward's bank records, but they couldn't possibly be correct.

It was common knowledge that Levi Seward was swiftly approaching trillionaire status, and yet his accounts showed him to be almost destitute.

Mateo dug deeper into the accounts. In the last two months there had been a number of large withdrawals into private accounts. Either Seward was squirreling away finds to keep them safe when he was charged, or someone had beaten Mateo to the punch and stolen his funds first.

"The money is gone. Seward is broke."

"My next payment is due in a week. They will take my eyes!" Natalia burst into tears. The glassiness made her purple irises sparkle.

WAITING GAME

Walt's eyes were itching with tiredness. He had been sitting with Sid in the ARC conference room for what felt like forever with nothing to show for it. They had gone over every piece of evidence but had uncovered nothing new of note.

"We need to interview Helena Cutter's husband. He is the only lead we haven't followed but if he has nothing new to tell us..." Walt scrubbed his face with his hands.

"All we can do is wait for him to kill again and hope he leaves some clues." Sid leant back in his chair and stretched. "I hate this. I hate always showing up after. It doesn't feel like we're the good guys when we're hoping for another body."

"I owe you an apology," Walt said with a sigh.

"What?" Sid asked in surprise.

"I'm sorry for getting in between you and Thea. It was petty among other things. I'm your boss. It was unethical and unprofessional, and it won't happen again."

"Why did you?" Sid swallowed. "Do you still want her?"

Walt ran a hand through his hair. "That's a complicated question."

"And what about Fen? I thought you guys were solid."

"Also complicated."

"Never pegged you as a girl on each arm kinda guy."

"I'm not."

They lapsed into silence for a moment.

"She called it off—Thea. Said it was too messy because I work with you. You two have a lot of history, huh?"

"I'm sorry. Really."

"I have no right to, but I feel robbed. I barely know her but she...there's just something about her."

"There's just something about her," Walt repeated.

I MADE A MONSTER

Thea could hear screams as she walked up the front steps of Levi Seward's mansion. The wails were that of a man destroyed and she knew exactly where they were coming from. Syed Seward's grief at the loss of his husband drowned out the noise of the police presence.

"Agent Williams," the police officer at the door said, holding it open for her. He looked strained; it was the kind of look that an officer got when they had seen something truly terrible. "Detective Wyndham is waiting for you inside."

"Thea." Alex said by way of a greeting. They stood at the kitchen entrance, the same grim expression on their face as the others in the room.

"How bad is it?"

Alex just shook their head.

Thea had seen some gruesome things in her time, but the body of Levi Seward very nearly took the top spot. There was something personal, almost intimate about his murder. He lay prostrate on the tiled kitchen floor in a slowly darkening pool of blood. His eyes were open and staring, his jaw was hanging from his skull and his tongue lolled out to the side. As he had bled out, the preacher had scrawled a message in his own blood. It read: 'I made a monster'.

"He knew his killer." Thea said, with a tired sigh.

"This wasn't your fault," Alex said, correctly interpreting Thea's furrowed brow.

"Wasn't it? It didn't even occur to me to put a protection detail on him."

"He said it himself. The monsters he made killed him. He's responsible for countless deaths and injuries and now his own. That's not on you."

"It's not exactly justice, is it?"

"I'm sorry, but I won't weep for Levi Seward, and neither should you."

"Have you spoken to Syed?"

"I tried but...he was here when it happened. He's...in and out."

"Did he see the killer?"

"I don't know. I couldn't get anything out of him. Maybe he'll talk to you. He's in their bedroom."

Two grief officers were trying to calm Syed down when Thea entered the bedroom, but he was refusing their ministrations.

"It's all going to be okay? How? How will it be okay? Did you see what he did to my husband? You!" he screamed when he saw Thea. "You did this. You should have protected him. You should have known there would be consequences. You did this."

He was right. She should have seen this coming.

"I'm sorry for your loss," she said numbly.

"You're sorry?" Slowly, Syed closed the gap between them. When he was less than a foot away, he raised his hand and slapped Thea across the face. It made her teeth rattle, but she didn't react. "You forced him to out himself and then you didn't protect him. Are you happy now?"

"That's enough, Mr Seward," one of the grief officers said softly. "Please, sit down. It's a lot to process."

"Don't try to handle me," Syed spat, swatting away the officer. He breathed deeply then turned back to Thea; all anger seemingly gone. She could see the hurt and the pain of his loss etched into every line of his face; it was hard to watch. "Have you ever loved someone, Agent Williams? Have you ever been in love?"

"Yes."

"Were they perfect?"

"No."

"But you loved them anyway, right?"

"Without exception."

"I think he might have been the devil, but I loved him anyway. What am I supposed to do now? He did what I wanted. What you wanted. This was supposed to be our new start." They looked at each other for a moment and then he crumpled to the floor in a dead faint.

"He'll be fine. We had a Medicus give him a sedative," the officer told Thea as they lifted Syed gently from the ground and placed him on a large bed.

Thea waited at his bedside for the better part of two hours, before Syed's eyes fluttered open again.

"You're still here. It wasn't a nightmare, then? He's really dead." He seemed beyond tears now. "Tell me again, so I can really believe it."

"Levi is dead, Syed."

"Oh."

"You were here when it happened. The officers downstairs told me that...they locked you in a closet while the attack took place. Mr Seward, did you see who killed your husband?"

"I saw his black eyes. There was evil in them. That sandy-haired boy that Levi plucked off the streets. I told him there was something wrong with him. I told him."

"Who?"

"Joel Curtis."

Evening

CALIGO TODAY

Edition

Keeping you in the know

LEVI SEWARD MURDERED

Police have confirmed that the body of Una Anima founder, Levi Seward, 51, was discovered today at his home. The death is being treated as a homicide by police. Early reports link his death to the serial killer known as 'The Zealot', with an unnamed source within CPD claiming that the murder was a direct result of the recent speech made by the victim. The preacher's spectacular fall from grace was witnessed by all in Caligo…

[MORE ON PAGE 9]

THE ZEALOT NAMED

A spokesperson for the CPD officially named Joel Curtis as the prime suspect in the ongoing investigation into the death of Una Anima founder, Levi Seward. The spokesperson also confirmed that they believe Curtis to be the true identity of the serial killer plaguing our streets known as 'The Zealot'. While identification of a suspect is a major breakthrough, police urge caution, particularly to those among the augmented community and their vocal allies. If you have any information that you believe is important to the case…

[MORE ON PAGE 4]

VIOLENCE GRIPS CALIGO

The city of Caligo has witnessed a seventh consecutive day of anti-aug violence with police urging anyone who does not need to venture out to stay at home. Since the hotly anticipated Una Anima march, tensions have been close to the surface, with several reported deaths, countless injuries and millions of credits in property damage. A streak of bombings in the city, which have yet to claim any fatalities, have also been attributed to an Una Anima affiliate - The Soulful Elite. There is a red terror alert active in the…

[MORE ON PAGE 12]

THE INVISIBLE MAN

Thea was struggling. Guilt consumed her. She couldn't strike the image of Syed's grief-stricken face from her mind. She should have seen it coming. She had been careless, caught up in her own petty dramas and it cost a man his life.

"He doesn't exist," Walt said, throwing the report he had been reading down onto the conference room table. "Joel Curtis doesn't exist."

"I can't find anything on him," Torrez said, shaking his head. He was sitting across from Walt next to Alex and Sid.

"Surface due diligence is here, and it's pretty strong. He could be charged and processed, and the system wouldn't flag the false data." Walt indicated the papers he had just tossed. "But dig deep enough and you start to see the holes. His name is fake—so is his ID number. There aren't any records of this guy. He's a ghost. He's the invisible man as far as our searches are concerned."

"Wait," Sid said, holding his hand up like he was in class. "He was photographed when you arrested him."

"Why isn't that flagging in any of our searches? What if someone is actively erasing traces of him? Could be doing it himself."

"What?" Thea said distractedly.

"Joel Curtis, remember?" Alex cocked their head to the side.

"I didn't find anything either," Thea mumbled.

"Can we talk outside?" Alex said pointedly.

"Sure."

Thea led them into an empty office and closed the door.

"What's the matter with you?" Alex asked as soon as they were alone. "You've been distracted and it's not just today."

"I had Curtis in custody and I let him go. I didn't act quickly enough to stop the riots. I threw Levi Seward to the wolves and now he's dead."

"Oh, so you're wallowing. How useful." Their tone was blunt but their expression was one of concern.

"I'm not—"

"Yeah, you are. Bad things happen. It's not your fault. But that's not all, right? It's the detective and the captain and your mom."

"And the guy who tried to kill me and kidnapped my sister. He's here in Caligo."

"That's a bad beat, Tee. You've been dealt some real shitty cards the last few weeks and I'm sorry, but you don't have the luxury of falling apart. You're calling the shots here. The city is on fire, and we're all looking to you to do something about it."

"Castillo called me reckless. He's right. I am, and that was fine when it was my life on the line, but someone is dead because of me."

"Stop it. Think about all the people you've saved. We have high pressure, high stakes jobs, but we're only human. We're gonna make mistakes. And you are reckless. It's dangerous but it's also what makes you so good at what you do."

"Alex—"

"The way Torrez tells it, you saved Tenebrium, almost single-handedly. Well, Caligo is your home now. The city is balanced on the edge of a knife. Get off your ass and do something about it."

Thea was stunned into silence. They were right, she had let her feelings about Walt, Sid, her mother and Bastion distract her. And it had made her sloppy. Levi Seward had paid that price, but no one else would.

"Well?" Alex demanded when Thea didn't speak immediately.

"I want to speak to Helena Cutter's husband. He's the only family member we didn't interview. We need to understand why Curtis is choosing his victims. That's the key."

"Well, all right then, Let's get to it."

"Thank you—for the tough love."

"I'll whip your butt into shape any time you need it." Alex winked.

"Tell Torrez to keep his mouth shut. He's such a gossip."

"Oh, but he has other, better qualities."

"I bet he does."

IS THIS SUCCESS?

Cleo's lab and the larger research division was part of an enormous centralised medical centre and as such had access to all the medical records in the colonies. Not from her office, however. There were far too many files, far too much data for the terminals in her lab to handle. For a full list of those with augmentations, she would have to go to the executive level.

I have every right to be here. I work here, Cleo reminded herself as she nodded to a colleague. It wasn't at all strange for her to be in the executive wing. It was part of her job to research medical data, but knowing she was about to steal was making her jumpy. Her Cicada rang in her ear, and she let out a little yelp. Thankfully, there had been no one nearby to hear it.

"What?" she snapped.

"Are you okay?" Thea's voice was a relief.

"I'm not good at subterfuge."

"I think the first rule would be to not say that that's what you're doing out loud."

"Why did you call me?" Cleo whispered.

"We have a suspect. His name is Joel Curtis, but it's a fake. We only need the records for men twenty to thirty, who have ocular augmentations. The operation would have happened when they were children. We need names; anything extra is a bonus."

"I'll see what I can do."

"You don't have to do this if you don't want to."

"I know, but this is important. I'll call you when it's done."

It didn't take Cleo long to find a console in a quiet spot of the case library, and it took her even less time to illegally download patient records and send them onto Thea. The walk back to her lab was a far more relaxed affair, until she saw the head of the medical centre, a tall man with long dark hair, half of which was tied into a bun on the top of his head. Dr Ed Cohen was tall with russet brown skin that reflected his Tongan heritage. He had deep, dark eyes and the best bedside manner she had ever witnessed. Cohen had a way about him that made a person feel instantly at ease. Or at least he usually did. Today, after she had committed theft, he was the last person she wanted to speak to.

"Dr James," he said by way of a greeting. His grim expression made a lump form in her throat. "Bad news."

"Oh?" The word sounded strangled, but Dr Cohen didn't seem to notice.

"Your research has caught the attention of the feds."

"Isn't that a good thing? The more interest, the more funding. The more funding, the more ghouls we can help."

"That's not what interests them. If you're successful, they want to repurpose Styxx as a punishment for tier one crimes."

"They want to turn criminals into ghouls?" All fear of being caught left Cleo as she reeled from the abhorrence of the idea.

"Prisons are overcrowded. They want to use the SubLevel instead of building more, or dealing with crime on a social level." Cohen's disdain for the establishment was another point in his favour. "Your monthly funding has been tripled. The government has a vested interest in your research. It's out of our hands now. If you don't finish it, someone else will."

"There must be something we can do to halt this."

"I already tried. The project is part of the deal you made to avoid prison. The government owns the project. So, they own your research."

"This can't be happening."

"Well, it is. I'm sorry, Cleo. There's nothing to be done here."

THE SURGEON

Thea and Walt stood outside penthouse three on the top floor of Lawrie Plaza in Tenebrium's Eltham District. Neither spoke. They had smelled it the moment the private elevator opened. The odour was pungent and unmistakable to a pair of former homicide detectives. It was the scent of death.

"Ready?" Walt asked Thea, resting his hand on the door handle. She nodded. He opened the door and a wave of warm, fetid air washed over them. Thea coughed and covered her mouth with her hand.

"Christ," Walt said, just barely managing not to wretch.

Thea stepped inside, raising her gun, Walt followed behind. The interior of the penthouse was immaculate. It was a large, open space decorated in pale neutrals. A glass staircase led to a second floor. Running water sounded from somewhere upstairs.

"TPD, anyone here?" Walt called scanning the room. "Dr Cutter?" There was no response.

Thea made her way to the stairs following the sound of running water. Each step she climbed, the foul smell intensified. Steam emanated from an open doorway on the second-floor landing. Holding her breath, Thea entered the bathroom. The shower was still running, filling the room with a hot haze, but it wasn't enough to obscure the body.

Crucified under the scorching spray could only be Dr Cutter. He had been dead for days. Flies buzzed around the shower cubicle and maggots squirmed in the mushy pile that had formed over the drain, flooding the room. The hot water had caused his skin to slough and accelerated decomposition to the point where the doctor's abdomen had split and his viscera pooled at his feet. His face was horribly burned, flecks of metal clung to what remained of his lips, and a scalpel lodged in each eye.

Thea's eyes stung and she kept her mouth clamped shut, afraid she would vomit if she opened it. She could hear Walt coming up the stairs having finished his sweep of the lower level. She stepped out of the bathroom to meet him.

"No one here," he said, screwing his face up against the smell. "I called in the team. He in there?" Walt nodded towards the bathroom. She didn't need to answer.

"I wouldn't," Thea said, but he stepped around her and entered the bathroom.

Shaking slightly, she sat down on the top step. Less than five seconds later Walt dropped down beside her, his face pale. Thea had worked around death for over ten years; she had seen some truly horrible things in her time, and for the most part she was desensitised to it, but the body of Dr Cutter was the kind of thing that would give her nightmares for weeks to come.

"We have to catch him," she said quietly.

He leaned his shoulder against hers. "We will."

THE LINK

Thea placed a cup of coffee in front of Fen then sat down in the chair opposite. They were in the conference room in The Orchard that had become a hub of sorts for the investigation of The Zealot.

"Ready?"

Fen nodded and gave Thea a small smile.

"Witness interview of Fen Yeoh. Conducted by SSA Thea Williams. Miss Yeoh, thank you for joining us today."

"This is oddly formal."

Thea smiled reassuringly but went on. "For her co-operation, Miss Yeoh has been granted immunity. Any information given that may incriminate her cannot be used against her in a court of law. Do you know who Frederick Cutter is?"

"Yes, he's a surgeon."

"How do you know him?"

"I was—am—a sculptor. To make money when I was younger, I created casts for black market augmentations. Dr Cutter was the surgeon. He performed the surgeries for lower prices and I was given a cut of the proceeds."

"How did the doctor get the materials needed?"

"He had a contact. He implied it was someone in the mob, but I never knew who."

"How did he find patients?"

"They weren't married when we met, but his girlfriend at the time, before she was famous and before she changed her name, worked at a non-profit – the Travis Mercer Foundation. She would refer those in need to him."

"Who are you referring to?"

"Sorry, Helena Cutter, but she went by Samantha Braxton then. I never met her in person, and we only spoke a couple of times. That's why I didn't make the connection. I didn't realise they were the same person."

"Where were the surgeries performed?"

"At the hospital the doc worked at."

"How?"

"Ranveer Baker-Singh would forge the required paperwork, so it would seem like the surgeries were legitimate. It allowed patients to recover at the hospital and allowed the doctor access to nurses, drugs and equipment."

Thea paused the tape. "You doing okay?"

"I'm nervous."

"You're doing great. Because of you we have a suspect and we know what links the victims."

"I feel dirty. Tainted by this."

"For the record, I think what you and the doctor and Ranveer did was great. You helped people."

"Thank you."

Thea restarted the recording. "Was there anyone else involved in the process, in the surgeries?"

"Nursing Staff, but they had no idea. I'm the last one left who knew." Fen let out an awkward laugh, but she looked afraid. "He's going to come after me again, isn't he?"

"He might, but I won't let anything happen to you. We're scouring Caligo and Tenebrium for Joel Curtis. I have his face on every billboard in the city. I don't need his real name to find him. Someone will see him and when they do, we'll get him. Witness interview concluded." Thea stopped the recording. "Thank you for doing this."

"Can I ask you something?"

"Of course."

"It's not about the case."

"Okay..." Thea was hesitant; she had a feeling she knew where this was going.

"Did he tell you about what I did?"

"Walt?" Thea considered lying for a moment but thought better of it. "Yeah, he told me."

"Do you think he'll forgive me?"

"I don't think I'm the person you should be talking to about this. I hope he does, if that counts for anything."

"I know about...I mean, he didn't say anything...but I know."

"I can't get in the middle of this."

"What was he like? Before? What was he like when you met him?"

Thea thought for a moment. "Arrogant. He could be a real asshole. But he was the best detective I ever met. He really cared about the victims and did everything he could to get answers for their families."

"When—"

"It's not my place. If you want to talk about it, talk to Walt."

"I'm not sure there's any point. I think we're done."

"He loves you. That has to count for something."

It was freeing to realise that she genuinely hoped they worked it out. Thea packed up her things and was at the door when Fen called her back.

“Wayland!” she all but shouted. “The kid’s mother. She was Mrs Wayland.”

CYNTHIA

"Guess how many people have the surname Wayland in the colonies?" Thea asked Torrez. He looked up from the report he was reading and leaned back in his chair frowning.

"A lot?"

"Two and a half million."

"Madre de dios."

The conference room door opened, and Walt entered carrying a tray of coffees. "Anything new?" he asked passing cups to Torrez and Thea.

"Wayland is a very common name."

"How many?" Walt asked.

"In Tenebrium and Caligo alone? About thirty thousand, seven thousand of which match the age range of Joel Curtis. You got anything?"

"Montgomery finished her autopsy of Dr Cutter. Nothing we didn't know. Molten metal was poured down his throat. He didn't have a message carved into his skin, but I think the scalpels in his eyes made the point. That was done first, and they didn't go deep enough to kill him." He paused. "Where's Fen?"

"Downstairs in protective custody. You can go see her if you like."

Walt shook his head.

"Wayland!" Torrez all but shouted waving a report at Thea. "Cynthia Wayland."

"Full sentences, Drew," Thea said.

"The mobsters who have been going missing are from the Russo family. The head of the Russo Family, Vinny, his wife was Cynthia Wayland and she had a son from a previous marriage. He's the right age. That can't be a coincidence."

"What's his name?"

"It's not listed, but Cynthia is here, Thea. In Caligo."

Less than half an hour later Thea was standing outside a rundown tenement in the Pleasure District. Her heart pounded with excitement. If Torrez was right, they were finally going to get some answers.

Adrenaline was making her slightly jittery as she stepped into the close. There had been no fire door protecting the building; the frame that should have held it was battered and bent. The stairs were crumbling and the wooden railings had rotted away in places. Graffiti covered the walls, litter and drug paraphernalia was scattered around the concrete floor. It was a dismal place marked by the kind of decay that came from being forgotten.

The smell of rotting food and faeces stung her nose as she clambered up flight after flight of dilapidated stairs. Some of the stairs had crumbled away completely and Thea was forced to jump over large gaps to continue her ascent. She wondered how anyone could live there day to day.

There were six apartments connected by a small landing on the eighth floor. All appeared abandoned except for one. The glass panels of the door were cracked or missing, Thea could have walked straight in if she'd had a mind too, but she raised her hand and knocked.

"I've been wondering when you'd find me," a rasping voice called from inside. Taking this as an invitation Thea pushed open the door. As she stepped inside, she was immediately greeted with the smell of damp mould and stale tobacco. She reluctantly followed the scent down a cramped and dirty hallway into a tiny living room.

Dirty dishes and clothes were piled on what must have been a sofa at some point. Whatever colour the walls had been was completely obscured by a thick layer of yellow tobacco grime. A dense haze of smoke surrounded a rickety armchair, but Thea could still make out the occupant. A White woman in her mid-fifties, with tangled and matted red hair sat smoking a long cigarette, an overflowing ashtray beside her. Her skin was as grubby as the rest of her home and her clothes were stained and threadbare. The only item on her person that wasn't encrusted with dirt was a gleaming watch. It was far too big for her delicate wrist, but it was clean enough to pass for brand new.

"Who the hell are you?" she rasped, squinting through the smoke. It was dull in the room and there was no lights Thea could see, only the streetlights from outside shining through the window provided any illumination.

"Not who you were expecting?" Cynthia Wayland didn't answer. "I've come to talk to you about your son."

"I figured someone might, though I thought he'd find me first. I'd say sit, but well..." she gestured at the mess with disinterest. "What d'you wanna know?"

"Could you confirm for me if this is your son?" Thea tapped her index and an image of Joel Curtis sprung to life in the air between them.

"Yeah, that's George."

"George?"

"George Wayland, though he's not gone by that in a long time."

"Cynthia—"

"Stop. You're about to ask the wrong question."

"How do you know?"

"'Cause you're going to ask about Georgie when you should be asking about Vinny." She took another drag of her cigarette with a shaking hand. "He's not only killing the people involved in his operation, is he? Yeah, I worked it out long before you pigs did. I've heard whispers of Russos going missing, too. It all started with Vinny."

"Then tell me about Vinny."

"When Georgie was five, we had a bad accident." She waved a soot-blackened prosthetic hand. "Jonk crash. He was blinded. Augmentations were still rare back then—this is over twenty years ago now. And there was no way someone like me could have afforded one. So, I walked into a casino I knew was run by the mob and I asked for a loan. That was the day I met Vincent Russo. He agreed to pay for Georgie's surgery if I went to him every Thursday night."

"He extorted you for sex?"

Cynthia gave a hollow little laugh. "That's what I thought I had agreed to, but no, he was just lonely and wanted company. There were no strings attached."

"Vinny didn't just pay for the surgery, though, did he?"

"No, he didn't. He put me in touch with that actress and her husband and he had me meet with the writer and artist. I'm the last one left."

"And after the surgery?"

"I had to keep to our deal. I was scared at first, I knew his reputation and it turned out it was all true. But he was kind to me. He made me feel safe, alive; I was free with Vinny in a way I never was with my husband." The resentment was clear on her face. "He showed me his darkness and I showed him mine and neither of us flinched. Nobody really knew Vinny. Frankenstein, they called him. Freak. Cyclops. But to me he was just Vinny. He was a monster, but he was my monster." Her eyes went glassy, and she wiped away a single tear. Thea said nothing, listening intently. "We fell in love and the deeper I got in with him the more I realised that if I stayed with my son, I'd be putting him in danger. So, I left. I loved Vinny more than I loved being a mother. I'm sure you have something to say about that."

"I'm not here to judge you."

"It's the thing I am most ashamed of. I don't regret Vinny for a second—he was the love of my life but I should have found a way to be there for George too. I got my comeuppance though." A bitter smile twisted her lips. "We got raided and he got arrested a few years after I walked out on my son. We had agreed that if the law ever came for him, I would turn witness and keep my freedom so I could go back to George. That's what I did. I ratted him out. I told them everything we had done together and I saved my own skin." Cynthia covered her face with her hands, tears slipping between her fingers. "We thought that if Vinny could tell them about other mobsters he would get life. But the judge refused the deal and sentenced him to death. I saw him," her voice faltered. "I saw him hanged. I was there when they put the noose around his neck and I watched him swing. His neck didn't break, so I gotta see him strangle to death. His eyes bulged and he went purple and..." she seemed unable to continue. "I knew it was my fault. I couldn't go back to my son, I couldn't go back to anything. I was too ashamed. Too lost without Vinny. You want to know my secret? The big one? I wish I'd died with him. To have lived these last years without him has been worse than any hell, but he wanted me to live. So, I live." She finished her cigarette in two long drags and immediately lit another.

"You left because you fell in love—I can understand that, but your son is involved with Una Anima, he murdered its founder." Thea pitied Cynthia, but she needed to find George Wayland before he killed again. "He isn't just killing those involved in the surgery anymore. He thinks he's damned. He thinks by getting him augmented you damned him. He may think that's why you left."

"I left because I'm weak. I love my boy, no matter what he's done. I won't help you catch him."

"Then why did you tell me your story?"

"I want you to understand. He didn't have it easy. His mom walked out on him, and his dad drank himself to death."

"Mrs Wayland—"

"Russo. My name is Cynthia Russo." Her tone was acid.

"Mrs Russo, you don't seem like you go out much," Thea said changing the subject. "Which means if people are talking to you, they're coming here to do it. What do you know about the missing Russos?"

"Clever girl," Cynthia said, though she didn't seem impressed. "He's trying to find me. To finish the job. That's why he's taking them."

"Whether you help me or not, I will catch him. But until I do, I would like to put you into protective custody."

"Let him come." Cynthia smiled weakly looking over Thea's shoulder.

"Hi, Mom."

Thea spun around, drawing her gun as she did so. Joel Curtis—George Wayland—was standing less than a metre away, lurking in the dimly lit doorway. The black bottomless pools of his eyes met hers for a second before he ran. Thea hurtled after him, knocking piles of trash over in her haste.

George bolted out of the apartment and down the decaying steps. Thea kept pace with him, down one, two, three flights of stairs.

The next flight had a large gap between the top and the bottom where at least six stairs had crumbled away. George jumped it with ease and Thea followed suit, but when she landed, the concrete of the landing below gave way. Huge chunks of grey rock surrounded her as she fell. The impact of the concrete on the landing below caused it to collapse too and she was falling again. When she finally came to a stop, battered and bruised, in a pile of rubble, George was nowhere to be seen.

Cursing, she got to her feet. A sharp stabbing pain that made Thea look down. There was something sticking out of her thigh—it was a rusted spike.

"Shit."

"All right, Agent Williams," the Medicus said. "I've given you a shot and taken some blood. You should be fine, but I'd like you to come back in a couple days just in case. It's a deep wound."

As soon as Thea realised she had been injured, she had headed straight for ARC's Medbay.

"Are you okay?" Torrez peeked his head into the small white exam room.

"I almost had him."

"That's not what I meant."

"I'm fine. Has someone gone and picked up Cynthia Wayland? I don't care what she says, she's in danger."

"Walt is bringing her in now. He took your team."

"Good. C'mon, get everyone in the conference room. We have a serial killer to catch."

IMAGE

The week following her meeting with Cynthia passed in a blur for Thea. She had done so much work leading the teams and the task force that ARC named her head of the entire operation to catch The Zealot.

The search for Joel Curtis was constant, with teams of police and ARC agents under Thea's direction searching day and night in both Caligo and Tenebrium, but to no avail.

Alex reported finding the bodies of three more former Russo family men, but found no trace of Curtis. Curtis's face was broadcast all over the colonies, but none of the reported sightings yielded any real leads. Calls to the tip line were constant and the various agencies involved in the search followed up on every one, but he was nowhere to be found.

On the Friday of that week, Thea found herself standing with Walt in front of an evidence board, trying to separate fact from fiction in a new round of reported sightings. They had been pouring over the footage for hours and both had stinging eyes.

"What if we released his backstory to the press?" Walt said, rubbing his eyes with the heels of his hands.

"What difference would that make?" Thea asked gratefully, turning away from the bright images.

"He wants to seem powerful, a warrior for God. That's his identity, it's how he sees himself and what he projects into the world. He's carefully cultivated that image. What if we shatter it? Spin a tale about the sad little boy who had an accident, whose father drank himself to death and whose mother left him."

"You want the public to sympathise. You want them to pity him."

"If we've profiled him right, he would hate people knowing where he came from and it might make him act out. Slip up."

"I bet Fen could help with that. I'll ask her—unless you want to?"

"No, you can talk to her." Walt looked away. "Just make sure she's safe."

"She's safe here, I'll keep her involvement secret. He failed to kill her, I don't want it to look like she's rubbing it in his face."

"That's a good idea. If we really want to shatter him, we should release more details about Seward's murder too. Make him face what he did to someone he loves."

"We need to be careful," Thea cautioned. "I want him to show himself, but I don't want anyone else to get hurt. Love him or loathe him, Seward is dead because of me. I don't want to rile him into another murder."

"He's a serial killer. He's gonna kill again no matter what we do. We just have to catch him. It sucks, but most of our job is after the fact. And Seward isn't your fault. This whole mess is on him, not you."

"But I knew better. I knew to protect Benny. With Seward I took it so personally, and I got so caught up in bringing him down...I could have stopped what happened to him and I should have. I lost sight of what was important, and a man died."

"Benny and Seward aren't the same. You're protecting Cynthia, you're protecting Fen—"

"You would have put a detail on Seward. I know you would."

Walt shrugged. "Look, if you want someone to guilt you, you're looking in the wrong place. You made a mistake. It happens. You have the weight of this operation on your shoulders. Hundreds of cops and agents all looking to you to make the big decisions and you can't always get it right. You do your best. That's the job."

"I'd hoped my best was better." She was wallowing and she knew it.

"Stop. If I can't have a pity party, neither can you. We both know what this is. You saved Tenebrium. You were the big hero and a lot of people who were involved in that are looking to you to pull it out of the bag again. It's a lot of pressure and you're worried that this time you'll fail."

Thea laughed uncomfortably. "It's like you know me."

"I do know you and that's why I know you can do this. Just remember you aren't alone. Think about all the people willing to fight for you, to fight with you. That should tell you something."

"Thank you," Thea said quietly. They lapsed into comfortable silence. "I have an idea," she said after a few moments.

"What?"

"A lot of augs have gone underground because of Una Anima and the Soulful Elite. If I had an augmentation and I didn't want to be found, I know where I'd go."

"Augs don't love law enforcement as a rule. Could be tricky."

Thea paused to scrutinise Walt's face. He looked expectant. "Cora knows where Bastion is."

"What? And you called me a liar."

"Don't. It is not the same," Thea said shaking her head. "The community trusts him. He might be able to help us."

"He's been on the run. He knows you'll arrest him on sight."
"What if I didn't?"
"Can you let what happened in Tenebrium go?"
"To save people's lives–yes."
"He'll need a guarantee."

MOTHER

Athena had no idea how her life had ended up the way it had. She had always dreamed of being a gymnast. She had been good too, but then she had met Harold. He had been driven and confident and their connection had been instant. Before she knew it, they were married and a few years later she gave birth to two beautiful twin girls. She turned to writing instead so she could stay home, and she loved her life; she loved her family; she loved being a wife but more than anything she loved being a mother. Where had it all gone wrong?

Now, she was sitting alone in her home drinking at midday. Her husband, a killer who was murdered himself. One daughter a liar and the other lost to her forever. She would forgive Cora in time, and until then there was sherry. Thea, on the other hand, there was no road back for them. Athena had failed her, and she knew it, but Thea had turned her back on the family, betrayed her father. Neither would forgive the other.

That had been why she had let him in.

"Can I get you a drink?"

"No, thank you," Joel Curtis said. He was pleasant and handsome, if a tad unsettling with his black, white-less eyes. If she didn't know what he was, she could be fooled into thinking he was just like any other nice young man.

"My daughter is looking for you."

"I know." He smiled slightly as if glad he didn't have to pretend to be someone else.

"Everyone's looking for you."

His smile widened.

"Thea is quite the woman. You must be proud."

"I'm not. What do you want? You're interrupting my drinking."

"I want to hurt her."

"I won't help you."

"Not physically. I want to wound her, like she wounded me. I had to kill Levi because of her. I want to know what she loves. Not you, or you wouldn't be here drinking alone. Her sister is too well-protected. But there must be someone, a friend or a lover perhaps?" His voice was calm and his tone even, yet there was a darkness and a danger to his words that shook Athena to her core.

This was one of those moments, Athena thought. One of those moments where she could stand for something. Curtis would surely kill her but at least she would be protecting her daughter. Or she could do something wicked; inflict pain on someone else to ease her own suffering. She chose to be like her late husband that day.

"There's a man." She hated Walt with every fibre of her being and would sleep better knowing he received a fraction of what he had done to her husband. "Walter James."

"The TPD police captain?"

"Yes."

"His death would hurt her? Ruin her?"

"His death would soothe me. But yes, she would be hurt if he passed."

"Are you going to warn them?"

"No." She expected to feel guilt or shame, but there was nothing but emptiness inside of Athena. Curtis stared into her eyes, as if boring into her mind.

"I believe you. But if you speak false, I will come back and cut out your liar's tongue."

"Cheers." Athena raised her glass of wine in the air as if in a toast, then drained it in two gulps.

MONEY

Mateo had been up all night following Levi Seward's money. He had told Thea just about everything, leaving out only Natalia's involvement, and she had been grateful when he had told her he would deal with that aspect of the investigation. It was a testament to their newfound trust that she hadn't questioned him, and it was with some guilt that he continued the work.

The money was gone, and no matter what Natalia wanted, it wasn't coming back. And if it did, it was no longer possible that it could find its way into her bank account. She would have to figure out her money troubles on her own. She hadn't taken the news well. He wanted to help her, but he simply didn't know how, so instead he turned his attentions to the task at hand.

He was struggling not to fall asleep at his desk as his terminal ran through hundreds of encrypted transactions, trying to find where Seward's money had ended up. He couldn't really do anything but watch the system work and no matter how hard he fought it, he could feel his eyelids drooping.

A loud *ping* shocked him back to consciousness. The programme had finally completed its work. Mateo glanced over at the small clock perched on his bookshelf. It was after midnight. He had been asleep for nearly three hours. Wiping the dried drool from the side of his mouth and stretching his neck and shoulders, Mateo gave himself a little shake before looking at the alert.

The programme had managed to track the funds to several accounts in Caligo and some on the surface. There had been several layers of fake names and details to confuse anyone searching, but the terminal had managed to decipher the twisted web to come up with a single name: 'Ralph Price.'

THE PAST

Nine years ago...

Cynthia felt sick as she sat on the bench in the back of the courtroom. It felt cruel to be so close to Vinny and yet so far away. As a witness for the prosecution, she hadn't been allowed to visit him. It was torture to stand up in front of the court day after day and incriminate him further, and yet every time she had taken the stand, he had looked at her with nothing but love in his eyes, so palpable it was like a caress.

Her part done, the guilty verdict had been a surprise to no one. The only thing left was the sentencing. She knew that Vinny was going to jail for the rest of his life for the many crimes he had committed, but that didn't stop a tiny foolish part of her hoping for leniency. She could wait ten years, twenty even, thirty, she didn't care if it meant she would be able to hold him again.

Her heart fluttered nervously as Vinny was brought in, flanked by two guards. He dwarfed the men in his grey suit but didn't struggle. He smiled at her as he passed and mouthed, *I love you.* Tears pricked her eyes; she had known he was lost to her, but today would make it final. It was like their relationship was surviving on life support and the sentencing would withdraw care.

"All rise," was called as the judge entered.

Everard Wolfsheim was aged and White. He was batlike with his sharp features and flowing black robes. "Don't bother sitting," he said as he took up his place at the head of the courtroom. "This won't take long."

Cynthia swallowed hard, nervous sweat slicking the back of her neck.

"Mr Russo, you have been found guilty of innumerable crimes including but not limited to, murder—including that of an officer of the law, assault, racketeering, smuggling, attempted murder, extortion, kidnapping, torture and many more that we do not have the time to list here today. In my extensive tenure as a judge, I cannot think of a career criminal more prolific and more sadistic. You have proven yourself a brutal and remorseless killer. A violent man who enjoys inflicting pain on others. The scope of your crimes is such that it leaves me in no doubt that true evil lurks within you. You are a danger to society, and it is my firm belief that were you ever freed you would continue your violent tyranny in the city's underworld. It is for this reason, Vincent Russo, that I today sentence you to death by hanging."

There was a collective intake of breath before clapping erupted in the gallery. Photographers snapped picture after picture of Vinny who didn't react. He just stared straight ahead.

The noise was such that no one heard Cynthia scream and in the flurry of activity that followed the verdict, no one noticed her collapse to the ground and begin to sob. No one but Vinny.

The two guards took Vinny by the arms and tried to pull him away, but he held his ground. He shouldered one of the men, sending him crashing to the ground before headbutting the other and vaulting over the railing that separated the courtroom proper from the gallery. Hands still cuffed in front of him, he made his way to Cynthia. She scrambled to her feet to meet him.

As soon as he was close enough he took her face in his hands and kissed her. "One life with you was never going to be enough for me. I'll see you in the next one, my love. Death is only the beginning." He kissed her again and then turned back to the guards who now surrounded them, guns aiming at his chest. He raised his hands as best he could with them handcuffed together and knelt on the hard marble floor in surrender.

Multiple court guards and police officers swarmed Vinny, dragging him from the room.

Cynthia's head swirled. *My life is over,* was the last thought she had before she fainted.

OLD ENEMIES

Caligo City Zoo had been abandoned for years. Pens lay empty, bars rusted and the plant life had taken over entirely. It was like something from another world, so different to Caligo which was a shrine to glass, metal and brick, the zoo was a haven for nature. A small pocket of the earth, thousands of feet in the sky.

Derelict and out the way, Thea supposed it was an ideal spot for a clandestine meeting. It had taken some convincing for Cora to get a message to Bastion and as Thea stood next to her sister in what had once been a lion's den, she could feel the waves of anticipation rolling off her body. Unbeknownst to Cora and so Bastion, Walt was hovering near-by in case they had to take the man by force. Thea hoped it wouldn't come to that.

"Thank you, for doing this," Thea said quietly to Cora, as they waited.

"I'll hold you to your word on this."

"I need his help more than I need him behind bars. That's the truth."

"I'm glad to hear it," a familiar voice said behind them.

Instinctively, Thea drew her gun as she turned.

Bastion was standing at the end of one of the zoo's streets. He looked much as she remembered him and much as he had when they had come upon each other at the shelter. Tall, Black and muscular, with a ponytail of long dark locs, it was as if no time had passed for him. His high cheekbones and full lips showed none of the signs of hard living. It would be just like Bastion to land on his feet.

"I came here in friendship," Bastion said, raising his hands and walking slowly towards them. Nothing about his walk betrayed the augmented limb Thea knew he had, but she hadn't expected it to.

Thea put her gun back in its holster but kept her hand resting on the butt. She wouldn't have been so easily swayed to do so if Walt wasn't lurking unseen and at the ready.

"Cora," Bastion gave Thea's twin the kind of secret smile that lovers share. "Thea, I'm glad you weren't hurt in the explosion."

Thea said nothing. She couldn't form words.

"You came," Cora said softly. "We need your help."

"Anything," he said benevolently.

"For a price," Thea ground out.

"Don't start," Cora said, swatting at Thea's arm.

Bastion drew his eyes away from Cora and narrowed them on Thea. "It's true, I don't want to go back to The Pit. Few would. That's not unreasonable."

"Yes, why pay for your crimes when you can pretend you're helping those in need?"

"Enough," Cora said more forcefully. "Tell him what you need."

Thea closed her eyes for a moment, willing herself calm. When she opened them again, she kept her voice neutral. "I'm sure you've heard about Joel Curtis, the serial killer styling himself as The Zealot." Bastion nodded. "We think he's hiding out with some of the displaced in the augmented community. ARC doesn't have the best track record of late with augs and any allies I had, have gone underground. The community trusts you. I was hoping you could point us in the right direction, maybe take us to some lesser-known refuges, anywhere someone like him could hide."

"You mean someone like me—a fugitive."

"Yes. That's what I mean."

"What do I get in return? I can hardly start keeping company with the law and not expect to get arrested."

"I have no powers to grant you a pardon and I wouldn't if I could. You'll be with Walt or me only. You won't have to deal with the wider teams. No one will know who you are."

"That's not much incentive."

"I'd have hoped catching a serial killer was incentive enough, but I'm giving you a pass. If I see you in the street after this, I'll just walk right on by. I'm not going to report that I've seen you now, and I won't ever. No investigation. Thea Williams has never heard of Bastion Tyrus after this. That's the deal."

"And if you were to see me in your home?" His eyes flickered to Cora.

"I would shoot you on sight."

"Thea!" Cora exclaimed.

"No, I'm not bargaining for a relationship with my sister. I don't care what went on between you two, you killed people. You tried to kill me. If you want to be with him," Thea turned to her sister. "You find a new place to live."

"You're more like Dad than you think."

"Spiteful and childish. You're more like Mom than I thought." Thea took a steadying breath regretting her retort. Cora was always prone to lashing out when rattled, but Thea refused to feed into it any more than she already had. "I've said my piece. If you want to pursue a relationship I can't stop you, but the things he's done should. There is blood on his hands, enough to fill an ocean."

"You're the one who wanted his help—"

"No. I don't want his help. I need it. If there was anyone else I could ask I would. I'm trying to catch a serial killer and avoid all-out war on our streets. Have you forgotten what we're doing here? This isn't about you or Bastion. He's a criminal, he should be in jail, that's a fact. But I'm willing to bend the law to save lives. Our history has nothing to do with it."

"I'll help you." Bastion said before Cora could reply.

"I need you to promise me you won't arrest him." Cora grabbed Thea by the forearms, imploring her.

"I give you my word." But she didn't look at Cora, she looked at Bastion.

"And what about Walt? I know he's here somewhere," Bastion said, gesturing with an airy hand. "You two are never far apart."

Cora looked angrily at Thea who ignored her. A few moments later, Walt appeared from a copse of trees. He walked casually to join them.

"I didn't search for you then; I'm not starting now," he said with a shrug.

"Good enough. When do we start?"

Thea couldn't shake the feeling that she had made a horrible mistake. Cora was already starting to act like her old self. The Cora who was deeply troubled. Bastion being back in her orbit was the cause and no good could come of them spending more time together.

PUNISHMENT

It was well past midnight, but Cleo couldn't bring herself to go home. She had spent the day in meetings with the medical board. The previously sceptical panel had been overjoyed to hear of Cleo's successes with Isobelle, but Cleo struggled to share in their delight.

The weight of what she had done was heavy upon her. All the pain, and suffering, all the trauma and death could be laid at least partially at her feet. The serum and the new implant had brought four ghouls temporarily back to themselves, but it had also killed six others. The cost of advancement already outweighed the benefits in her mind. More than this, the worst thhydeing she had ever done, the things she was actively trying to correct was going to be used as a punishment, inflicting the old horrors anew.

She felt stupid for not realising before that some people may have seen so many things and done so many things under the influence of Styxx that they didn't want to come back. She herself had witnessed things and done things that would haunt her for the rest of her life.

Isobelle had refused any further treatments while lucid and even despite pressure from Hyde, Cleo had rejected the notion that the treatments should be forced upon her once she had reverted to her feral state.

On top of this, Cleo worried that at any moment it would be discovered that she had stolen records. Thea had obtained a warrant after the fact to protect her, but if anyone dug too deeply Cleo would have to answer for her actions. Every time she thought about it, her mind was drawn back to the night Dr Maxwell caught her snooping, drugged her and dragged her off to the SubLevel.

All of this however, paled in comparison to the dread that roiled her stomach after a visit from Betty Charles. Betty had confirmed to her that the plan to use Styxx as an alternative punishment was officially in motion.

Cleo had never felt more like a villain and yet she could see no clear path to the right thing. What followed was yet another sleepless night.

MESSAGE

The Grove wasn't really part of any district. It was made up of the poorest neighbourhoods of several adjacent areas. It was purely residential and extremely rundown. The buildings, even though they were less than thirty years old, looked like they were from another era. Many were crumbling, with broken windows and gaps in the roofs.

The deeper into the region Thea got, the buildings became shorter and shorter, until they weren't buildings at all, but tents and shacks made from corrugated metal and dark fabrics. The atmosphere was joyless, and the poverty palpable.

Bastion had told Thea to wait until it was dark before heading there, the obvious law enforcement presence in broad daylight being likely to spook anyone hiding out. She had taken his advice and waited until the evening before venturing out, taking him with her.

They walked down a muddy track that led to the most decrepit parts of The Grove. The people there looked hungry, and the longer they walked the more augmentations they saw.

"I see Walt is still mooning over you," Bastion said. His tone was pleasant, conversational, like they were old friends.

"You don't get to talk to me about Walt. You don't get to talk to me about anything that doesn't help me catch a serial killer."

"It wasn't fake, you know."

"What?"

"You have this warped idea of me in your head and I understand why, but it's not the truth. I wasn't some secret psycho-killer with a pile of bodies in the basement."

"No, you kept yours in the SubLevel."

"We were friends. I was greedy and ambitious. I was selfish. I didn't care who I hurt—I just wanted more power. But we were friends. I cared about you. I cared about Walt. It wasn't all an act. I have changed. Just like Walt, I have changed."

"I don't believe you."

They were passing a row of tents with corrugated iron roofs. Just barely audible in the chill night air was the muffled sound of shouts. "You check that row, I'll check these," Thea yelled as she ran. People darted out of her way, scurrying out of sight. The tents were small and open, and it didn't take long to search them.

"Over here!" Bastion called after only a few minutes. Thea darted over to where he had called from.

Bastion was standing inside a small shack that looked like a wooden outhouse. The smell as Thea approached was appalling, like sewage mixed with rotting food. Bastion stepped back to let Thea look inside. There was a man in a soiled suit, bound and gagged in the prayer position. His lips were cracked from thirst and his features were sunken. He was Middle Eastern, with warm brown skin that was caked with dirt. It was clear he had been held captive for several weeks.

Thea could hear Bastion calling for Medicus as she knelt to untie the man. His eyes darted around wildly, and he shifted back as if afraid she was going to hurt him. "It's okay, I'm here to help. My name is Thea, I'm with ARC. You're safe now."

She pulled the gag out of his mouth first. It was rough and dry. "Please get me out of here," the man croaked, his voice barely more than a rasping whisper.

"I will. I promise." She pulled a small knife from her pocket and cut through his bonds. "What's your name?"

"Duke. Duke Goodman."

"Okay, Duke. You're safe now. Can you tell me how you ended up here?"

"The black-eyed man. He kidnapped me. He wanted me to tell him where his mother is. But I don't know. I don't know."

"Are you a family man? A Russo?"

He nodded warily.

"When was he here last?"

"Days. He's not coming back. He told me I was going to die in my own filth like the sinner I am."

"He was wrong. We're going to get a Medicus and you're gonna be fine. Can you stand?"

"Did you say your name was Thea? Are you Thea Williams?"

"Yeah, that's me."

Duke grabbed the arm she offered and let her pull him to his feet. Panting, he leaned against the shack wall. With shaking hands, he lifted his shirt. Carved into his flesh, the wounds puckered and red, with yellow pus seeping from them, were the words, 'I will cut out your deceitful tongue.'

"He said the message was for you."

BOMBING

The emergency room at the MedTech Medical Centre was in chaos and Peggy Simone was run off her feet. She hadn't been home in days, but with the continuing violence in Caligo, there was a constant stream of patients needing treatment from the emergency medicine team and no end in sight.

"We're out of O-Neg. Have one of the nurses call the blood bank." Peggy said to the intern beside her as she pulled off her apron and gloves and put them in the medical waste bin. The team had managed to save the patient, but only just. There would be more deaths, it was unavoidable now. Peggy cursed under her breath; the ER was getting dangerously low on supplies and there weren't enough beds. Treatment rooms that were meant for single occupancy were housing multiple patients. It was dangerous and against protocol, but they had no choice. The alternative was turning patients away.

Peggy walked to the nearest vending machine and got herself a bottle of water. She was hungry but there was no time to eat.

"Dr Simone," one of the trauma surgeons called to her. "Next transporter is three minutes out."

"I'll meet you in the docking bay." Sighing, she gulped down the water then jogged after her colleague.

There was a distant *BOOM*. The ER shuddered and the lights flickered. There had been another bombing. Cursing, Peggy grabbed another set of gloves and made her way to the docking bay, praying they could tend to the new patient, before the casualties from the latest bombing rolled in.

ELITE LEADER

At Thea's request Alex had taken Duke to the CPD. They had only just left him in the medbay when the CPD SWAT team arrived in the detectives Bullpen.

"Alex," SWAT Leader Ibrahim said by way of a greeting. "That's all of them. All the major players in Una Anima and Sewards inner circle have been rounded up. They're being charged now."

"Hopefully that will temper some of the violence. They can't preach from jail."

"The DA has agreed to charge them with hate speech and inciting violence against a minority. The ones we caught at the riots are being charged with assault and the red-head, Muller, he's been charged with attempted murder for the initiations."

"Good work."

"It was all you. We just go where you tell us."

Alex smiled. "I'll head downstairs to start the interviews. There are going to be a lot of lawyers here. Gimme a second." Alex's Cicada buzzed in their ear.

"Detective Wyndham."

"Detective, this is Assistant Director Castillo with ARC."

"Thea's boss? How can I help?"

"Actually, I think I may be able to help you. I've been following up on the funds missing from Levi Seward's estate. I'm sure SSA Williams has been keeping you apprised. The credits appeared to go to a single account, but the tech team has dug a little deeper. It seems that Seward was paying for the bombings. We traced the accounts owner. A man named Ralph Price. We have been able to confirm that he's one of the bigger players in The Soulful Elite. I know you have been liaising with ARC and it's technically our jurisdiction, but Thea said that you were running point."

"This is great. That's excellent news." Alex was elated to finally be making progress. "How did you make the connection?"

"His bank accounts have vocal recognition. We ran the sample through the database and got a hit on one of the videos claiming responsibility for the bombings. Honestly, it was complete chance."

"Now all I need to do is find the S.O.B. Thank you, sir. We're a bit stretched here— I'm sure you understand. Would it be possible to take one of ARC's teams?"

"Certainly, Thea's team is ready and awaiting your command."

"Detective," Fry called to them across the bullpen. "There's been another bombing."

"I think I could use that team now, AD Castillo."

TARGETED

As bombings continued to plague Caligo, Thea, Walt and Torrez followed every lead Bastion gave them, went to every secret place and spoke to many members of the augmented community. The augmented people they spoke to wanted to help, fearing The Zealot as much as the rest of the city if not more, but the killer was an expert at covering his tracks. They found traces of Joel Curtis at many of them, but he had always moved on by the time they arrived.

It was barely eight o'clock in the morning when Thea made her way into the conference room at The Orchard to meet with Castillo, Walt, Sid, and Torrez. Alex was still dealing with the bombings and Thea's team was with them.

"I am sick of being given the run around by this cocky shit. We are running out of time. He will kill again, and soon."

"He's taunting us. Torrez found another former Russo with letters carved on his back this time. Another message for you," Walt said.

"If he wants me so badly, he can come and get me."

"Don't joke about that," Walt said seriously.

"What if that's exactly what we want?" Sid said. Thea could see a plan forming behind his eyes.

"What d'you mean?" Torrez asked, curiosity tinged with hesitance.

"He's coming for you one way or another, but he's being careful. He's taking his time. You've already got Fen writing an article. Why not hold a press conference? Have it play on every channel and every screen in the city."

"It's worked before. If I get him mad enough, he might show himself."

"He wants you dead; let's not make it easy for him," Torrez said with concern.

"I'm not going to dangle myself on a hook, but Sid is right. I'd rather meet him on my terms and...it worked before."

"You were shot last time." Walt said. "Maxwell shot you."

"The press conference was why we were briefly fugitives, it wasn't why I was shot. The article was thinking too small. We have to draw him out."

"It's too dangerous, Querida."

"No, what's dangerous is having a serial killer out there who could attack at any time. I could come home one day and find him in the apartment. He could surprise me on a mission. We know how he operates. We profiled him and we have all dealt with killers like him before. He's sadistic and he likes to be in control, he likes to play games, but so much of it is about ego. We challenge him, he won't be able to resist coming to get me."

"I don't like it." Walt said, shaking his head.

"It's not your call. Fen, Cynthia, there are so many people that will be safer once he's behind bars."

"For the record, I know it was my idea, but I'm not crazy about it either," Sid said. Their eyes met. The concern that shone out of his face was heartening.

"It's a good plan."

"If it was good enough for the Gold Legion..." Torrez winked.

Two hours later, Castillo and, to Thea's great surprise, Vargas, had called in every favour they had to get the press conference broadcast on every channel all across the city. That hadn't been the hard part however, the hard part had been convincing Cynthia to stand beside her. Joel's mother was warped by loss and regret; she felt it was a betrayal to help law enforcement. Thea only succeeded in convincing her to join the press conference when she pointed out that the longer the manhunt went on, the more likely it was that her son would be killed by police.

"You're not wearing a vest?" Walt asked as they stood in The Orchard's lobby, waiting to meet the press outside.

"I have my aegis," Thea said, tapping the button under her shirt.

"That only works if you see it coming."

"Ninety seconds," Castillo called from where he stood several feet away next to the ARC press liaison. Thea nodded.

"A vest will make him think we're scared," she said, turning back to Walt.

"Then you haven't lined up enough security."

"It's not your job to worry about me anymore."

He looked as though he was going to say more, but Castillo moved to join them. "Time to go."

Guided by the press liaison, Cynthia fell into step beside Thea, as both walked out onto The Orchard's front steps. Thea had never faced a bigger crowd, but she was glad to see it. She took her place in front of the podium and waited for the assembled press to quiet. When they finally did, she began.

"Good evening. I'm Supervisory Special Agent Thea Williams. On behalf of ARC and the CPD, I would like to thank you for joining us. As you all know, times in our city are hard. You're probably wondering why you've been called here. I will state officially and for the avoidance of doubt that I am standing here in the company of my law enforcement partner agencies, to give you an update on the serial killer styling himself as 'The Zealot'. We want all of the information here to be reported accurately and as such there will be press packs issued to all major outlets." Thea paused. "This week the name Joel Curtis was released publicly as a person of interest in the investigation. Today, I can confirm that both ARC and the CPD are treating him as the prime suspect and major focus of our joint investigation. With the evidence we have gathered so far, we can say with certainty that we believe he is the killer.

We believe Curtis is responsible for the murder, torture and mutilation of, Travis Mercer, Ranveer Baker-Singh, Helena Cutter, Dr Frederick Cutter and Levi Seward." An outbreak of mutterings followed the last name. "The kidnap and attempted murder of acclaimed journalist Fen Yeoh who thankfully was rescued from his clutches, assault of an officer of the law – for the purposes of full transparency, I, SSA Williams am the officer in questions. Curtis is also wanted in connection with the kidnap, torture, and murder of several former members of the defunct Russo crime family. He is extremely dangerous and any and all sightings should be reported to the Caligo Police Department, The Tenebrium Police Department or ARC. I repeat he is extremely dangerous. Under no circumstances should a member of the public approach the suspect.

We are releasing the following in the hope of discovering new leads that will aid us in apprehending the suspect.

Joel Curtis, born George Wayland, was injured in a Jonk accident at a young age. His mother, with the help of Vincent Russo, arranged for life changing augmentative surgery to be performed on Curtis to restore his sight. We believe Curtis to have an antisocial personality disorder, as well as autophobia – fear of abandonment - and believe this is why he was vulnerable to indoctrination. We have a witness that has confirmed that Levi Seward took a young Curtis into his care after the separation of his parents and used his position as a father figure to radicalise Curtis for his own purposes. Curtis believes that he is a warrior for God, but this could not be further from the truth. He is a troubled individual who has been victim to a master manipulator. Levi Seward used him and when he revealed this truth, we believe that Curtis murdered him. At this stage, his mental state is impossible to predict. The Zealot taskforce fully intends to posthumously charge Levi Seward in connection with the violence in the city and the serial killings. He has also been named in several hate crime and hate speech libel suits, however, these are out with the scope of the taskforce. We can confirm that ARC and CPD fully intend to have stochastic terrorism added to the list of charges being brought against both Curtis and Seward."

Thea nodded to Cynthia to join her. "With me today is Curtis' mother Cynthia who would like to make an appeal." There was a flurry of whispering as Thea moved back to allow Cyntia to step in front of the microphone.

"I know I wasn't there for you, Georgie, but this has to stop now. Please turn yourself in. I still remember the sweet little boy who cried whenever I left the house, who was afraid of the dark and who wouldn't go anywhere without his robot teddy bear. I refuse to believe that he is gone. I love you. Please turn yourself in." Cynthia dabbed at her eyes with a handkerchief as Thea stepped back in front of the podium.

"Thank you for joining us. We will not be taking questions at this time."

"Do you think we went far enough?" Thea asked Castillo ten minutes later in her office.

"I think any further and it would have been obvious you were goading him. Our profile was good; he'll want to be talked about like a master criminal, not a fool. He will act, and soon, so be careful."

"Yes, sir."

"You should get some rest. Do you have assignments for your teams?"

"I want Walt and our informant checking the Una Anima churches and Torrez and Sid can follow-up on the tip line. Most of the field agents are still tied up with CPD and the bombings— I don't want to pull them back yet."

"And you?"

"I'll be here, right where he expects me to be."

THE CHURCH

The Church of the Single Soul was a huge gaudy building emblazoned with bronze suns. Walt imagined that usually it was alive with activity, today however, the windows were boarded and a large 'CLOSED' sign has been posted on the front steps. Since the arrest of all of its major leaders and the brutal murder of Levi Seward, Una Anima had all but up shop and the usually vocal followers had gone suspiciously quiet.

Walt and Bastion had decided to search the main building first, though both thought the smaller more secluded buildings were far more likely candidates for The Zealot's hideout. They planned to give the building a quick sweep just in case before moving on.

The large wooden front doors weren't locked, but Walt couldn't be sure if that was odd or not, as many of the followers and staff had made quick exits to avoid law enforcement.

They shared a quick nod before Walt pulled the door open and entered. The nave was dark, with all light barred from the inside by thick shutters, Walt couldn't see past the pews to the altar.

"Something isn't right here," Bastion said. "I can feel it."

No sooner had he spoken than the door slammed shut behind them. "I came here for one beauty, and I found two," said a rasping female voice.

Walt spun to see Denise Barone standing just inside the church illuminated by the lights attached to the guns of her henchmen.

"You just couldn't stay away," Walt said flirtatiously, playing for time. "I'm glad our brief time together meant as much to you as it did to me."

"Not your usual type, buddy," Bastion added, catching on at once.

"Well, when you know, you know."

"Cute," Denise rasped. "But you can't sweet talk your way out of this one, darlin'. We've got the place surrounded."

"You're not still mad about that little bust, are you?" Walt squinted, scanning the dark recesses of the church. There were shadows looming and Walt was sure they were thugs in Denise's employ.

"All my boys are in jail because of you. I had to hire these bozos. You think that's cheap?"

"I think your boys are in jail because you're criminals. How did you escape justice?"

"I was already in the wind when they kicked down my door. I knew you'd bring more pigs with you."

"Why don't we cut to the chase?"

"Who's your little friend?"

Bastion, who towered over every other person in the room, chuckled. "You don't need to know."

"Fair enough." Denise shrugged. "Best be on your way then. This doesn't concern you."

"I'm fine right here."

"You won't be if you stay. Leave. It would be a shame to mar such a beautiful package."

"Careful, you'll make Walt jealous."

"You boys are real fun, but this is serious business. I have a message for your girlfriend from Joel Curtis."

"You're working for a serial killer now?" Walt said, dropping the friendly pretence.

"Who d'you think paid for the help?" She indicated the heavily armed thugs that stood around her.

"What's the message?"

"It's not really one you can give her...it's more of a 'she finds you dead' kind of message."

Everything happened at once. Bastion grabbed the gun from Walt's holster and brought it to bear on Denise as two of the looming shadows took form and grabbed Walt from behind dragging him between the pews. A thick arm found its way around Walt's neck, and he kicked out madly but could do nothing to shake the iron-clad grip. He was only vaguely aware of Bastion locked in combat with the four men who flanked Denise as he struggled in vain.

Walt was panicking and he knew it. He hated having anything around his neck, it reminded him of a noose, but he had to relax or he had no chance of getting free. Either the man with his arm around Walt's neck was unskilled or he wasn't actually trying to kill Walt, rather, just to restrain him. Walt took full advantage of this. Forcing the men holding him to take all his weight, Walt lifted his legs off the ground and bucked. The explosive power of the move caused the men to lose their grip. Walt tumbled forwards into one of the pews as they fell backwards into another.

The two men were upon him again in seconds. One of the attackers pulled a pair of handcuffs from his pocket and managed to get one of the bracelets around Walt's wrist, before he wrestled himself free. He could feel the subtle magnetic pull as it searched for its twin. Using his free hand, Walt threw a heavy cross, followed by a thunderous hook that floored his would-be captor. His friend lunged for Walt, who grabbed a Bible from the nearest pew and hurled it at the man. It hit him hard in the face and caused him to back off. Walt put the distraction to good use and dove forward tackling the man to the ground, but before Walt could advance any further something hit him in the back. The impact was soft at first, then a jolt of electricity shot through him, bringing him to his knees as his legs gave out.

"The boss said a small pinch would work. You should really get that augmentation upgraded. Being paralysed leaves you in a very vulnerable position."

Walt ignored the jibe and used his arms to pull himself away from the man who had gotten the first cuff around his wrist.

"Not so fast, Captain." The man leaned down and placed a small circular device on Walt's chest. Walt immediately tried to pull it off, but it gave him a painful shock. "Don't want those legs working any time soon."

"Walt?" Bastion shouted from somewhere out of view. There was an odd *thunk* like metal hitting flesh, then the unmistakable *thud* of a body hitting the floor.

"Bastion!" Walt yelled, still trying to drag himself away.

"I think he's having a little nap. Maybe you should too."

The last thing Walt remembered was seeing a boot moving swiftly towards his face.

MOTHER

It was getting late. Thea was tired, but it had been agreed she wouldn't go home in case Joel Curtis was waiting for her. Cora remained at ARC as well, though she was still ignoring Thea and had sequestered herself in her office. Thea sat in comfortable silence with Castillo in the Directors' Lounge, waiting for Walt, Bastion, Torrez and Sid to return from their missions.

Mateo lay across a cushy sofa that was nicer and more expensive than any of the furniture Thea had at home, while Thea herself curled up in a squashy armchair.

"I hate waiting. I should just go home."

"Do you hate waiting more than you hate the idea of being attacked by a serial killer?" Castillo asked, covering his eyes with his forearm.

"Right now, yes."

Castillo gave a short sleepy laugh. "Can I ask about Tenebrium?" He said after a long pause in which Thea thought he might have dosed off.

"What about it?"

"What was it like when the Gold Legion took over?"

"Quick. Everything happened so fast. One minute we were on the trail of a cult and the next they'd taken over the city. We became public enemy number one overnight. Nowhere was safe. The city was on fire, ghouls roamed the streets. It was us against the world. A lot of good people died in the fight. But it was nothing like this if that's what you're getting at."

"Sure feels like we've been taken over by a cult."

They lapsed into silence again. Thea had just fallen into an uneasy dose when her Cicada rang.

"Sir," Thea said, throwing a pillow at Castillo to wake him. "Unknown caller."

Castillo touched his hand to his ear and said, "Hasim, record and trace the call coming through to SSA Williams." Thea couldn't hear the reply, but Castillo nodded letting her know she could answer the call.

"SSA Thea Willaims here."

"You weren't home, Miss Thea. I waited."

"I'm sorry, who is this?"

"Don't try that with me."

"I thought you liked games."

"You used my mother against me. You paraded her in front of the city."

"It was her choice. She doesn't want you to get hurt."

"No! She damned me and then abandoned me. She doesn't care about me. You manipulated her like you manipulated Levi. I had to kill him because of you. It's your fault. It's all your fault."

"That's a great way to deflect blame, but you killed Levi. You. I didn't make you. That was your choice. But none of that is why you called, is it?"

"We're tracing the call. Keep him talking," Castillo all but mouthed.

"I want to meet with you."

"Where?"

"So eager. But that's not how we're going to do this."

"It's your game. Why don't you tell me the rules so I can play?"

"Some things are going to happen—"

"What things?"

"—And how you react to them will dictate how we play."

"That's it?"

"That's all you get for now. By the way, your mother is a lovely host."

The line went dead.

"What is it? What's wrong?" But Thea was already on her feet.

"I need you to check the protection detail we put on my mother. Make sure they're still there."

"All right."

"And make sure Cora is still here."

"Done, but what did he say?"

Thea shook her head and stepped out into the corridor with her hand to her ear. She paced as the call rang. "Come on. Come on. Come on. Come on."

"Thea? It's late." Her mother's voice was slurred. She was drunk.

"Mom, are you okay?"

"You care now, do you?" The words were garbled.

"Are the officers still outside your house? I need you to check, right now."

Thea heard her mother stumble as she made her way to a window. "Still watching." She hiccupped drunkenly.

"Mom, have you had any strange calls? Has there been anyone lurking around? Even before the agents were put outside?"

"The man on the news..." Her voice was sly.

"What do you mean, Mom?" Thea heard another little hiccough. "Mom. This is serious. Did you see him?"

"He was here."

"What? When? Are you all right?"

"He's a nice talker. He just wanted to talk. It was days ago."

"What did you tell him, Mom?"

"He wanted to hurt you like you hurt me."

"What did you tell him?"

"I told him about Walter James."

"You sent him after Walt?"

"He deserves to pay for what he did to your father."

Thea hung up and immediately called Walt. "Please. Please, please, please. Pick up."

"This number is no longer in service."

"Fuck!"

"Thea!" Bastion was running up the corridor towards her.

"What the hell are you doing here?" she snapped at him.

"He took Walt."

"I know. Follow me."

Thea led Bastion back into the Directors' Lounge where Mateo was waiting.

"The officers at your mother's residence are still in position. There has been nothing unusual. And Cora is asleep in her office; I've posted an agent outside the door. Who's this? What's going on?"

"Sit down, I'll explain everything."

"So, you think Joel Curtis has taken Captain James because of your past personal connection?" Castillo asked after Thea had filled him in. "And this man—" He pointed at Bastion. "—Is a fugitive from the Gold Legion that I'm going to forget exists?"

"Yes, and yes."

"We can't just sit here and wait," Bastion said, crossing his arms. "We have to get out there and look for him."

"Where?" Thea demanded. "He could be anywhere, but if you have any leads, I'm happy to follow."

"Track his implant."

"I tried. It's been shut down. Any other ideas?"

Bastion said nothing and Thea returned her attention to Castillo. "We need to make sure someone has eyes on Cynthia at all times and someone needs to check on Sid and Torrez. I have a personal connection to both."

"They checked in less than five minutes ago," Castillo said, tapping his index.

"All we can do now is wait for his call."

It was the longest forty minutes of Thea's life, but there was no relief to be had when her Cicada finally buzzed.

"I'm here."

"Are you missing someone, Miss Thea?"

"Where's Walt?" Thea kept her voice as calm as possible, giving nothing away.

"He's safe for now. But he won't stay that way forever."

"What do you want?"

"A trade, Mr James for my mother."

"Not a chance."

"All right, fine. I'll just kill him."

"You do that, and this becomes personal. Are you ready for that?"

"Ah, so you do care. That means we can negotiate."

"Even if I wanted to, you know I can't give you Cynthia."

"Don't be so hasty; a man's life hangs in the balance. I'll give you some time to think about it. Gives me some time to play with my new toy."

The line went dead.

BOURBON BLUES

Walt was bleeding. A steady stream of red was trickling across his face, stirring him back to wakefulness. He was lying on his side on a cold, painfully hard floor, something tight around his wrists. He opened his eyes slowly, blinking away the blood that had pooled in the corner next to his nose and tried to sit up. His head swam and it took him a moment to bring his surroundings into focus.

The walls of the room were invisible to him having been engulfed by darkness. Walt had no idea how big the room was, yet something in the feel of the air told him it was a vast space.

He felt his wrists. There were heavy manacles around them, with chains that had been bolted into the floor. They gave him just enough leeway to allow him to stand and take a few steps. Walt pulled with all his might at his shackles, but it was no good. He brought a hand instinctively to his ear but drew it away sharply with a wince. Where his Cicada should have been, was an oozing wound. If he had harboured any doubt about who had captured him, that certainly put an end to it. Like Mercer, Baker-Singh, Cutter and Fen, he had been taken by The Zealot.

A flash of how he was apprehended came to him and he brought a hand to his chest. The little device was still affixed to his shirt. He tried to pull it off, but it sent a shock through him that caused him to crumple to the ground, his legs numb.

"I wouldn't do that if I were you. You'll want to keep your sea legs."

Walt whipped around. Standing in the shadows, barely visible, was a young, fair-haired man with a smattering of stubble and black ink-pools for eyes.

"What do you want?" Walt struggled to pull his legs from underneath him.

Curtis didn't answer at first. He stepped out of view for a moment. When he came back, he was carrying two yellow tripods of around five feet tall, each with a rectangular bulb at the top. They looked like miniature floodlights. He placed one either side of Walt and turned them on.

A deluge of light flooded the room and Walt brought a hand to shield his eyes from the stark white glare. He had been right about the size of the space. It looked like a massive stock room. The floor was bare concrete. Steel shelving, taller than a five-story building, lined the walls. Wooden boxes and metal containers had been cleared from the central space to sit haphazardly against the shelves.

"What do you want?" Walt asked again, but again Curtis ignored him. The Zealot just stood there, staring at him as he sat helplessly on the ground.

"You should have the feeling back in your legs by now," he said after a few minutes. "Stand up."

Walt did as he was told, feeling that regardless of what Curtis wanted, it put him in a much better position to attack.

"Take off your shoes." Curtis demanded abruptly. "And your socks."

"Why?"

"Do as I say, or I'll give you another little jolt and do it, myself." Curtis waved a little remote control that Walt was sure was linked to the device on his chest.

Never taking his eyes from Curtis, he lifted each foot so he could remove his socks and shoes without leaning over. When he was done, he tossed them out of reach.

"Good." Curtis turned and left the room again. This time, Walt could see that he left through a heavy grey door marked 'Delivery Office'. He didn't return as quickly this time, but when he did, he was carrying two large bottles of water, the type that fitted into water coolers. Without speaking, he pulled the tops off both and poured them out onto the floor.

The cold water flooded over Walt's feet, sending a shiver through him.

"What now?" Walt asked. He kept his tone calm, though he felt anything but. He was in a bad situation; a very bad situation.

"Take off your jacket and your waistcoat."

"That's going to be a little hard." Walt shook a wrist making the manacles jingle.

"Hhm." Curtis made his way to one of the containers and rifled through it. A moment later he was back in front of Walt holding a large pair of scissors. "Do I need to shock you, or will you behave?"

Walt weighed up his options. If he fought back and won, he was still chained to the floor. He thought it was better to play along, for now.

"I won't fight you."

Walt tensed; he couldn't help it as Curtis stood behind him. He felt the fabric shift as his jacket and waistcoat were cut from him. When Curtis was finished, he stepped back taking the tatters of Walt's clothes with him.

Barefoot, wearing only his suit trousers and shirt, arms chained and with a device that could paralyse him attached to his chest, Walt was feeling very vulnerable.

"You are a liar. You have damned yourself by receiving an augmentation and you now try and convince others to get them, damning them with you. You and all the others like you are the snake, with its many heads."

"Is that why you do this? Because you think you're already damned? Your bible says 'thou shall not kill'."

"I am a warrior for God, but we aren't talking about me. You have been judged and you have been found wanting. Athena Williams told me you're an alcoholic, is that true?"

Walt said nothing.

"What was your drink of choice?"

Again, Walt stayed silent.

"You must have noticed the water on the floor," Curtis hopped up onto the nearest crate, so his feet dangled. He reached into a small box that sat there and pulled out a hollow black circle. It was what the TPD weapon techs called a 'taze grenade'. "I can tell by that glint in your eye that you know what this is. So, you answer my questions or the next jolt you get is going to be a big one."

"Bourbon," Walt said with a sigh. "My drink of choice was bourbon."

"I guessed correctly."

For the third time, Curtis left the room. When he returned it was with a room service cart filled with glasses of dark amber liquid. The scent alone told Walt it was top shelf bourbon.

"What are you doing?"

Curtis smiled widely. He parked the cart just out of Walt's reach and began to unload the glasses, placing them in a ring around Walt. When he had finished, he left again, returning with more bourbon. The new glasses were placed in a second ring. On and on it went for the best part of an hour until the entire floor for several metres around Walt was covered in gleaming glasses of liquor.

The smell was heady. His sobriety had been tested over the last few days, but nothing like this. The temptation was almost too great. Walt may have been an addict, but he wasn't an idiot. He was willing to bet the glasses had been tampered with and no matter how much he wanted to drink, and he really wanted to, he wouldn't.

"I'm not playing," Walt said, clenching and unclenching his fists.

"But you don't know what the game is yet. You see, this isn't really about you. It's about your girlfriend."

"Thea can take care of herself, she's tougher than you'll ever be."

"I was wondering if you'd think I meant the journalist. I'm glad I made the right choice."

Walt closed his eyes, internally cursing himself. A personal connection could be exploited.

"There's only one rule. Drink and it stops, but if you do, I won't just kill Miss Williams; I'll destroy her."

"Make what stop?" Walt asked, feigning indifference.

Curtis ignored the questions. "I will torture her. I will rip her apart. She will beg for death before the end."

Walt could feel the vein in his temple pulsing, but he kept his voice calm. "She's too smart for you, she won't play your games."

"You think her my equal?"

"I think her your better."

"She's already playing. If she brings me my mother, I'll let you go."

"She won't make the trade."

"So, I should just kill you now? Where's the fun in that? Drink."

"No."

"She will die screaming no matter what you do."

Without warning, Curtis threw one of the black circles at Walt's feet. He looked at it for a moment before it glowed blue and emitted a wave of electricity. Amplified by the water on the floor the jolt that surged up his legs was immense. It prickled at first, then his muscles spasmed. Pain roared through him and he was thrown into the air. The chains round his wrists served to yank him back to the ground. He landed painfully on the wet concrete, panting, his legs numb, a faint burning smell tingling in his nose.

"You stay there, I have a call to make."

GOOD NEWS

As it neared midnight, Alex realised that today had been the first day with no rioting. Caligo was finally seeing some form of betterment after the rounding up of the major players in Una Amina. Yet, the streets were still plagued by fear. The riots had been bad enough, but the bombings were something different entirely.

No one in the CPD had ever had to deal with a serial bomber. Uncommon as a rule, the sheer amount of bombings and the devastation they caused were unheard of. The death toll was mounting and more than this, food was starting to run low at many of the aug safe houses.

Alex couldn't help but feel frustrated. Objectively, they'd had one of the best months of their career. They had been front and centre of an operation that had crippled one of the biggest crime families in the city. They were the CPD face of the joint Zealot task force, and they were leading the investigation into the bombings—not to mention the work they were doing to ensure the safety of the augmented community. Alex knew that they were in for a promotion and several commendations and yet, they weren't satisfied. All their achievements of late looked impressive on paper, but the city was still divided by hate and until The Soulful Elite were caught, its citizens were in danger. All the praise in the world couldn't make up for that.

Alex hadn't seen Torrez in days and wasn't at all surprised to find that they missed him. The relationship was progressing quickly, but it felt right. Torrez would have to wait however; the bombings were Alex's only priority.

"Detective," Officer Fry called from across the bullpen. "I've got good news."

"Please tell me it's about Ralph Price."

"Facial recognition got a hit in the database, and he's turned up on a street cam in the Church Ward." Fry smiled in a 'gotcha' sort of way.

"Get a team together. We're heading out."

WAITING GAME

Walt had been missing for eighteen hours. Joel Curtis had been in contact once to tell Thea she had until midday the next day to hand over his mother in an exchange, or Walt would be crucified like the other victims.

"What do we do if we haven't found him by midday?" Torrez asked Thea as they poured over a city map trying to pinpoint places for the ground teams to search. It was four in the morning, and both were somewhere far beyond tired. Thea was running on coffee and unease; she knew she would be more useful if she slept and yet she couldn't bring herself to close her eyes even for a second.

"I don't know. I can't hand Cynthia over. I can't let Walt die. And he could be anywhere. He might not even be in the city. The TPD should be checking in any minute, maybe they'll have some news."

"Anything from Bastion?"

Thea shook her head.

It had taken some coaxing from Bastion to get Cora to aid in the search, still bitter as she was about their argument and even more so about the fact Thea had allowed Bastion into The Orchard, where any number of the agents inside might recognise him. To avoid further conflict Bastion was personally following up on any leads Cora generated focusing on Denise and her hired goons while the other teams focused potential hideouts for The Zealot.

"I can't just sit here," Thea said. She picked up a file from the desk and threw it across the room.

"Why didn't you tell me?" a voice shrieked. The conference room door burst open to reveal Fen; a rather bedraggled witness protection agent following closely behind.

"Miss Yeoh, please," the agent said, tugging gently on Fen's arm.

"I'll handle this," Thea said to the agent, who took the statement as a dismissal.

"I don't need to be handled. I need you to tell me why?" Fen demanded through gritted teeth.

Guilt bubbled up in Thea's stomach. "I forgot about you," she admitted.

"You forgot? I had a right to know. You should have told me."

"I'm sorry," Thea said. "You're right. I'm sorry."

Thea's calm contrition seemed to catch Fen off guard. It was hard to maintain her anger when Thea displayed none.

"Why Walt? What does he have to do with this? Is it because of the press conference? Is it because of me?"

"No. It's because of me." Thea stooped to pick up the file she had thrown and replaced it on the table.

"I don't understand."

"My mother told Curtis that Walt and I..."

"Why would he care? Why would your mother do that?"

"It's complicated."

"What does that even mean? Complicated how? Tell me what's happening!"

"Walt murdered my father." Thea heard Torrez's audible intake of breath beside her but ploughed on regardless. Fen's mouth opened ever so slightly in shock. "It wasn't his fault; but he did. My mother never got over it. She hates him. So, when Curtis asked her how he could hurt me, she told him about my past with Walt."

"I don't care about your past. What are you doing to find him? Why aren't you out there looking?"

"I'm doing everything I can to find him. We have teams—"

"Are you though? If he killed your father I would understand—"

"I want to be out there," Thea cut across her, keeping her voice measured but firm. "It's taking everything I have not to be out there, but I'm more use here. We have no leads and nothing to go on. This is a big city. We need plans, information; not blind searches." Their eyes met. Fen's gaze was intense, like she was trying to read Thea's mind. "I will find him. I promise."

Fen nodded. "What can I do to help? Please, let me help."

"Come with me. The officer guarding Cynthia is due for a break, and I can't spare anyone from the search. I want you to watch over her and see if you can get any information that might help us find Walt. Since the press conference, she won't talk to me."

Thea left the room and Fen followed her without hesitation.

"I'm sorry about your dad," Fen said as they stood in an elevator together.

"It wasn't Walt's fault. He was forced to do it against his will."

"Still. That must have been hard for you."

Thea nodded her thanks.

The protective custody wing was underground much like the lock-up, but it was far more inviting. There were private rooms that looked more like self-catering hotels, and common areas with televisions, pool tables and arcade games.

Cynthia had been given a large room with a rare skylight window. When they arrived at her door, Thea wasn't surprised to see it shut. It had been with a distinct lack of grace that Cynthia had agreed to protective custody.

Thea knocked. "Cynthia, it's Agent Williams."

No response.

"Agent Clawson?"

No response.

Thea grabbed the door handle. It was locked. "Fen, go down the hall and the first agent you find, tell them we have a situation in WitPro." Fen turned on her heel and jogged back the way they had come.

"Stand back," Thea called before raising a leg high and kicking the door. It snapped open ricocheting off the wall. Inside, Thea could see that Agent Clawson, a muscular White man with long curly hair, lying face-down on the floor of the small room. She darted to his side and turned him over. There was a large gash on his forehead. She checked his pulse; he was alive but out cold. Scanning the room, her eyes came to rest on the single window. It was open. The blind billowed slightly in the breeze that creeped in from the outside. Cynthia was nowhere to be seen.

"What do you mean she's gone?" Torrez said nonplussed when Thea and Fen arrived back in the conference room to tell him and AD Castillo the news.

"She knocked out the guard and climbed out the window."

"What are you going to do?" Torrez asked.

"I don't know."

"Thea..."

"I don't have enough agents. With the bombings and everything else in the city, it was a struggle to get a team to search for Walt. Everyone is in danger, and it's my job to keep them safe. How am I supposed to make this choice? I can't take anyone from the bombings, so either we search for Walt, or we search for Cynthia. There is no right choice here, but it's Walt, Drew. It's Walt."

"I know. I wish this wasn't on you."

"But it is on me." Thea rubbed her eyes. "You keep searching for Walt. Keep everyone looking for him. I'll find Cynthia myself. She can't have gotten far."

"You can't go out there alone. That's exactly what Curtis wants."

"It's Walt," she said again. "I can't let him die. That's my choice."

WHISKEY KICKER

Walt was in pain. He had been electrocuted over and over again. His skin tingled. His feet were burned, but more than anything, he was mentally and physically exhausted.

"Stand up."

It cost Walt something to force himself onto his feet. His heart was beating erratically and that mixed with the strong smell of bourbon was making him feel lightheaded.

Curtis smiled, enjoying Walt's obedience. He pulled the small remote out of his pocket and pressed the button in the centre. There was a jolt and then it felt like someone was pouring warm water down Walt's spine. For what felt like the hundredth time, Walt collapsed to the ground, his legs numb.

"Just to make things more interesting..." Curtis shortened the lengths of chain attached to his wrists, so that Walt could sit up and no more. Then he moved to one of the shelves and picked up a red metal toolbox. He sat it on the ground next to Walt, opened it and pulled out a hammer and a box of thin, inch long nails.

"What the hell are you doing?"

"Drink."

"No."

"Why do you fight it?"

Walt watched on in horror, unable to stop him, as Curtis pulled a nail from the box and placed it against his right shin. He raised the hammer and struck, embedding the nail into Walt's bone. He did this three more times, Walt yelling all the while, before he finally said, "It's not like you can feel it."

"What the hell is wrong with you?"

The familiar tingling sensation was making its way down Walt's legs. He was regaining the feeling and with that, the pain would come.

"You're a strong one. I didn't want Eddie at a disadvantage. He's a little starved."

"Who's Eddie?"

"Stand up."

"What's the point? I'm just gonna end up on my ass again anyway."

Curtis raised a leg and stomped down on Walt's shin driving the nails in further. Walt cried out as pain ricocheted through him.

"Get up!" Curtis snarled as he reached down to loosen the chains slightly. "Or I hammer."

Walt dragged himself to his feet. "Now what?"

"Now you show me what you're made of."

Walt took a reflexive step back as Curtis picked up the hammer again, but he didn't raise it to strike. Instead, he moved over to a stack of wooden crates off to one side and used the clawed end to pry one open. A dishevelled man in a soiled three-piece suit crawled out. He was White and emaciated, with greasy blond hair and a scraggly beard. He was very tall, though he stooped, clearly stiff from being crammed into the crate. He looked scared yet defiant.

"Eddie, meet Walter," Curtis said to the man. "Kill him and I'll let you go."

Life seemed to return to the man's eyes as he took in the chains around Walt's wrists.

"Wait, wait, wait," Walt called, raising his hands. "Just like that?"

"Eddie here is the brother of Vincent Russo. The man who ruined my life for the first time."

"Who is he?" Eddie nodded to Walt. His voice was horse.

"Walt here," Curtis said, gesturing with the hammer. "Is very important to the woman who ruined it for the second time. Kill him and you're free. Fail, it's back in the box with your friends—the rats."

"I'm sorry, buddy," Eddie said, taking a step closer, and he almost looked it.

"You trust him?" Walt asked, tentatively checking his reach. He could take two steps in all directions and had just enough leash to punch.

"No, but I can't go back in."

Curtis stepped back to perch against the crate he had taken Eddie out of, as Eddie rushed at Walt. He sent glasses of bourbon skittering away, sloshing their contents on the already soaked concrete as he ran.

The slight down-tilt of his head was enough to tell Walt that the mobster was going to tackle him. It would be very dangerous to allow this fight to go to the ground. As Eddie reached him, bending low to trap Walt's waist, Walt brought up a knee that connected audibly with the mobster's chin. Walt heard his teeth snap shut with a crunch as the mobster staggered back but didn't fall. He reached forward to grab Eddie, but the chains held him back. Walt kicked out instead but missed as Eddie stepped out of reach.

"That's the only one you're getting," Eddie said, spitting blood onto the floor. "I won't die here."

Eddie stooped and grabbed one of the glasses. He hurled it at Walt. The tumbler bounced off his chest splashing his face and neck with bourbon.

"Was that a drink, Captain?" Curtis sounded positively gleeful. "Poor Agent Williams."

Walt spat on the floor trying to get it out of his mouth. "You touch Thea and I'll kill you." His distraction cost him dearly.

Eddie unleashed a devastating flurry of blows upon Walt's face and torso. Walt had taken several heavy hits before he had managed to bring his hands up to guard. As Eddie showed signs of tiring, Walt used the chain around his right arm to trap the mobster's fist and pull him in range of a vicious headbutt. The impact dazed Walt, but the effect it had on Eddie was far worse. Clutching his nose, the mobster dropped to his knees.

Walt took full advantage of the opening and slung the slackened chain around Eddie's neck. He pulled as hard as he could while Eddie fought and spluttered, his face slowly purpling. As the mobster's eyes rolled back and he slipped into unconsciousness, Walt let go of the chain, panting.

"You're not done," Curtis said, moving closer. "Kill him."

"No."

"Kill him."

"No," Walt snarled, his hands curling into fists.

"Do it or you die." Curtis raised the hammer, his intentions clear.

"Fine. Kill me because I won't do it."

"Pathetic," Curtis spat. "A man who can't kill, even to save his own life."

"I've killed before, but I won't kill for sport, and I won't kill for you."

Cursing, Curtis pulled the little remote from his pocket and pressed the button. The shock ran through Walt, causing his muscles to spasm and sending him crashing to the ground. He landed lying side by side with Eddie.

"You're pathetic. Weak. Broken. That's why they left you. That's why everyone leaves you." Curtis's eyes seemed to go out of focus as he raised the hammer and brought it down on Eddie's skull. The sound was revolting, like a coconut being split, but duller and wetter.

Walt was splattered with blood and brain matter, the ichor getting in his mouth and eyes. He scrambled away as far as the chains would allow, as Curtis brought the hammer up for another devastating assault. Again and again, blow after blow landed on Eddie's face and skull until nothing was left but a bloody red pulp. Walt felt sick.

Curtis turned to look at him then, murderous intent plain on his face, tinged with a terrifying sort of madness. But before he had made even the slightest move towards Walt, they both heard a familiar voice calling, "Walt? Walt? Are you here?"

A truly chilling grin seemed to almost split Curtis's face in two.

"Thea!" Walt bellowed. "Run! Get out of here!"

Curtis dropped the hammer next to Walt. "I'd better go greet our guest."

"Don't you touch her." But Curtis was already halfway to the exit. Walt grabbed the hammer and attacked the chains. It took multiple hits and far longer than Walt wanted to free himself, but when he finally managed it, he sprinted after Curtis, remnants of the chains still dangling from his wrists.

STING

Rain poured, the droplets landing on Alex's visor making the neon lights all around seem kaleidoscopic. Alex and their team had the old nightclub surrounded. Once a dazzling venue for those of a bohemian spirit, The Green Fairy was now little more than a battered husk.

A tall archway of carved peacock feathers was all that stood between Alex and their quarry. They nodded to the officers on their left and right. Alex could feel the tension emensting from them and they understood. This raid was more dangerous than any they had been on before. The headquarters of a terrorist organisation was likely to be trapped and with the group known for bombings, a single step inside could spell the end of them all. It was for this reason, that the team favoured a stealthier approach. Large groups were stationed at the entrances and exits, while smaller groups, like the one Alex led, would attempt to breach from other, less used, access points, remaining unseen.

Alex watched as the officer next to them used a crowbar to pry the boards off the old exit. The officer was quiet, but the sound would still carry. Once clear, Alex gently pulled the door open and stepped inside.

Everything inside the club was dark glittering greens and deep purples, from the walls and the floors to the old furniture pushed roughly to the side of the dancefloor. Even the overhead lights were green. Absinthe was the running theme, with bottles depicted on every surface. When the club was in operation it must have been a trip, Alex thought.

Their team fanned out behind them. The room they had entered was a smaller bar, not big enough to be confused for the main club floor. Huge pallets sat in the centre of the room, holding large white barrels filled with liquid and marked 'flammable'. They were in the right place all right.

There was a small opening on the opposite wall, covered by a curtain of green beads. The closer they got to it, the more voices they could hear.

"...dumb bitch," a rowdy male voice floated between the beads. "Told her the burn was from a barbeque."

"She bought it?" another replied.

"Well, I didn't marry her because she was smart."

Alex slipped between the beads. They were in the back corner of the main dancehall, obscured by shadows. Eight men sat on rundown and mismatched couches drinking beers and surrounded by tables of equipment that Alex was sure was used to make bombs. The décor on the larger dancefloor was much the same as the previous room's, with one exception. High above where the men sat, there was a huge disco ball made from empty absinthe bottles.

"Everyone on me," they murmured so quietly it was almost inaudible. They waited until they heard a double tap of static over the open line and then Alex took careful aim at the enormous disco ball. They fired a well-placed shot and the disco ball crashed to the ground in between the men. They leaped to their feet startled.

"CPD, nobody move!"

"Put your hands behind your head and get on your knees!"

Officers had the men surrounded and they quickly complied.

"Where is Ralph Price?" Alex demanded of the man nearest them. He was White and portly with a bald head and long beard. He spat at their feet. "Talk, and I'll put in a good word. Otherwise, take a good look, boys, because this is the last taste of freedom you're ever gonna get."

"He's in the office." The bald man nodded his head to a set of spiral stairs behind the bar. Alex gestured to two of the other officers to join them. They ascended to the top and were faced with a trap door. They could hear movement from inside.

Without missing a beat, Alex burst through the door and found Ralph Prince dousing the office in vodka, a book of matches in hand.

Ralph was White and in his late forties, he had dark blond hair flecked with grey and pale blue eyes.

"Freeze. Ralph Price you are under arrest for domestic terrorism."

"I want to make a deal."

"Oh yeah?"

"I'll tell you where we get our funding from and our targets."

"We already know that. Levi Seward."

Price's lips curved into a smile full of malintent. "It's his money but he isn't the one spending it. Ready to deal now?"

THE PAST

Seven years ago...

The glacial wind whipped through the threadbare blankets George had tried to fashion into a tent. The sleeping bag he had stolen when he was thrown out of the halfway house and the newspaper he had stuffed into his jacket were poor protection against a Tenebrium winter.

No one camping in the underpass had paid any attention to him, but he was too nervous to approach the larger group around the fire pit. He curled up in the foetal position and prayed that no one would come into his tent in the small hours of the night. He was so cold that he was dangerously drowsy when he heard it.

Shouts and clapping were coming from the park nearby. Afraid that if he curled up and attempted to sleep in the freezing weather he would never wake up again, George let his curiosity guide him.

The park was small but well-manicured. It had only two benches, and a single ring of trees with a patch of grass in the middle. A group of people were sitting on the grass, listening intently to a dark-haired man in his early forties. Even from a distance, George could tell that there was something about him. He had a charisma that seemed to sweep over everything around him.

George huddled in the shadow of one of the trees listening to the man speak.

"We are society's unwanted, the least desirables, but that doesn't mean that we have nothing to give. We are—well, hi there." The man had spotted George. "It's all right, friend. Come and join us. What's your name?"

"George."

"Hi, George, I'm Levi. Welcome to the flock."

THE SEARCH

Four days. Walt had been missing for four days. The tension inside ARC was palpable. Every single one of those involved in the search knew that with every passing hour it was becoming less and less likely they were going to find him alive.

Torrez had become broody, preferring to go out on the search missions with the field agents, rather than sit going over plans. Sid had taken on the role of the enthusiast, refusing to give up hope and jumping on every possible lead with fervour. Bastion, who Thea would never forgive for his actions in Tenebrium, has been so devoted to the search that she was surprised to find herself genuinely glad of his help. She might not have entirely believed his purported contrition, but the one thing they did have in common was their desperate desire to find Walt alive and well. Castillo, who didn't really know Walt, was maintaining a professional detachment. And Fen had shown that had journalism not been her calling, she would have made an exceptional agent. She was quick to notice patterns.

"I can't just sit here knowing Walt is out there somewhere!" Fen railed at no one in particular as she stood in the conference room that had become the de facto headquarters for the search. She looked strained, like she hadn't slept as she joined Alex and Castillo who had been helping Thea draw up plans for the next round of searches.

"You heading out again?" she asked Thea, taking in her tactical gear.

"Cynthia has to be somewhere."

"Do you have a minute before you leave? Coffee?"

Down in the break room Thea could feel Fen's eyes on her. "Are you okay?"

The truth was, she was spiralling. After Thea had refused to return Cynthia to The Zealot, he had cut off all contact. That had been three days ago. Since that moment, fear had an icy and unrelenting grip on Thea's heart, one that was only tightening. A trade was out of the question for so many reasons, but had she been of a mind to, it was impossible since Cynthia had fled protective custody.

She couldn't let herself think about the possibility of Walt being dead. Every time she did it stopped her cold. The only thing she could do was keep searching, because to stop was to give up on him and that felt like a bigger betrayal than any they had inflicted upon each other in the past.

"I'm fine. Really. I'm just tired. Like everybody else."

Fen nodded slowly, her mouth twisting.

"I overheard some of the field agents talking. They said it's been too long. Is it true? Is he dead?"

"I don't know."

"What do you think? As a cop. Have you ever found someone after this long?"

"Yes, I have. I've found people after years."

"If he's still alive, he doesn't have years, does he?"

"No. Curtis wants to hurt me. Levi was the only emotional connection he had and that's gone now. He's untethered, ungrounded. That makes him extremely dangerous. He blames me because he isn't capable of taking responsibility for what he did." In her heart of hearts Thea believed that Walt was alive, but being subjected to unspeakable horrors. It made her feel sick to think about.

"You aren't telling me something. Thea, please. I love him, I need you to tell me the truth."

Thea surveyed Fen before speaking. "Curtis wants to hurt me. I don't think killing Walt would be enough. I think he would want him to suffer and he'd want me to know about it."

"My god. Do you think...is he...d'you think, he's out there crucified?"

"I think the crucifixions were symbolic to him. He thinks his augmentations damned him, so those involved had to die to rid him of his sins. He didn't crucify any of the mobsters. I don't know what he's doing to Walt."

"My god," Fen said again.

"We'll find him."

"You don't believe that." Tears leaked from her eyes. "You are as worried as I am."

"We *will* find him," Thea said firmly.

"Thea?"

"Yeah?"

"It's the way he looks at you. I think he loves you and I hope he knows you're coming for him. I'd feel better, knowing you were looking for me. Be safe out there."

Thea didn't know what to say to that, so she didn't say anything. She took Fen's hand. They walked like that until they reached the lift. Fen went back to the conference room and Thea set out to look for Cynthia.

LOST BOY

Tears pricked Cynthia's eyes as she stepped into the small park. The faux moon reflected off the small pond and gave the place an ethereal quality. It was beautiful, with its ring of trees and perfect grass.

"I met Levi in this park. You left me in this park," George said as she approached. He was sitting on the little bench where they had fed the birds when he was a boy. Her beautiful boy was all grown up, but there was still the trace of the sweet child he had been in his boyish features. His eyes, however, told darker stories. It had nothing to do with his augmentation, there was just something inhuman about the consciousness that peered out of the inky pools.

"I missed you. I'm so sorry I wasn't the mother you deserved. My Georgie."

Anger flickered behind his eyes. Her beloved son was dangerous, more dangerous than Vinny or any of his men, and yet all she wanted to do was take him in her arms and tell him she loved him. Perhaps she was as broken as she felt; in that moment she didn't care.

"You damned me. You realised you had damaged my soul and you fled."

"No, it wasn't like that—"

"You brought me to this park and you left me on this bench like trash and you never looked back."

"I told you I loved you and then I took you home. It wasn't safe for you to be around me."

"But you never came back! You were disgusted by the creature you'd made."

When she imagined their reunion, it was never like this. She had made so many mistakes in her life but being a mother to George wasn't one of them. "You aren't damned, you're just lost." Looking at her son, it was as if all the years she had spent with Vinny had disappeared. Washed away. She felt like the timid and desperate woman who had wandered into a casino to make a deal with the devil. "You aren't damned. I should have been there for you, should have taught you that and I'm sorry I wasn't. I'm sorry that I didn't. But I love you and we can make up for it now. Just stop. Please stop what you're doing." Cynthia closed the distance between them to sit down on the bench beside her son. "I won't abandon you again. I swear."

"There is no stopping. I'm not going to let them take me."

"George, you're confused. If they catch you, they will kill you. You've hurt people. They won't understand that you didn't mean it."

"I did mean it. I enjoy it. I'm doing God's wet work. It's exhilarating to strike in his name."

"Listen to me, Georgie. What you are doing is wrong. You aren't damned. I don't think you're damned—I wasn't repulsed by your beautiful black eyes. They are unique; they are as much a part of you as your sweet smile."

"Liar!" he bellowed, flaring up at once. "The Devil has black eyes! You threw me away like trash. Do you know what it was like after you left? Dad never got off the couch again. He drank himself to death. Because of you!"

"I'm sorry. I'm so sorry. I know I've made mistakes—"

"He drank away all our money, I couldn't even afford a funeral. They took our house! I had to live in a group home and as soon as I turned eighteen, they kicked me out."

"My poor baby..."

"I was homeless, starving, sleeping under bridges and praying that no one came searching for company during the night. Where were you then, huh? You didn't care about me! You weren't the one who rescued me. Levi did. He saved me. He gave me a home. He was more of a parent to me than you ever were and now he's dead!" George let out a moan like a wounded animal. He curled forward hugging his knees and began to sob.

"My sweet boy..." Cynthia gently put her arms around him. He froze, not pushing her away but not giving into the embrace either. Then, almost instinctively, he turned to her, putting his head in her lap as he continued to cry. She held him like that for she didn't know how long. "I love you, Georgie. I love you and I'm sorry I wasn't there for you, but I'm here now. I want to help you."

"How can you help me?" he sounded so lost that it made her heart constrict in her chest.

"Tell me where the police captain is. Maybe if you let him go they'll go easy on you."

As soon as she said it, Cynthia knew it was a mistake. George stiffened and sat up, it was like shutters had closed behind his eyes. All traces of the lost little boy gone to be replaced by a cold fury that sent a shiver down her spine.

"You nearly had me, Mother. She sent you, didn't she? The one who made me kill Levi. She sent you to trick me. Didn't she? ANSWER ME!" George lunged for Cynthia pinning her to the bench.

"I came for you! She has no idea I'm here. I swear."

"I don't believe you. You left me! Why would you come back now?"

"I was too ashamed to come back before. I thought you'd hate me for leaving, for being selfish. But I realised that even though you're grown, you need your mother. I just want to help you."

"I have no mother." George pulled a long bloody shard of glass from inside his jacket and plunged it into her chest. Her breath caught as the pain radiated through her. There was no air in her lungs to cry out. She couldn't breathe, she couldn't fight back, she could only watch as her son began to carve.

She turned away. She didn't want to see what George had become. The pain was so intense and then it just faded. She saw a familiar figure standing in the tree line. Tall and scarred but beautiful. He gave her favourite crooked smile and then she thought no more.

Cynthia was dead long before George succeeded in cutting out her heart, but the jogger who found the body the next morning would never forget the gruesome sight.

THEFT

When Cleo arrived at her lab sometime after midnight, there were already security and police officers waiting for her. A small cordon stopped her from entering her office.

"Excuse me, Officer?" she asked the nearest member of law enforcement. A Black woman with a long afro and freckles. "What's going on?"

"Dr James, I am Detective Michaels. Your in-house security reported a break-in in your lab. I need to accompany you while we do a sweep and assess if anything is missing."

When they stepped inside, nothing seemed out of place. Cleo searched her cabinets, but all was accounted for. She checked her journals, the test logs, patient files and still found nothing missing. It wasn't until she searched her fridge of drug samples that she realised what was gone.

"Detective Michaels. I am missing several samples of pure Styxx."

"You carry that here? How much is gone?"

"If taken or administered, enough to create maybe fifty ghouls."

RUSTY NAIL

Walt had been searching for hours. He ran through corridor after corridor, each the same as the last, but he found no trace of Thea or Curtis in the white cinder block maze. He ached all over. The nails embedded in his shins caused shooting pains with every step he took, and his bare feet stung as they slapped the hard floor. He was starving, thirsty and sleep deprived. But he couldn't stop.

Walt was starting to think he had gotten turned around in the featureless corridors when he finally came across a door. It was narrow and metal, like the side door of a nightclub. He reached a cautious hand towards the push bar and was equally surprised and suspicious when the door opened.

He had found himself in an alley like any other in Tenebrium, shrouded in shadows punctuated by the glow from the neon signs posted on the buildings that towered above. Walt saw instantly that he had been right to be suspicious.

Four men stood half-way down the alley. All wore waistcoats; the sleeves of the shirts underneath were rolled up. It was too dark for Walt to make out any features.

"More Russos, right?" Walt said blandly, mentally preparing himself for a fight. "Any chance you could just let me leave?"

"You will be punished for your sins." The man that spoke hurled something as he did so. Walt only just moved out of the way as the heavy object clattered to the ground. It was a brick.

Another was thrown and then another. Walt barely managed to dodge out of the way. Finally, a brick hit its target, skimming his face. He doubled over clutching his cheek and another collided painfully with his back.

Walt straightened, keen to keep his eyes on the men, lest another brick hit him. He squinted into the gloom and saw one of the men stoop to pick something up. It was long and thin and made a metallic noise as it was scraped along the ground. It was a pipe.

This was his chance. Walt moved forward knowing it would make it easier for the others to hit him and waited. As soon as the pipe was thrown Walt extended a hand to catch it, and he did so, deftly.

"That was stupid," he said, charging forward to meet his attackers.

The first man he reached was Indian, with dark hair and several gold teeth that glinted in the low light. Walt brought the pipe down hard on the top of his head, following up with a huge swing that clattered across the man's jaw. Walt gave him a last jab to the stomach with the end of the pipe and the man crumpled to the ground unconscious.

His fellows were upon Walt in seconds. Walt swung the pipe low, sweeping the legs from a White man with a significant scar that distorted his bottom lip. The scarred mobster toppled over, landing painfully on the uneven cobbles.

One of the two mobsters left standing, raised a baseball bat Walt hadn't noticed and tried to bring it down on Walt's head, but Walt parried with the pipe, holding it horizontally in both hands. He thrust the pipe forwards, the metal crushing the man's nose. While he was distracted, Walt grabbed the bat and threw it out of reach before landing a knockout-blow on the man's temple.

As the scarred man scrambled to his feet, his remaining comrade threw a heavy haymaker at Walt's face. Walt trapped the extended arm with the pipe. He gave a vicious twist that snapped the man's arm with a crack so loud, it reverberated off the alley walls. He didn't have a chance to cry out, as Walt unleashed a haymaker of his own that sent the man to the ground.

The scarred man lunged for Walt who surprised him by closing the gap between them with a flying knee. The strike settled right on target and sent the man careening through the air to land on his back. Walt didn't waste any time. He brought a foot down hard on the man's stomach, once, twice, three times, before setting off at run.

As he came to the mouth of the alley something hard collided with the back of his head. His vision went fuzzy and his legs unsteady. He was unconscious before he hit the ground.

When Walt opened his eyes, he was lying on his back in a pool of shattered glass, a rabid ghoul advancing on him. He was on his feet in less than a second and had struck out with his fists, before the first droplets of blood had soaked onto his shirt. The onslaught he unleashed was brutal, ending with a push kick that sent the ghoul tumbling backwards to land in Thea's shower.

There was no time to relax, another ghoul was already close enough to bite him and it tried. Walt grabbed it roughly by the shoulders and spun it round so he could wrestle it into a chokehold. He torqued his body and the muted crunch that followed told him he had broken its neck.

Walt put his hands on his knees, panting. He could feel his broken ribs trying to break through the skin. He looked around to make sure he was safe and saw Thea lying on her back between the coffee table and her sofa. All pain forgotten, he sprinted into the bathroom and grabbed the MedKit from under the sink. He rushed back to Thea, dropping to his knees at her side. Walt checked her pulse. There wasn't one.

"No, no, no, no. Don't you dare. Don't you fucking dare."

Walt pulled a syringe-like device from the MedKit and jabbed it into Thea's neck.

"Analysing," a robotic voice said in his ear.

"Come on. Come on."

"Analysis complete. Substance unknown."

Walt was at sea. He didn't know how to fix this, but he couldn't let her die. He plunged a hand back into the MedKit and pulled out a large needle and a small bottle. He loaded the syringe with adrenaline and plunged it into Thea's chest.

Nothing happened.

"This isn't happening. This isn't happening. Don't do this to me, Thea. Please."

She remained motionless before him.

"Fuck, fuck, fuck."

He cradled Thea in his arms, holding her close to his chest as despair threatened to overwhelm him. Tears fell unbidden and unchecked down his face, landing in Thea's hair as he rocked her back and forth, muttering pleas. On and on it went as the horrible realisation hit Walt. She wasn't going to wake up.

Something inside him cracked, broke wide open, a void threatening to swallow him whole and then he remembered— "She woke up."

Relief surged through him so forcefully it made him shiver. "She woke up. This already happened and Thea survived. This isn't real." Reality flooded back as the pain in his ribs left him to be replaced with pain in his legs and a clawing hunger. "Curtis, you bastard! Where are you?"

Walt's eyes raked over Thea's apartment. It was as he remembered and yet not quite right. It looked like it had after the explosion had caused it to be rebuilt and that had happened after the ghouls had attacked. Even more proof to his mind that it wasn't real.

"That was heart-wrenching."

Curtis stepped forth from the shadows, the edges of his form seeming to undulate.

"This isn't real."

"How sure are you?"

"Why are you doing this? What does this accomplish?"

"Lucifer was an angel once, his father's right hand. Aren't these the eyes of a Devil?" He pointed to his black sclerae.

"You hate them that much, why not get them removed or updated to look more like natural eyes?"

"Hiding the sin doesn't absolve one of it," Curtis spat. "Enough. How sure are you that this isn't real?"

"It's not. Thea survived." It was a fact and yet Walt was still careful not to let his eyes stray to the pale and cold Thea on the ground at his feet. "And you don't have her."

"Not yet. Eddie, be a dear and join us."

Eddie, alive and well, his skull intact, stepped into the living room through the broken glass window. He appeared thinner than he had before and far more afraid. "Please just let me go. I'm not my brother."

"I know that, but he went and got himself hanged, so you'll have to do. Kill the Police Captain here and you're free."

"No. No way. I'm out of the life. Please don't make me do this," Eddie begged.

"I will dip you feet first into a vat of molten metal and I'll do it slowly." Curtis growled the words.

Once again, Eddie peered at Walt sizing him up. "I'm sorry, buddy." This time it seemed like he meant it. *Nice touch*, Walt thought.

Curtis picked up the metal pipe that had appeared on the coffee table and threw it to Walt, who caught it lazily.

"I'm really sorry," Eddie said again. He ran for Walt who wasted no time in swinging the pipe. The metal collided with Eddie's kneecap and brought him to the ground. Walt followed up with a thunderous strike to the face which sent a tooth flying, following in the wake of the pipe. Now that Eddie teetered on his knees, Walt stepped behind him and used the pipe to choke him. Eddie fought hard at first, but then his protests became more and more feeble until they stopped entirely.

"None of this is real," Walt yelled, throwing the pipe aside.

"How sure are you?"

The room around Walt dissolved. It was like watching a water balloon burst in slow motion, except the droplets were square and then he was standing in the same large storeroom. Thea's body was gone. The pipe was nowhere to be seen, neither were the chains that had held him, but the hundreds of glasses of bourbon were still there, and the lifeless corpse of Eddie remained.

"No. It can't be..." Walt didn't know what to believe. His heart rate quickened and nervous sweat slicked his palms.

"The first fight wasn't real. The alley wasn't real. The apartment wasn't real. But Eddie was real."

"No..." Walt felt numb.

"Now you're a fallen angel."

"Why are you doing this?"

"Why won't you drink? Why won't you just give in? Why do you fight your nature? I've been in your head. You are broken. Damaged beyond repair. You feel everything. Loss. Pain. Greed. Anger. Why aren't we the same? Why aren't you a killer? Why doesn't it bring you peace? Your memories...you've suffered... so...why aren't you like me?" He looked so childlike that Walt almost felt sympathy.

"We aren't the same kind of broken."

Walt blinked and he was standing in his apartment. In his open plan living room. He was enraged and for a moment he couldn't remember why. And then he saw Thea. She was standing next to the sink in the kitchen, the counter covered in bottles, as she poured his bourbon down the sink.

"What the fuck are you doing?" he bellowed stalking towards her.

"I'm done, Walt. I'm done," she said, opening another bottle and sloshing it down the drain.

"Then be done. Leave! Get out!" He snatched one of the bottles from the counter before she could reach for it. "I told you I didn't want anything to do with you at Boulevardier. Are you so pathetic that you would cling to a man who hates you?"

Thea scoffed loudly as she rounded to face him properly. "Today you hate me, yesterday I was the love of your life. The day before that, you wished me dead and the day before that, you couldn't live without me." She reached for another bottle.

Walt hurled the bottle at the wall. It smashed soaking the floor. Thea didn't flinch, and didn't that make him want her more. "I don't want you in my life," he snarled.

"Well tough shit. You nearly got us both killed today because you were drunk off your ass! This has to stop. I know my Walt is in there somewhere."

Her Walt.

"You really think I'm worth saving?" He grabbed another half-drunk bottle from the counter and was about to put it to his lips and drain the contents when something caught his eye. There was a man with black eyes standing in the corner.

"Who the hell are you?"

TICK, TICK, BOOM

Ralph Price sat on his chair inside the small metal cage like it was a throne. He leaned back, lifting two of the chair legs off the ground and watched Alex as they circled.

"For someone desperate to make a deal, you've sure clammed up," they said, stopping in front of Price. "Are you worried the ghost of Levi Seward will haunt you if you squeal?"

Price snorted at that. "It's not Seward you need to be worrying about, but I'm not saying anymore 'til I see that sweet pardon paperwork."

It was Alex's turn to laugh. "D'you actually think there is a single thing you could tell us that will get you out of this one? The best you can hope for is the death penalty is taken off the bill."

"What?"

"You're a domestic terrorist. The powers that be don't look on that too kindly."

"If there's no pardon, I'm not talking."

"Fine, good luck with your trial. I'm sure the jury will love you—you're a real people person."

Alex turned and walked towards the door.

"Wait," Price shouted after them.

Alex was pleased to hear a note of panic in his voice, but they kept their face impassie as they turned back to him.

"No life term and no death penalty. That's the deal."

"I'll see what I can do."

It took over an hour to get the paperwork from the District Attorney but that was fine with Alex—they were happy to see Price sweat.

"You took your time," he said when they returned to the interrogation room.

"I'm glad to see your bravado has returned now you aren't gonna swing." Alex held the deal document up to the bars. "Happy? Now, talk."

"Seward always had this creepy little kid with him. Kept to himself. Then one day, he comes to us and says that he has bigger plans than preaching and hoping dipshits do the dirty work for us. He gave us the money and the targets. Even taught us how to make the bombs."

"The kid?"

"Yeah."

"Give me the name."

"Joel Curtis or The Zealot or whatever you guys call him."

"How was he paying you?"

"Transfer. Skimming from Levi's accounts. He put us in contact with some mob goons, too, when we needed muscle."

"What family?"

"The Barones."

"So, you're telling me that Joel Curtis is the mastermind behind the bombings?"

"Yup."

"Thank you for your co-operation. I'll let you know if the DA thinks your information merits a deal."

"What the fuck does that mean? You said I got the deal!"

"It's not my problem that you can't read. I showed you the docs. It says you get the deal if your info is useful."

"And I almost felt guilty about holding out on you."

Alex had expected this. "Oh yeah? Might wanna spill it if you want your deal."

Price's grin was almost perverted as he said, "There are more bombs in the city and a big surprise for your agent pal. Yeah, I know who you are, and I know you hang out with the Williams chick. Hope you say your goodbyes before she goes boom!"

"Where are the bombs? How many are there?"

"How the hell should I know? I've been here with you officer. Tick, tick, boom!" Price laughed but Alex ignored him as they sprinted from the room.

They tried to call Thea, but the line was engaged. They called Torrez next. "Babe, where is Thea right now?"

KENNETH

Thea had never been more surrounded by people and yet, she had never felt more alone. The streets of Caligo were full. Full of police, full of agents, full of people trying to go about their business and people who were afraid. And there was Thea, alone in the crowd.

She had searched everywhere she could think of for Cynthia. Every old Russo haunt. Every abandoned Una Anima building. She needed to get smarter with her search. Since Curtis had killed Levi Seward he had been fixated on her. Blaming her for the death because he couldn't handle what he had done. What if that was the key? What if she should be focussing on herself?

Her home was too obvious. The Orchard was too well guarded, but her mother's house...Curtis has already targeted Athena. It was a Hail Mary, but it was the only idea Thea could come up with. If she found Curtis, or rather she let Curtis find her, she would find Cynthia and Walt.

Athena lived in the closest thing Caligo had to a suburb. It was eerily quiet as Thea arrived. The agents that should have been posted outside her mother's house were nowhere to be seen, but someone was sitting on the bench on Athena's front porch. Fear caused the hair on the back Thea's neck to stands on end.

"If I go inside, what will I find?" Thea asked when she had made her way onto the porch.

Curtis looked peaceful. Oddly at ease. "Your mother, passed out on the couch. Drunk, but otherwise unharmed."

"Where is Cynthia?"

"Dead. I'd imagine she's already in a morgue somewhere waiting to be identified."

Damn. There was an undeniable truth in the casual way he had said the words.

"Where's Walt?"

"That's the question you really want to know the answer to. He's alive. For now."

"Where is he?"

"You see this?" Curtis pulled a small remote from his pocket. "This is attached to the bomb I placed under your mother's house. If you don't want me to push the button, you'll hand me your gun."

"You'd kill us too."

"We're at the win or die stage of the game. So, you can refuse and I press the button, killing you, me, and your mother. Maybe some of her neighbours. And Mr James, because without me, no one will find him. I'll be a martyr remembered in the annals of history and you will be a footnote at best. A bloody smear."

Slowly, Thea pulled her gun from its holster and tossed it to Curtis who caught it with ease.

"What now?"

With a speed and accuracy Thea could not have predicted, Curtis brought her own gun to bear on her and fired a single shot. It hit her squarely in the chest. Darkness claimed her before she could process what had happened.

When Thea opened her eyes again her first thought was that she was cold. She was lying on an icy floor. She sat up and looked at her surroundings. It was an atrium of some kind, perhaps that of a hotel or resort. It was a huge circular space, with a glass water tank in the centre that rose up out of sight. The water inside was murky, the skeletons of what looked like sharks lay at the bottom. Behind the tank, there were multiple sets of black and gold double doors. The once gleaming brass floors were now covered in dust and dirt.

Thea got to her feet. "Show yourself." Her voice echoed around the room.

There was a crackle as the intercom came into life. "Welcome, Miss Thea."

"Where's Walt?"

"He's around here somewhere."

"What do you want?"

No response.

Thea cursed loudly and brought her hand to her Cicada.

"Drew, I need a trace on my location."

"Thea—" but the rest of his sentence was cut off by a horrible high-pitched screech. Thea yelped, clutching her ear in pain. Curtis had engaged some sort of coms-jammer.

Her ears still ringing, Thea examined the room. There was a reception desk off to one side and stairs to the left and right, each set leading up to the next floor. The subtle hum as Thea approached them told her they had been electrified. Her path was through one of the sets of double doors then.

There were four sets, each with a sign above denoting the destination. Above all four was the same scrawled writing, it read:

There is no fire and yet there is smoke.
There is no wood and yet there is oak.

I bite without teeth; I burn without flame.
When memories are gone, I am to blame.

Thea chuckled in spite of herself. The answer was as plain to her as it would have been to Walt: whiskey. Shaking her head, Thea made her way through the door marked 'WATERING HOLE'.

The room Thea had entered was another smaller circular atrium, this time the centrepiece was a decrepit fountain. It had long since dried up, dead plants and fish mixed with coins to form a sludgy mess at the bottom of the pool. It was cold and dark, the air filled with the smell of turned wine. There were several separate bars, but the choice of which to enter was easy.

A dim but warm light emanated from the furthest venue. The front facing wall of which was made from oak whiskey casks, with red letters emblazoned on the front proclaiming the name to be 'FIREWATER'. Thea glanced around quickly, but there was nothing she could use as a weapon.. She was alone with no idea of where her enemy was, though she was sure he was watching her. It was unnerving.

No matter how sure she was of the dangers, Thea had to press on. She didn't trouble to be quiet as she ran towards the entrance. The Zealot knew she was coming.

When Thea entered the bar the first thing she noticed was the overpowering smell of alcohol. It was enough to make her head swim and it was everywhere. The second, was how the bar seemed to be an exact replica of French 75 in Tenebrium. It was unnerving. There were thousands of glasses all filled to the brim covering every surface. But that wasn't what kept her attention. Hanging from the ceiling by his wrists, with a noose around his neck was a man. He looked half-dead, starved. White, with grey hair, he was deathly pale. His face was drawn and his lips were chapped and cracked. He was filthy and bloody in equal measure.

"Wait!" he cried, his voice hoarse. Thea stopped dead. She saw at once what had the man staring wide-eyed and panicked. Partially hidden by the glasses, were thin wires running this way and that, criss-crossing along the floor. They were connected to the single pin in the ceiling that the man was suspended by. If she disturbed any of them, the wrist restraints would fall, and the man would hang.

"I'm Thea, what's your name?" Thea said, trying to keep her voice light as she struggled to see a way to free him.

"Kenneth...Russell. Pl-please get me down from here." His voice was shaking, and Thea could see in his eyes that he was barely holding on. He shivered in a way that made her nervous. Even the slightest movement could cause one of the wires to snap.

"I will, I promise. I will figure this out." But how? There were so many wires, and she had no idea where to begin. "Tell me about yourself. Where did you grow up?"

"P-p-please. Help m-me."

"I need a minute to think. So, talk to me."

"About w-what?"

"Anything. Tell me about yourself."

"I grew up in Tenebrium. I was an in-investigator for the DA," he said breathily. "I know you're trying to keep me calm."

"So, humour me. Keep going. Did you know Harold Williams?"

"Yes, he was my boss b-before he died."

"He was my dad." What the hell was she going to do?

"He was a bastard."

"Yes, he was."

"I retired after...everything." He gave an uneasy laugh, but stopped immediately when it made his restraints rattle.

Thea was only half listening. No matter how she looked at it she couldn't see how to free him safely.

"Kenneth," Thea said seriously.

"I know that tone. I don't know you, but I know that tone. You don't think you can do th-this. You seem nice. Competent. You have to do this b-because I don't want to die."

"There are so many wires. Touching any one of them could cause you to drop. If your neck doesn't break, I can free you, but I don't think we want to take that gamble."

"I can't take this much longer."

"I'm going to try and use the tabletops to get to you without touching the floor."

"If you knock a single glass over, I'm d-dead."

"I know. I'm sorry. I don't know what else to do. We can't wait for anyone else to get here. We don't have time."

"You mean I don't have time."

Thea could tell he was fighting panic. He wanted to struggle, and it was costing him everything not to. She looked him straight in the eyes as if trying to bore into his brain. "I will fix this. Trust me."

"I'm the guy who caught Vinny Russo."

"What?"

"If I die. It might be important. Wayland wanted to kill Vinny, but he was executed before the kid was old enough to kill."

"Okay. Here we go."

Careful not to nudge any of the wires, Thea stepped on to the first table. It groaned under her weight and shuddered slightly, causing the glasses on the top to quiver. The nearest table was an easy step and she made it over with no issues. The next table, however, would require a lengthy jump. She looked over at the long bar, it was too far away, then up at the ceiling. There were thin pipes running all along it. If she jumped, she could grab a pipe and shimmy across to Kenneth, but she had no idea if the pipes would hold her weight and if she fell, he would swing.

The chances of her making several table-to-table jumps without nudging a wire or a glass seemed astronomical. Seeing no other option, Thea raised her arms and jumped upwards. Her hands clasped around the pipe, and she sighed audibly as it held.

Kenneth closed his eyes in prayer.

Slowly and deliberately, she shimmied her way along the pipe, as if it was a set of children's monkey bars. She let out a sigh of relief when she reached Kenneth, that quickly turned to a groan as she realised she had no way of undoing the noose. It was knotted tightly on a pipe similar to the one she was holding, but she couldn't undo it with one hand, and if she let go of the pipe to stand on a nearby tabletop, she wouldn't be able to reach.

Kenneth was wriggling gently now, agitated and somewhere far beyond afraid. "Why did you stop?" he said, opening his eyes. "Why are you just hanging there?"

"I don't know how to untie you."

"No. No. No. I can't take it anymore. I've been up here for days, and I can't take it." He was shaking, tears rolling down his cheeks.

"You have to stop moving. Kenneth. Stop moving."

His breathing was erratic, and he was struggling more and more.

"Kenneth. Listen to me." Thea dropped carefully onto the nearest tabletop. "You have to calm down."

"No. I just need to be down. Let me down."

"Kenneth if you keep moving—"

SNAP.

The wires holding Kenneth's arms broke away from the ceiling. There was relief on his face for just a second, before the rope around his neck went tight. The short drop came to a sudden stop as the wires all around the room snapped or slackened. Thea jumped to the floor and ran forward. She grabbed Kenneth around the legs and lifted, trying to take the pressure off his neck, but he was heavy, she wouldn't be able to hold him forever.

Cursing, Thea gently let go. She rushed to the bar searching for anything she could use to cut him down. She grabbed the fruit knife stashed under the counter and used it to release him, laying him gently on the sopping floor. She knew before she took his pulse that he was dead. She had heard his neck break.

Thea's hands were shaking as she got to her feet. Adrenaline pulsed through her body as tears pricked the corners of her eyes. She looked sadly down at Kenneth. She had known him for less than fifteen minutes, but they had been briefly together, partners against a common threat.

Through a tiny gap in his shirt, she noticed something in his chest. Carefully she undid the buttons to reveal another message just for her. Carved into his flesh were the words, 'You can't save them all'.

A crackle overhead announced the return of The Zealot. "You failed. Just like you will fail to save your precious Captain and fail to save the city."

"Save the city from what? Una Anima? Already done."

"I will bring this city tumbling to the sea, taking every sinner with me. I will cleanse Caligo with fire."

My god, Thea thought. Curtis was behind the bombings and he had more planned. She felt stupid for not realising it sooner but there was no time to dwell. She had to find Walt and get out of wherever she was to warn the people of Caligo.

Clutching the fruit knife, Thea made her way out of the bar. There were no other exits in the fountain room. She had no choice but to go back the way she came. As she pushed through the double doors and into the atrium with the huge aquarium, she saw that the other sets of doors, still inscribed with the riddle, were now barred shut. She was being herded and she hated it. She had faced legions, one serial killer was not going to get the better of her.

Thea couldn't hear the subtle electric current from the stairs when she neared them and guessed that was where she was supposed to go. She walked slowly, staying vigilant for any traps. The stairs ended in a small balcony that was perfect for viewing the aquarium. There was a defunct restaurant called 'Anasui' and another set of large black double doors.

Thea pushed on. As soon as she opened the doors she knew something was wrong. She stepped into a corridor lined with doors on both sides. It was clinical, with its white walls and marble floors. It was like she had somehow found herself back inside Medicorum, but it couldn't be. It didn't make sense.

Holding the knife in an ice-pick grip, Thea pressed down the corridor as quickly as she dared. It was dark near the junction at the end, the corridors either side were completely obscured by darkness but Thea could hear a sort of skittering. She could feel that she wasn't alone.

"Walt?" she whispered. The response was an all too familiar growl, then several things happened at once. Strip lights flared into life overhead. A metallic *click* told her that she was trapped, and a horde of ravenous ghouls barrelled towards her.

Instinctively, Thea raised her leg and kicked. Her foot landed in the centre of the nearest ghoul's chest, sending it careening backwards, taking several of its fellows with it. She turned to run but gnarled and grasping hands took hold of her pulling her back towards the throng. She managed to spin out of the ghoul's grip, using the momentum to slam it into the nearest wall.

Another was on her in seconds. Thea never killed if she could help it, but the situation was leaving her little choice. The ghoul grabbed her by the hair, attempting to drag her close enough to bite. Thea elbowed blindly behind her, then twisted around. She had plunged the tiny knife into the ghoul's armpit before it knew what had happened. Its arm went limp, nonetheless.

Thea dodged back out of the reach of the next ghoul who tried to bite her. She dropped low, sweeping her leg around in an arc that sent the ghoul to the ground. She sprinted through the gap into the left-hand corridor. There were fewer doors there. Thea ran to the end and tried one of the many handles. Mercifully, the door was unlocked. She dived through, slamming it shut, and locking it with a deadbolt.

Breathing heavily, she took in her surroundings. It wasn't possible. She was standing in Walt's Tenebrium apartment. It looked exactly as she remembered it, with its bookcases and the dented gramophone.

The room was awash with an amber glow, and the smell of bourbon was so strong it was heady. Just like Firewater, there were glasses everywhere. The room was so dense with them that Thea couldn't see the floor. She knocked several over as she stepped further into the room.

There was a tiny circle in the middle of the living area, where the coffee table used to be, that was clear of glasses and inside it, sitting with his knees pressed to his chest, was Walt. He looked hellish. He was barefoot, filthy and bloody—even more so than Kenneth. He looked thin, starved. His eyes were sunken and had a wild quality that came from being subjected to something horrible. The last time she had seen that look on his face, he had just murdered her father.

"Walt?"

He didn't move. Thea carefully stepped between the tumblers and bottles. When she was within feet of Walt, she gasped. Nails. More nails than she was willing to count protruded from his legs. More than this, Walt was shaking, clearly struggling with the urge to drink.

"What if I just took a sip?"

"Walt," Thea crouched in front of him.

"You aren't real. None of this is real. He's just showing me what I want so I'll let my guard down."

"Walt, it's really me."

"No, it's not." He surged forwards and captured her lips. She didn't stop him. His hands found her hair as he kissed her with a ferocity that left her breathless. "See?"

"What're you doing?"

"You aren't you." He held her face lightly between his palms. "I am this close," he brought his thumb and his index finger together. "To giving in. If I can't drink, I might as well do the thing I've wanted to do since I stepped out of that elevator and saw you. The real you." He kissed her again. It was feverish and desperate, charged like it had been in the past. Gently, Thea pulled away and sat back so she could look at him.

"It's really me," she said again.

"I don't believe you."

"Well, I'm still gonna get you out of here. Can you stand?"

With difficulty, Walt dragged himself to his feet. He took a tentative step, then let himself fall back onto the sofa, clearly in pain.

"Pull them out," he said, indicating the nails.

"No way."

Now Thea looked at them, the majority of the nails were embedded in his shins, with only a few dotted around his thighs.

"Fine." And Walt reached down and pulled a nail out of his thigh.

"Okay, okay," Thea said quickly.

"I need to get out of this room. If you are really you, you'll understand that."

Thea could see Walt's eyes darting from glass to glass. Alcohol was, historically, how he coped with stress. She couldn't imagine how strong the urges he was fighting were. Tortured and in pain, surrounded by booze, whiskey soaking his clothes, he must have been in hell.

"It's going to be okay."

"Is it really you?" He looked unsure, almost childlike.

"It's me."

Walt didn't reply, but she could see mistrust in his eyes.

"It's me," Thea implored. "We met when I was nineteen. You were thirty-one. You hated me at first. We became partners when I was twenty-two. We worked the Salome bust together—it was the first time I realised I had earned your respect." Still nothing. "The last thing I said to you before I left Tenebrium was 'loving you means hating me, and I'm not gonna do it anymore'. It's really me."

Something passed over his face. His eyes traced her lips, then moved up to meet her gaze. "Pull them out," Walt said with a small nod.

"I'm not sure that's a good idea..."

"Thea, please get them out. Wrap me up and I'll be good to go."

Against her better judgement, Thea searched the room for something to help her remove the nails. She found some old hand towels and a pair of pliers under the sink. She tore the towels into strips, ready to use them as bandages and dipped the pliers into the nearest glass of alcohol.

"Put this in your mouth," Thea said, handing Walt the cleanest of the rags. He did as she asked. "Ready?"

Before he had replied, Thea gripped the first nail and tugged. Walt groaned in pain. She lost count of how many times she repeated the process. Walt's knuckles were white from gripping the counter. "I'm nearly there." When she pulled the final nail from his shin, she poured one of the glasses of bourbon down each leg, causing Walt to yell out, then used the strips of towel to bandage him up.

Walt stood up and Thea was glad to see he was far steadier on his feet.

"You okay?"

"I didn't think you'd come."

"Then you're an idiot."

Their eyes met for a moment and the dull echo of a familiar electricity passed between them.

"Take this." Thea pulled her aegis out from under her shirt.

"No way."

"You're hurt, I'm not. Don't argue, just take it."

Walt looked down at the offered protection, a crease between his eyebrows. After a moment he took it. "We have to get back to the precinct," he said, attaching it to his chest.

"Walt, we're still in Caligo."

"Look around. You can't tell me you don't know where we are."

Thea checked her index. "It hasn't been long enough. We're in Caligo, I swear."

"I can't tell what's real and what isn't anymore. Curtis is using VR—"

There was a horrible high pitched whine in her ear and then a static sort of crackle.

"Thea...we can't...you...blocked."

"Drew? I found Walt. There are more bombs. Curtis said he wanted to destroy the whole city. You have to find them."

"Querida—"

There was another awful high-pitched sound, and the line went dead.

"Looks like we're on our own," she said with a wince. "What's that?" She said, noticing the small device on the front of his shirt.

CALIGO FALLING

"Please tell me that connection was long enough for a trace?" Torrez said to Mateo, who shook his head sombrely. "Damn."

"I want to help Williams as much as you do, but if Price wasn't lying, the people of Caligo need more help than she does."

"Thea said he wanted to destroy the whole city," Torrez said slowly.

"We've already sent teams to the major population centres to clear the area and search for bombs."

"Pull them back." The realisation hit Torrez like a wrecking ball.

"What?"

"Does this city have a SubLevel?"

"Yes. Yes, all the colony top cities do."

"Pull back all the teams. Get Sid and Alex and everyone you have with bomb disposal experience to meet me at the entrance to your SubLevel."

"Why?"

"Bombing buildings creates fear and suffering. It destroys lives, but not the whole city. If he wants to destroy the whole city and everyone in it—"

"My god. Collapsing the SubLevel could cause the whole city to crumble. Go! Go now, I'll get you your teams. You better hope you're right about this, Andrew."

"I'm willing to bet the lives of everyone in this city on it."

FAMILY MEN

Thea pressed her ear to the door, but all that she heard was silence.

"What's at the other end of the corridor?" she asked Walt.

"I've no idea." Walt's voice was odd, it had a dream-like quality. Thea turned to look at him. Blood was still trickling lazily down his chest, from the wound where she had cut the shock device from him. He had his hands planted on one of the kitchen counters, his shoulders hunched, as he stared at a large glass of bourbon. The scent of it was everywhere. It was so strong it was giving Thea a headache and making her feel tipsy.

"Hey. Look at me. You're doing good. You're gonna be okay."

"No alcoholic is ever doing *that* good, Thea. It's been days. I need to get out of this room or we'll have more problems than just Joel Curtis."

There was nothing she could say to ease him, this was likely his worst nightmare, so she focussed on their immediate problems.

"None of those ghouls were bloody or dirty or ragged." Walt didn't respond. She pressed on. "Come on, work it with me. Like a case."

"You think they're fresh? Or new?" He was breathing heavily. "If we're still in Caligo, where the hell did he get Styxx?"

"I don't know."

"We could funnel them. Let them in one at a time and take them down."

"I don't relish the thought of killing these people."

"Me neither."

They lapsed back into silence. Thea dropped down onto the floor, resting her back against the door. She was struggling to think of a way out that wouldn't get them or a large portion of the ghouls killed and yet, they couldn't just sit there waiting for Curtis to strike.

CRASH

Without warning, Walt swept his arms across the countertop knocking glass after glass to the floor. He kicked the glasses at his feet and threw several against the wall. When he was done, not a single glass remained. The floors were hidden by jagged shards and a centimetre of amber alcohol.

Thea hadn't moved, even when the bourbon seeped onto her trousers, she just let him get it out of his system. "Do you want to talk about it?"

"About what?" Walt had his back to her, hands resting on his hips.

"What he did to you."

Walt nudged some glass with his toe, still facing away. It was a few seconds before he spoke. "He shocked me. He hammered nails into my legs, and he had me fight. I killed someone today because I thought he wasn't real. Curtis is messing with my head. He's using VR...you might not even be here." He gave a hollow laugh. "This could be another one of his games. How am I supposed to know the difference? Is any of this real?"

"The building is. It has to be. The ghouls are, if the scratches on my arm are a good indicator. And you are."

"You sound sure."

"I am. Maybe this room isn't real. Maybe the ghouls aren't real, but the situation is. We both know how dangerous being tortured in VR can be. We need to try and hold it together. Are you gonna be okay?"

"Survive now, everything else can wait." Finally, Walt turned to look at her. The wild look he'd had in his eyes since she had found him was gone. He looked steady. "Real or not, I'm glad you're here."

"What if we move all the furniture, create a sort of barricade, let them come and slip behind them. You and I can vault a table no problem."

"You can. I don't even know if I can run."

"Right. Shit."

"I guess we're gonna have to find out."

Together they moved all the bookcases, tables and chairs, as well as the sofa into an open square shape, facing the door.

"Ready?"

He nodded.

Thea hammered on the door before she opened it, then turned and retreated behind the barrier with Walt. It was like a flood. The ghouls rushed in; hands raised in front of them. They pushed and scrabbled, tripping over each other, as they shambled across the glass-strewn floor.

"Let's move!" Walt yelled, but Thea ignored him. She waited until the last ghoul was inside, until they were pushing against the barrier. When the first ghoul had clambered onto the table, Thea vaulted over it. Walt swore loudly and followed. They sprinted past the horde, out into the corridor. Thea turned and grabbed the door handle, slamming it shut and trapping the ghouls in the apartment.

The corridor was brightly lit now, and a messy trail of blood led to the body of the ghoul Thea had stabbed. She kept her eyes averted as she checked to see how Walt had fared.

He looked pale out of the warm glow of the living room, his complexion almost as grey as the ghouls. "We need to get you some water. Come on."

They made their way out of the corridor and into what looked like a buffet restaurant. It was a large open space with tables and chairs spread out in front of the different food counters. There was a wide staircase on the opposite side. This odd change of scenery only further confirmed to Thea that she couldn't take what she saw at face value.

She made her way to the nearest buffet counter. It had been a burger place when it was functioning, but now a thick layer of dust covered all surfaces. Thea fished a cup from one of the long dormant vending machines and prayed that the building still had water. She let out a sigh of relief when murky liquid burst forth from the tap. Once it had cleared slightly, Thea filled the cup and brought it back to Walt, who had sat down at a nearby table.

"Thank you," he said, draining the glass in one long gulp.

"I'll get you another."

Thea watched as Walt drained yet another glass of water and took a bite of the stale protein bar they had found under a till.

The water and the food had done him a world of good, though he still looked drawn and tired. There was something slightly hollow behind his eyes and Thea wondered grimly what exactly had been done to him.

"Where the hell are we?" Walt said finally, his frustration clear. "And where is Curtis? Is this what the building really looks like or another trick?"

"An old resort hotel, I think. It doesn't matter. We need to get out of here. I think there are more bombs in the city."

Walt got to his feet. He was steady enough, though it looked like the movement was painful. They followed the stairs down to an archway and walked through it.

"This is where I woke up after he took me," Thea said as they found themselves in the atrium again. As if her words had triggered it, there was a thunderous crash and sturdy metal shutters dropped over the atrium doors. "I'm starting to think this kid likes us," Walt said flatly.

"Up it is." They made their way past the murky cylindrical tank to the curved stairs that led to the next floor. "We have to find him."

"You make that sound easy." Walt winced slightly as he climbed and Thea noted with concern that blood was already starting to show through his make-shift bandages.

The more they saw of the place the more Thea was convinced it was one of those one stop shop resorts, filled with restaurants, bars, entertainment venues and hotels. The signage told her it was called 'Little Vegas'. It was eerily quiet as they made their way through the derelict passaged and abandoned outlets. It was so long before they encountered anyone that Thea was starting to think that Curtis' plan was just to leave them there to rot, but all too soon she was proved wrong.

They were walking past an arcade when she heard the first signs of life. Thea tapped Walt on the shoulder and moved closer. There was the distant echo of some discordant jazz.

"Sinners this way." He nodded to a scrawl across the arcade window when Thea gave him a questioning look.

Dull neon lights gave the arcade a moody feel. It was clearly trying to market itself as an adult's playground. Mannequins dressed like flappers were positioned next to many of the games, with creepy plastic grins and blank eyes. Fluorescent arrows had been painted haphazardly on the carpets leading the way to a faux chariot racing track called, 'Circus Maximus'.

Thea opened a set of double doors into a small hippodrome. The entire venue was made to look like something from Ancient Rome. The track was covered in sand, with chariots on rails. There were rows and rows of seats, each with a betting console attached. In the very centre of the arena, tied with barbed wire to crudely made crosses were four men.

All were in their forties or fifties and all looked terrified. Thea made to move towards them but Walt grabbed her elbow and pulled her back. "There has to be a catch here," he said, scanning the room.

"I'm sure of it, but we can't not help them."

"What if they aren't real?"

"What if they are?"

Thea half jogged down the stairs into the arena, Walt right behind her. The men were gagged but she could still make out their muffled pleas. Ignoring the pain in their fingers as they untangled the wires, Walt and Thea managed to free the men.

"You're Russos, right?" Thea asked as she helped one of the men into a sitting position.

"How did you know?" the man asked. He was medium height, Turkish and slim. His hair was almost completely white.

"Where is he? The man who took you?" Walt said, still scanning the large room.

"I don't know. He said I was to tell you that your time is running out."

The buzzing in her tragus made Thea jump. "Torrez?"

"Querida!" Torrez sounded harassed and worried.

"I found Walt."

"Get out of there, Thea. He's going to—"

The horrible ringing sound made her feel like someone had put an icepick in her ear and she knew that coms had once again been disabled.

"He also said, we had to kill you and if we did, he'd let us go."

"There it is," Walt said with a grim smile. "You can try."

"He's just one man, and we make six. We don't have to play his games."

"I won't risk him taking me again. I'm really sorry about this."

The four men got to their feet and formed a tight circle around Thea and Walt, who immediately moved so they were back-to-back. Thea didn't wait for them to attack, she kicked sand in the face of the white-haired man and lunged forward to follow-up with a series of well-placed punches while he was blinded. He was on the ground before he could even lift a finger.

One of his fellows grabbed Thea by the shoulder and spun her around. He punched her in the face and the gut in quick succession. She doubled over only dimly aware of Walt with one of the ex-mobsters' hands around his throat, but she had no time to react, the man who had hit her, grabbed her again and pulled her upright so he could headbutt her squarely in the face.

As she felt blood spill from her nose, she fell back onto the sands. The man advanced, but Thea quickly spun where she was, bringing her leg up to land a brutal blow on his kneecap. There was a disgusting crunch as he cried out, but the yell was cut short as she got to her feet and kneed him in the face, sending him crashing to the ground unconscious.

When she turned to look back at Walt, he too was standing triumphant over two unconscious foes.

"Are you all right?" Walt asked as Thea dabbed at her bloody nose.

"They're gonna wake up any minute."

"We should tie them back up," Walt said, nodding to the mobsters with an unforgiving expression on his face.

"Curtis will kill them for failing him."

"They just tried to kill us, I'm finding it hard to feel sympathetic. For all we know it's just another trick."

"Come on. We have to find him before he gets tired of waiting and blows up half the city."

BOMB DISPOSAL

Caligo's SubLevel didn't have gates out in the open like Tenebrium. The underground tunnels could only be accessed through specific entry channels. The nearest one was in the Entertainment District, concealed by a circular manhole cover.

Torrez watched as Sid and Rosenburg lifted the iron slab to reveal a long dark shaft. It was claustrophobic with a narrow ladder that descended beyond Torrez's field of vision.

"Castillo and Alex should be heading down now. Who's first?" Rosenburg asked, stepping away from the opening.

Torrez raised a hand half-heartedly and clambered onto the ladder. It was rough and rusted, as if no one had used it in years. The shaft was barely wide enough to fit his shoulders and it got tighter as he descended. All light disappeared as Sid and Rosenburg began climbing down above him.

The descent took Torrez a full ten minutes. It was pitch black at the bottom. Torrez tapped his index and a sea of green developed around him. The passageway they had entered looked like a subway tunnel, with its rounded walls and track along the ground, except it wasn't track, it was piping.

"Okay," Sid said, coming to stand behind Torrez. "The first support column is about half a klick north."

They walked in silence. Torrez knew these tunnels were empty. He knew there were no ghouls, and yet he still felt uneasy. His relief at reaching the support column died before it was fully formed.

There was a large explosive attached to the pillar. It was embedded into the concrete. It was sleek and silver and glowed with a faint blue light.

"Torrez," Castillo called over their open comms channel. "We have a bomb here. A big one. Other teams are reporting the same. You were right."

"I have never been less happy to hear that in my life. Billy, can you diffuse it?"
"Honestly, I don't know."

GHOULS

The floor above the arcade was home to what would have been a plethora of expensive jewellery stores. Some of the derelict shops still had displays that twinkled beneath the layers of dust. Thea peered through the nearest one, checking it was empty.

The street was dark and the night wet. The cool rain was a salve to Thea's aching bones. Neon lights blared all around and yet there was almost complete silence.

Thea was racing through the TPD, Onyx Legion soldiers close behind. She burst through the set of double doors that led to the morgue and found herself in a graveyard.

The warm sun beat down on her as she panted trying to catch her bearings. A small distance away there was a crowd of people dressed in black overlooking an open grave. It was a funeral.

Thea edged closer, unsure of how she got there and was surprised to see faces she recognised in the crowd; but they didn't look how she remembered them. She saw Cleo and Walt. Both were younger, and still wearing wedding rings. They clung to each other embroiled in the grief of the funeral. And then it hit her. She came back to herself with such speed and clarity that it felt like an elastic band snapping inside her mind. It wasn't real.

Thea ran forward, pushing between the crowd until she reached Walt. "We have to find a way out of here," she said, pulling him away from the graveside. She glanced at the headstone. The name upon it was 'Arthur James'.

"Get the hell off me," he spat angrily. His assembled loved ones gasped and tutted, some even stepped forward to intervene.

"Walt. It's me, Thea"

"Have some respect," an older White woman, who Thea knew to be Walt's mother, said weakly.

"Walt—"

"Stop saying my name like you know me. Just leave us in peace." He tried to shake Thea's grasp on his arm, but she held on tightly.

"Walt. It's me. It's Thea."

The anger faded slowly from his face to be replaced by a confused curiosity. "How do I know you?"

"We were partners."

"But we were more than that. Right?" He cocked his head to the side as if trying to see through a dense fog.

"Yes, we were more than that, a long time ago."

"You need to leave," Cleo said, stepping between them. It was unnerving and something Thea was very happy had never happened during their affair.

Walt shook himself and Thea could tell he was slipping back into the fiction.

"This already happened. Your dad died when you were twenty-five. You're forty-three. You are the TPD Police Captain. You are divorced. You are an alcoholic. We had an affair, and it blew up in our faces. Think about Fen. I know you love her. Remember," Thea implored. "Curtis is playing with us, and this is just another one of his games. Walt, I need you to come back to me. I need you to remember."

"Lady, you're crazy," Cleo said, trying to pull Walt back to the funeral. "You need to leave."

Thea ignored her. She had to do something to make him remember. Throwing caution to the wind Thea moved to the graveside and jumped down on top of the glossy wooden coffin. There were shouts and yells of protest, but she pushed on. She reached forward and wrenched the coffin open. Thea let out a yell of surprise. There was no body but what looked like a window into the execution chamber of the TPD. Before she knew what was happening, Thea tumbled forwards and landed painfully on the concrete floor, Walt falling after her.

The shock of the landing seemed to bring Walt back to himself.

"Thea?"

"Thank God."

"How did you get out of Virtual last time?"

"I didn't. Torrez saved me."

Thea got to her feet and looked around the room. There was no one there and no sounds from outside. This wasn't a memory.

"It has to be on us. There are no VR suites this big. It's on us."

Thea moved behind Walt and ran her hands along his shoulders and down his back. "What are you doing?" he asked with a shiver. Thea didn't respond. She checked behind his ears and ran her hands through his hair. Hidden in his hairline at the base of the neck, she felt something small and cold. "Hey!" he yelped as she gripped it between her fingers and pulled.

The device was black and round with rough edges. It looked like a tiny spider. Thea dropped it on the ground and crushed it under her heel.

Walt found her device in the same place and removed it just as she had.

The TPD dissolved around them and they were back inside Little Vegas. They had moved, though Thea wasn't sure how far. The nearest point of egress was a set of double doors marked 'Adults Only'.

Walt stumbled slightly as they walked towards it.

"Are you okay?"

"I'm fine, I'm just tired." He sounded sure but looked pale.

"Look at your legs," Thea said in surprise. There were no bandages, just four nails in his right shin. "It wasn't real. None of it." Thea brought her hands to her face, there was no blood and no pain in her nose.

"Come on," Walt said. "He can't get inside our heads now." He moved past Thea to push open the doors. They stepped through into complete blackness. As the doors slammed shut there was an electronic *CLICK* and Thea knew they had locked behind them. The darkness was so complete it was almost painful as it pressed against her eyeballs. She could feel the heat of Walt next to her, but there was something else; a strange charge in the air.

"There's something in here," she whispered.

Out of nowhere, Thea felt a tearing pain in her shoulder as something took a bite out of her flesh. She grunted in pain as Walt let out his own yell of surprise. Thea threw an elbow out wildly behind her and hit something hard and fleshy.

"Run!" she yelled, setting off blindly.

Hands tried to grasp at her as she collided with bodies, wildly pushing them out of the way. There was a buzzing sound and dim red neon lights sprung to life along the ceiling casting an eerie crimson glow on the terrifying scene in front of them.

They had stepped into a large strip club. There was a main stage in the centre of the room as well as smaller stages dotted around between tables and booths. Scattered amongst them, in numbers Thea had thought she would never see again, were ghouls. Black goo oozed from their gnashing mouths as they advanced on Thea and Walt.

"Fuck," Walt said on an exhale somewhere behind her.

"More Russos."

Thea had no time to process this horrific turn of events. She darted between the tables avoiding gnarled clutching hands. A ghoul in a three-piece suit lunged over a table forcing Thea to stagger back. She tripped over an upturned chair and came clattering to the ground. Immediately, several ghouls threw themselves to the floor attempting to catch her. She rolled over and began to crawl between the tables.

"Walt?" she shouted, having lost sight of him.

"I'm here! Get to the stage."

Thea kicked at a ghoul who had taken hold of her ankle and scrambled back to her feet. She picked up the nearest chair and hurled it at the advancing ghouls before pushing past to the stage. Walt had already climbed up when Thea came to the edge, and she gratefully grabbed the hand he offered her. The ghouls were right behind them.

The stage itself was long, with mirrored tiles running the length of it. At the end was a set of curtains that appeared undisturbed. Thea set off after Walt, dodging the frenzied ghouls who were trying to drag her back down into their hungry clutches.

The curtains led a to small backstage area. The first glimmer of hope since Thea had set foot in the Little Vagas resort, came in the form of an emergency exit.

A mass of ghouls breached the curtains just as Thea opened the door. She and Walt darted through and slammed it shut, both breathing heavily.

The exit had taken them onto a glass catwalk that overlooked the atrium. Thea could see the outlets, and restaurants, bars and casinos, far below. Directly underneath them was the murky aquatic tank. Thea imagined that when Little Vegas was new, it would have been beautiful to watch the fish swimming in the water. Dilapidated as it was, standing on the catwalk, was like looking out over a ghost town.

The catwalk itself had several dormant restaurants and bars dotted along it, but the only other area it led to was the Vespasian Hotel.

Thea groaned and clutched her ear as her Cicada let out a high-pitched shriek.

"What's wrong?" Walt said, turning from where he had been using the dining tables to barricade the door into the brothel.

"...Found...bombs...run...get out..." Torrez's voice was interspersed with a horrible keening static, so much so it was a relief when the line went dead.

"Drew found more bombs."

"Then we need to get the hell out of here."

"That would be cheating."

Both heads whipped around. Emerging from the hotel entrance, finally, was Joel Curtis with a gun in his hand and a grim smile on his lips.

"You've ruined the game," he said with a delicate ferocity.

"What was the point? What message were you trying to send?" Thea shouted.

"We are all damned. Every one of us. And it's because of people like my mother and you and Vincent Russo. You protect the wicked. Mother was weak like so many others and Vinny, he and men like him are devils that hide in plain sight. It is not enough to root out the evil of augmentations, because it has tainted us all. We accept it in our bodies, in our homes, in our friends. I am the reckoning for these doomed cities. I am enacting God's will. As he cleansed with the floods I shall cleanse with fire."

"What do you want with us?" Walt demanded.

"You? Nothing. This is about her." He turned his pitch-black gaze onto Thea. "You are the reason Levi is dead. He was my world. My saviour. His legacy has been destroyed, his church torn down and why? Because you decided he was wrong? What gives you that right? You talk of tolerance, but you didn't tolerate our beliefs."

"Yes, we did. I even thought I was saving his life when you staged that shooting. I put my life on the line for him. Freedom of speech doesn't mean you deserve a platform and it doesn't mean you get to spew hate. Your beliefs breed violence against innocent people. No one in their right mind would stand for that."

"You are blind to the hold the Devil has over you."

"You're a victim too. Levi used you. He took a vulnerable kid and twisted him into a weapon. Augs aren't the villain of your story. Levi Seward is."

Thea saw, as if in slow motion, as Curtis raised his gun and took aim, a look of pure rage on his face. She brought her hand instinctively to her chest before realising she had given her aegis to Walt. Walt had realised too, and he dove for Thea, sending them both to the ground as more shots pelted the glass around them.

They both scrambled to their feet and ran towards the nearest place of cover, a pillar outside one of the restaurants. Pressed together behind the narrow pillar, Thea could feel Walt's thunderous heartbeat matched only by her own.

"Can you draw his fire?"

Walt nodded.

"The shield gives you ten seconds."

He gave one of her hands a quick squeeze and darted out from cover with a defiant shout. Thea waited a fraction of a second to ensure that Curtis was focussed on Walt, before creeping out from behind cover. She ducked between tables, keeping low as Walt stood out in the open and yet Curtis didn't fire.

"You don't want to kill me now? I'm hurt. This isn't the time to lose your nerve," Walt goaded. "Not so brave without your little buzzer, huh? You had to tie me up to beat me. You are a scared little boy playing at being grown."

Thea edged closer, but still Curtis didn't shoot. He just stared at Walt as if he was a complicated problem that he was trying to solve. It didn't matter if he didn't want to fire at Walt as long as Walt kept his attention. Seizing her opportunity, Thea moved slightly past Curtis, before slowly creeping up behind him. Moving silently, she pounced and grabbed him in a half nelson.

"Got you," he choked out as he began to fire at the glass catwalk. The fourth shot caused the glass to crack, the sixth caused it to shatter and the seventh saw both Thea and Curtis falling into the water tank below.

The water was freezing as Thea landed. She was disoriented as the murky putrescent water stung her eyes. She couldn't tell which way was up. Something metal made contact with the side of her head and she was sure Curtis had hit her with the barrel of his gun. Maybe his augmentations meant the water didn't hinder him. She heard the blast as if from a mile away, then something blunt hit her in the chest sending her backwards. Her head collided with the glass of the tank and darkness claimed her.

NO HOPE

Alex tried not to panic as they stood in the dark tunnel in front of a bomb, listening to Rosenburg's grim assessment.

"There's nothing I can do. There is nothing any of us can do. We need to evacuate the city. Save as many lives as we can."

"What? That can't be it. There can't be no hope."

"There's a remote detonator and a jammer trigger. If we try to block the signal—the bombs explode. If whoever holds the remote detonator pushes the big red button—they explode. We have at least forty devices in the tunnels under the city. If they detonate, Caligo is ash. We don't have enough people to disarm them all."

"Are we agreed that this is Curtis?"

"Yes."

"Have the rest of the teams start the evacuation. Get Castillo to lead it. You, me, Torrez and Sid have to find Thea. If she found Walt, she found Curtis. She's our last hope."

THE TANK

Walt realised a second too late what Curtis had been planning. He sprinted forward, shouting warnings to Thea, but it made no difference. The glass beneath her feet shattered and she and Curtis fell from the catwalk into the gigantic aquarium below.

Walt dropped to his hands and knees at the edge ignoring the pain in his shin. "Thea? Thea!" Neither surfaced. Walt was pulling off his jacket when a blond head surfaced. Curtis fired wildly, but the gun only spluttered. The time it had taken for Curtis to swim to the top, an injured Thea could have sunk to the bottom.

Walt looked around wildly, ignoring Curtis as he attempted unsuccessfully to climb out of the tank. He didn't matter anymore. All that mattered was Thea. Walt sprinted towards the hotel, bursting through the double doors with such ferocity that one of them came off its decaying hinges, but he didn't stop. As he had hoped, he was confronted immediately with stairs.

He ran down all twenty flights, the pain in his shins and the burning in his lungs nothing compared to the fear that was grasping at his chest. At the bottom of the stairs was the hotel lobby and another set of double doors. Walt flung the doors wide and gave a cry of relief to find that he was exactly where he needed to be. The atrium. He grabbed a brass stanchion from reception as he ran and raised it over his head. As soon as he reached the aquarium, he swung it with all his might. Again and again, he hit the glass until it started to crack. Another well placed hit and the glass shattered, water exploding outward, it swept him off his feet as the deluge flooded the atrium. The putrid tide slammed him back against the hotel doors, but he fought to his feet, pushing through the water.

As the deluge began to slow, Walt clambered through the gaping hole he had made in the tank. Inside the water was still waist deep. He didn't care as Curtis pushed past him to climb out of the tank. He waded through the water with searching hands until he made contact with a body.

Walt pulled Thea to the surface and dragged her out of the water. He laid her flat on the cold atrium floor. She wasn't breathing.

"You don't get to do this to me again." Walt pushed hard on her chest to force the water out of her lungs. "This isn't how you go out." He pushed again. "No fucking way." Walt pushed for a third time. Thea opened her eyes and coughed, greyish water spilling from her mouth.

"Be...hind..." she spluttered.

Walt turned just in time to see the stanchion he had used to break the tank collide with his temple.

When Walt awoke someone was shaking his shoulders.

"Walt, buddy, are you okay?"

It was Bastion, a look of concern on his face.

"Where's Thea?"

"Some things never change."

"I'm serious, is she here?"

"No," another voice said. Walt sat up, his head throbbing and looked around. Alex, Bastion, Billy, Torrez and Sid were standing over him. He felt sick as he tried to get to his feet, but Bastion pushed him back down.

"You're hurt. Let us take it from here."

"No, no way." Walt tried valiantly to stand but he was too dizzy. He slumped back onto the wet floor.

"C'mon, big guy," Bastion said, pulling Walt to his feet, and putting an arm around his waist. "Medicus is waiting outside. We'll find Thea and your serial killer."

"She's a big girl, she can handle herself," Alex said, though it was obvious they were worried.

Barely conscious, his vision blurred, the exhaustion and the pain of his recent ordeal finally catching up with him, Walt could do nothing but let Bastion drag him outside.

THE TRUTH

Thea was only dimly aware of being carried through the hotel. Curtis dropped her heavily into a service lift, he himself panting. Her mind felt foggy. She knew she was in danger, but when she tried to compel herself to do more than acknowledge it, her body wouldn't comply. It was like being very drunk.

She must have blacked out because when she awakened again, she was in an enormous laundry room. Washers and dryers were stacked four high, with sets of stairs on wheels to allow access to each. The floors were concrete like the walls and metal support pillars interspersed the large space.

As the haze in her mind finally dissipated, Thea assessed her situation. She could hear movement, meaning she wasn't alone, but couldn't see Curtis from her positions. She, herself, was tied to a rusted metal pipe that ran from the high ceiling into the concrete floor. She was sore. Her throat ached from her near drowning, and her body was starting to feel the effects of the many beatings it had taken of late.

The section of the room she was in was brightly lit by overhead lamps, but she could tell that the space extended further into the darkness. Curtis came into view at the very edge of the illumination. He was carrying torn bedsheets and several planks of wood. He dropped his heavy load and Thea watched with a sinking feeling in her stomach as he started to assemble a cross.

She twisted her hands in her bonds trying to work out what was restraining her. It felt like more strips of bedsheet. She was careful to be inconspicuous as she pulled, stretching the fabric with every tug. Thea kept a close eye on Curtis, but he was engrossed in his cross-making.

She gave a sharp intake of breath as another tug caused a ripping sound, but it didn't seem to travel to Curtis who still paid her no mind. With one last pull, there was enough room to wiggle one of her hands free and then the other.

BANG

A shot hit the ground less than an inch from her right foot. "Stay where you are."

"And wait to be crucified? I'll take my chances."

"Why can't you people see what I'm trying to do here?" Curtis asked, abandoning the cross and stepping closer to Thea, gun raised.

"What you're doing is wrong. And you're doing it for the wrong reasons."

"A blasphemer like you will never be able to understand."

"Nothing you're doing has anything to do with any God, and you pretending it does is an insult to people with faith."

"Don't preach to me,' Curtis spat.

"You don't have to do this. You can stop now. Levi took advantage of you."

"You have no idea what you're talking about."

"Yes, I do. Your mom left you when you were just a kid, and your dad wasn't much of a father. You felt abandoned and alone until you met Levi. He told you that your mother left you because of your augmentations. And he made you believe that to be augmented is to be damned. But none of that is true."

"Yes, it is! She damned me when she had me augmented and then abandoned me. She realised that I was tainted, and she couldn't stand the sight of me, so she left." He was almost frothing at the mouth.

"That's not true. Your mother loved you. She made a deal with a dangerous man because she wanted you to have the best life possible. She wasn't perfect, but she did love you. She didn't leave you because you're damned. She left because she fell in love with Vinny Russo, and she didn't want to put you in danger. It was selfish, but it doesn't mean she didn't care, and it certainly doesn't mean you're damned."

"That doesn't matter. The why isn't important. She cursed me."

"No, that was Levi Seward. He lied to you; he told me so himself. He saw a lost and vulnerable young man and he took advantage. He indoctrinated you into believing you're damned."

"He is the only person who ever loved me!" Curtis bellowed hysterically and Thea could see the cracks beginning to form.

"He didn't love you. He used you. He made you into something that other people would fear to further his agenda. But he didn't believe any of it. All he cared about was money and when you got too dangerous, he cast you aside as easily as he abandoned Una Anima."

"That's not true!" Curtis screamed. He fired wildly, but none of the shots came close to Thea.

"It's the truth and you know it. You were lost and in desperate need of a parent. He exploited you. Levi turned you into a monster. Levi is the one who damned you and he is the one who rejected you, cast you aside."

"None of this would have happened if it wasn't for you."

"Maybe not, but did you want to live a lie forever? Levi ruined your life. He turned you against your mother, he manipulated your faith, he made you hate yourself. He made you his weapon and when you started to think for yourself, he got cold feet and instead of helping you, or caring for you, he abandoned you. That's not love. Levi isn't capable of compassion, he isn't capable of nurturing, he could never be what you needed, and he only pretended to be because it helped him. He didn't care about you."

"No!" Curtis shrieked. He threw the gun aside and pulled a small remote out of your pocket and held it up high.

"Joel...What are you doing?"

"I am a warrior for God. I am one of the chosen. Levi loved me. He loved me."

"You don't have to do this. Let me help you."

"Now you want to help me? You want to walk me to the gallows. You think I'm a monster."

"I never called you that, the only person who did was Levi. He told me you were a monster, but you can help me prove him wrong. You're confused. You're hurting, you've been manipulated, and it isn't your fault."

"I've killed people and revelled in it. There is no way a cop can help me."

"You'll have to pay for what you've done. There's no excuse for the hurt you've caused but that doesn't mean you aren't a victim too. I can talk to the DA, take execution off the table. Put down the remote and we can leave here together. I won't abandon you. I give you my word I will help you through this."

"I've already killed one mother. I don't need a replacement."

Thea lunged forward and grabbed his wrist. He punched her with his free hand, and she retaliated by kneeing him in the groin. His grip slackened on the remote. She pulled it free and threw it far out of his reach.

He roared with rage, shooting upwards and grabbing Thea around the neck. But he was clumsy in his fury and before he could really establish the strangle hold, Thea had thrust the heel of her hand into his nose. He staggered back. She closed the distance and threw a hook, then a cross, then another hook, followed by an uppercut. She sent him to the ground with a final round kick to the face.

"You can't win this fight," she said looking down at him. "It's over."

Curtis smiled, the blood from his nose staining his teeth red. "Not yet." He pulled another smaller remote from his pocket and pushed the button.

NO WAY BACK

BOOM

The explosion was visible from outside Little Vegas. Smoke billowed as the flames licked the sky. Walt pushed away the Medicus who was treating him and sprinted back towards the resort.

"Thea!"

Alex tried to grab for him, but he shook them off.

"Walt! It's too dangerous." They shouted, as a secondary explosion shook the resort. Part of the façade crumbled to the ground as flames consumed the atrium. There was another explosion and then another.

Walt was almost at the door when Bastion grabbed him around the waist.

"Get the hell off me!" Walt roared. "Let me go."

"It's too dangerous!" Bastion shouted, dragging Walt away from the doors. It was lucky he did, as yet another explosion sent a jet of flames shooting outward. It missed them by inches. The heat was painful on Walt's skin, but he didn't care.

Walt spun in Bastion's grip. He pushed him away and when Bastion made to grab him again, he punched him hard in the face. Bastion stumbled back, but recovered quickly, regaining his grip on Walt.

"Let me go!"

"You can't help her!" As if to make his point, part of the building cracked and crumbled in on itself.

"Let me go!" Walt struggled with all his might, but Bastion held strong, pulling him away from the doors.

"There's nothing we can do. If you go in there all that will happen is you'll die too."

"You don't know that she's dead." The thought was too painful to acknowledge.

"You're right, I don't, but I do know that you'll die if you go in there after her.

I don't want Thea to be hurt, but there is nothing we can do. The Fire Department will be on their way. Let them search for her."

Alex shook their head blankly. "There is a mass evacuation going on."

"They aren't coming." With a herculean effort Walt managed to shake off Bastion. He ran to the doors, but the flames were so fierce, there was no way for him to enter. All he could do was drop to his knees and watch the flames grow.

INFERNO

Red. All Thea could see was red.

She was lying on her back covered in debris. She coughed as smoke invaded her lungs and nostrils. The heat was so intense that she thought she might pass out. Her ears rang, and her eyes were blurry.

An explosion...there had been an explosion.

Everything was on fire. The walls, the floors, the ceilings. The building was crumbling around her as the spreading flames caused secondary explosions. Thea staggered as she tried to stand, blood dripping from a cut on her forehead.

She squinted through the inferno. Beams had fallen, barring her path. She lurched from side to side as she tried to find some way to escape.

"Help me..." a strangled voice cried, barely audible over the roar of the flames.

Thea teetered through the wreckage of the building. She fell to her knees more than once and had to drag herself back to her feet. But she could still hear the pleading voice.

She followed it as best she could to the edge of a crater in the floor. The force of the blast had split the concrete, and Thea could see the sewers many feet below. On the other side of the gap, trapped underneath a slab of concrete, she saw Curtis. "Help me," he begged, a bloodied hand reaching out to her.

He had killed so many people, was she really going to risk her life to save him when, not for the first time, he was the reason she was in danger? Seconds ticked by. She would have walked away if you could, but it wasn't in her nature. She had promised not to abandon him.

Thea took a few steps back, then made a running leap over the fissure. It was further than she thought. In her weakened state she couldn't clear the gap. Her chest collided with the other side, knocking the wind out of her and she only just managed to hold on to the ledge. With great difficulty, Thea heaved herself up. Ignoring the suffocating smoke, she quickly made her way over to Curtis.

He didn't look good. Only his head and shoulders were visible, the rest of his body was buried deep underneath the debris. Blood was trickling from his mouth, and it was starting to pool from somewhere under the rubble.

"I can't feel my legs," he choked out.

"It's okay," Thea lied. "You're gonna be fine."

She knew it was fruitless, but she had to try. She began to move smaller bits of concrete as more explosions shook the building. She had to be quick, she was coughing so much it was hard work and she knew that meant that she was going to succumb to carbon monoxide poisoning soon.

"If you are right, I'm going to Hell."

"I don't believe in Hell."

"Then I'll see you there." He coughed, sending flecks of blood into the air.

There was another rumble and Thea looked up just in time to see a huge chunk of concrete falling from the ceiling. She threw herself out of the way just in time, but there was nothing she could do to help Curtis. He let out a shriek that was cut short when the concrete landed, silencing him forever.

"I'm sorry," Thea murmured quietly.

She had no time to think about how horrible an end it was to a troubled and sad life. She had to escape. She was not going to die here, not like this; she refused. She clambered over the fallen rubble, back to the edge of the fissure.

The dank sewer pool was some twenty feet below, but it was either that or die in a fire. She was already feeling faint, and she half jumped; half fell. The cold air whooshing past was sobering and all too soon she broke the surface of the water. It was fast moving, and she gratefully let the water carry her away.

After a few seconds Thea saw a ladder in the gloom. She could barely summon the energy to reach out for it. Using every ounce of willpower she had left, she extended a hand. Thea just caught the ladder as the water continued to sweep past her and began to climb.

There was a manhole cover at the top. It was dark and rusted, but there were no bolts. Thea only just managed to push it open. She let out a laugh of joy as she felt the cool night air wash over her. It felt like an eternity since she had been out in the open.

She had come out into the docking junction of Little Vegas. Thea climbed out of the sewer and lay flat on her back, allowing the fresh air to fill her lungs.

"Thea!"

She turned to see Bastion, Alex, Torrez, Sid and Walt sprinting towards her. She closed her eyes and let them come.

TWO MONTHS LATER

CONSEQUENCES

Thea looked at her reflection in the bathroom mirror. The last traces of her ordeal with Curtis had finally faded from her face. The weeks that had followed had not been easy. There were questions that needed answering. The city was still on edge and while there was a marked reduction in anti-aug violence, the peace that Caligo had once enjoyed was yet to be restored. The rehoming centres had been dismantled, and with the threat of more bombings unlikely, the augs who had been situated there were allowed to return to their homes and business. But the rebuilding of their lives had only just begun, and it would be a long time before things in Caligo resembled normal.

For Thea's part, she had kept her head down, working through the final stages of the investigation and presenting reports to the directors. In her down time, she was volunteering at several city projects, aimed at helping the augmented community recover from their own ordeals.

Today, however, was the first step she was going to take to instigate real change.

She moved out into the living room, ignoring Bastion and Cora as they sat at the little table by the window eating breakfast. There would be time to address their relationship, but it wasn't now.

Alex and Torrez emerged from Torrez's bedroom, both dressed like Thea in the clothes they usually only have donned when attending court to give evidence. They were holding hands.

"I probably should have mentioned that Alex was staying the night," Torrez said with a reasonable attempt at apologetic.

"This is your home, too," Thea shrugged. They had decided that Torrez would be a permanent resident.

"I know you've been worried, and we talked, and we're taking things slow. I have a tendency to jump headfirst into things—"

"I'm not your mom. I worry about you, because I love you both. But you're adults. Just be good to each other and be happy."

"Speaking of mothers," Alex said. "Walt declined to press charges against yours in Tenebrium, but the CPD is moving forward. I'm sorry."

"Actions have consequences, and it's about time she learned that."

"She asked if you would come visit her and help her get a good lawyer."

"No. She's on her own. Being blood doesn't make someone family."

"Are you sure, Querida?"

"Yeah, that relationship is broken, and it has been for a while. You can ask Cora though; she might still want to be involved."

"We found the body of Eddie Russo in the rubble of Little Vegas. I was wondering if you wanted to tell Walt?" Alex offered tentatively.

Thea shook her head. "No, you tell him. He was fighting for his life. He did what he had to. I think he knows that. What happened to Eddie Russo and Kenneth Russel, the ghouls, it was all Curtis' doing."

"You ready for the hearing?" Torrez asked, straightening his tie.

"I am. It was a fight to get here, but I really think we can convince them. They can't ignore us all."

"Change is coming." Torrez smiled.

"About that. I've been speaking to Castillo. How would you feel about joining ARC? As a Special Agent on my team?"

"I think I'd be honoured to work for you."

"With me."

"I've said it before, and I meant it. There is no one I'd rather follow into battle."

BREAKING NEWS

Fen checked her lipstick and gave herself a quick shake. Winter had faded into spring, but the chill of the cold season still lingered in the early morning air.

"How are we looking?" Fen asked her camera operator.

"Ready when you are."

Fen made sure her mic was on and nodded.

"Good morning. I am Fen Yeoh with Caligo Central News reporting live to you from City Hall. In less than an hour's time, prominent figures from all facets of government and law enforcement will meet here to discuss the rights of the Augmented community in a historical first. The hearing is expected to last for days with over forty witnesses to recent events and specialist testimonies expected.

Mayor Goodwin and the directorial board of The Augmentation Regulation Committee issued a joint statement just after midnight saying that it is their aim to provide new protections to the city's augmented population and to ensure that violence the like of which the city faced earlier in the year will never happen again. They are yet to give any clarification as to what these new protections will be, leaving some in the augmented community to fear that these will be no more than pacifying measures like the previous protections.

This first of its kind hearing isn't the only remarkable event taking place today. In a bombshell that has left Tenebrium City's law enforcement reeling, Dr Cleo James, one of the original creators of the drug Styxx—which ravaged Tenebrium City three years ago—has revealed, that Colony Six's Department of Justice, has tabled plans to use Styxx as an alternative to standard custodial sentences.

Dr James, who has been working to reverse the effects of the ill-fated drug, has had some success with her research, combining drug therapies with augmentation devices. She claims that because of this success she had been approached by members of the project's funding body who were eager to monetise Styxx. Dr James has gone on the record to state that she believes the motivations for this plan were to ease overcrowding and prison costs, with the expectation that those who had been turned into Ghouls as a punishment would be housed in Tenebrium's SubLevel, with other victims of the drug.

Prominent Pro-Aug activist Marielena Torrez, Dr James' partner, has also gone on record to lend credence to the reports. Coincidentally, Ms Torrez is also scheduled to speak at today's hearing.

Stay tuned for updates on these stories and more, after the break."

Fen held her expression until the camera operator confirmed she was no longer live. "How was it?"

"Good. It's gonna be a long day."

"Get some coffee and settle in. Today we are part of history."

THE HEARING

The antechamber was small, but comfortable. Thea knew most of the people sitting there with her, though there were several she didn't. Of the ones she did, there was Walt, Torrez, Alex, Rosenburg, Castillo, Vargas, Sid, Marielena, Syed and Cilla Cone. Among those she didn't, there was the CPD Captain, several prominent pro-aug activists as well as the families of several of Joel Curtis' victims.

Collected and confident at first, the longer they waited the more nervous Thea became. She could feel the same energy reflected in the room and when she caught Torrez's eye, he gave her a reassuring smile that she returned.

It was another fifteen minutes before an aid came to collect them. As a group, they filed into the debate chamber and took their seats.

The debate chamber was frequently used as a court and it showed in the décor. Everything was dark lacquered wood, the desks, the railings and the top bench where the judge or in this case the committee members were seated. Glimmering chandeliers hung from the ceiling, but they were rendered useless by the tall windows allowing the artificial sun to flood the room.

Thea and her fellows were ushered to the left side of the chamber to sit on three rows of benches. The right side was reserved for city officials and select members of the press.

Preset were Caligo's District Attorney, two of ARC's Directors, the Police Commissioner, three Senators, the Chair of the Law and Order Committee, Colony Eleven's Equality Minister, and a Supreme Court Judge. Mayor Goodwin was acting as the presiding authority who would lead the hearing.

Goodwin waited for all attendees to be settled before getting to her feet. Harveen Goodwin was a handsome woman in her sixties. Her bold red lipstick perfectly complimented her deep brown skin. She had a formidable air about her only further accented by her bright eyes that gave the impression of being all-seeing.

"This hearing has been convened to discuss the causes and impact of the recent violence in our city, and to make recommendations to the relevant lawmakers on future prevention. I speak both for myself and the committee when I assure all present that we are committed to ensuring there is never a repeat of the tragic events of the last few months. Before we get into the testimonials that will allow us to make these important recommendations, Supervisory Special Agent Thea Williams will provide an overview of those unfortunate events. SSA Williams, please take the floor."

There was no podium, rather just a space for Thea to stand before the committee and the assembled crowds.

"For the record, please state your name," Goodwin said.

"SSA Thea Persephone Williams."

"SSA Williams, please summarise your investigation and its findings to provide context to this hearing."

"Myself, my fellow agents and ARC as an organisation had been keeping tabs on The Church of the Single Soul for some time before the violence started. This was due to its troubling stance on augmented individuals. However, it wasn't until the summer of 2426 that we could concretely tie the church to an uptick in anti-aug sentiment and violence. It was around this time that Levi Seward's popularity came into the mainstream. Some years before this, Seward had taken several younger unhoused individuals in under his wing with a view of radicalising them to further his own goals. One of these individuals was Joel Curtis.

Curtis, born George Wayland, was manipulated by Seward into believing he was damned due to his augmentations. Seward manipulated Curtis's faith and vulnerabilities to turn him into a weapon to achieve his own ends. Curtis however was unstable and became the serial killer the media have dubbed The Zealot. This resulted in several deaths under horrific circumstances including that of Levi Seward..."

It took Thea nearly two hours to explain the full scope of what had happened. The longer Thea talked the more it felt like a weight was being lifted. When she finally concluded, Goodwin said, "Myself, this committee and the city of Caligo would like to thank you for your efforts to protect the citizens of this city."

Next to testify was Alex, who told tales of their hunt for The Soulful Elite and Curtis's connections to the Mafia, as well as the arson of The Kelpie Clinic, perpetrated by an Una Anima devotee. They also detailed how Joel Curtis had paid the group to carry out lethal bombings.

After Alex, Cilla Cone told the story of recent events from the perspective of someone in the augmented community. She painted a damning picture of the ARC response and then gave harrowing testimonial about the hate that the augmented community faced on a daily basis.

Walt and Torrez's statements were comparatively short, with Torrez speaking only of his involvement with the Baker-Singh murder and the bomb disposal efforts. Walt gave a succinct but detailed account of the TDP's role in the investigation, including the kidnapping of Fen. He spoke of how the fact his augmentation was invisible, meant that he didn't receive the same abuse as others and understandably kept the portion about his own torture very brief.

When they finally called an end to the first day of testimonials it was late into the evening. The second day began much as the first had. There was an opening statement from Mayor Goodwin, a summary of the previous day's testimonials and then it was time for new statements to be given.

First on the roster was Natalia Vargas. Thea had been extremely interested to hear what she would say.

"I am Natalia Vargas, Deputy Director in charge of the investigation wing of The Augmentation Relations Committee. I was diagnosed with a degenerative eye disease late last year. The surgery to correct this and provide an augmentation to return my sight was more than I could ever hope to afford. That is when I came into contact with Levi Seward. Maybe it was a coincidence, maybe he sought me out. I don't know. But he offered to pay for my augmentations in exchange for favours. They started small at first, but he demanded more and more each time. Before his death he had asked that I ensure ARC would not intervene during an Una Anima march where he expected violence to break out. He also gave a false tip about illegal firearms at a shelter."

"Did you comply with these demands?" Goodwin asked.

"Yes, ma'am. I'm ashamed to say I did. He threatened to stop payments for my augmentation, and I was worried about losing my job...and my eyes. It seems so stupid now to have been so selfish."

"And what, in your opinion, was the effect of your actions?"

"There were several casualties and one fatality, as well as the destruction of innumerable livelihoods and homes. I can't express how grateful I am to SSA Williams and AD Castillo for taking charge and putting ARC's investigation unit back on track. I fully expect to be charged for my crimes and will willingly accept the consequences."

"It has already been decided that this committee will expunge your debts, allowing you to keep your sight. You will, however, be charged for your part in recent events."

After Vargas, the ARC Directors gave an impassioned speech promising to restore ARC back to its intended purpose.

Then it was Marielena's turn to speak. She was superb. She gave a wonderful speech detailing her journey to become augmented, the backlash she experienced, the bombing of her apartment and an in-depth look into what life is like within the augmented community. Thea couldn't think of anyone better to speak for those with augmentations and the community seemed to agree. There was an outpouring of love and support for Marielena, with many demanding that she be appointed to the equality committee.

Castillo, Sid and Rosenburg took the stand together, all sharing insights into the operations and aftermath of the anti-aug riots, the bombings, and serial killings.

After weeks of witness testimonials, the final day saw discussions of the previous statements and expert witness findings as well as counter arguments from those who still wished to outlaw augmentations and segregate those with them from those without. By the end Thea was surprised to find herself hopeful. The trials and hearings in Tenebrium dealing with the fallout from the Gold Legion had been fruitless. With gag orders served, no real change could be made, but here, it really seemed like there might be a positive outcome.

"Thank you all for your time," Mayor Goodwin said, getting to her feet for the last time. "The committee will deliberate all that has been shared here and make our recommendations to the relevant authorities. We will notify you when we have reached our decisions."

Back in the antechamber Torrez demanded they all go out for dinner and Thea was happy to be dragged along for the ride.

She was delighted to find Cleo and Marielena waiting for them. *I had needed this,* Thea thought as she laughed at a story Sid was telling. They had all needed this. They had been through so much, but she could finally see the light at the end of the tunnel.

FORGIVENESS

Walt was glad to leave the restaurant. He had been going to meetings daily since his encounter with Curtis, and while his resolve was strong, he was most definitely in the throes of addiction. His every thought was about the sweet smell of bourbon that seemed to perpetually pervade his nostrils. He was twitchy and on edge, but he refused to give in, he had come too far. He hadn't drank. He had maintained his sobriety even in the darkest of moments, a fact that gave him a fierce sense of pride. What he was feeling would pass; it was a strangely hopeful thought.

His feet had carried him to Fen's hotel without him really realising it. She was still in the suite they had shared.

"It's me," he said, knocking gently. "Can we talk?"

The door opened a moment later. Fen looked beautiful; her hair framed her face with soft waves. She was wearing pyjamas, and a pencil was tucked behind her ear. Clearly, she was working on her next story.

"Congratulations on the new job. You always wanted to be an anchor."

She looked conflicted, neither happy to see him nor like she wished him to leave.

"Why are you here?" she asked neutrally.

"I met Thea when she was nineteen and I hated her. I couldn't stand that she had a rich father. I was an asshole back then and the fact she was a rookie made me hate her even more."

"Why are you telling me this?"

"Because you want to know me. You want to know about my past. I owe you that."

Fen stepped aside to allow him entry. She sat on the bed and crossed her legs waiting for him to continue.

"I spent the next three years ignoring her on principle. When my old partner retired, I was so pissed when I found out that she was going to be my new one, but the longer we spent together the longer I realised how brilliant she was. How brave. I was in awe of her, but she was too young. I was married and I loved my wife, so, I pushed those thoughts away. For over a year I knew I was slowly falling for her, but I didn't act on it until one day I just...I don't know...couldn't resist anymore. I had never done anything like that before in my life, I was so ashamed, but I always found myself going back to her. We had an affair for over two years. We knew it was wrong, but it was like we were in each other's blood. Then Cleo—my wife—walked in on us in our marital bed. She ran from the room and I thought she was crying, little did I know she had already been poisoned with Quietus—a Styxx variant...she turned into a ghoul before our eyes and the Onyx Legion dragged her away." Walt shook his head sadly.

"Oh my god."

"I thought she was dead at first, but not long after I found out she'd been locked up with the other ghouls. I was wracked with guilt. I turned to drink. I pushed Thea away. I stopped doing my job and became someone I didn't recognise. And then the Gold Legion happened. They were a cult who took over the city. Thea nearly died and I realised that the guilt I was feeling was nothing compared to how awful it felt when I thought she was dead.

We worked the case, I tried to get sober, and we tried to be together. But then Cleo came back to me and begged me not to leave her and even though I knew it was wrong, that I was in love with someone else, I told her I would stay from some misguided notion of doing the right thing." Walt laughed bitterly. "I was an idiot. I hurt Thea badly then, it was the second time I'd abandoned her, and we haven't been together since. I was forced to kill her father, against my will, and it still haunts me to this day. That's really how my spine was injured. The cult put a device on my back that could control me. Thea saved me in spite of what I'd done. We dismantled the Gold Legopn and she left. I got sober, became captain, and met you."

Their eyes met for a moment.

"I'm sorry I pressured you. I can see now why you didn't want to talk about it. But I'm glad you shared. It just proves you are exactly who I thought you were." She smiled warmly. "I'm sorry for what I did to you. It was ruthless and heartless and manipulative. I thought you were an easy mark. But I never realised how much I would love you. You aren't damaged."

"I am. But so is everybody else." He smiled.

"I am so sorry."

"I know."

"But you can't forgive me." Her eyes were glassy and over-bright.

"I do forgive you. I forgive you. But I can't be with you. Our feelings were real, but what you did means nothing else in our relationship was. There isn't a single moment that wasn't part of the lie. I love you, but I don't trust you and I'm more in love with someone else."

"I love you, more than you know." Fen paused, blinking back tears. "I think we could have been something really special if Thea hadn't come back into your life. But she did. If she had been gone just a few months longer, I think we'd have been solid and there would've been no question."

"Our problems go way beyond Thea. Would you ever have told me? Would you ever have stopped using the tap?"

"I don't know. I wish I could say that I would have, but I get so blinded by the job sometimes." She smiled sadly. "I'm a workaholic who always put the job first, but I never meant to hurt you. I did a terrible thing to you and I'm going to have to live with the fact I killed us, but I need you to know that."

"I know."

"We missed our chance, that's all." She wiped a tear from her eye. "Don't miss your chance with her."

"She doesn't want me." Walt smiled in a reigned sort of way.

"Then that's the choice you have to make. Are you willing to risk it for the chance to start again or will you choose to play it safe and say nothing, but live with not knowing forever?"

Walt moved to the bed and sat down on the edge. He leaned towards Fen, making it clear what he was going to do. She raised her lips to meet his. The kiss was sweet and final.

"I'll miss you," she said against his lips.

THE RIGHT THING

Bastion was packing a bag when Cora entered the living room.

"What are you doing?"

"Turning myself in."

"Why? I made Thea and Walt swear that they wouldn't tell anyone that you're here."

"I trust them to keep their word, but that's not what this is about. I love you. I know that it's real now. I don't deserve you, but I want to."

"What are you talking about?"

"I want a life with you, but I won't let you be on the run because of me. I'm turning myself in and Walt said he would speak to the DA about how I helped here. Maybe get me a lighter sentence. I want to start fresh. I want my life to be honest. I want to be a better man. Living among the augs for the last few years gave me a sense of purpose, of family. People looked up to me and relied on me, but it wasn't real. I want to feel that again and I want to have earned it. I did so many terrible things, it's time I paid for them."

"But I only just got you back."

"We'll be together again. I know it."

He kissed her deeply, threw his bag over his shoulder and left. Walt was waiting for him outside with a police transporter.

"Are you ready?" he asked sombrely.

"I want what Cora and I had to be real. No matter how it started."

"You were holding her captive, Bast. You slept with her sister."

"How did you do it? How did you cope with guilt of the things you did?"

"I became a raging alcoholic. I don't recommend it. Come on."

NEW DAWN

Marielena's hand shook in Thea's as they stood in front of the committee waiting for Mayor Goodwin to speak. It had been two weeks since they had given their testimonials and they had been starting to worry that a decision would never be reached, but then they had been summoned to appear that very afternoon.

Thea couldn't help but feel hopeful. She knew there was every chance the hearing would yield no meaningful results, but she was desperate to believe it would.

"Thank you for joining me on such short notice. I would like to begin by thanking each and every one of you for your contributions to the city and to this hearing. You all exemplify what we want Caligo to stand for."

"Get on with it," Torrez muttered on Thea's other side. She smiled and gave him a gentle nudge.

"Having taken all that was presented to us into consideration we will be making the following recommendations. Both Una Anima and The Soulful Elite will be branded as terrorist organisations. They will be banned within Caligo City."

"Yes!" Alex exclaimed, punching the air. A number of heads turned to look in disapproval, but Alex ignored them, beaming.

"The rhetoric of both organisations is harmful and dangerous. We are recommending that it is formally recognised as hate speech and is punishable by fines and custodial sentences where appropriate. We will propose amendments to our equality laws to include and protect those with augmentations from discrimination and we are proposing that new laws specific to the augmented community be drawn up to ensure they are protected in our city. We are also requesting the formation of an Augmentation Committee, with a focus on providing funding and resourcing to those who need augmentations and aftercare for those who already have them, including trade-in and upgrade schemes. We feel that it is of the utmost importance to see those with augmentations in higher levels of public office, so that they can be actively involved in the decisions that affect their community."

It was better than Thea could have imagined. Marielena dissolved into tears beside her and Thea pulled her into a tight hug. Finally, they had made a difference.

"We hope that these recommendations are upheld and form the beginning of a new dawn for Caligo as it recovers. We hope that these changes will foster and grow a sense of community and togetherness. We are weaker divided."

DAVID

Alex and Torrez were sitting on the sofa when Thea came home from work. Each had a glass of wine in their hand.

"Want us to move?" Torrez asked.

"No, I'm glad you're both here."

"You look serious, Tee. Everything okay?" Alex gave Thea a scrutinising look.

"Yeah. Can I sit?" Thea indicated the armchair opposite.

"You're freaking me out, now," Alex said.

"Drew told me about your brother, and I did some digging."

"Did you find him?" They sat forward so quickly that wine sloshed on the floor. "Do you know what happened?"

"I did and I do. I have a file, but I can tell you if you'd like."

"I'd prefer it came from you." Alex grabbed Torrez's hand with of both their own. "Please, just tell me."

"Your brother joined the Onyx Legion a year before the battle of Medicorum. He was reprimanded for asking too many questions. I think he was suspicious about what the legion was doing. He marched on Medicorum with his fellows on October 22nd, 2425. When he arrived he knew what he was doing was wrong and he turned on the legion to help the remaining TPD officers who were fighting to protect the city. He was shot and he died trying to protect a very good friend of mine, named Bill. He was identified and cremated, his ashes scattered over the sea as per his will. He was a good man."

"Thank you," Alex said with a sob. They got unsteadily to their feet and crossed to Thea. They laid their head in her lap and sobbed as Thea rubbed gentle circles on their back.

OLD HABITS

"Mind if I come in?"

Thea looked up from her desk and smiled at AD Castillo. "Of course, take a seat. How was your holiday?"

"Well needed. We loved every second of it. On the transporter home all I heard was 'Daddy, can't we stay just one more day'. I'm not sure she'll ever forgive me for bringing her home. I'm surprised you haven't taken any time away. Aren't you sick of this place?" He waved an airy hand around the office.

"No, this is where I'm meant to be."

"I'm glad you think that, because I want to run something by you."

"Shoot."

"You are a natural born leader. The way you handled yourself, the teams, the investigations around Curtis and the riots was nothing short of superb. You are smart, fast, cool under pressure. We need people like you in positions of power. I've been given Vargas's Deputy Director position, and I was hoping you would consider taking up the role of Assistant Director."

"Congratulations on the promotion. I can't think of anyone better. And thank you for the offer, but I'm supposed to be out in the field. I'll lead teams and task forces, co-ordinate missions, but I'm not ready to sit behind a desk yet."

"There's still fighting to be done, right? It's a shame, but I'm sure a lot of people will sleep better knowing you are out there on the front lines."

"Thank you, sir."

Castillo smiled, then added, "Before I forget, you have a visitor waiting in the Executive Lounge."

"Walt? I thought you'd left."

They had shared a glance and a nod after the hearing, but Thea had assumed that Walt had gone back to Tenebrium. It was with great surprise that she found him standing alone waiting for her in the Executive Lounge.

"Not yet." He seemed nervous.

"Is everything okay?"

Walt took a deep breath. "I still love you," he blurted.

Thea's heart dropped into her stomach. "Please don't do this."

"I loved you when I was married to Cleo. I loved you when I was your mentor. I loved you when I was your partner. I loved you when I was drunk. I loved you when I was in love with someone else. I loved you at my worst and now I'm sober, I still love you."

"You can't do this to me again. It's done. We're done."

"I'm not asking you for anything, I'm just telling you the truth. I came here with every intention of trying to get you back, but that's just...crazy. I've known for a long time that you were right to leave. You were right to leave when you did. I was a mess and if we had been together, I would have stayed that way. You were the only thing I cared about; you were my only goal. My sobriety would have hinged on you; it would have been all about you because everything was all about you back then. You were right to leave. If you hadn't, I would have convinced myself I had everything I needed and I never would have gotten sober."

"Why are you telling me this? Why now?"

"I'm not a month sober. I'm three years sober and counting. I got sober for me, not for you. I worked my way back from hell. I worked my way through the ranks. I'm the Captain just like I always wanted. I'm together. Really together. Happy. And I still want you."

"Walt..."

"But I finally understand. I get it now. I didn't before, but I do now. It's not just that you've moved on. It's that we changed each other. We made each other worse. You and I have thrived apart. I used to think losing you would end my life but it didn't. I can live without you." He paused, his eyes searching her face. "Neither of us want to be the people we are when we're together. What I did to Sid was petty and I hate that I'm still capable of that when it comes to you. You were right; we're bad for each other. But none of that changes the fact that I still love you. I don't even know how to begin to stop. But I'd like to—stop loving you."

"You have changed." There was a lump in Thea's throat, but she couldn't help but smile.

He returned her smile with a wistful one of his own. "I can't have you in my life and not have you *in* my life. It's too hard. I'm leaving Caligo and I'm not coming back. I have no right to ban you from Tenebrium, but I hope you stay here. You're thriving."

"What if another case crosses city lines?"

"The TPD will always be at your disposal. Anything you need. Just not me."

"I don't know what to say."

"There's nothing left to say, except goodbye."

"Goodbye, Walt," she said softly.

Walt didn't say anything. He just looked at her as if trying to memorise her face. Then he was in front of her, and his lips were pressed against hers. It was different from the other times they'd kissed. There was no desperation, no need that pushed the borders of sanity. It was just pure electricity. And then it was over.

"Old habits," he said, resting his forehead against hers for a moment. "Bye." It was barely more than a whisper.

He turned and walked away without a backwards glance.

Thea watched him go. She hadn't realised she was still carrying the weight of all that had transpired between them, until she felt it lift. They had finally put an end to things. There was nothing left unsaid or undone. It was freeing. It felt like a new beginning.

EPILOGUE

There you have it, my chronicle from Caligo. It was a city set ablaze by hate and yet it is a city that has come together. In the years since the disbanding of Una Anima and The Soulful Elite, Caligo has evolved. Caligo is thriving.

The city will never be able to erase its bloody legacy, but what was birthed from the struggle is something new; something better.

Time has eroded the intricate details of how this change came about. My tale differs from the official narrative in many ways, but I will say as I always do, that I believe what I have presented here to be the truth.

Caligo's legacy is a cautionary tale to those who would let hate, money, power, and privilege drive them, but it is also solid and undeniable proof that it is not foolish to hope for change.

No city is perfect because the system is still broken, and attitudes can't be changed overnight, but Caligo has shown that we need not accept the status quo. Change can be won if there are those willing to fight for it.

Fight on. Fight hard, and never give up.

ACKNOWLEDGMENTS

Thank you to my 'gals'. To RJ Ruthless for being the fastest and most dedicated reader I have ever met, and to Downtown for her never-ending support.

Thank you to my beloved Gage for his endless patience and ability to make the bad days good. This book isn't dedicated to you, because Tenebrium was, and two dedications would just be greedy.

I would also like to apologise sincerely to my dear friend Lu who really really really wanted Walt to die. I'm sorry that he did, in fact, survive this book.

SPECIAL THANKS
To Stephanie Francis of The Abundant Word

Printed in Great Britain
by Amazon

9b8447d4-8d62-465a-91a4-563b0d7a5deaR01